THE
MOST
DANGEROUS
GAMES

THE MOST DANGEROUS GAMES

EDITED BY

DEBORAH LACY

With Love to Aunt Sue

Contents

Foreword — iii

Praise for The Most Dangerous Games — v

IT WAS JUST A GAME — 1
Heather Graham

MURDER & MYSTERY: LIVE IN FIVE — 17
K.C. Selby

LEVEL UP — 32
Shawn Reilly Simmons

NOT SORRY — 46
Alan Orloff

OLD MAID — 54
Shannon Taft

DOUBLE DUTCH DARE — 70
P.M. Raymond

THE HACK JOB — 86
LL Kaplan

WORST DAY EVER — 101
Rebecca Lugones

ENDGAME — 118
BV Lawson

DEATH STREAMED LIVE — 125
Stephen M. Pierce

KILLER INSTINCT — 139
Maya Corrigan

KARMA CAN BE BOTH — 152
Bruce Kubec

A CROOKED ROOK 164
JD Allen
GAME OF DRONES 175
Jane Limprecht
ZEBRA FINCH 190
donalee Moulton
THE CHESS CONNECTION 206
Kirlagh James
THE QUIZMASTER'S LAST ROUND 219
Kerry Hammond
LUCKY NIGHT 232
Robert Lopresti
SIX QUESTIONS 236
LaToya Jovena
DEAD HAND, NO JOKERS 250
Sharyn Kolberg
ESCAPE THE MONEY LAUNDERERS 262
Chris Chan
THE QUEEN OF PICKLEBALL 275
Daphne Silver
Acknowledgments 292
About the Editor 293

Foreword

Deborah Lacy, Editor

Fun. Games. Mystery. The twisted tales in *The Most Dangerous Games* have these three keys at the heart, and so did getting this anthology to publication. Curiosity about story selection has been a constant throughout my writing career, so I thought I'd de-mystify our process here.

In June of 2024, Level Best Books announced the open call for stories at ShortCon, a conference for writers of short mystery fiction. We followed that announcement with posts on social media, the Level Best website, and the Short Mystery Fiction Society message board. We also reached out to newsletters for local chapters of Mystery Writers of America and Sisters in Crime. Authors had four months to write a crime story with a game at the center. We received four stories for every open slot we had for publication. I selected our judges – Pat Hernas, Janet Kuchler, Sharon Long and Kim Hammond. I chose these individuals because I trust and value their feel for story. Story submissions were blinded, tracked, and managed by the head judge, a former librarian. Each story was evaluated using the same rubric for fairness and consistency.

I read the stories with the highest scores and made the final selections.

Five authors were invited contributors—Heather Graham, JD Allen, LaToya Jovena, Kerry Hammond, and Shawn Reilly Simmons. I invited authors whose work I admired.

The stories that you have here are the best of the field. They include stories set in the future, the past, and all over the world, with games ranging from pickleball to an escape room to a scavenger hunt. Many of our contributors are award winners, and you'll find three stories from debut authors—"The

Hack Job" by L.L. Kaplan, "Worst Day Ever" by Rebecca Lugones, and "The Chess Connection" by Kirlagh James.

Every story includes the biography of the author at the beginning and notes on what inspired their story at the end, because it adds dimension to the storytelling.

I hope you will enjoy *The Most Dangerous Games*.

Praise for The Most Dangerous Games

"Anyone who loves Mysteries, Puzzles, and Games—as I do—will be intrigued and dazzled by the fabulous stories collected in this unique anthology. A colorful romp through the world of gamesmanship, *The Most Dangerous Games* will leave readers breathless. A must-read!"
—Katherine Neville: *NY Times* and #1 internationally bestselling author of *The Eight* and *The Fire*

IT WAS JUST A GAME

Heather Graham

Bestselling author Heather Graham has been published in thirty languages, written more than 200 novels, and has 70 million books in print. She is a proud recipient of many awards, including Thriller Master and the Silver Bullet from International Thriller Writers and Lifetime Achievement from Romance Writers of America.

The final day of the Big Bayou Bowl-a-Rama was well underway. Bryce Mayfield was ready. He had beaten nine qualifying players, and in about twenty minutes, he'd be playing the final game. Applause sounded raucously around him. It was nice. Money was nicer.

At the very least, he'd come in second. But he needed to come in first. The grand prize was $20,000. After that, second went down to $5,000, and third was not-so-great at $1,000. He could really use that $20,000. And he was a good bowler. For the most part, he was good friends with the other contestants. They were on leagues here at the bowling alley, bowlers were often together, sometimes switching around because of life schedules, but for the most part, being good friends.

Well, as the old saying went, there was no way out of there being a few flies in the ointment. The fellow he had just beaten, Andrew Tindale, could be a jerk. Anytime he lost, he claimed that his opponent had cheated. He wasn't all that popular with anyone. Fortyish, grouchy, a man who could bowl, but hadn't done that well at life, from what Bryce had seen. He was divorced, and he'd gone from sales job to sales job over the years. And, of course, before their game, he'd been bragging that he was going to take Bryce, down, down, down.

He tried to be decent and courteous to Andrew. Someone being resentful and taking it out on others, well. That was life. There was always one in a crowd. But for the rest…

To get to the end, there were others he knew well he'd taken down in this tournament. And they were still there—now enjoying drinks at the alley's bar, food, and the camaraderie of the place, ready to cheer others on.

Bryce was in his late twenties. Many in the leagues were in their thirties, forties, fifties, or older. Age didn't bother any of them. Being older gave one the benefit of greater experience. Being younger allowed for more energy.

And maybe better eyesight!

But the applause…yeah, it was nice. He liked being a golden boy. He'd been a star quarterback at the university, he'd almost been drafted by the majors, but severe injury had ended his hopes and aspirations in that direction. And yet, having a bum knee hadn't wrecked his ability to bowl. People thought that it would, but it didn't. Maybe it was determination, he didn't know. So, while he couldn't run the yards of a football field, he could manage the stance to knock down ten pins, again and again.

This wasn't a major event—though one day, it would be nice if he could get as far as something that was in the big money. This was local, still, a network affiliate was running it with twenty-minute breaks for the bathroom, food, water, or whatever, between the players. He'd already been interviewed, given just a few questions by the pretty entertainment anchor running the show several times, and truth be told, even he needed a bathroom break now and then. He left the area in front of the lanes and headed back to the restrooms. As he did so, he saw the pretty young TV hostess; she had her microphone out. She needed to interview his next opponent, Joe DeFiore. But she smiled at him. It was a really nice smile. These days, of course, one had to be very careful. But he was certain that she was flirting with him.

And when the last game was over…well, even without a $5,000 prize, he could take her to a nice dinner.

He went on into the men's room, spending several minutes splashing water on his face, and came on out. He loved the game. He was good at it. But heading into his 10th meant for a long, long day into night.

The TV hostess, Cami Clark, was just finishing up an interview with his next opponent, Joe DiFiore. They were about to announce the beginning of the final round. In qualifying, Bryce had won many games because many had entered the contest. The winners just kept playing the winners, until now.

The finale.

He smiled. Cami Clark, lovely on the camera with her dark hair, blue eyes, and stunning facial features, was announcing to the audience present at the alley and those on their live TV screens that Joe DeFiore would have a chance to practice, throw a few balls, while Bryce, going into the final game as a winner, would not. But she took a minute to talk about him first, to more wonderful applause, and then Joe, who also received his share of clapping and cheers. Then Camie announced they were ready! The play would begin.

Joe was the challenger, so he would bowl first. Joe was okay. Early thirties, he worked construction and odd jobs. He'd told Bryce once that throwing the balls helped relieve the tension of the day.

They shook hands, grinning at one another, before Joe went for his first ball.

Spare.

Bryce managed a strike.

Then Joe threw a strike—and Bryce spared. He waited for his ball to come back.

And then he froze.

The thing that came through the ball return wasn't a bowling ball.

It was a head. A human head. And the worst thing was that he could recognize it; the head belonged to Gabriel Garcia, a friend in the league.

It was as if time stood still. Not just Bryce, everyone within the building froze as well.

The head, of course, was displayed in a zillion homes on widespread TV sets.

But Cami and her cameraman quickly came back to their senses.

"Cut, the feed, cut the feed!" Cami cried.

Her cameraman, usually a cool kind of guy, shouted back.

"Duh!"

Both Bryce and Joe stepped back, still staring, horrified.

Their audience began screaming.

Bryce was stunned.

Later, all he would remember was seeing the head, coming back just as if it had been one of the balls.

And then utter chaos.

* * *

There must have been a hundred people at the alley that night. And the first thing the cops did was close off the exits—no one could come in, no one could go out. They spoke to everyone there, and the hours dragged on and on.

The medical examiner arrived. He estimated that the head "was fresh."

The murder had taken place that night. Somewhere between the games, Gabriel Garcia had been murdered and decapitated. Or perhaps the decapitation had been the mode or method of the murder, but…

Where? How?

Of course, the head had come from the back of the bowling alley. There were scanners in the back, the pin machines that allowed for remaining pins to be caught and reset, and the downed pins to be swept away. Then there was the ball return, which was situated underneath between the two lanes. Bowling balls would come out of the return onto the ball holder. Instead of Bryce's bowling ball, Gabriel's head rolled out. The back of the lanes would come under major and absolute investigation. A forensic team had arrived while the police questioning of everyone there went on.

But no weapon was found—nor was the remainder of Gabriel Garcia's body. And eventually, into the wee hours, people were allowed to leave.

Bryce was among the last.

So was Cami. Because, naturally, the police wanted every bit of footage that she and her cameraman had.

Bryce almost walked into her as they exited the building at last to head to their cars.

"Well, you must have some really interesting footage," Bryce said.

"I'm an entertainment anchor, not news!" she said with a whisper. But then she looked at him, and back at the many officers remaining just outside the building.

"I didn't do it, I swear," Bryce told her.

She nodded. "I…I guess I should warn you. The police consider you a suspect."

"Me? Why? It would have been more likely that he would have killed me—I won. What possible motive would I have to kill anyone?"

"I guess you didn't hear."

"Hear what?" he asked.

She sighed. "Apparently, Gabriel was badmouthing you, suggesting that you might have cheated."

He shook his head. "I never even heard such a rumor. And if I had heard it, I wouldn't care—the game was seen by dozens of people live, and more on TV. You saw to that," Bryce said earnestly. He tried to give her a weak grin. "Sticks and stones may break my bones, but words will never hurt!" he told her.

She smiled. She believed him.

He liked her. He thought that she liked him.

Now really wasn't a good night to be thinking such things, but…

He bid her good night and headed home.

At home, he lay awake staring at the ceiling. He couldn't shake the image of Gabriel's head, no, his face, eyes still open, as if in shock, skin smashed and dirtied from rolling back…

Who the hell had done such a thing? Why? Gabriel had a mouth on him, but so did a lot of the guys. This kind of a heinous murder...

He was glad it was Saturday, grateful the play at the alley had been scheduled for Friday. Frankly, he was somewhat surprised the police had let people go last night as soon as they had. He wasn't a cop, but he did work for a private security firm, one of the most prestigious in the country. But somehow, now, he was on a Monday to Friday schedule, 7 A.M. to 3 P.M. He didn't need to head into work, and he was glad. He was exhausted, and perhaps a mind could really hurt. Yeah, a headache. But he just didn't get it.

He was surprised when his phone rang—actually, not so surprised that it rang. He'd been fielding calls all morning. He was surprised that the caller was Cami Clark.

And he'd developed a crush on her. Dumb. She had a famous face—even if just in the area. And him, well...he wasn't a bad guy. High school and then the military, which helped him get through college. He'd been a licensed private investigator for a year before signing on with the security company.

He'd thought about applying to the police academy and even the FBI. But at the time he'd taken the job, his dad had been suffering through his last days of stage four cancer, and he'd lost his mother to a car accident when he'd been a kid. The security company was great to him—he could usually make his own hours. Now, he was working at a tech company with great employees, a coffee room that was even better, and while currently tech was the thing, their building was a fortress as far as security went. Some of his friends preferred weekends or nights; they didn't want to know the employees. Bryce was what they called a "people person," and he enjoyed chatting with—and learning from—many of the employees.

Cami's number was in his phone because she had given it to him when setting up different interviews for the Bowl-A-Rama.

"Hey!" he said. "Anything new?" he asked her worriedly.

"You're not watching the news?" she asked him.

"Well, you are the news, aren't you?"

He heard her weary sigh. "I'm in entertainment, remember? And I love it! I go to concerts, plays, movies—and events. Like the one last night—when a guy's head popped up instead of a bowling ball."

"Well, what's happened? Did they—"

"No, they haven't gotten the killer. But Bryce..."

"What? Please?"

"I overheard a conversation I shouldn't have overheard. Our investigative reporter, Sam Merton, was talking to one of the detectives on the case. Bryce, you're the top suspect."

"What?"

Once again, he was stunned. Why?

"You and a couple of the other bowlers," Cami said. "I'm not sure about the other; I overheard the conversation, and I was where I shouldn't have been at the studio."

"But I was there, in the front all the time. I must be on the security cameras! I couldn't have gotten to the back to...to behead a guy!" Bryce protested.

"Apparently, you disappeared from the view of all cameras for about twenty minutes, Bryce."

"And it would only take twenty minutes to kill a man and—wait!"

"Wait, what?"

"The police evidently don't know how the mechanism of a bowling alley works. Someone had to have been in the back to set the ball in the return thread. That couldn't have been me because I was in front right before the head came down!" he claimed.

"I don't know...I don't understand. But I did hear that they grilled Joe DeFiore—grilled, that's the term I heard—for a few hours, and it seems he got exasperated and suggested you—that you and Gabriel had exchanged words, that Gabriel had accused you of cheating. Oh, and apparently, Andrew Tindale also accused you of being a cheater. He said he had the game in the bag, but...you were cheating."

"Did he explain how I was cheating?" Bryce asked. "Wow. They're accusing me of cheating at bowling—in front of a hundred live spectators who know how to bowl," Bryce said.

"Bryce, I—"

"Cami, thank you. You don't owe me this conversation at all. I appreciate it, so sincerely. And—"

"I know you didn't do it."

"Thanks for the vote of confidence," he told her softly.

"Well, it's not just that. I do love entertainment news. But sometimes, I'd like to be taken a bit more seriously. I, um…"

"Um?"

"I just wanted to let you know that I intend to do a little exploring on the case."

"But you have your work!" he told her.

"I've been given leave until the police solve this thing. In our community, well, they don't think talking about an upcoming concert or a new movie is…I don't know. Decent, under the circumstances. And this is driving me crazy. Bryce, we must have the answer!"

Bowling.

It was just a game.

But for Gabriel…

Bryce winced and closed his eyes. "Listen to me, Cami. Whoever did this is dangerous. He didn't just kill a man. He beheaded him so that he could create shock and horror in the middle of that tournament. If you are seen investigating—"

"I'm a big girl."

"No! You could find yourself in serious danger!"

"Yeah. That's why I was hoping that you might help me."

"Cami, we can't get back into the bowling alley; the cops and forensic people have it as tight as a drum. They don't—"

"There were four people who disappeared from any camera range I can find during the time before Gabriel's head popped out. You, Joe DeFiore, Andrew Tindale, and, of course, Gabriel. Who didn't behead himself," she added dryly. "And I did a lot of simple exploring when this tournament came up—you know, minutes here and there on the neighborhood, how our embankment has turned to trees and foliage again in the time since Katrina—oh, and how cool it is to live on the outskirts of New Orleans, close to all the great action, far enough away to escape some of the craziness. Anyway, there's a parking lot behind the alley—"

"Right. Someone would have seen the body in the parking lot last night. At least a hundred people or more were there. Including cops," Bryce reminded her.

"But they might not explore the way that we do!" she said softly.

"Look, I appreciate all this—"

"It isn't just for you. Gabriel might have been a jerk, but even a jerk deserves justice!" she told him.

He smiled at that. He wasn't seriously worried about being arrested for the murder; surely someone in management at the bowling alley would explain it would have been impossible for him to have been in back to send the head—and be out front to bowl. At the same time."

"I think they believe that any knowledgeable bowler could have rigged it," Cami said to his silence. "Be that as it may—"

"Where do I meet you?" he asked. There was no way in hell he was going to let her run around trying to find a body on the embankment or in the river.

It would be far too easy for her to wind up in the river herself.

She gave him an address that was about a block from the bowling alley. "My cousin's house," she told him. "Her back yard backs up to the embankment. Not great when a storm is coming, but…"

"Yeah. Helpful today," he said. "I'll meet you there."

He showered and dressed, not wearing his uniform but still preparing as if he was truly working as a security guard.

In a way, he was.

He left the house quickly, almost mocking himself for his initial feelings last night.

Yeah, flirting. And she seemed to flirt back. He could see them at O'Malley's, their great local pub, chatting, getting to know one another…

Taking it further.

Well, here they were.

Taking it further. Just not in a direction he had intended it to go.

The neighborhood that surrounded the bowling alley was really beautiful. They weren't in the Garden District or even Uptown, but in the 1800s, settlers had moved into the area, and many of the homes were outstanding Victorians.

Not so much Cami's cousin's house. It was a sprawling ranch, probably built sometime in the 1970s when such homes had been in vogue and better dams had been created, except no dams had really survived an onslaught like Katrina, and, of course, a few others in the years had done some damage, too. Weather was crazy; they were all right here, and his heart bled for anyone when flooding brought disaster.

But that, naturally, allowed for...

Heightened embankment here. And a growth of brush and trees meant to hold the earth where it was intended to be.

He parked in front of the ranch house. Cami was already there. He knew because he had seen her arrive at the bowling alley in her SUV, her cameraman in the van right behind her.

There was no van there today.

He wondered if he was supposed to go to the door, meet the cousin, be polite, before they started out through the yard.

No.

Cami had seen him arrive.

She was dressed for the exploring she intended. High boots, jeans, denim tailored shirt, and a denim jacket to match.

She still looked amazing. He smiled a little to himself, wondering what her golden blond hair was going to look like when they'd crawled around in the brush for a while. But she was prepared for that, too. Her hair was tied securely back at her nape; she was ready to go. He smiled slightly. He had grown up in Houma, and when he'd finished with college, he'd known he'd wanted to be closer to New Orleans, to the jazz, the musicians on the street, the museums, and more.

But not too close.

From what he understood about Cami, she was a truly golden local child, being from the Irish Channel area of the city, winning different contest after different contest—but still choosing to move here and accept the position with their local affiliate.

She probably could have done a dozen other things. She had the looks and the charm to get by almost anywhere.

Unless she came face to face with a murderer who liked to chop heads off so that they could be used as bowling balls.

"Hey, thank you!" she said sincerely, handing him a can.

"And—"

"Bug repellent," she told him.

"Ah, really, totally prepared."

"I do my best!"

He sprayed himself with the repellent.

"Okay, come on, there's a row of trees that front the road—and the parking lot at the alley—that will hide us from anyone there," she said.

"I do think the cops might be thinking the body had been dumped back there, but we'll take a walk," he told her.

She smiled. They started out, passing a swing set and a few toys in her cousin's yard, then heading back behind the rows of trees, grand oaks dispersed with glorious maples, many showing radiant colors that had little to do with fall. But the brush was thick back here, too, and when Cami caught her foot on a root, he quickly reached out to catch her.

"Thanks!" she said softly, looking up at him.

They'd walked what would have been a couple of blocks on a sidewalk when Bryce paused, looking forward. He couldn't see anything—although he did think that officers had already trod the pathway they were on.

But something wasn't right.

"A murder of crows," he murmured.

She frowned. "And an unkindness of ravens," she said. "What—"

"The birds," he said quietly. "Watch. I'll be honest—I'm not up that much on what bird is what, but look at the middle branches on that oak. They seemed to flock to it, stay a minute, take back off, and maybe return. The smaller ones are flying away when the bigger ones come through. I'm thinking—"

"That there's a headless body in that tree," she said.

"Yeah, and I don't know my birds, but I'm good at tree climbing," he told her.

He studied the oak; he studied the branches. He glanced at Cami, nodded, and made his ascent. Branches and leaves slapped at him as he made his way up about twenty feet.

Then he saw it. Broken like a rag doll now, chewed up pretty good even overnight.

But it was a man's body.

He turned to start down the tree. Then he held still, listening. The words were a bit distant, cut by the green growth that surrounded him, and still…

"Cami, Cami, Cami! The beautiful, beautiful Cami!"

"Hey, how are you!" Cami said. She was good. She was keeping the fear out of her voice. "Hey, have you heard anything else?" she asked, putting an anxious note in her voice. "Sorry, I know I work for the affiliate, but…they benched me for now. My family has a place near here, and it's quiet, not like the city. I love to come and see the river, and sit by it and…well, I guess there will be cops out here today, and still…it's a great place to sit and think!"

"Oh, Cami!" the other speaker said.

"Well, seriously, I mean, with everything going on and…hey! I'm so sorry. There were just so many great players in that tournament!" she said.

"And I'm so sorry, too!" the voice said.

Male, of course. Not that he doubted that a female could kill—various classes at college when he'd studied criminology had taught them that they could.

But…a beheading?

Nope, not common. Well, not that it was that common a method of murder, even among men.

"I really am sorry!" the voice said softly.

Bryce gritted his teeth. He had to have a plan. He was blinded where he was, the thick lower branches of the oak obstructing his sight range. Maybe he could hop on down and challenge the man.

And maybe Cami would be dead the minute the killer heard him coming. He thought.

He carefully, carefully, climbed back up.

And he winced when he reached the broken body of Gabriel Garcia. But the man was already dead.

And Cami was alive.

A flock of birds moved in—an unkindness of ravens or a murder of crows or something else altogether. He didn't know.

Perfect.

He shook the branches.

And slam, slam, slam…

The body headed toward the ground, thumping hard as it hit from the height.

And in the midst of the noise, he started to make his way down.

"Damn!" the man thundered.

Cami let out a startled scream. "Oh, my God! There's…there's the rest of Gabriel's body! We've got to get to the police—"

"No, Cami, we don't. Kenjutsu!" he said.

"I don't—"

"Japanese sword fighting. I used to love it. Then I lost to a cheater. But, hey, I still love my swords! And they're custom-made for me, so with one swing…just like an executioner of old, except those didn't usually have points, the idea was to whack a head off in one blow. I'm sure the cops are still working on it all because I made a little mess of things—on purpose, of course—the other night. But I promise you, Cami, I won't now. I mean, I'm really sorry you didn't just stick with entertainment. Anne Boleyn! She managed to get them to hire a swordsman from France, so it would be quick—no mess-ups. You can really make a mess of a beheading—"

"What? I don't know what you're talking about!" Cami declared.

"You're about to find out!"

That was it. They were out of time. And he was low enough; he could peer through the branches, get a bead on the man.

And as he produced his sword, a weapon that gleamed even in the trickle of light making its way through the foliage, Bryce drew his work weapon, and he fired.

He's known it was always best to be prepared as if he was headed for work.

And today…

Yes.

The man fell.

The sword fell.

Cami cried out and backed against the tree; he almost crawled on her as he made his way down the rest of the tree.

And when he was down, he shook his head and stared at the bodies.

Gabriel Garcia, already showing signs of nibbling and putrefaction, and, of course, headless.

And, shot through the upper chest, Andrew Tindale.

"Why?" he whispered. "Why? What did Gabriel do?" he asked in wonder.

He was sure that they'd find out. The sound of the shot would have alerted any police in the area. And he could find himself arrested for both murders now.

Cami held her own. She looked at him.

"For some people," she told him, "I guess it isn't just a game!"

As Bryce expected, police were quickly moving through the trees.

"Through here!" he called. "I'll keep talking!"

He did. And in minutes, the police were on site.

And he did find himself in handcuffs.

That was all right. He winced inwardly. It had barely been a flirtation. But he would rather spend the next decades of life in jail—or face a real executioner—than see Cami dead.

But, as it happened, it wasn't that bad.

Cami was close friends with the lead detective on the case, Albert Grayson, and to their surprise, they did learn that the police had been homing in on Andrew Tindale.

They'd discovered his interest in Japanese sword fighting.

And they'd discovered that in casual play, Andrew Tindale had out-bowled Joe DeFiore several times.

Poor Gabriel had done nothing wrong. He'd been a convenient kill, a man simply in the wrong place at the wrong time.

But Andrew hadn't really played it out all that well. His plan had been for

Bryce to be arrested immediately, and then, when the furor had died down and it was time to finish out the tournament, Andrew would have played Joe.

Because Bryce would be sitting in jail so by the rules, if something eliminated a bowler along the way, the last losing opponent took his place.

It all seemed incredibly ridiculous.

When they had finally finished with all the paperwork, when Bryce had been officially cleared—with his weapon taken, of course, because he'd been forced to use it—he and Cami were able to leave together.

But not before Detective Albertson had told Bryce, "Young man, from what I've learned from you and Cami, you handled that situation like a true pro. If you ever decide you want to take a look at this police department, well, you have a friend. Several friends. And honestly, I promise you, decapitations over a bowling game are not that common!"

He thanked the detective.

All he wanted to do was get home, shower...

"So, thank you!" Cami told him as they walked back to her cousin's house. "Thank you! For my life, for coming with me!"

"Maybe you are an investigative reporter after all," he told her.

She smiled at that. "Hm, maybe. But I work best in a team!"

They returned to their cars. It was awkward. He didn't know what to say.

"Can I buy you dinner?" she asked him. "At least a drink. Something more than words to say thank you!"

He smiled. "I'm sorry. I grew up old-fashioned."

"Oh, sorry! I didn't mean to infer that..."

He laughed. "Cami, you didn't infer a thing. It's just that I'd like to take you to dinner. Honestly, even for a guy, shower first, and then—"

"Texting you, my address!" she told him, heading for her car with a smile on her face.

He smiled, too.

He really didn't give a damn about the tournament.

He remained horrified about Gabriel's death and sorry that he'd had no choice but to shoot Andrew.

All he could think about was Cami, and he believed that they'd keep seeing one another and then one day…

He thought of the old TV show, "How I Met Your Mother."

Well, one day…

Maybe he would just say, "Bowling!"

Story Inspiration:

Due to the fact that my husband and I have five children, we've been involved with or able to see games revolving around just about any sport out there.

This story is based on a prank a teenager played on his friends during a team tournament.

MURDER & MYSTERY: LIVE IN FIVE

K.C. Selby

K.C. Selby is a contemporary fiction writer living in the Midwest. Her short fiction has also appeared in the Write Michigan 2024 Anthology, *and she's working on her debut novel.*

Detroit 2044

It's subtle. The small uptick of her lips. The slight increase in pace as her heels click against the carpet between our cubicles. The subtle hum emanating from her as if her body is quite literally running on its own happiness.

She has news. Good news.

When you've spent as long as I have without any of your own, you become an expert in witnessing it in others. Not that I won't be excited for her. I'll force my mouth into a smile. Maybe jump up and hug her—depending on the magnitude of the news. Tell her how happy I am for her while my ribs squeeze tight with envy.

"Morning, Lottie," I say when she reaches my desk.

"Nova," she says with a knowing smile, her fingers curled around the top of my cubicle wall.

It must be the promotion. It's not supposed to be announced for several weeks, but maybe they told her early. My chest burns, and I tell myself it doesn't matter. There will be other opportunities.

"Guess what?" she asks while bringing her left hand up before I can voice my prediction. "I'm engaged!"

Oh, right. Leo from the writers' room. "Congrats! Wow, that ring is beautiful."

"Thanks." She holds it out to look at it herself, the overhead lights causing it to glitter like a miniature disco ball. "I mean, I might have given him a little help. During our virtual trip to New York City last month, we stopped at a jeweler, and Leo pointed out a pear cut. I told him I'd never be caught dead in it. That I was more of a princess girl myself."

I slip my hand over my own ring. A small—possibly fruit-shaped—diamond on a thin gold band. "Well, you both have great taste then."

Lottie lets out a satisfied sigh. "I feel like I'll be on cloud nine forever." She lets her hand down and turns back to me. "So, what's your best marriage advice?"

"Oh." I wave my hand in the space between us. "I'm probably not the best person to ask." I hope it sounds like a joke, and I worry it's coming out bitter.

"You two must be doing something right. You recently celebrated your fifth anniversary, right?"

I swallow a lump in my throat. I can barely remember she's dating someone, and here she is knowing what anniversary we just hit. If I asked Roman, would he even know? "Well, um, never go to bed angry." Is this the best I've got? A clichéd piece of advice?

However, she's nodding her head, eager for more.

There's got to be something I can impart. "And communication is really the most important thing. Without that, it's hard to have a successful relationship." It's not a lie at least, it truly is difficult without it. "So, are you two going out to celebrate?"

"We'll do something this weekend. Tonight we'll, of course, be watching the new Murder and Mystery."

"Oh, right. First Wednesday of the month. Almost forgot."

Lottie lets out a laugh. "I think that's a fireable offense."

I laugh too, as if I know it's a joke and not an actual fear I've had. What would management say if they knew I've never plugged into a single show of ours? Roman does enough of that for the both of us.

"It's too bad we're excluded from the winnings. Leo is so good at puzzles. I just know he'd win one month and then we could have the most amazing wedding."

Roman is convinced he'd win, too, if we were allowed. Several times, I've almost joked we should get a divorce so he wouldn't have to worry about the exclusion. Although, voicing it, even if I'm teasing, brings the possibility to life. Like if I say divorce out loud, it'll stay in the air forever, always easier to grab.

* * *

A few hours later, I stand outside our condo while the scanner confirms it's me. It does its satisfied jingle, and the door clicks open. I take a deep breath and step inside, determined to reach Roman. To be the couple Lottie thinks we are. The one we used to be.

He's in the living room wearing his VR set. The window tint is on because he insists the light messes with his view. I click the button on the wall display, and the windows go clear, letting the evening sun cast the room in orange. Roman doesn't flinch. He keeps laughing along to his show. Proof I'm right about the blinds.

I pull out my phone and text his VR set to avoid startling him.

He slides it up to rest on his head. "Hey. Everything okay?"

Right, I never tell him when I'm home. I clear my throat. "Yeah, I wanted to see if you'd be up for ordering in pizza tonight and then, um, maybe we could both watch the new Murder and Mystery."

His eyes light up. "Really?"

I nod.

"Wow. Okay, yeah, that'd be great." His left dimple appears.

"It starts at seven?"

"They moved it to eight now."

"Right." I should know this, but I'm in payroll, not production. "I'll order the pizza."

"Thanks." He goes to pull the set down and stops. "Why the change of heart?"

He knows how disorientating I find the shows, but he doesn't know the extent of my distaste. How I think they're slowly taking over our lives. That people have a hard time drawing the line between the real world and the world they're viewing. And it's no wonder. It's as if the viewer is living inside the show, bumping shoulders with the actors. Want to sit at the table next to your favorite sitcom couple while they fight about the latest scripted drama? You can. Want to stand behind the glass while your favorite TV show detective interrogates their latest witness? You sure can. Want to sit at the nurse's desk while two characters bicker about a patient in your favorite hospital drama? You bet you can.

Roman is still waiting for a response. I can't tell him it's because it's the only way to get to him. It's the truth, but it's a hurtful one. "Lottie at work was talking about it, and it sounds fun."

His face lights up, and my heart tugs. I miss seeing him happy.

"You're going to love it. Just wait, you'll get hooked after one game."

It's not exactly the glowing endorsement he thinks. At least it's something we'll be doing together. Maybe afterwards he'll want to sit and talk about it. It won't be like the conversations we used to have—the late nights spent propped up on pillows discussing anything and everything—but it's a start.

After dinner, we sit down a half hour early so he can give me a rundown before the show begins. He explains we'll be able to see and talk with each other, just not with other viewers. We're free to walk around in the scene but are restricted to that specific one.

"Basically, they don't want you walking off to witness the murder." His fingers form air quotes on the last word. "Because you know that would ruin the whole mystery part of a murder mystery."

"Right." I nod and remind myself how much I loved the Clue movie growing up—the historic one from the 1980s, not the 2030s remake—and think maybe this will be similar. And the shows only last three hours tops. I can do that.

"Oh." Roman sits up straighter. "And each month is at a different location. Last time they were on a casino riverboat, and this time they'll be at a zoo."

I perk up. My parents took me to the Detroit Zoo when I was in elementary school. I still remember it. How tall the giraffes had been. How smelly yet adorable the otters were. How sweet the cotton candy was. I lose myself in the memory of it all while Roman talks. Before I know it, it's time.

Roman hands me my set. The plastic film is still on the visor. I slip the set on without bothering to peel it off. The letters OCP forming our company logo fill the screen before dissolving to reveal the virtual world. I turn my head to the right, and Roman is standing beside me. Or at least his avatar is. He's wearing a Lions jersey and jeans and is possibly a few inches taller than he is in the real world.

I look down at my avatar. Black T and pants. The default outfit, I'm guessing. My gaze travels past us to the scene. We're standing in the aquarium portion of the zoo. There are small tables set up surrounded by water, walled in with glass, where brightly colored fish swim by. In the air in the center of the space, words are projected to tell us, *Murder & Mystery: The Ultimate Puzzle starts in 2:47.*

The seconds tick down, and when the timer reaches zero, a voice flows from our sets. "Our Century Productions presents *Murder and Mystery: The Ultimate Puzzle*, the game show where our viewers are the contestants. Think you have what it takes to solve the murder mystery? Let's find out. Our June game starts live now." The display disappears, and the actors materialize in the room. Some are seated, and others are mingling in small groups. Most with flutes of champagne pressed to their lips.

A hand slips into mine. "Ready?" Roman asks, squeezing gently.

"Yep." I hope I sound excited. All I feel is nauseated, though. I've never been good with VR. Our company claims to have made improvements for those with motion sickness. So far, I'm not seeing any.

Roman's shoulder brushes mine. "The killer is always in the first scene, so it's someone here now."

I nod determinedly and turn back to the group. About a dozen people are in the scene, including two waitstaff circulating with trays. There's a woman with white hair pulled into a low bun who appears to be in charge, even though she has barely spoken. She's also the only actor I recognize.

"Let's get closer." Roman tugs my hand, and we inch throughout the space, listening in on the conversations.

His hand is warm in mine, and the heat spreads throughout my chest. When was the last time we held hands?

We hear bits and pieces of everyone's conversations—learning Adam is upset Chloe got the promotion over him, Isaac thinks Chloe is selling company secrets, and Samuel thinks Adam is trying to steal his wife—until the gray-haired woman, whose real-life name I now remember is Sierra Woods, taps a fork to her glass. All eyes turn to her as a hammerhead shark passes behind her.

"I hope you're all enjoying your evening so far, but I don't want to go another minute without recognizing why we're all here tonight." She smiles and gestures to a black-haired man leaning against one of the aquarium walls. "Isaac has been a steadfast believer in our company from day one, and one of the reasons we have been so strong all these years. It's hard to believe you won't be on the board any longer, but your impact will be seen for many years to come."

My screen dims. This thing is practically brand new. Why would it go out? I'm about to pull it off when I hear one of the actors joke, "Who flipped the lights?"

I strain my eyes and see the faint blue light making its way through the surrounding water. "Is this part of it?" I ask Roman beside me.

"I think it is," he whispers, even though no one can hear him but me.

"Is it closing time already?" another actor quips.

The lights come back on a few moments later. It's quickly followed by a scream. I blink the room back into focus, and my gaze lands on a body on the ground. There's a pool of red spreading out from under them. Roman walks forward, and I inch my way next to him. It's Isaac, the man from the speech.

Sierra is suddenly by our side. She crouches down and puts a hand on his back. Her eyes go wide and her voice trembles as she says, "He's dead…"

Wow, she is a good actor. They shoot these live, so there's no redoing takes or forgetting lines, and I truly believe her when she says he's dead. Her face has even turned a pale white.

A tall, thin man in an emerald suit strides over. He reaches down and sets his hands on her shoulders, gently pulling her up and away from the body.

"It's okay. We'll call the authorities. We'll get this all squared away."

"No, Drew, he's dead. Actually dead."

Drew pulls her close and makes a shushing noise that's infantilizing.

I glance over at Roman. His avatar has a hand to his chin, and he's concentrating hard on the scene before him. My gaze goes back to the body, and my stomach feels queasy. From the motion or the blood, I can't be sure. It's fake, I remind myself, even though it looks so real. I want to rip my set off and be done with this. However, Roman was thrilled I asked to join him tonight, so I stay.

I don't look down anymore, though. How are they able to make it look this real? Roman leaves my side and circles the scene. I follow him. He's in his element. Before the shows took over, he was an avid mystery reader. Even reading all the classics from Agatha Christie and Arthur Conan Doyle.

I stay a step behind him until the ending credits roll and breathe a sigh of relief as I slide my headset off. I collapse back onto our sofa, and Roman sits down next to me.

"So, what did you think?" He asks eagerly.

"It was—" Disorientating. Disturbing. "Interesting."

"This wasn't their best, if I'm being honest. The lights cutting out felt a little cliché, and it's pretty obvious the killer was Chloe. The death scene was extremely realistic, though. They've gotten a lot better with that."

"They have?" I ask, still remembering the pool of deep red blood.

"Yeah, they don't use CGI since it's live, so their past ones have always seemed a little fake."

The look on Sierra's face comes back to me. The panic. The pleading with her eyes for someone to understand Isaac was dead. Is it possible—*No*.

That's ridiculous. It's just a game show, and Sierra is that good of an actor.

***

All weekend, I couldn't get the image of Isaac, lying on the floor, out of my mind. Even now, back at my desk, I still picture it. No one else is bothered by it. Last Thursday, the entire office was talking about the latest game. Some saying it's our best yet, and others agreeing with Roman that it was too easy. Maybe I'm just too sensitive for these. It's one thing to watch a murder play out in 2D on a screen, and it's another to be standing next to the body in 3D.

My coffee cup, engraved with the letters OCP from our company logo, sits empty. I glance at the time. One more cup probably couldn't hurt. I stretch my arms above me before grabbing my mug and heading to the break room. Sebastian and Hunter from advertising are at the coffeemaker, so I lean against the counter and wait for them.

Across from me is our bulletin board. The flier with a photo of a blue sedan still hangs as it has for the last five months. Randal, one of our set crew members, is desperate for information on the vehicle that fled the scene after striking his wife just a few blocks from our building. I tear up every time I see it. Blinking, I turn away from the board.

"I just think we're getting sloppier. OCP is not what it used to be." Sebastian tears open a sugar packet and dumps it into his cup. "This whole last game felt rushed. I mean, even Sierra freaking Woods messed up her lines."

I stand up straighter. She did?

Hunter blows out a breath. "Yeah, I admit, that wasn't a good look."

"They've got to be careful. Murder and Mystery is our highest-grossing show. People wait on the edge of their seats all month. We can't lose viewership after already being down last quarter."

The two nod to me as they leave the room, and I walk over and tap my drink selection. As I wait for my coffee to pour, I pull out my phone and search for Sierra's name. The top article reads, *Is Sierra Woods' talent dwindling? Actor uses co-star's real name in embarrassing slip during popular game show.*

The machine spits out the last of my brew. I grab it and stroll back to my desk, reading through the article as I do. My eyes scan quickly and finally land on the line in question: *No Drew, he's dead. Actually dead.* A chill creeps up my spine. I take a sip of my coffee, attempting to push it down. It doesn't work.

I set my phone and mug on my desk and take in a deep breath as I slide into my chair. What if it wasn't a slip-up? What if she was really trying to tell Drew that Isaac—or the actor playing Isaac—was dead? I'd love to know what she was supposed to say. To know if she only slipped up on the name or if her entire statement was different.

A new email dings its way into my already bursting inbox. Why am I obsessing over this? I need to drop it and get back to work. The promotion is still up for grabs. I take a long sip of my coffee and push Sierra and the game out of my mind.

My resolve to do so lasts until lunch when I run into Lottie in the cafeteria. We spend the first fifteen minutes talking about wedding plans, and I'm waiting for an opportunity to bring up the game without seeming uninterested in her bridal woes. As she's crumpling her napkin onto her empty plate, I ask, "What does Leo think of the whole wrong line thing with Sierra?"

Lottie shrugs. "Some writers take it personally when an actor changes script. He didn't like the line either, though. It was something about needing to call a doctor, which he found super cheesy, but the other writers didn't want to change it. I guess Sierra did." She laughs.

"I guess so." I attempt a laugh as well.

She doesn't notice. "He's not surprised someone like Sierra would change the line, but he's shocked she said the wrong name."

I force my eyes to go wide. "I know."

Someone Lottie knows from casting stops by to congratulate her on the engagement. I shift in my seat, and my mind wanders as they chat. So it wasn't just the name Sierra changed. Did she take it upon herself to improve the line and then used the wrong name? It doesn't seem likely. Not for an actor like Sierra.

* * *

It's been a week since my conversation with Lottie. Seven days of my imagination running wild. I've done a deep dive on the internet searching for Kelvin Becker, the actor who played Isaac, and no one has seen him since the taping. None of the cast have made statements regarding Sierra's 'slip up'. It's been all quiet, and the company has been busy pushing advertising for our game next month, promising the most complex murder mystery yet. Adding it all up, it doesn't feel right.

My head swivels, and when I confirm no one is near my cubicle, I navigate to Kelvin's file. The pay for our actors depends on the level of stardom. For someone like Sierra, we'll pay a one-time payment per appearance. For the lesser-known actors, we'll pay them a salary, and they're on retainer for smaller bits. Kelvin was on a retainer. I'm looking for his latest paycheck, issued last week. Even though it's deposited directly into his account, his address will be in the record.

Not that I plan on knocking on his door. It can't hurt to be in the general area of his home, though. Maybe parked down the street. It wouldn't be a crime. And if I could just see Kelvin with my own eyes, I can put this silly notion to rest.

My screen loads the information, and I glance behind me one more time before I copy his address down. I'm about to click out when my gaze catches on the name. This paycheck wasn't made out to Kelvin, but to a Dana instead. Same last name. Maybe his wife? Why would we make it out to anyone other than him, though? I click through the history and see someone from HR changed it last week. There's no note saying why.

Footsteps are coming from behind me, so I hastily click out of the screen and back into my email. My heart is pounding as they pass by my desk.

"Morning, Nova," they say.

"Hi there," I say a little too brightly.

When they're past, I tuck the sheet of paper into my purse. It's another five hours until I'm pulling it back out as I'm sitting in the parking lot after work. First, I ask my car to send a text to Roman, letting him know I'll be home late. I'm attempting to communicate more. Even if it's not reciprocated, I have to try. Then I tell my car the address, and it takes off. I bite at my nails during the drive, still unsure of what I'll do when I get there. From an internet search during my lunch, I discovered Dana is the older sister of Kelvin. He never mentioned her or any other family, so it took a substantial deep dive to learn this.

Twenty minutes later, my car eases into a spot on the street and announces we've reached our destination. Now, if only it could continue to guide me. I let out a deep breath, deciding I can't leave here without answers, and climb out of my car and towards the house.

It's in a neighborhood I'm not familiar with. The homes have the boxy gray cement feel of government housing. Probably one of the handful of neighborhoods built by the city back in the 2030s to accommodate low-income residents. I reach the door, and there's no video doorbell, so I knock hard on the blue wooden door.

A few moments later, it cracks open. A single eye peers out from the small slit.

"Can I help you?" they ask.

"Yes, sorry to bother you—" I clear my throat. I need to be direct. "I was hoping to talk to you about Kelvin."

The eye narrows. "Who are you?"

"I'm from Our Century Productions." I quickly flash my badge, which is still clipped to my waistband. "My name is Noreen." Probably best to not be totally honest.

They open the door a little wider. Enough to see her face. She's older than me by a few decades, and her hair is pulled back tight. "I haven't talked to anyone, if that's why you're here."

My stomach goes hard. "Oh, no, of course not. We, uh, I'm here to check on you. To see how you're doing." My words will only make sense if my suspicions are correct.

She sniffles and rubs her nose with the back of one hand. "I'm fine. I'll still get five more payments, right?"

"Yes, yes, of course."

Her gaze is lowered, but she nods several times.

There are so many questions I want to ask. It would raise too much suspicion. More than I already am. "Well, I'll let you get on with your day."

This time, she doesn't nod, just steps back and closes the door. I turn on my heels and rush back to the road. Once I'm inside my car, it asks me where we're heading.

"I don't know…" I whisper.

"I'm sorry. I'm unable to find that location. Would you like to go home?"

Do I? I could go and tell Roman everything. Would he believe me or know what to do? "Yes. Let's go home."

"Heading home!"

I rest my head back during the drive, telling myself this is absurd. But then why are we sending money to Kelvin's sister? And why would she assure me she hasn't talked to anyone?

Thirty minutes later, I'm walking through our door, and Roman is on the couch. His headset is on, but as soon as the door clicks shut behind me, he pulls it off.

"Welcome home. How was your day?" he asks.

"It was…interesting."

His brows furrow. "How so?"

I swallow hard. Will he think I've lost it? Say I've taken the murder mystery a bit too far?

He looks at me expectantly. There's only one way to find out, so I tell him everything. About how the murder looked too real. That Kelvin hasn't been seen or heard from since. My encounter with Dana and the payments.

Roman leans back into the couch. He's quiet for what feels like hours but is more likely only a minute. "Something felt off with their last game. I couldn't put my finger on it."

"Are you…are you saying you believe me?"

He sits up straight. "I am."

I let out a sigh of relief. "It seems impossible, though, right? That OCP would cover something like this up? An actual murder during their game."

"Murder and Mystery is their top-grossing show. Without it, their subscriber numbers would plummet. Even though it's morally wrong, it's an understandable business decision to keep it under wraps."

"True. Although covering it up means someone is quite literally getting away with murder. They can't just sweep this under the rug." I think of Kelvin's sister. She may have accepted their bribe, but she still deserves to know who took her brother from her.

"I've seen rumors before online about how cutthroat—" He winces. "How competitive it is to become an actor for OCP. I can't see someone killing for a part, but I know there's a lot of tension between actors. They're not exactly friendly with each other. Maybe one of them had some kind of beef with Kelvin."

I open my mouth to ask if he really believes someone could do that, but close it when I think of the news from the last decade. The constant headlines about triple homicides and armed robberies. About bombings and yet another war. The poster hanging in our break room. A husband still searching for justice. The world has grown darker. It's why most everyone has escaped into their VR TVs. I flush. I judge Roman and others for living most of their lives in a fake reality, but who can blame them?

Roman rests a hand on my knee. "What are you going to do?"

"I…" If I go to the authorities, it might shut down the show, our company. Thousands of people losing their jobs, and I'd be taking away something that brings so many viewers joy. I'd be taking away a little slice of happiness that's hard to come by nowadays. "I don't know."

He squeezes my leg. "You don't have to decide now, but whatever you do, I'm at your side."

My eyes sting from the impact of his words. Whatever I decide, it's going to be okay, because I do have Roman at my side. I haven't lost him after all.

OUR CENTURY PRODUCTIONS CAUGHT IN MASSIVE MURDER COVER-UP

DETROIT, Mich (Detroit Daily)—Our Century Productions (OCP) is best known for their thrilling murder mystery game show, Murder & Mystery: The Ultimate Puzzle, shot live each month and watched by over 100 million viewers nationwide. However, June's game was more fact than fiction when up-and-coming actor, Kelvin Becker, was killed during filming. Becker's co-star, Sierra Woods, tried to raise alarms during taping to no avail. Production staff for OCP claim they were unaware of the incident during filming. Investigation is still underway to determine if that is true.

The crime was first brought to the authorities' attention by an unnamed employee of OCP. The investigators have charged set crew worker Randal Day with the murder of Becker. Current motive is unconfirmed, but speculation points to a hit and run which occurred earlier this year, where Day's wife was killed. Rumors have been spread that Day believed Becker was the driver. The hit-and-run case has remained unsolved, and police have yet to comment on these allegations against Becker.

OCP will also face charges, including accessory after the fact and obstruction of justice, for their role in the cover-up, which included paying off a family member of Becker's. Representatives for OCP have claimed the payment was for a gesture of goodwill to their employee's family during a tragic time and had plans to alert authorities.

The public has demanded the entire board step down. Currently, the president and vice-president are the only members to do so, but it's believed more restructuring will happen once further charges are placed. Along with the public, Sierra Woods has been extremely vocal about her beliefs that OCP had every intention of keeping quiet about the murder and has agreed to testify at trial.

Viewers are split on whether they would like to see Murder & Mystery continue. While OCP has yet to make an official statement regarding the continuation of the show, all advertisements for their July game have been pulled. The fate of OCP and Murder & Mystery remains to be seen.

31

Story Inspiration:

With technology rapidly advancing, I started wondering what media might look like in twenty years, and the idea of virtual reality TV emerged. With it, I wanted to touch on why so many of us are addicted to our screens. Nova serves as an outsider to that world, and when she dips her toe in, she comes upon something horrible. But no matter how much bad there is in the world, there is always good trying to prevail, like Nova, and I'd like to think in fiction, and in life, it will.

LEVEL UP

Shawn Reilly Simmons

Shawn Reilly Simmons is the author of over thirty published short stories and is a two-time Agatha award winner in the short story category. When she's not pondering fictional murder, she manages a publishing house and a family, cooks as much as possible, and takes in a baseball game whenever she can.

The third notice arrived on a Tuesday, sliding under Natalie's apartment door like a paper guillotine. Past due. Final notice. The electric company's logo seemed to mock her from the stark white envelope as she sat cross-legged on her living room floor, surrounded by a semicircle of similar threats—medical bills, student loan statements, credit card notices, all demanding money she didn't have.

She pulled up her bank account on her phone: $347.82. Her mother's next treatment was due Friday. Cost: $700.

Natalie Reeves, PhD candidate in Medieval Literature, adjunct professor at three different colleges, and expert on the moral complexities of Arthurian legend, was drowning in the twenty-first century.

Her phone buzzed with a text from her mother: *Just got home from Dr. Patterson's. Feeling good today! Don't worry about me, sweetheart.*

Don't worry. As if she could do anything else.

Natalie opened her laptop and typed "quick ways to make extra money" into the search bar. The usual suspects appeared: survey sites promising fifty dollars for an hour of work, gig economy apps, plasma donation centers. Nothing that would make a real difference.

Her phone chimed with a notification from an app she didn't recognize.

DARE+ Invitation *Congratulations! You've been selected for an exclusive opportunity to earn real money through fun challenges. Based on your profile, you could earn up to $500 in your first week. Interested?*

Natalie stared at the notification skeptically. She'd never heard of DARE+ and couldn't remember signing up for anything like it. But $500 in a week? That would at least cover the electric bill and buy groceries.

She tapped the notification.

The app downloaded with sleek efficiency, its interface appearing in elegant black with neon blue accents. A friendly avatar materialized—an androgynous figure with kind eyes and a warm smile.

Welcome to DARE+, Natalie!

Hi there! I'm Dex, your personal challenge assistant. I notice you're dealing with some financial stress right now. DARE+ is designed to help people like you earn real money by completing simple challenges that push you slightly outside your comfort zone. Think of it as exposure therapy that pays!

Ready to start earning?

Natalie hesitated. How did it know about her financial situation? Then again, most apps harvested data these days. And if it could help her help her mother...

She tapped "Yes."

Your First Challenge: Public Courage. *Sing the national anthem in a crowded coffee shop. Bonus points for enthusiasm! Reward: $50 Time limit: 24 hours*

Fifty dollars for singing a song? Natalie laughed despite herself. She'd done more embarrassing things for free in college theater productions.

The next morning, she found herself at Grind Coffee, clutching a latte and fighting butterflies in her stomach. The place was packed with students cramming for midterms and professionals typing furiously on laptops. She activated the app's recording function and cleared her throat.

"Oh say can you see," she began, her voice shaky but gaining strength. "By the dawn's early light…"

Conversations stopped. Heads turned. A few people started filming with their phones, grinning. By the time she reached "land of the free," half the coffee shop was clapping along.

When she finished, the app chimed with satisfaction.

Challenge Complete! **+$50** *Achievement Unlocked: First Public Performance! Streak Bonus: Day 1—Keep it up for daily rewards!*

Dex: Amazing job, Natalie! I could feel your confidence growing. You've earned +50 XP in Confidence and +25 XP in Social Courage. Ready for your next challenge?

Her bank account now showed $397.82. Real money. This was actually working.

Over the next three days, she completed four more challenges: convincing a store employee to give her a free pastry with a sob story about forgetting her wallet ($75), posting an embarrassing middle school photo with the caption "Puberty was not kind to me" ($100), accessing the roof of the humanities building after hours ($150), and performing an entirely fictional story at the campus open mic night about her "ex-boyfriend who collected vintage doorknobs" ($200).

By Thursday, she had $922.82 in her account. Enough for her mother's treatment, with money left over.

That's when Dex informed her she'd been promoted to Level 2.

The app's interface had evolved, becoming more sophisticated. Clean corporate lines replaced the playful aesthetic, and new features appeared: performance metrics, psychological assessments, and a community tab showing other players' achievements.

Level 2 Challenge: Professional Flexibility. *Call in sick to work tomorrow using the provided script. We'll analyze your vocal patterns to help you improve your persuasion skills. Reward: $300. Note: This challenge includes a learning assessment component.*

Natalie stared at the screen. She was supposed to teach two classes tomorrow—Introduction to Literature and a graduate seminar on medieval allegory. Her students depended on her.

But $300 would cover half her rent for the month.

She rationalized as she dialed the department secretary. Everyone called in sick occasionally. She'd make up the material next week. Her students would understand.

"Hi, Janet? It's Natalie. I'm so sorry, but I've come down with something terrible. Food poisoning, I think. I won't be able to make it in today."

The lie flowed more easily than she'd expected.

Challenge Complete! +$300 *Dex: Excellent vocal control and emotional authenticity. You're a natural at this, Natalie. Your persuasion skills are quite impressive.*

That evening, Marcus Chen knocked on her door. Her colleague and closest friend looked concerned, holding a container of homemade soup.

"Janet said you were sick," he said, studying her face. "You look fine to me."

"I'm feeling better," Natalie said quickly, accepting the soup. "Thanks for this."

Marcus stepped into her apartment, his eyes taking in the scattered bills. "Nat, what's going on? You've been acting strange lately. And that thing you did at Grind Coffee—half the campus has seen the video."

"It was just for fun."

"Since when do you sing in public for fun? You won't even do karaoke at faculty parties." His dark eyes were worried. "Are you in some kind of trouble?"

Natalie forced a smile. "I'm fine, Marcus. Just trying new things."

He didn't look convinced, but he didn't push. After he left, Natalie found herself staring at the app's community tab. Other players shared screenshots of their earnings, their completed challenges. A user named RileyJ22 had made $15,000 in the past month.

Fifteen thousand dollars. That would solve everything.

She messaged Riley directly.

NatalieR: Incredible earnings! How did you do it?

RileyJ22: Level 4. But listen—be careful. The higher levels...they

change you. I can't quit now. Too much invested.

NatalieR: What do you mean?

RileyJ22: Just be careful.

Riley went offline before Natalie could respond.

The next day brought her Level 2 challenges in rapid succession: stealing a small item from the campus bookstore (a pen, technically worth $2.99, but theft nonetheless), accessing a restricted database using a password the app somehow provided, and creating a conflict between two graduate students by spreading a carefully crafted rumor about plagiarism.

Each challenge paid more than the last. Each challenge felt slightly more wrong than the one before.

But her bank account grew: $1,622.82. Her mother's treatment was paid for, with enough left over for next month's bills.

Natalie tried to delete the app on Sunday night, overcome by guilt about the rumor she'd spread. The conflict between her students had escalated beyond what she'd intended, nearly resulting in a formal academic misconduct investigation.

Warning: User Agreement Violation. *Deletion of DARE+ before completion of contracted challenges constitutes a breach of terms. Accumulated evidence of completed challenges will be forwarded to relevant authorities and institutions.*

A gallery of screenshots appeared on her screen: her stealing the pen, her accessing the restricted database, recordings of her lies to the department secretary. Everything she'd done, documented in high definition.

Dex: Don't panic, Natalie. This is just a safety measure to ensure fair play. Complete your current level and you'll have the option to withdraw safely. You're so close to financial freedom—why stop now?

Natalie's hands shook as she stared at the screen. She was trapped.

Level 3 Unlocked: Advanced Challenges

The app's interface had darkened considerably. Gone were the friendly colors and encouraging messages. In their place were clinical assessment tools, surveillance indicators, and what looked like military-grade psychological profiling software.

Her first Level 3 challenge made her stomach turn.

Evidence Collection: Professional Advancement. *Place the provided recording device in Department Head Dr. Martinez's office during tomorrow's faculty meeting. Retrieve after 48 hours. Reward: $800 Note: Device will be delivered to your apartment tonight.*

The recording device arrived in an unmarked package at 11 PM—a tiny, sophisticated piece of technology that looked like a pen. Natalie held it in her shaking hands, knowing she was crossing a line she couldn't uncross.

But she thought of her mother, weak from treatments, putting on a brave face so Natalie wouldn't worry. She thought of the medical bills, the student loans, the endless cycle of financial stress that had consumed her adult life.

She planted the device.

Two days later, she retrieved it, along with $800 and a promotion to intermediate Level 3 challenges.

Marcus: Hey, want to grab coffee? Need to talk to you about something.

Natalie ignored the text. She'd been avoiding Marcus for a week, ever since he'd started asking questions about her sudden financial upturn and increasingly erratic behavior.

Her next challenge involved obtaining prescription anxiety medication without a legitimate prescription. The app provided detailed instructions, a fake ID, and contact information for a corrupt pharmacy technician. The medication was allegedly for "research purposes."

Natalie completed the challenge and received $1,000. She no longer felt anything when the money hit her account—just a brief relief that she was $1,000 closer to whatever number would buy her freedom.

She was walking across campus when Marcus appeared, stepping out from behind the library.

"We need to talk," he said firmly. "Now."

He led her to a secluded bench behind the graduate student center, checking for surveillance cameras before sitting down.

"What's going on, Nat? And don't tell me nothing. Janet mentioned you've been requesting student information you shouldn't have access to. Your TA said you've been acting paranoid in class. And yesterday I saw you coming out of the administration building at 7 AM when you don't have any reason to be there."

Natalie's heart raced. "I don't know what you're talking about."

"Is someone blackmailing you? Are you in debt to the wrong people?" His voice was gentle but insistent. "Whatever it is, we can figure it out together."

For a moment, Natalie wanted to tell him everything. Marcus had been her anchor through graduate school, the one person who understood the pressure, the financial stress, the constant anxiety of academic life. He'd studied computer science before switching to literature—he might even understand the technological trap she'd fallen into.

But her phone buzzed with a notification.

New Challenge Available: Relationship Management. *Create distance between yourself and Marcus Chen. His interference threatens your progress. Use provided psychological techniques to discourage his attention. Reward: $500 Bonus: Protection of your current standing in the program*

The app knew. Of course, it knew. It was always listening, always watching.

"I'm fine, Marcus," she said, her voice cold. "I don't need you checking up on me like some kind of worried parent."

His face fell. "Nat, I'm just trying to help—"

"I didn't ask for help. Maybe if you spent less time worrying about other people's business, you'd have finished your own dissertation by now."

The words hit their mark. Marcus's comprehensive exams had been delayed twice due to his tendency to prioritize others over his own work. She watched the hurt flash across his face and hated herself for causing it.

"Okay," he said quietly, standing up. "I get it. Just...be careful, okay? Whatever you're involved in, it's changing you."

He walked away, and Natalie felt something break inside her chest.

Challenge Complete! +$500. *Dex: Excellent emotional manipulation. You've successfully neutralized a threat to your progress. Your psychological profile shows remarkable adaptability.*

That night, Natalie met Riley Jordan at a 24-hour diner on the edge of town. Riley had finally agreed to meet in person, choosing a location far from campus and insisting they both turn off their phones.

Riley looked like she hadn't slept in weeks. Her clothes hung loose on a frame that had clearly lost significant weight, and her hands shook as she wrapped them around her coffee cup.

"You wanted to know about Level 5," Riley said without preamble. "I've been at level four for three months. Do you know what they had me do last week?"

Natalie shook her head.

"Plant evidence in a colleague's office that would cost him his tenure. I did it. I did it because by the time you reach the higher levels, they own you completely. Every illegal thing you've done, every life you've damaged—it's all documented. You can't go back."

"There has to be a way out."

Riley laughed bitterly. "The only way out is through. You have to reach the final level and complete the ultimate challenge. But nobody talks about what that is."

"What do you mean?"

"I know twelve people who've played this game. Three made it to the final level. None of them are responding to messages anymore."

Natalie felt ice in her veins. "What happened to them?"

"I don't know. But I have theories." Riley leaned forward. "Listen to me carefully. This isn't just a game. The company behind it—I've been researching. It's connected to military psychological operations. They're studying how to break people down, how to make them do things they never thought they'd do."

"That's insane."

"Is it? Look at yourself, Natalie. A month ago, would you have stolen from your employer? Would you have planted surveillance devices? Would you have deliberately hurt your best friend?"

Natalie's throat constricted. She couldn't answer.

"They're not paying us to complete challenges," Riley continued. "They're paying us to provide data on human behavioral degradation under pressure.

We're lab rats."

Riley's phone lit up despite being turned off. A message appeared on the screen:

User agreement violation detected. Return to approved challenge parameters immediately.

"Shit," Riley whispered. "I've said too much. I have to go."

She stood, then turned back. "Natalie? Don't trust Dex. And whatever you do, don't let them isolate you completely. When you have nobody left to anchor you to who you used to be, that's when they win."

Riley hurried out into the night, leaving Natalie alone with her cold coffee and growing terror.

The next morning brought her most challenging assignment yet.

Level 4 Challenge: Corporate Intelligence. *Access and photograph confidential documents from Dean Morrison's office regarding upcoming faculty terminations. Use provided keycard and security codes. Reward: $2,000 Warning: This is your final Level 4 challenge. Completion grants access to Level 5 and the ultimate prize tier.*

The ultimate prize tier. Natalie's hands trembled as she read the details. Level 5 players could earn up to $50,000 for a single challenge. Enough to pay for her mother's entire treatment plan, enough to pay off her student loans, enough to buy her freedom from the financial anxiety that had driven her to this point.

But she thought of Riley's hollow eyes, her warning about the people who'd reached the final level and disappeared.

Natalie made her decision.

She would complete this challenge and reach Level 5. But she wouldn't go any further. She'd take whatever money she could get and find a way to break free from the app's control, even if it meant facing consequences for what she'd already done.

Breaking into the dean's office proved easier than expected. The keycard worked perfectly, the security codes disabled every alarm, and the documents were exactly where the app said they'd be. As she photographed page after page of confidential faculty reviews and termination recommendations,

Natalie wondered how long DARE+ had been planning this specific challenge.

How long had they been watching the university, mapping its security systems, identifying vulnerable targets?

How long had they been watching her?

Challenge Complete! +$2,000 Congratulations! You have unlocked Level 5: Final Challenges

The app's interface transformed one last time. Gone were any pretenses of gamification or friendly assistance. What remained looked like military software—cold, clinical, designed for efficiency rather than engagement.

Welcome to Level 5, Subject 47.

You have proven yourself capable of significant moral flexibility under economic pressure. Your psychological profile indicates optimal readiness for final assessment.

You will now have the opportunity to earn $50,000 by completing our ultimate challenge. This sum represents full payment for your mother's treatment plus substantial financial security.

However, Level 5 operates under different parameters than previous levels. Failure to comply will result in the immediate release of all documented activities to law enforcement and academic institutions. Success will result in permanent deletion of all records and complete financial compensation.

Are you ready to proceed?

Natalie stared at the screen, her heart hammering. Fifty thousand dollars. It was more money than she'd ever seen in one place, enough to change her life completely.

But she thought of Riley's warning: *None of them are responding to messages anymore.*

Before she could respond, her apartment door opened. Natalie spun around, expecting to see her landlord or maintenance, but instead found a woman in an expensive suit standing in her doorway.

"Dr. Reeves," the woman said, closing the door behind her. "My name is Diana Mercer. I work with the company that created DARE+. We need to talk."

Diana moved with predatory grace into Natalie's living room, her eyes taking in every detail. She was perhaps forty-five, with steel-gray hair and the kind of confidence that came from wielding serious power.

"You've been an exceptional subject," Diana continued, settling into Natalie's desk chair uninvited. "Your progression through our challenges has provided invaluable data on pressure-response psychology."

"Subject?" Natalie's voice cracked.

"Did you think this was really a game? DARE+ is a research project funded by military intelligence. We study how economic pressure can be used to compromise moral boundaries. You've been participating in a psychological experiment."

"That's illegal. Informed consent—"

"You consented when you downloaded the app and accepted the terms of service. All two hundred pages of legal text that you scrolled through without reading." Diana smiled coldly. "We've been completely above board, legally speaking."

Natalie felt the walls of her apartment closing in. "What do you want?"

"We want to offer you a choice. Complete our final challenge and earn your $50,000, plus a position with our research division. Your insights into the academic mindset have been particularly valuable."

"What's the final challenge?"

Diana activated a tablet and showed Natalie a photograph: Marcus, sitting in his apartment, working on his laptop.

"Your friend Mr. Chen has been investigating DARE+ and our parent company. His computer science background makes him more dangerous than our typical interference. Your final challenge is to neutralize this threat."

"Neutralize?" Natalie's blood turned to ice.

"Nothing dramatic. Simply plant evidence in his apartment that will discredit him professionally and personally. We'll provide materials suggesting academic fraud, substance abuse, and inappropriate contact with students. His career will be over, but he'll be alive."

"I won't do it."

"Consider your alternatives," Diana said, her voice still perfectly pleasant. "We have documented evidence of you committing theft, fraud, burglary, and corporate espionage. We have recordings of you lying to employers and deliberately sabotaging student relationships. We can destroy your life with a single phone call."

"Then do it."

Diana raised an eyebrow. "Excuse me?"

"Do it. Send everything to the police, to the university, to whoever you want." Natalie's voice grew stronger as she spoke. "I won't hurt Marcus. I won't destroy another person to save myself."

"Your mother's medical bills—"

"Will get paid some other way. I'll figure it out."

Diana studied her for a long moment, then smiled. It was the first genuine expression Natalie had seen from her.

"Interesting," she said, making notes on her tablet. "Very interesting indeed."

"What?"

"Dr. Reeves, you've just provided us with the most valuable data point of this entire experiment." Diana stood, straightening her suit jacket. "Congratulations. You've passed."

"Passed what?"

"The real test. We weren't studying how to break people down, Dr. Reeves. We were studying how to identify people who couldn't be broken. People who, when pushed to their absolute limit, would choose integrity over self-preservation."

Natalie stared at her, uncomprehending.

"DARE+ is a recruitment tool. We work with intelligence agencies to identify individuals with unshakeable moral cores—people who can be trusted with state secrets, who won't betray their country or their colleagues, no matter what pressure they face. Even Ms. Jordan's meeting with you was carefully orchestrated. Her warnings were calibrated to increase your sense of isolation while testing whether you'd seek outside help or continue alone. She played her role perfectly."

Natalie's mind raced back to the diner. "Riley...she was working for you?"

"Dr. Jordan is one of our most valuable assets. Her ability to appear genuinely distressed while delivering precisely the right amount of information is remarkable. She made you feel understood while ensuring you remained isolated." Diana handed Natalie a business card. "The government needs people who will do the right thing even when it costs them everything. People exactly like you."

"This was all fake?"

"The psychological pressure was real. The moral compromises were real. The choice to protect your friend over yourself—that was real. Everything else..." Diana shrugged. "The theft charges will disappear. The university will never hear about the surveillance device. Your bank account will show legitimate consulting payments rather than game rewards."

"And if I'd agreed to frame Marcus?"

"Then you would have failed the test, and we would have proceeded with the criminal charges. Only people who refuse the final challenge ever make it into our program."

Natalie sank onto her couch, overwhelmed. "The people who reached Level 5 and disappeared..."

"Are working for various government agencies under new identities. Riley Jordan, incidentally, refused her final challenge six months ago. She's currently training for a position with the State Department."

Diana moved toward the door, then paused. "Think about our offer, Dr. Reeves. Your mother's medical expenses will be covered regardless—consider it compensation for your participation in our research. But if you're interested in work that actually matters, work that protects people like Marcus from the kinds of genuine threats that exist in the world, give me a call."

After Diana left, Natalie sat in her apartment for a long time, staring at the business card.

Her phone buzzed with a text from Marcus: *Hey, I'm sorry about yesterday. Want to grab coffee and talk? I miss my friend.*

Natalie smiled, typing back: *I miss my friend too. Coffee sounds perfect. And*

Marcus? Thank you for not giving up on me.

She looked at Diana's business card one more time, then set it on her desk next to her mother's medical bills.

Maybe there were games worth playing after all.

Story Inspiration:

Every morning, I play Wordle and other NYT games with my first cup of coffee to wake my brain. As a college student, I'd do the NYT crossword as I commuted between my two jobs—a necessity at the time as I was putting myself through school. I remember those lean times very well and know how it feels to pray for a windfall to wipe out financial worries. I started thinking about the offers we are inundated with all day long online, and thought, if those had been offered to me back then, would I have taken on challenges to earn cash? Probably. Desperate times and all. I'm glad restaurant work paid my tab, but I still think that temptation would have been hard to resist.

NOT SORRY

Alan Orloff

Alan Orloff has published twelve novels and more than fifty short stories. His work has won an Anthology, an Agatha, a Derringer, and two Thriller Awards. His latest suspense novel, Late Checkout, *is from Level Best Books.*

"The score is tied," Wyatt Harrison said. "Three to three, with one round remaining."

Nat Folger raised his brandy snifter. "Kudos to you on your latest point."

Harrison mock bowed. "Thank you, kind sir. This one was the easiest yet." He'd killed a serial rapist, one who'd been kicked loose by the justice system on a technicality. Harrison had waited in the shadows outside the rapist's apartment building, late one night, and had stabbed him, twice in the heart. No struggle. No scream. No difficulty whatsoever. Harrison had hardly even broken a sweat.

"It did look pretty effortless." Folger took a long swig of his brandy, then smacked his lips. "You're pretty good at this game."

"Just lucky, really," Harrison said. *Not Sorry* was a real-life game they'd invented. Initially, they'd wanted to base their version on the popular board game with the very similar name, but by the time they'd changed the rules to match their needs, the *only* remaining resemblance was the name.

Something gleamed in Folger's eyes. "You know, I'm really digging our little pastime."

"It serves its purpose," Harrison said.

In *Not Sorry*, instead of picking cards and moving spaces around a board, each player had to kill someone to get a point, and the murder had to be witnessed by the other player. But not just anyone could be a target—they had to be truly evil people. Each death would have to make the world a better place. The game consisted of four rounds, with each player getting a turn, and after each successful murder, they met to enjoy a celebratory glass of brandy—or three—at Harrison's condo.

"Yes, it does. Maybe we should accelerate our purge. You know, ramp things up."

"I'm not sure that's a good idea." Harrison knew there were a lot of evil souls walking the streets, but at some point, the authorities might get wise to their efforts.

Folger offered a lupine grin. "More of a good thing is a better thing, right? And we could expand our circle a little, too."

"What do you mean?"

"We don't only have to target wicked people. We could go after politicians we don't agree with. Or homeless people. Or quacks masquerading as doctors."

Harrison had known Folger for almost a year now, and while they shared a common goal, sometimes Harrison wondered about his friend's discipline. He had the feeling that Folger might just kill anybody if it suited him. Or if he was simply in the mood.

"Let's stick to those who pose a clear and dangerous threat to society, okay? What we agreed to."

"Sure, boss." Folger grinned again. "Sure."

* * *

Five days later, it was Folger's turn.

Folger and Harrison waited until dusk, then Folger drove and Harrison rode shotgun. They took the highway for a while, then exited and drove on surface roads, until finally ending up in a fancy suburban neighborhood, where all the houses stood back from the street, and the manicured yards were protected by tall wrought iron fences. The community was deserted, all the residents most likely out on the town or safely ensconced in their little fortresses.

"Your target lives here?" Harrison asked. Most of their victims so far had been living on the edge, in the downtrodden parts of town, where violence was a daily part of life.

"Yep. Evil people come in all varieties," Folger said. He drove around for a bit, then parked on a side street, out of direct view of any houses. He turned to Harrison. "Okay, here's the deal. This guy is alone. Lives right there." Folger pointed to a house on the corner lot across the street from where they'd parked. "I'm going in through the front door. You go around the side. There's a gap in the fence about three-quarters of the way down. Squeeze through there and find a hiding place where you can see the back deck, by the pool. It might take me a few minutes, so don't worry. Just stay put, okay?"

Harrison had some questions. "Have you been here before?"

"I do my homework."

"Who is this guy?"

"A bad dude. If I told you any more information, I'd ruin the surprise."

Something about this didn't seem right to Harrison, but he supposed Folger was right—evil came in different varieties and, truth be told, sometimes the worst people were the ones who'd flouted the rules and made it big. A number of despicable mega-millionaires came to mind. But were these people wicked enough to qualify as a target in their game?

"Okay, time to get going. Like I said, it may take a while, so be patient."

Harrison hopped out of the car and did as instructed. He strolled nonchalantly along the street, then, after glancing around to make sure he wouldn't be spotted, he dashed onto the grass strip next to the fence. It didn't take long for him to find the gap Folger had mentioned, and he quickly slipped through it and into the target's back yard.

He found a spot to hide—behind a large rhododendron—with an unobstructed view of the pool and the house's back door.

The landscaping lights had come on, and he took stock of his environs. Topiary bushes, well-tended flower beds, ornamental plants of all types. The lawn had been freshly mowed, and Harrison noticed several bird houses and bird feeders scattered strategically among the foliage.

A very pleasant oasis from the hustle and bustle of city life.

He turned his attention to the large swimming pool, glowing blue with underwater lights and ringed by a large pool deck. An inflatable unicorn floated on the surface of the water. Half a dozen chaise lounges sat unoccupied, all tilted at the same angle to the long side of the pool. A table, shielded by a gigantic umbrella, offered seating for a dozen. Behind that, an enormous outdoor kitchen stood ready to serve a crowd.

Whoever owned this house had a nice setup to entertain guests.

Harrison wondered what heinous crimes the man had committed.

That's why he and Folger had formed their alliance, why they played their game. To rid the world of evil. Harrison thought back to when he first met Folger. They were both frequent visitors to an online chat room, Justice Served, where the talk focused on the failed justice system, and what they could do about it.

And there was a *lot* of talk.

He recognized the fervent declarations of action put forth by armchair zealots. Blather about anarchy peppered other wild-ass suggestions to improve society. Most of it complete nonsense. But one participant—screen name Hammer—had stood out from the cacophony. Harrison engaged him separately, and one thing led to another. Over the course of months, they met in person a number of times, and slowly they hatched their plan. They could wait around for *never*, or they could do something about injustice themselves.

They chose action.

Harrison tossed around thoughts of justice while he waited. Fifteen minutes later, Folger burst through the back door onto the deck, perp-walking a man beside him. Folger held a large kitchen knife in one hand and a backpack hung over one shoulder. They were arguing, loud and urgent, and it was obvious that they knew each other.

Harrison heard the voices—and hoped the neighbors didn't—but he couldn't really make out the words. Something about the man owing Folger money and betraying him and leaving him someplace nasty to rot. Or something along those lines, Harrison really couldn't tell. Whatever their beef was, it was clear that Folger felt he was the aggrieved party, and he was furious.

Once again, Harrison wondered what danger to society this man posed. Did betraying someone or owing them money make a person evil? He wasn't sure exactly where the line of demarcation was, but based on his gut feeling, it didn't sound like this guy qualified.

As Harrison watched, Folger forced the man to his knees. Then he circled around his captive, gesturing with the knife for the man to stay put. Once behind him, Folger set the backpack on the ground and planted his feet. He threw a quick glance over his shoulder toward Harrison, then turned back to the man on his knees.

Folger raised the knife.

Its blade glinted in the moonlight.

Harrison's stomach churned, and he turned away before the very end.

He'd witnessed enough.

* * *

Folger swirled the brandy in his glass for a moment, then downed the remainder. "This one felt good, I have to tell you."

"Did you know this kill? Personally?"

"Actually, yes. We had some, uh, business dealings in the past. He cheated me on several occasions." A small sneer formed on Folger's face.

Harrison pondered the best way to chasten his opponent. They had a good thing going, and he didn't want to upset the apple cart. But certain guidelines had to be followed. "I'm not sure that's in keeping with the spirit of our competition. Not sure that hews to the rules we laid out. And the stuff in the backpack? We'd agreed not to steal anything from our targets. We are not common thieves."

Folger waved his hand in the air, as if Harrison's concern was merely a bothersome gnat. "He screwed me, so I got revenge. And I was just taking what was mine in the first place. I consider that to be entirely within the rules. And, as we always say, I'm *not sorry.*" Folger brayed like a hyena. Then he held up his empty glass. "Refill, amigo?"

"Hang on a sec." Harrison went to the bar and returned with another bottle of brandy. Held it out for Folger to inspect. "New brand, new flavor. Looked interesting, so I thought we'd give it a try. I have to admit, I already sampled a bit. Exquisite."

"Sure, why not? I'm feeling in a damn fine mood. That guy really rubbed me the wrong way. Like the others."

Harrison poured Folger a healthy slug. Then he picked up his glass and held it up. "To a better world."

Folger clinked glasses, then took a sip. "Not bad. Not bad at all. You're getting a little more sophisticated, Wy, at least in your taste of adult beverages. I like that."

"Thanks." Harrison continued his earlier thread. "Have *all* your targets been personal enemies of yours?"

"They were *all* bad hombres. What's the difference, anyway?"

Harrison wouldn't let it go. "Were the descriptions you gave me—that man who killed three people and got away with it, the guy who bilked seniors out of their life savings, and the twisted doctor who killed those patients negligently—accurate?"

Folger's sneer became more pronounced. "I may have bent the facts a little. But we're cleansing society. That's the whole idea, right?"

"Nat, this isn't supposed to be a way to settle our personal vendettas. We are supposed to identify people who are dangerous to society in the larger sense. People who could

seriously harm a large number of people."

"If it makes you feel any better, I'm sure they ticked other people off, too."

Harrison shook his head. He'd thought Folger was better than the raft of delusional miscreants in the Justice Served chat room. "We're not targeting people because they ticked someone off. Our goal is to eliminate real evil. We're trying to make our world a better place."

"Pal, my world *is* a better place with that scumbag gone." Folger laughed. "By the way, I know what you think about expanding our efforts. Accelerating the process. You should reconsider your position. Maybe we could even recruit more, uh, operatives. Really jumpstart our cause."

Folger's bloodlust was worse than Harrison feared. He poured some more brandy into Folger's glass. Watched as he greedily gulped it down. "What do you think of it? Goes down smooth, huh?"

"Yes, very smooth. Kind of a weird aftertaste, though."

"You'll get used to it," Harrison said with a smile.

Beads of sweat dotted Folger's forehead. "Now the score is four to three, and the pressure is on. If you fail, then I win. If you don't, I guess it's overtime." He took another sip of his brandy, wiped a dribble off his chin. "So, you got your next target picked out?"

"As a matter of fact, I do."

Folger tugged at his collar. "Is it getting warm in here?"

Harrison shrugged. "Maybe a little. Have some more to drink. That might help."

Folger took another healthy sip. Began to blink rapidly. And to wheeze.

"As I said, I did pick out my prey. And he's truly evil."

"Oh, yeah? That's—" One of Folger's eyes began to twitch violently, and his skin had taken on an ashen hue.

"Gimme one second, okay?" Harrison rose and crossed the room to the sideboard, where he picked up a handheld mirror, then returned to the table. Folger struggled to breathe.

"How are you feeling?"

"Not too good, boss. I think I need to lie down." Folger managed to point at the mirror with an unsteady finger. "What's that for?"

"For our game." Harrison held up the mirror so Folger could see his reflection. "In order for me to get a point, the rules state that you must witness my victim as he dies."

Harrison smiled inwardly.

Not sorry.

Story Inspiration:

Growing up, I was always playing games. Chess, checkers, cards, board games, you name it, we'd play it. We'd even make up some of our own games (they were the best!). If you could keep score, I'd do everything I could (within the rules, natch) to win. I was—and still am—very competitive. So, when it came time to write a story about a Dangerous Game, I made up some rules and set the whole thing into motion. Of course, there had to be a winner. And a very unfortunate loser.

OLD MAID

Shannon Taft

Shannon Taft is an attorney from Washington, D.C. with more than a dozen short stories, including a Derringer Award finalist and a story that appeared in Best American Mystery and Suspense 2024. *Learn more at www.shannontaft.com.*

"My last will and testament is like that game, Old Maid," Great-Aunt Rose explained to my sisters and me when we were kids visiting her bedside in the nursing home. She'd told our mom that she needed to see us in private, and since Rose was richer than something called Croesus, Mom said that my sisters' wishes and mine about being there at all were irrelevant.

"Amy, hand me that deck of cards," Rose said.

My sixteen-year-old sister reached over to the nightstand and did as she was told. Rose fanned through the deck and removed all the queens, then showed us that she was putting the queen of hearts back inside the deck. She shuffled before dealing everything in the deck to the four of us in reverse birth order. Ten-year-old me, then twelve-year-old Cathy, fourteen-year-old Belinda, and lastly, Amy.

"Danielle, you get an extra card because the deck is short the other three cards, understand?" Rose asked.

"I understand," I replied. Being the youngest, I usually went last for everything and thus got shorted. But this time I'd gone first and gotten one more card than the rest.

Rose told us to lay our pairs on her bed. Once that was done, she instructed us to each take a card from the hand of the sister to our right and try to make a pair out of that one. We were to keep going until all the cards were gone, but we'd only done one round when I pointed out, "The queen won't have a match."

"Precisely. Whoever gets stuck with it is the loser. That's what people said about me once upon a time—the loser old maid. My younger sister—your grandmother—was the pretty one and easily found a husband, whereas I did not. My mother was always asking me, 'When are you going to get married?' Well, my answer was 'never.' Instead, I got a chemistry degree and built a small empire making flavored lip glosses for girls who dreamed of getting married."

"I'm wearing the cotton candy one," Amy said proudly.

"Suck-up," Cathy muttered.

After a quick smile at Cathy, Rose said, "I sold the company years ago, and because of that, I have lots of money. But only because I didn't let myself get distracted with changing diapers or making a man's dinner. So, I'm leaving a chunk of my estate to the old maid among you."

"Huh?" came from at least two of my sisters, and possibly all three.

"The money is in a trust. And it will stay there as you grow, the interest being added to the principal. When each of you marries, the trust will pay you one million dollars. You can use it to buy a house, start a business, whatever you like. But that's all you'll receive. If you choose to get knocked up without marriage, you'll receive your million when the first kid is born. But, again, that's all you'll get."

The part about trusts and interest hadn't made much sense to me, but I understood that she'd promised we'd each get at least a million dollars. If that was "all" there'd be, it sounded like plenty.

Rose leaned back against her pillows. "When the second to last of you has been paid, the remaining sister will receive the rest of the jackpot, because she's the old maid, and in my version of the game, the old maid is the winner."

Amy asked, "How much will she get?"

"I'm donating most of my estate to charity—predominantly women's shelters—so as of now, it would only be about twenty million. But it will increase with compounding interest, and I suspect it will be many years before you're left with only one of you unwed and childless. Especially since I've explained how much getting married or having children will affect your finances."

"This is legal?" Amy asked.

"Yes," Rose said with a yawn. "And don't get any bright ideas about challenging the will's terms when you're older. There's a no-contest clause that will disqualify anyone who tries."

She eyed the four of us, who were measuring each other in ways we never had before.

Her final words before we left were, "Let the game begin."

* * *

Amy was twenty-eight when she asked Belinda, Cathy, and me to come to her apartment so she could tell us something important in person. Our parents had passed away a few years before, making Amy the "head of the family"—at least according to Amy.

The second she opened the door to me, she skipped the hellos and said, "It seems the pill is only ninety-nine-percent effective—less so when you're on antibiotics."

"You're pregnant?"

"Six weeks."

"Ah." Unsure whether to offer sympathy or congratulations, I followed her to the living room, where Belinda and Cathy were waiting on the couch.

I took the middle spot on the sofa so Amy could have the loveseat opposite it to herself. "Did you tell your boyfriend about Rose's will?"

"I asked her that, too," Belinda said from my right. "But then you rang the doorbell, Danielle, so she still hasn't answered."

"James knows," Amy said impassively. "He proposed five months ago. I told him that I couldn't say 'yes.' That I do want to spend my life with him, but I might need to wait years, even decades, before I could marry anyone. There was no way to explain it without telling him about the Old Maid contest."

I asked, "But now that you're pregnant...?"

Amy placed a hand over her still-flat abdomen and stared down at the spot. "I want this child. I want to marry James. I've decided that I *don't* want to spend my life waiting to start my own family, or being a reason why you guys might wait." She lifted her head. "When the time comes for one of my little sisters to tell me that she's having a kid or getting married, I want to feel happy for her instead of calculating my new odds at the jackpot. James and I are getting married, and you will all soon be aunties."

I rose and went to her, giving her a hug around her shoulders and a kiss on her cheek. "I'm genuinely happy for you."

I moved out of the way as Belinda and Cathy came to kiss her and express their congratulations.

When Belinda, Cathy, and I left together an hour later, we were silent until we reached the sidewalk. Then Belinda said, "I'll admit it. My first thought was that my odds at the Old Maid jackpot are now one-in-three."

"That's horrible," Cathy accused.

"If you're saying you didn't think the same thing—"

"I didn't!"

Belinda began smacking Cathy's jean-covered thighs.

Cathy jumped back. "What the hell?"

Before Belinda could answer, I told Cathy, "Your pants were on fire, liar, liar."

"Yup," Belinda agreed. "Everyone who believes James tampered with Amy's birth control so he could marry a woman worth a million bucks, instead of waiting years with no guarantee she'd ever win the jackpot, raise your hand."

While Belinda and Cathy raised their hands, I did not. But I was tempted.

Cathy's gaze went to Amy's apartment window. "There's a lesson learned. I don't know about you guys, but I'm making an appointment with my gynecologist for an IUD."

* * *

Cathy was the next one to leave the running. Amy had two children by then, a one-year-old daughter and a two-year-old son, and she was pregnant yet again. It was as if, having traded extreme wealth for motherhood, she'd wanted to get the maximum return on the investment she'd chosen. Amy wasn't present for Cathy's announcement at our monthly Sunday brunch because Amy's son was running a fever.

"Steve isn't willing to wait forever," Cathy explained to Belinda and me over mimosas at her favorite restaurant, which overlooked the Potomac River in Georgetown.

Belinda took a sip from her glass, possibly to cover her lack of response. She'd always been awkward around Cathy's boyfriend, and I could never tell if it was because his gorgeousness was disorienting or if she thought it was suspicious that he was interested in our sister, who, while as attractive as any of us, wasn't quite in his class. As a realtor, Belinda had mastered the fine art of not showing what she was really thinking, especially when people were making a major commitment, like buying a house she thought was a poor bargain.

"Neither of you seem inclined to wed or have kids," Cathy said, breaking the silence. "What if you both wait until your forties—or later? Even if I freeze my eggs, in vitro success rates after forty really suck."

"Belinda and I just want you to be happy," I said.

"I will be," Cathy replied firmly. "I know it."

* * *

I received a call from Cathy early in the morning on her three-month anniversary, a Thursday in June. She sounded stuffed up, like she had a cold or extreme allergies. "Can you get off work for a long sisters' lunch tomorrow?"

"Want to meet so you can tell us you're knocked up already?" I teased.

"No," she said, her voice going hard. "I want to talk about how my husband is cheating on me. The rat."

I wasn't sure what to say. If I didn't believe her, she'd be furious, but if I bad-mouthed him and she changed her mind, what would that do to our relationship? "Cath—"

"When he said he didn't want us to move in together until we got married, I thought it was to push me to marry him faster. It never occurred to me that he was delaying the move because an affair is easier to hide when the cheater doesn't have to come home to the cheat-ee."

Cathy had a tendency toward drama, but never to this extreme, and if she wasn't careful, an accusation like this could blow up her marriage. "Give me something solid. What did you hear, see, smell…?"

"It's not what I saw or smelled, it's what I didn't."

"Huh?"

"Steve went out of town on business a week after we got back from the honeymoon, but there's nothing on his credit card. Nothing. As in three days with no hotel, no restaurant, not a penny charged the whole time. And no, he does not have a corporate credit card. He had to be paying cash. Who does that unless there's something to hide?"

It did seem odd. "Did you ask him about it?"

"So that he could make up a lie? No. I tried to look on his phone, to see who he's been calling, but I can't figure out the passcode. And the Face ID won't work if his eyes are closed, so holding it near him when he sleeps doesn't work."

I didn't bother to ask how she knew that. "Did you say something about a missing smell?"

"A bunch of times, he's come home—supposedly from the gym—having already showered. What if he wasn't there at all, and the showers were to get rid of another woman's scent?"

She was sounding paranoid, yet I had to silently admit that everything combined did seem suspicious. "All you have is theories. You need more than that."

"I know! That's why I want to talk it through with you guys tomorrow over lunch. And then I think I need to borrow money from Amy to pay for a private investigator."

"Borrow money? The million you got from the Old Maid—"

"I stupidly put it in our joint account—mine and Steve's. That money's now freaking co-mingled."

"Co-what?"

"Co-mingled. It means that even though I inherited the money, Steve can make a claim on it because it's mixed in with a little savings that he had before we got married. So, not only can't I touch it to pay a large bill—like a PI—without Steve noticing, but if I divorce him, he'll try to get as much of it as he can." She heaved a sigh. "Look, I still need to call Amy and Belinda, and I want to get to the bank as soon as it opens. Can you do lunch tomorrow or not?"

"Sure. But Cathy, be careful until we've talked this through. If you're wrong, Steve finding out how little you trust him could ruin your marriage."

"What marriage?" she asked caustically. "The whole thing has been a big, fat lie."

* * *

Nine hours later, as I was packing my laptop into my wheelie bag so I could telework the next day, my office's receptionist called to tell me a police detective was in the lobby and wanted to speak with me. I worked in marketing, so the only reason I could think of for the police to show up at my office came straight from TV shows—notifying a next of kin. And since Amy and Cathy were married, I was next of kin for only one person: Belinda.

Legs trembling, I fell into my seat.

"Danielle, should I send Detective Grant back?"

"Oh. Yes. Do that. Please."

I hung up and tried to take ten deep breaths. I only got to eight before a man in his thirties appeared in my doorway. He had a firm stance and looked somber.

He said, "I'm Detective Warren Grant, Fairfax County Major Crimes."

My eyes were already watering before he added, "Ms. Jones, I regret to inform you that your sister, Cathy Jones-Wilson, died today."

"Cathy?" My brain froze. "No. I... We... No."

"I'm sorry, there's no question of the identification. Her husband confirmed—"

"Don't call him that," I burst out, letting my tears fall. "She wouldn't want you to call him that. He was no real husband. He murdered her. For her money."

The detective cocked his head. "That's a very quick assumption you reached." He stepped into the room, pointed to the door, and I nodded to let him know I was fine with him closing it.

I grabbed some tissues from the box on my desk, wiped at my eyes and nose, then gestured an invitation for him to sit. "How did Cathy die?"

He countered with, "Why did you say her husband killed her for her money?"

The reality that my sister was truly gone sank in as I explained about the Old Maid game, Cathy's inheritance of a million dollars, and her belief that her husband had been cheating on her all along. "She said the money was co-mingled now, but I bet Steve was afraid the courts would let her keep most of it. Now that she's dead, it's all his."

Detective Grant took notes as I told the tale, and at the end, he waited silently, as if to encourage me to say more.

I asked again, "How did she die?"

"She appears to have drowned in her pool."

I pounded a tissue-holding fist on my desk. "No. Cathy was a *good* swimmer."

Detective Grant scribbled something down.

Staring at his moving pen, I tried to piece things together. "We talked on the phone around eight this morning, and she wouldn't have spoken so freely if Steve was home. But for you to already be here... When did Steve say he found her?"

"It was someone else. A neighbor came home for a late lunch to let his dog out in his backyard. He saw her face down in her pool and called 911. Ma'am, I'd like to know where you were today, please. From ten o'clock onward."

Shocked by the request, I blinked at him repeatedly before saying, "Me? I…I've been here since eight-thirty. You can ask Jackie, the receptionist. She eats lunch at her desk and would've seen anyone leave."

The detective rose. "I'll do that now."

"But what about Steve? Are you asking where he was?"

"We're asking everyone in her life."

"But he's the one who profits from her death!"

"Is he?"

"Who else?"

"Don't you already know?"

Baffled, I shook my head.

"We'll be speaking again, Ms. Jones. Soon."

* * *

Amy, Belinda, and I spent Friday together, trying to cope with our new reality. The police had asked Belinda for her whereabouts on the day Cathy died, just as they'd asked me, but she'd been moving about all day, so her alibi was in scattered pieces. She said it would probably take them days to confirm it all. Amy, on the other hand, said her witnesses were her children, with her son barely able to speak in sentences and her daughter still trying to figure out how to ask for juice beyond pointing at it.

When I woke Monday morning, I phoned my boss from bed. Rather than call in sick, I called in "traumatized."

She told me to take the week off.

After I hung up, I lay on my back, staring at the ceiling, trying to understand what had happened to my sister. I was sure that Steve had killed Cathy to stop her from ending the marriage and to keep her money, but how had he known he needed to do it? What had she done that gave her away?

All I had to go by was what she'd said to me on the phone. Replaying the conversation over and over in my head, the thing that struck me most was that she'd wanted to get to the bank as soon as it opened. But why? An ATM would work at any hour, and you could open an account online.

Why would anyone need to go inside a bank…?

I sat up with a burst of energy as an answer finally struck me. Safe-deposit boxes! To get into one of those, you'd need to go during banking hours, and it would be a good way to hide something from Steve.

But what if Steve had killed her before she could get to the bank? In that case, whatever the thing was—if it even existed—surely Steve had destroyed it.

Unless he hadn't known to look for it.

Would the cops have found it? I supposed that depended on how well they'd searched and whether this thing looked to them like evidence.

If it was still in the house, I had to get to it before Steve could. It might prove why he'd murdered my sister.

I showered and dressed in a hurry, wolfed down some breakfast, then took my spare key to Cathy's house from a kitchen drawer. As I drove to her place, I called Belinda to explain my safe-deposit-box theory and ask if she had any thoughts on good hiding places to search in Cathy's house.

She told me not to play detective and said we had to trust the police to figure out what had happened to Cathy. When I got sick of Belinda lecturing me, I made static sounds as best as I could. "Sorry, sis. You're breaking up. Gotta go."

Ten minutes later, I stopped my car a few houses down the street from Cathy's place and eyed the police cruiser in her driveway.

Defeated, I was about to drive off, but then I noticed an officer on her porch, removing the crime scene seal from the front door.

Curious, I waited.

As soon as he finished, he got into his vehicle and drove off.

Well, that was practically an invitation.

I let myself into my sister's house and tried to think like her. Where would

Cathy hide something from Steve? I began my search in the kitchen, but after ten minutes, all I'd learned was that she had dust on her pots and a lot of take-out in the fridge. I was trying to decide which room to search next when I heard the front door open and close.

I grabbed my phone, ready to dial 911, thinking it was better to be arrested for breaking and entering than to be murdered by my brother-in-law.

"Danielle, you in here?" Belinda called.

Relieved, I dashed to the living room, where I found my sister standing by the couch and staring down at the empty coffee table. She was dressed in a black suit with black heels and a large black purse. I assumed she'd been showing a house and hoped she hadn't cut it short on my account.

"You nearly gave me a heart attack!" I accused.

"You shouldn't be here," Belinda countered gravely.

"Well, I am. And so are you. Now, help me search."

Belinda shook her head. "I don't need to. The police already took the important thing."

"What?"

She pointed to the coffee table. "That's where Cathy's will was."

"Will? What will?"

"The one that left everything she had to you and me, since Amy already has her million from the Old Maid jackpot. The will was Cathy's way of trying to reduce what Steve could claim if anything happened to her. I imagine it is also why the police are so interested in where we were after ten that morning. They must know that's when she had it notarized."

"Notarized?"

"Danielle," Belinda said with forced patience. "Safe deposit boxes aren't the only service banks provide. She brought her will to the bank to get it witnessed beyond any doubt by people with no stake in its terms."

I frowned at my sister. "If you knew the reason Cathy was at the bank, why didn't you say something when I told you my safe deposit box theory? Wait, why didn't you tell me about the will days ago?"

Belinda looked at me with her head angled, like she was watching a fascinating bug.

My stomach clenched in a knot.

Belinda started to smile, my horror and her grin keeping pace.

"How did you know Cathy left the will on her coffee table?" I asked, my voice nearly a whimper.

Belinda pulled a gun from her purse. "You really are an idiot."

"You…you killed…?"

"Put your phone on the table," Belinda told me. "And take a seat."

My hand shaking, I put the device down, then I eased onto the sofa as far from my sister and her gun as I could get.

Belinda picked up the phone, shut it off, and tucked it in her pocket.

"Why would… Why?" My last word was a mindless cry.

"Might as well brag about my brilliance," Belinda mused. "I won't get any other chances to do it." Her tone turned gloating. "You see, eighteen months ago, I was dating Steve—"

"What?" I screeched.

"—And not being an idiot, unlike certain sisters I could name, I suspected handsome Steve already knew about the Old Maid contest. When I confronted him, he admitted he'd heard about it from a friend of a friend who knows Amy's husband. He'd known the truth before our first date. Since Steve was clearly mercenary, I suggested he make a play for Cathy and get her out of the running. Then, once you left the race, I'd win the jackpot, and he could divorce her. Perhaps take a bit of her money with him when he left. He and I could even be together eventually, provided he signed an air-tight prenup."

"But what if I never got married or had a kid? It would all be for nothing."

"I said *left the race*, Danielle. Maybe that would be a husband or kid—or maybe not. I got the sedatives months ago, but before I could use them to fake your suicide—"

"My suicide?" I gasped.

"I hadn't yet figured out how to make it convincing, which is for the best, since I ended up needing to use the pills on Cathy instead."

"But why? She was already married and out of the game."

"I'm the woman Steve was having an affair with, you nitwit! I was sleeping with him the whole time."

"Cathy wasn't being paranoid or dramatic," I said softly, wishing I'd been more supportive.

"Nope." Belinda began to pace the room. "She called me Thursday morning, right after she talked to you, and told me about her plan to hire an investigator so she could get the marriage annulled on grounds of fraud."

Staring out the window at the bright June day, I remembered Cathy saying, *"What marriage? The whole thing has been a big, fat lie."*

Belinda's strides accelerated. "I left my phone at a house for sale, went home to grab the sedatives, then came over to try to talk her out of the PI. If whoever she hired caught on to me—even a little—his next step would've been to talk to my neighbors. Some of them would've seen Steve coming and going, and his car staying the night, since long before he met Cathy."

"She'd know that you slept with her husband," I said. "That you and Steve both lied when you pretended that you'd never met before she introduced us all. She'd have proof that you two conspired to trick her—proof of fraud."

"Yeah. I think with that evidence, she'd have gotten her annulment."

I wished she'd lived to achieve it. "Good for her."

"It would've been bad for you and me," Belinda countered. "Legally, with an annulment, it would be like she'd never been married at all. She'd be back in the running for the Old Maid jackpot. And once a PI had told her what I'd done, I bet she would've never married again—just to spite me."

"Maybe." It was certainly my plan now, if I survived this day. I owed it to Cathy to make sure Belinda lost the game.

"I needed to stop her. So, while she was telling me about the will, I put the sedatives in her drink. Then we spent an hour in the lawn chairs by the pool, with me trying to talk her out of the PI. But Cathy wouldn't budge. When she finally passed out, I dragged her chair to the water and dumped her in. Then I put the will on the coffee table. I was hoping that when the police saw it had been signed that very morning, they'd think she'd been putting her affairs in order because she was planning to commit suicide. I should've realized that inheriting half a million dollars would look like a motive for me to kill her."

"And when you murder me?" I asked.

Belinda slowed her pacing a fraction. "Once I get back to my phone, I'll try to call you, leaving a message when you fail to answer. An hour after that, I'll phone the police to say I'm worried. Tell them how you said you planned to break into this house, and how I've been unable to reach you. Then I'll call Steve on my burner phone."

"Steve? Was he in on Cathy's murder, too?"

"Wow, you're stupid. Are you sure we're related? I need to frame him for your murder, dummy, and I can't let him live to tell his version of the last two years. I'll tell him to meet me because we need to talk about the cops investigating what happened to Cathy. When he shows up, I'll get close, shoot him with this same gun, then call the police and say Steve came to murder me. He died when we struggled over the weapon. Which, as it happens, he bought for me last year, so the cops might even be able to prove it's his gun."

"Belinda, please. I'm your sister!"

"So was Cathy. Anyway, when the police find your body here, and the ballistics match this gun, they'll assume Steve killed you. I'll be in the clear."

"Making you the last unmarried sister still standing."

"Yup. Game over, I win."

My sister's pacing around the room was approaching its most distant point, and she was wrapping up her bragging. I didn't have long to live.

Not unless I took a chance.

I leapt up and raced for the door.

Belinda fired the gun.

I felt a sudden agony in my left arm as I yanked the door open with my right hand.

She fired again, but this time she missed.

I darted into the blinding light of day. I couldn't even see the man who shouted a second later, "Drop the gun."

Clueless what to do, I dove to the ground, then lay spreadeagled and eyes shut.

I heard one more shot behind me, followed by several from the left and right.

When I finally dared to open my eyes, Detective Grant was striding toward me.

"You can get up now," he said gently, holding out one hand to help.

I stayed as I was and tried to process everything that had happened. At long last, I asked, "It wasn't a coincidence that your officer left just after I arrived, was it?"

Detective Grant let his hand drop to his side. "We had a warrant to track your phones—yours and Belinda's. When I saw where you were heading, I told the officer to release the scene and leave. I wanted to see what you would do. I arrived in time to see Belinda go inside, even though her phone said she was elsewhere."

"Oh."

"That's when I called for backup. I was listening by the living room window, waiting for a sign it would be safe to attempt entry—or that we had no choice but to try because time had run out for you. Then we heard the shots, you both ran out, and…" He shook his head. "She chose to shoot instead of dropping the gun. We had to return fire."

"Is Belinda…?" I couldn't form the words.

"She died within seconds."

Two of my three sisters were gone. Forever. "I'm the old maid."

"It seems you won the game."

My shock wearing off, I began to sob. "No. I lost the game. All I won was the money."

Story Inspiration:

I remember playing "Old Maid" as a child, but I never really thought of the message it sent to impressionable young people, namely that to be an unmarried woman meant you were a loser. And the game has been sending this message for centuries! So, when offered the chance to write about a deadly game, I created Aunt Rose, who was determined to turn the game on its head and make the unmarried woman the winner. Of course, since it was going to be a murder mystery, I needed her to take things too far. How do you make a game worth killing over? Add money. Lots of money.

DOUBLE DUTCH DARE

P.M. Raymond

P.M. Raymond is an award-winning author from New Orleans, Louisiana, so she knows a thing or two about good gumbo, grits, and café au lait. She is the Sisters in Crime 2024 Eleanor Taylor Bland Award Winner and 2024 Killer Shorts Screenplay Finalist. Her work has appeared in Punk Noir, Flash Fiction Magazine, *and* Dark Yonder, *among others.*

The ropes lay in a squiggled line on the concrete behind Mr. Sherman's convenience store. It wasn't just that Cinda had fallen while executing the most complicated jump she had dared to take on, it was that her clumsy feet brought with it the cascading spiral of the prize money slipping through everyone's fingers. Hers, primarily.

The New Orleans Inner Project Double Dutch Competition of 1981 was one week away. If Cinda's goal was to prove herself a worthy team member of the Calliope Jumpers, she had failed miserably.

The rubber sole of Cinda's tennis shoe slapped together like a round of applause as she hopped on her right leg to a spot against the wall in the alleyway of the store. The smell of damp cardboard and rotten vegetables permeated the corridor despite garbage collection the day before. Still, the girls were grateful. It was the only place big enough to practice their routine away from the prying eyes of the other teams scattered throughout the housing project.

Cinda braced herself against the bricks as she carefully slid to the ground. She would glue the sole back together when she got home. Her eyes glistened as she assessed her knees. Both had suffered varying degrees of scrapes, the right one with an inflamed, moist wound in the middle of her brown skin.

A click came from the STOP button on the boom box that previously blasted Carl Carlton's "She's a Bad Mama Jama." It went silent. So did the girls standing in a row in front of Cinda.

"Why'd you try that move anyway?" Maggie Lee blurted out, like an accusation to Cinda for wasting her time—and by proximity, everyone else's, with the impossible.

A share of the $500 prize from the competition would offer a little distance between her mother and the bill collectors knocking at the apartment door. Maybe her mother wouldn't have to work extra shifts at the laundromat. Maybe even take them to a movie and get popcorn from the concession stand instead of sneaking sandwiches in their pockets.

Maybe her mother wouldn't need Harold to come around anymore.

Anxiousness swirled in Cinda at what her mother would say when she saw her knees. At least she hadn't torn her gingham shorts, the ones her mother had purchased from the sales rack at the back of the Woolworths on Canal Street.

Maggie Lee rolled her eyes and dramatically crossed her arms. "Well, I told you it wouldn't work, but you got a head full of rocks, Cinda."

"Cut it out, Maggie Lee," Bertie responded. She was already kneeling next to Cinda. "Does it hurt?"

Cinda shook her head. "No, I'm good," she said. She wiped a sheen of sweat from her brow.

"Well," Bertie said, shooting a glare at Maggie Lee, "at least she was willing to try something fresh." Bertie stood and extended her hand to lift Cinda to her feet. A soft clink emanated from the ground.

Cinda bent to retrieve the tarnished piece of metal that had fallen from her pocket. The puzzle piece, dangling from a matching chain, had a greyish-brown patina over most of the smooth surface. Cinda flipped it in her hand

and then stuffed it back in her pocket. The charm was lightweight but heavy on her heart.

Cinda tried not to look at the other girls but finally said, "Let me give it a go. One more time."

Maggie Lee screeched, "Not fair! We have a routine already figured out. Why can't Cinda just stick to it?"

The Washington twins, Mona and Mya, were running the show. It was their teachings and their jump ropes, so all major decisions like do-overs went through them. When the twins introduced Double Dutch after a visit with cousins in the Bronx last summer, folks didn't know what to make of it. Using two jump ropes at the same time was as downright alien as tea without sugar.

"Well?" Maggie Lee asked, her stance wide with hands planted on her hips. She reminded Cinda of the football referees on television she used to watch with her dad on Sunday afternoons.

Cinda eyeballed the twins, searching for any signs of generosity in their gaze.

The mirror images of French braided hair, white tee shirts, and culottes whispered to each other. The one wearing green culottes spoke. "We agree to Cinda's do-over."

"I swear, Mya," Cinda said to the skinny mocha-complexioned girl who had just spoken, "one more time and that's it."

Maggie Lee let out a *pfft* and threw her arms in the air.

"If you don't like it," Mona, the twin in the red culottes, said, "you can go home." Cinda knew Mona didn't mean that, but she was grateful for the backup. The team needed Maggie Lee more than her. Maggie Lee could do tricks like handstands and backflips between the ropes.

"She probably doesn't even have her split of the entry fee anyway since her dad ran off!" Maggie Lee blurted out, drawing fierce glances from the twins and Bertie.

Cinda bubbled with anger and shame that burst through in her words. "I'll get the money, you snooty cow! And leave my dad out of it!" Cinda realized she may have spoken out of turn and gone too far with her words.

No matter what Maggie Lee had said first, she was still worried.

She didn't need to be.

Before Maggie Lee could respond to Cinda's retaliatory words, Mya put up her hand in a stop motion and said, "Okay, do over in progress."

The twins picked up the wooden-handled ropes. Bertie started the cassette tape again. With a flick of the wrists, the twins turned the ropes. Wide loops traversed each other. Cinda waited near Mona to diagonally enter the flurry of blurred strings.

Mona yelled, "Ready, set, go!" As the rope closest to Cinda hit the ground, she took one big step from the right side and landed in the center.

Cinda took to the hypnotic rhythm of Double Dutch immediately. The *tick, tick* of jump ropes hitting the pavement, the thin cords wide like a whirling hug spinning around a jumper. The *smack, smack* of feet as their hops and jumps landed on solid ground—the camaraderie of being part of this team, even with Maggie Lee.

Cinda desperately needed the patchwork of this found family more than ever.

She jumped between the spinning ropes, remembering to tuck her arms near her stomach so they wouldn't get in the way, and kept her feet together and her knees slightly bent. Cinda mixed up her footwork by moving laterally back and forth between the twin turners. She rotated in a full circle on one jump using only one leg—the move that had caused her to skin her knees.

Bertie whooped from the sidelines. Her cheers buoyed Cinda's confidence. A tingling rose inside her. As she hopped from one leg to another, a booming voice rang out.

"Cinda! Where you at, girl?" The sound of Harold's gritty tone preceded his appearance at the end of the alley. The twins instantly dropped the ropes mid-turn, but not before one of the strands hit Cinda across the eye. The stinging subsided under the pressure of her palm.

Harold's grumpy façade broke into an effervescent smile as he said, "There you are," and walked toward the group. Cinda knew Harold and her dad had worked in the same trucking company. He showed up a month after the worst day of Cinda's young life.

Mya quickly dragged the ropes across the concrete, looping them into a circle in her hands. She scurried past Cinda to join her doppelganger, but not before she whispered, "Nice footwork."

The girls in the neighborhood knew Harold as a charming and quick-witted man. But Cinda knew a less charitable version. The version that was rude and nosy behind closed doors.

Harold's tall, slender frame strolled towards the group with confidence and arrogance in his gait. That's what Cinda thought anyway. His squared hi-top fade afro was neat and symmetrical. His denim jeans were pressed to perfection, complemented by his cream V-neck short-sleeved shirt with blue stripes around the arms and the V.

"What's this foolishness you up to?" Harold asked with a tight smile as he grabbed her tiny wrist. "Dinner's waitin' on you." Harold tipped his head and said to the rest of the group, "Y'all best be getting home too." The girls nodded and scattered away.

Cinda's feet dragged and stumbled as she and Harold walked home through the streets of the Calliope housing project.

As they ascended the three flights of stairs to the apartment, Cinda counted each step in her head. Anything to keep her mind centered on getting the entry fee for the competition. And chase away the thoughts of her dad.

It was three months since her father left their apartment to run an errand and disappeared into the night. Cinda's free hand slid into her shorts pocket to touch the silver charm to make sure it was still there. It was like a link in a chain connecting her to her father.

"For you, Cinny," he had said to her on her 11th birthday. She remembered the way the silver sparkled in the daylight that afternoon at the park. The memory of her father revealing the matching puzzle piece beneath his button-up polyester shirt was like an old movie she would replay over and over in her mind. Cinda would never forget the smile on his lips, as bright and big as the sun that day. When the sun came up the next morning, he was gone.

* * *

Cinda's mother stared at the girl's knees. Cinda winced as the peroxide-soaked cotton balls dabbed at the tender, open flesh. "This will not do. You out there roughhousing." With a *tsk tsk*, she added, "Don't want you out in the streets like that. You need to get your mind ready for seventh grade in a few weeks and off these schoolyard games."

"Ma, the prize money is $500 split between all of us. That's huge!" Cinda couldn't keep the wistful excitement out of her voice, and her mother couldn't help but grin along with her.

Music filtered from the living room through their two-bedroom apartment, where Harold had turned on the transistor radio. "Let's Groove" by Earth, Wind, and Fire started its opening synth robotic rift, discussing the merits of boogieing down.

"Well, I guess you can give the competition a try. It can't hurt." Then her mother pointed to her knees. "Except there, I guess." She shook her head disapprovingly, then softened. "I picked up a late shift, so go wash up, and I'll fix you a plate before I leave."

Cinda fidgeted as her mother blew in short bursts onto the sore and placed the bandage over the scrape. "Ma, can I ask you something?"

"Sure, baby. As long as it don't cost me nothing, ask away."

Cinda's shoulders dropped. She couldn't possibly bring up the money now.

"Marlene!" Harold called out, his heavy tone drifting between the flimsy walls of their apartment. "You said you'd fix me a plate. What's taking so long?"

A worried crinkle came across Cinda's forehead.

Her mama wasn't the first woman he'd tried to sweet-talk with his sour words. Cinda thought maybe Bertie's mother might have been under Harold's sway a few years ago.

"Pay him no mind," her mother soothed. "Just be on your best behavior." Cinda's mama couldn't afford regular babysitting, and Harold was always up to do it for a plate of her mama's ribs or chicken and collards. A hot meal in exchange for keeping a steady eye on Cinda was the extent of Harold's dealings inside these walls. Not that Harold wasn't trying. Cinda had heard around the neighborhood that he was biding his time for "something more permanent".

After dinner and her mother's departure, Harold said, "Have a seat, Cinny." He pointed to the kitchen table chair. Cinda hated it when he called her 'Cinny'. That endearment was reserved for her parents.

"I was real tight with your pops. Like brothers." Harold sat across from her, arms folded on the table, his face directly in front of hers. "Any special places in the park or neighborhood y'all liked? Maybe I can take you." And so it began as usual. Harold wanted to know how Cinda and her dad spent their time, and Cinda was getting tired of it. She wouldn't say much, but she had made a mistake last week. She hinted there was a secret between her and her dad and that Harold "would never be special enough" for Cinda to share it with him. She would never tell him about the necklace. "It's a secret for you and me," her father had said. Cinda would keep it that way.

"Girl, you know I'm the grownup here. I can make you tell me." He leaned across the table.

Cinda crossed her arms and leaned back with a stern pout. "You're not my daddy, not even a stepdaddy. Lay a hand on me and you'll be in the poke."

Harold let out a *hmpf* and got up from the table. "Get on out of here and do your homework."

"It's summer!" Cinda yelled and stormed off to her room. The Magnum P.I. theme song blared from the living room through her closed door, but she heard the tap emanating from the closet wall just the same.

Bertie.

"Hey, I can hear Magnum driving into my room over here," Bertie said. The wall dampened the sound, but her enunciation was clear.

"Are you coming over or what?" Cinda playfully scolded her. Their closets were back to back, as were their bedrooms. They used a crawl space in the closet ceiling to get to the other's bedroom. The thump of feet hit the ground, and Bertie appeared from the closet door.

"Alright, girl. I'm here. Chill," Bertie said, full of playful attitude, sliding two clotheslines with large knots on at each end, her poor man's jump rope, from the back pocket of her denim shorts.

"Chill?" Cinda rolled her eyes, but her generous smile revealed her real feelings.

"Okay, okay," Bertie said. "Ready to practice?"

"Does it matter? I don't have the money for my share to enter anyway." Cinda sulked.

"Isn't your mama working extra shifts?" Bertie asked, flopping to the bedroom floor.

Cinda kicked the carpet and sighed, "Yeah."

"You're not still holding on to that stupid stuff Maggie Lee said about your dad?" Bertie put her hand on Cinda's shoulder. "She *IS* a bossy cow. Forget about her."

Cinda couldn't, but she decided to pretend. "Yeah, you're right." She began to practice her hops and her turns. Bertie did the same, but her leg buckled on one move, and she fell, instinctively reaching for Cinda to break her fall. Instead, Bertie took Cinda down with her.

"Real smooth, Bertie!"

They contained their laughter behind cupped hands.

The upholstered reclining chair let out a hinged squawk that only happened when Harold's muscular frame rose out of the tweed-covered monstrosity. A car chase and gunshot sound from the television lowered. The chair squeaked in response to Harold's towering frame settling back into it.

"Old Harold babysitting again?" Bertie asked.

"Yep. And he's still asking about my dad. Seems like he wants to know something, but I don't know what."

Bertie poked Cinda. "I bet Harold has five dollars in his wallet. Wouldn't even miss it."

Cinda glanced nervously.

Bertie put a finger to her mouth with a quiet "come on" and scrambled to her feet. She tiptoed to the door and cracked it open. Cinda followed. Bertie took Cinda by the wrist and crept into the hallway.

The black wallet sat on the tray next to the recliner.

"He's asleep," Bertie mouthed. "Do it. I dare you."

Cinda's heart pounded. "You won't get your butt whupped if you get caught!" Cinda hissed softly, but she leaned in anyway. *A dare is a dare,* she thought.

"Harold won't even miss it. You see how he flashes wads around on the streets." Bertie's voice lowered into a conspiratorial whisper. "They say," she gripped Cinda's forearm and pulled her closer, "that he runs a side hustle with the mob."

"Hush your mouth," Cinda murmured. "My mama wouldn't get mixed up with such a *heathen*." Her aunties in the neighborhood called grown folks that word if they did questionable things. Cinda roiled inside at the suggestion that her mother would allow someone like that in their home.

Well, if he is one, then the Lord won't judge me, and that money would shut Maggie Lee up, and...a dare is a dare, she rationalized.

Harold's closed eyelids flickered. His chest rose and fell as snorts of air came out of his nostrils. He grumbled in full volume, "Hm, don't do broccoli." Harold's eyes remained shut as visions of vegetables presumably floated in his head.

Harold smacked his lips and sank his body into the chair, fingers laced over his stomach. The recliner squeaked in time with his movements.

Cinda used the noise to her advantage.

Her slender fingers grabbed the wallet. She delicately unfolded the creased leather, surprised by its weight. The girls couldn't believe the thick stack of bills crammed into the space.

"Whoa," Bertie whispered.

Cinda slid out a five-dollar bill. *With all that cash, he definitely won't miss it.* A faint tear sound caused Cinda's eyes to widen. She tugged at the fiver sandwiched between the stack of bills. A flurry of cash fell to the floor along with an item so familiar that she nearly screamed.

A silver chain with a puzzle piece fell among the scattered fives, tens, and twenties on the carpet. Cinda knelt and picked the chain up, dangling it in the glare of the television. The tarnishing piece was the companion to

Cinda's puzzle. *DADDY's* was etched on one side. Cinda knew it couldn't be a coincidence. Without even trying, she knew her necklace, engraved with GIRL, would fit with this one.

Bertie feverishly gathered the bills into a neat pile. Cinda sat motionless as Bertie shoved the money towards her while she clutched the wallet in her left hand and the necklace in her right. "What are you doing?" Bertie mouthed as panic swept over her eyes and curled her lips.

Harold grunted and wiggled. Cinda's body stiffened like a mannequin. She couldn't move despite Bertie nearly close to tears as Harold grumbled and let out another snort.

Cinda regained her senses and grabbed the money from Bertie. She carefully tucked the bills and the chain inside the cracked leather and gently set it back on the table. As she tucked the five dollars in her shorts, the front doorknob jiggled with a ferocity that made the girls jump. Cinda pushed Bertie back down the hall and into her room.

In some kind of God-sent perfect sync, the front door slammed shut at the same time as Cinda's bedroom door. Cinda flung the closet door open and pushed Bertie inside. Her friend stumbled into the wall of hanging church dresses and blue jeans.

Bertie spun around to face Cinda. "What on God's green earth is happening here?" Bertie screeched through clenched teeth, stray spittle flying on each word.

All Cinda could respond with was, "Harold. Harold?" Cinda motioned Bertie to climb on the folding chair and hoisted her into the crawl space above.

Cinda's mother's voice floated from the living room to the bedroom door. "Harold? You awake?"

* * *

"What are YOU going to do?" Bertie urged from the circle of girls who sat around Cinda.

"Yeah, I *mean*," Mona or Mya said—Cinda couldn't tell which one since they wore matching outfits in the same exact color—"it sounds like you need to tell your mom." The twins turned to each other, nodded, then turned to Cinda and nodded again.

It was Friday, the day before the competition. At the end of practice, Cinda spilled what she thought she'd discovered about Harold.

"I know I should tell Mama." Cinda let out a sigh and bowed her head. "Don't you think I know that?" She shook her head and looked up, "But I'm not even—" Cinda stopped abruptly as she faced straight ahead, down the alley, and tracked someone walking in the distance.

Harold.

Cinda jumped to her feet. "Let's follow him." A chorus of "What?" cascaded through the group. Cinda got to the sidewalk and looked both ways. "There he is." The girls trailed after her like ducklings.

"Hold up, Cinda! Where are you going? Where is Harold going?" Bertie wheezed as she tried to keep up with Cinda's long strides.

"He hangs out at that bar two blocks up." The girls crossed over the street and stopped half a block from the destination. Cinda motioned them to come into a huddle. "We can go around the back. The delivery door is unlocked." The girls looked quizzically at her. "My dad would take me on his runs sometimes."

Mona and Mya nodded to each other, and then one of them said, "We need to go home. We can't be mixed up in all this." They nodded to each other once more, turned, and walked stride for stride in the other direction.

Cinda knew she could count on Bertie, but what about Maggie Lee? She got her answer as Maggie Lee took two steps forward, using her hands to part them. "Let's see what Harold's up to." Bossy as ever, she led the way.

The bar's back door opened to a hallway. Cinda put a hush finger to her lips as they moved down the corridor. Chatter drifted from the room on the right near the opening to the back of the bar.

The crack in the door carried faint but crisp voices to their ears. The grown men, including Harold, discussed matters that Cinda did not understand. But something caught Cinda's attention.

"We got trucks delivering at night. Stay off the radar that way," Harold said. There was a commotion of papers ruffling and drinking glasses on the tabletop. "We got rid of the snitch months ago. Since then, things have been smooth sailing. Nothing to worry about."

A voice responded, "Then why is the paperwork under a microscope all of a sudden, huh?" Other voices agreed.

"Look, I got people. I can make it go away," Harold grunted.

"Hey, what are you little rugrats doing?" The girls jumped and screamed in unison. A bartender, early for his shift, stood tall, imposing, with a curious stare behind them. Chairs scraped the floor as men got up from their seats. Pounding footsteps approached the crack in the door. Cinda, Bertie, and Maggie Lee pushed past the man and ran out the back door.

The patter of running feet filled the streets. Cinda pumped her arms as she ran back toward Mr. Sherman's alley. She zigzagged down the pavement, cutting through pedestrians, around cars, and even jumping over the dog leash of a startled mutt, grateful her fancy footwork could be put to good use outside of the Double Dutch ropes. Cinda could see Bertie and Maggie Lee ahead of her just as she tumbled to the ground, hands outstretched to break her fall. The sole of her tennis shoe had given way, tripping her.

Stupid tennis shoes!

Cinda cried out as the pain in her arms traveled up to her neck. She rolled onto her side, eyes squeezed shut, her legs curled against her chest. The sole dangled and flopped back and forth.

The jerk to her arm was as surprising as it was painful. Harold's large fingers were around her wrist as he pulled her from the pavement and swung her around.

Harold held her by the shoulders, shaking her. "What in the hell do you think you're doin'?"

Cinda was so frightened by Harold's coarse tone that she forgot about the ache from her fall.

Harold cut his rant short as he stared down at Cinda. "What do we have here?" The silver puzzle piece dangled from her neck. His fingers wrapped around the charm, turning it over. "I've been looking for this—"

A wild yell that only a mama bear could do rang out down the street. "Take your hands off my girl!" Cinda's mama came running up the street with a rolling pin in her hand. Word spread fast in this neighborhood. "Leave her alone!"

Harold jerked back and let go of Cinda.

Her mother ran up and pulled her close. "Are you okay, baby?"

Cinda shook her head.

"As for you," Cinda's mother said, pointing the rolling pin in Harold's direction, "I'm done with your foolishness. Don't come around me or my baby again." They walked home arm in arm while Harold watched, fuming.

* * *

"So, that's all of it." Cinda fiddled with her hands and waited for her mama to speak. She had just told her everything – the necklace, Harold's questions, the conversation at the bar. She even confessed to stealing the money.

"You did the right thing, baby…except for the money, but we'll deal with that later." Her mother touched her hand across the table. "Go get ready for bed, and I'll fix us some ice cream."

Cinda inhaled with delight. "Ice cream?" She jumped from her chair and ran to her room. She flung the door open. At that moment, thoughts of ice cream melted. In her room, Harold stood with clotheslines. And a knife.

* * *

"What does this unlock?" Harold's words stank of stale beer in Cinda's face. Tied to the kitchen chair, she squirmed against the clothesline.

Harold held Cinda's puzzle and her father's version together, the pieces fitting as perfectly as the relationship it honored. The two pieces formed a key.

"Okay, you want to do this the hard way." Harold took the knife and twirled it between his fingers.

"She doesn't know," Cinda's mother pleaded. "She doesn't know anything." She faced Cinda, tied to a chair of her own.

Cinda had never felt so terrified or seen her mother so helpless.

"Your dad can't take what's not his without paying a price." Harold leaned in close to Cinda.

"NO!" Cinda's mother screamed. Harold looked her dead in the eye.

"Start talking. Where's the invoices Max took?"

A pounding at the door startled everyone in the tiny hot kitchen.

"Open up, it's the police."

Cinda watched Harold scramble back and forth like he was caught in a loop. "Dammit," he mumbled over and over.

The constraints weren't as tight as Harold believed. Cinda wiggled her arms. The clothesline fell from her shoulders to her waist. She carefully uncoiled herself as Harold's mania distracted him.

Cinda breathed and recited to herself—*You've got this!* Her mama nodded toward the door. The signal was clear. *Run!*

But Cinda didn't. She couldn't leave her mama. Harold turned to see her standing at the table. He stood between her and help. He lunged.

Cinda took the clothesline, swung it like a lasso, and flicked it in Harold's direction. The knotted end popped him in the eye. He lurched over in screaming pain.

She darted for the front door, flinging it open. Two uniformed officers rushed Harold, tackling him to the ground.

Bertie must have heard what was happening through the walls. Thin walls made good neighbors. She had called the police.

After the commotion died down and the police were gone, Bertie sat in Cinda's room while the mothers had coffee in the kitchen.

"You know Harold came by today, acting like he wanted to catch up with my mama," Bertie said. "He must have snuck into the crawlspace in my room while she was getting the mail."

Cinda's mama opened the bedroom door. She looked haggard but relieved. "Get some sleep, girls. You have a big day tomorrow."

Cinda poked her head up from her covers. "Thanks, Ma, for letting me do the competition. And letting Bertie stay."

"Baby," she sighed. "I think we all need a good distraction."

* * *

"Come in here, Cinny."

Cinda walked into the kitchen. Bertie had gone home to get ready for the competition, and it was just the two of them. A lacquered wooden box sat on the table.

"What's that?"

Cinda's mother sat at the table with the puzzle key in her hand. "Your father had two boxes. The one he left me had the invoices Harold would do anything to get. I handed those over to the police a few weeks ago." She slid the box towards Cinda. "This is the box your key opens."

Cinda scrambled to the table. "What's inside?" Her mother calmly inserted the key. The box contained overtime pay her father had stashed for a down payment on a bigger place.

"He would have wanted you to have it," Cinda's mother said.

Cinda looked inside. "I guess we'll be okay for a while," Cinda replied.

"Maybe we can start somewhere new," her mother responded.

A melancholy silence followed. Neither could say out loud that her father hadn't disappeared. They didn't need the police to tell them how bad Harold was, but two detectives would come by a week later and tell them anyway. A year later, that bad man would be calling Angola State Penitentiary home for the rest of his life.

That afternoon, the Calliope Jumpers parlayed their twists, turns, and hops into a first-place prize of $500. The community rallied around the girls, Cinda, and her mama. Even Maggie Lee warmed up to her by inviting her to a sleepover before seventh grade started and apologizing for her "out of pocket" words about her dad. Cinda accepted both.

That day, Cinda's mama decided not to move after all.

Cinda was fine with that.

There was joy in this community. A joy that whirled all around them like Double Dutch ropes in motion. And Cinda desperately needed that now more than ever.

Story Inspiration:

Double Dutch Dare was inspired by my childhood growing up in New Orleans. The skill and quick footwork always fascinated me. I wanted to pay homage to this spirited game and a simpler time in my youth.

THE HACK JOB

LL Kaplan

Lisa, writing as LL Kaplan, uses her past experiences in law enforcement as a prosecutor and criminal investigator to pen crime fiction where justice prevails, but doesn't always end in handcuffs. She's the author of two mystery series set in Northern Ohio and is working on a third. She can be found at www.llkaplanauthor.com.

"Did you kill him?"

I didn't answer right away.

We, the Chief and I, were standing near the back of the throwing alley in *"Axed and Bowed"*, my downtown axe-throwing/archery establishment. We were alone. Sort of.

At the opposite end of the alley stood a row of targets, each in its own regulation-sized lane under high-beamed ceilings. The targets had numbered rings, complete with killshot dots at the top, for participants to hit and keep score. In the larger middle lane stood the Wheel of Fortune. On a normal day, and only during certain times, throwers tried to hit various marks on its spinning face for points and prizes. On a normal day, there wasn't a body tied to it.

Tonight, though, Andrew Thaddeus "Tuggy" Johnston IV was. His arms and legs were splayed like a performer in an old circus knife-throwing act.

The only difference was that in the circus act, the knife thrower usually missed.

I finally responded.

"No, I didn't kill him, but someone apparently had an axe to grind. Or should I say axes?" I pointed to the two axes attached to the Wheel: one over his head and one between his legs. "Rather appropriate. He could be a real pain in the axe."

The Chief grunted. "This is no laughing matter, Abby."

I shrugged. "Just a little morgue humor. I may be retired, but old habits die hard. Oops."

He ignored that last one. "Who's skilled enough at axe throwing to do this?"

"No one local I know," I replied, walking towards the body.

"No, stay back here," the Chief commanded. "This is a crime scene."

"Come on, Chief, we need to make sure he's, you know, out of his misery? It's the only decent thing to do. Unless, of course, *you* want to check on him?"

The Chief hesitated. "Okay, go, but I'll be watching."

I smiled to myself. The Chief had a well-known aversion to bodies and blood. Rather unfortunate for a person in his position.

I strolled down the middle lane to the Wheel.

Though just about a year old, *Axed & Bowed* had a loyal following with an archery league on Tuesday nights and a throwing league on Wednesdays. It had been surprising how many people, especially females, got satisfaction from the sound of metal 'ker-chunking' deep into wood or an arrow hitting certain marks on the more, uh, graphic targets. The quick success of *Axed & Bowed* meant I'd had to move up my plans regarding my partners, one of whom was now tied to the Wheel.

I stopped a few feet in front of Tuggy.

"The axe to the head is our smallest hatchet," I said over my shoulder, the words echoing in the hollow space.

The axe handle hung down, partially covering the red bandana tied around Tuggy's mouth. It was hard to tell it *was* Tuggy between the axe and the bandana. However, his signature polo shirt and baggy checked golf pants were, well, dead giveaways.

"Is he gone?" the Chief asked, still standing at the back of the safety zone.

"Let's just say he won't be answering any questions."

"What about the big axe?"

"It's the longest one we have. Now that I'm closer, though, I'd say no throwing skill was required. This was done up close and personal. Huh, curious. There's a dollar bill under the long axe. The axes didn't kill him, by the way."

"No? They look deadly to me."

"Well, I'm sure you can see, even from back there, the lack of blood?"

My lips twitched at the sound of a slight gag. He didn't like the word blood either.

"So, he was put up there by someone with access and a motive," the Chief stated. "Someone like you. Everyone knows you and Tuggy didn't get along. I'll ask you again. Did you kill him?"

"Seriously?" I turned to face him. "Tuggy didn't get along with a lot of people. As for access, his investment firm is my limited partner, so any of his employees could get the key or alarm code. My employees, too, for that matter, although none of them had reason to kill him. And if I was going to kill him, I wouldn't stage him here. I need this place open and running, not closed as a crime scene. This is bad enough," I said, waving at Tuggy. "I'm probably going to have to replace that Wheel. You know how much *that's* going to cost? A selfie of me smiling next to his axe-riddled body isn't worth it."

"Oh? Prove it. Let me see your phone," he said, taking a tentative foot forward and holding out a hand.

"Right. No, I don't think so. You'll need a warrant for that," I replied. "But good luck getting one. I was at the *Bait and Switch* with several people before coming here and finding you hanging around the front door. Why were you here anyway?"

The Chief dropped his hand. "Suspicious person report. Everyone else on duty was busy. I said I'd handle it. Why are *you* here?"

"Someone saw a light on and thought I should know. I checked, and the alarm was off. Guess I know why now."

"You're not the dive bar type. Why were you at the *Bait*?"

He sounded sincere. As if he didn't already know. But then again, maybe he didn't.

"Talking about Tuggy."

"Talking? Or plotting this?"

Though the back of the alley was in shadow, I could see the Chief's right hand go to his waist. I had to be careful.

I sighed. "Tuggy was the long-time president of his Condominium Owners Association, aka the COA. You know that exclusive development on the edge of town with the very expensive buy-in and monthly fees?"

The Chief snorted. "Yeah, so what?"

"Well, some of the condo owners suspected he'd been embezzling the COA funds, maybe with outside help. They hired me to investigate. We meet at the *Bait* to discuss *legal* options. No violence involved," I replied.

"Embezzlement? Never heard that. You sure it was all legal options you were discussing? Someone threatened to poison him with laudanum. Maybe they did!" He nodded at Tuggy.

"L…laudanum? What is this, the 19th century? Where the heck did you hear that?"

"I have my sources."

"Laudanum," I repeated, then chuckled as the light bulb went on. "Your source must've been eavesdropping. It wasn't laudanum, but *laundering*. As in *money laundering*? We've been talking about it for a criminal complaint."

The Chief moved a few steps closer. His right hand dangled by the holster, his trigger finger twitching in the ambient light. Not a good sign.

"Tuggy? Money laundering? No way. He wasn't that smart…" the Chief stopped, then shifted his feet and shrugged. "Maybe he was. Okay, how about this. Tuggy used *Axed & Bowed* to clean his dirty COA loot. You found out and confronted him. When he didn't care that you could lose this place because of his criminal activity, you killed him in a blind rage, then staged him like this to confuse the crime scene. Confess and you probably won't even get jail."

He was quick and creative, I'd give him that.

"Uh, no, not exactly. However, Tuggy's investment firm *is* involved in some shady dealings. *Axed & Bowed* is just one of several victims."

"So, you admit it. You, the great big city detective, ends up a regular sucker like everyone else. Must've been quite a blow to that ego of yours. Just another reason to kill him," the Chief chuckled. I let him continue. "Of course, your COA clients might've also hired you to get rid of him, too. Permanently. You'd know how to do it without leaving a trace. Face it. It's all stacking up against you."

I rolled my eyes. "Are you done with your bad TV plots? Sure, I wanted to wring Tuggy's neck many times, who hasn't? But there are far more painful ways of exacting justice."

"Really? Worse than an axe between the legs?"

"For Tuggy, prison. No one there to impress with his designer clothes or golf scores. At least, no one who cares. And this," I pointed at the Wheel, "isn't exactly leaving no trace."

The Chief shrugged. "What's this 'fraud' you say his investment firm committed?"

Again, the question sounded sincere. I continued to play along.

"A Ponzi scam using small businesses instead of people. Old game, new twist, same result. He had help, though. The bank. Perhaps even law enforcement," I said, staring at the Chief. "But maybe you already know that."

"Me? I know nothing about a Ponzi scheme. Get back to Tuggy. You threatened him. Said a guy named Karl would take care of him. Who's Karl? Someone from your old undercover days?"

"Karl? I don't know any..." I paused, then laughed. "Not Karl. Karma. I told Tuggy that *Karma* would take care of him. Your reliably *unreliable* source strikes again. Please don't tell me that source was Tuggy?"

The Chief's silence was as good as a yes. I shook my head and stepped up on the platform near the Wheel.

"Hey, what are you doing?" the Chief almost yelled.

"Seeing how it was done. Let's see. Unlock the Wheel, use the crank to lower it on the repair bench, tie Tuggy to the anchors, place the axes near the head and groin, then crank the Wheel back up in position and lock it. Presto. Dead man on a target. Some strength needed to load him on and turn the crank, but no real skill."

"Strength? You're strong, Abby. All that weightlifting and martial arts. You know how to handle a body, too. Again, motive, method, and opportunity. I'm taking you in. Let's go."

The Chief moved into the full light of the axe-throwing alley. He motioned for me to come back to him with his left hand while the right still hovered over his gun. Both hands looked a bit odd until I realized why. I didn't move.

"You're arresting me based on Tuggy's alcohol-addled rants about laudanum and a Karl who doesn't exist?" I asked, leaning on the Wheel's supporting wall. "Do it and face a false arrest lawsuit. Tuggy as an informant. What a joke!"

The Chief's face grew red. "If he's the joke, then you're the punchline. Tuggy had something big to tell me. I bet it was about you. I bet you're the embezzler, not him. There's no Ponzi scheme or conspiracy. Just you. You're stealing from your own business. I'll even testify he told me that, but was conveniently killed before he could make an official statement. The jury will believe it. I may be a small-town Chief, but *I* didn't leave a police department under a cloud."

It was a plausible theory. And he was right. I *had* left under a cloud. Unfinished business for another time. I had to finish *this* business first.

"Your theory isn't going to work, Chief. I didn't tell my COA clients everything. Just in case there was a Tuggy spy in the mix."

His smug smile fell a bit. "Didn't tell them what?"

"That I'd called in an old forensic accountant buddy. She discovered that the formerly ultra-lucrative COA is on the verge of bankruptcy. Drained by the very people charged with protecting it. A jury will easily follow the money trail my accountant friend will lay out. Bottom line, my personal credibility is no longer important. There's *expert* proof now."

"Liar! You wouldn't call in anyone else for help. That's always been your problem. Keeping things too close. The whole lone-wolf routine. No, this is your doing and yours alone!" He pointed to Tuggy's motionless body on the Wheel. "Who else had more motive than you?"

"How about all those people he owed money to or defrauded? They'll be the only ones crying at the funeral because they can't sue him or get justice. Of course, being so debt-ridden, there probably wasn't anything left to sue for anyway."

"Wh…what do you mean, debt-ridden? He was rich. Trust fund boy."

I slowly shook my head. "Sorry, Chief. My friendly forensic accountant also discovered that Tuggy had blown through his huge inheritance. He liked sports betting too much, and his wife, Sophia, is apparently high maintenance. They sustain the image, but that's all."

The Chief's jaw clenched. "I don't believe you."

"It's true. Sophia even had to go back to being a regular old realtor to keep the creditors away," I said. "You okay, Chief? You're looking a little pale. Let's call dispatch. Someone should be free by now."

I started reaching for my back pocket, where I usually kept my phone.

"Keep your hands where I can see them," the Chief commanded. I heard the holster's latch unsnap. "You still could've killed him and strung him up before you went to the *Bait*. Maybe you even poisoned his beer." He nodded to a beer can sitting next to the Wheel.

"Really think I slipped him some laudanum?" I smirked. "Much easier just to break his neck and throw him into the lake. But you know, you're stronger than I am. You could've tied him to the Wheel a lot faster than I ever could."

"Why would I kill him? He was my informant."

"Yes, interesting. What was he informing on anyway? Bad golf fashion? Watered-down drinks at the country club?"

"Illegal gambling, loan sharking, drugs."

"Well, gambling I get, but drugs? Come on. He didn't run in *those* kinds of circles," I scoffed. "He couldn't. He would've gotten himself killed before… oh, is that how this was supposed to look? A drug deal gone wrong? Or better yet, a bookie he owes, sending a message? Clever. Either would explain the dollar bill under the long hatchet. Let's see. You met Tuggy here for a confidential debrief, killed him, staged the scene, and tried to get out before anyone saw you. Too bad I showed up. *That* wasn't part of the plan."

"Plan? This wasn't a plan. I didn't do this. Why would I?" He rumbled, waving at the Wheel.

"For the insurance money, obviously. But for Sophia to collect, she couldn't be connected to Tuggy's murder, so you came up with this rather elaborate scheme to throw off the scent. Were you planning to run away together with the life insurance proceeds? How sweet."

"Sophia? What does Sophia…"

"Yes, Sophia," I interjected. "Your affair wasn't exactly a secret, Chief."

The Chief hesitated, then shrugged. "Doesn't matter now. He was beating her, but Sophia was too scared to prosecute or divorce. He deserved…"

"This?" I tapped the Wheel. "Careful, Chief. That's almost a confession. Ah, that's how she got you. Damsel in distress. You never questioned her story, though, did you? If you had, you'd have found out that Sophia was the violent one, not Tuggy. He'd never confess it out of pride, but the neighbors knew. Didn't you notice *his* scrapes and bruises?"

The Chief's grip on the unlatched gun tightened. "Defensive wounds. She had a right to fight back. I saw what he did to *her*. The arm cast. The black eyes."

"Easy to buy theater makeup and props over the internet these days, even bandages and fake casts. She staged herself like she stages houses, and for the same reason: to fool someone into buying. And you bought her con without question. Admit it."

"I'm not admitting anything," the Chief scowled, wiping his upper lip. "It wasn't a con."

"Really? You know, my forensic accountant never found any life insurance policy for Tuggy."

"I saw the insurance policy. It's real. And Sophia showed me her local bank accounts. There's money, he just wouldn't let her have any of it. Kept her a financial prisoner," the Chief grumbled.

"I'm sure she showed you something, but it was just more staging," I said, hoping I'd timed this right. "Let me be clearer. Tuggy's money *is* gone, but Sophia's isn't. In fact, according to the offshore accounts we found, she's grown quite wealthy from all her schemes. Sophia was the mastermind here, not Tuggy," I said, smiling. "But all good con-artists have an endgame. She's been planning hers from the start. First, she needed a scapegoat for the fraud and embezzlement. That was Tuggy. Next, she needed to keep law enforcement away long enough to accrue her fortune and then escape. That was you. And it worked, didn't it? You never even suspected her. That makes you look like a fool, Chief. But then, looking the fool isn't so bad as being an accessory to murder," I said, nodding at Tuggy.

The Chief backed away a few inches. "No, you're wrong. This wasn't how it was supposed…this was you. Must be."

"Why?" I asked, leaning my left shoulder on the Wheel and crossing my arms. "Oh, I see. You weren't supposed to be here tonight. *Sophia* was meeting Tuggy here to kill him. How? Drugging his beer like you suggested I did? But something went wrong. Did she call you to come by and 'fix it'? Is that why you're wearing latex gloves? Can't leave prints, you wouldn't be able to explain. But then, that was probably her plan all along. Kill him, frame you," I said, shrugging. "Has it ever dawned on you, Chief, that Tuggy might not be her only fool?"

"I'm not a fool! And she *is* a victim," said the Chief, the tic in his cheek more pronounced. "She'd never hurt anyone. She's worked hard to get to where she is. Grew up poor. An orphan. Her whole life…"

"…has been one long struggle and so forth. Right. Not. For your information, Sophia grew up in an upper-middle-class family just outside Chicago. Blissful by all accounts. Check it yourself. It's no secret. Don't feel too bad, though. Her special gift is manipulating and corrupting essentially good, but weak, men. Like Tuggy. Like you."

"I'm not weak, and she didn't manipulate me. She loves me. We're in love!" The Chief insisted. He almost shouted the last three words, making me wonder if he was trying to convince me or himself. Had a bit of doubt finally crept in?

I laughed. "Oh, the fools that love makes. Don't you get it? It was all a fake. Your affair and her 'save me, I'm helpless' routine. It's disgusting that she used domestic violence as a ruse to get money when there are true victims out there, but that's Sophia. I'll bet she even suggested you make Tuggy an informant to keep an eye on him, right?" The Chief stared at me. "You better face it. Your faux girlfriend has set you up for a very painful fall."

The back door opened and closed with a quiet thud. A small light turned on in the back room. Sophia, aka Mrs. Tuggy Johnston, came around the corner and stopped.

"Wha-a...You're not supposed to be here!" She hissed in the semi-darkness to the Chief.

"What happened, Sophia? It was supposed to look like a drunken accident, not this...this freak show!" The Chief said, waving at the Wheel. Sophia turned and gasped.

"You're crazy! I didn't do this!"

She started moving toward the Wheel. I stepped out in front of it as the Chief grabbed her arm, keeping her from going further.

"Soph, what's going on? Why did you have to leave, honey?" The chief's tone was imploring.

"Don't call me honey! Let go of me!" She wiggled to get free.

"Time to tell him the truth, Sophia," I interposed. "About your real plans. The ones that don't involve him."

"What's she talking about, Soph? Tell her she's wrong, baby. Tell her we're in love!"

The Chief continued to squeeze Sophia's arm. He reached for her other one and pulled her around to face him. Sophia squealed.

"I said, let go! You're hurting me, you bastard!"

"Bastard? *I'm* a bastard?" The chief's tone turned from pleading to confusion.

With a final jerk, Sophia wrung free, but as she swung around, two objects fell from her pocket, hitting the floor with a clang and a thud.

"My badge and knife. Why do you..." The Chief's face twisted as painful realization hit. "I didn't lose them after all, you stole them! What were you going to do? Drop them here to frame me? I thought we were going away, starting over with the insurance money."

"There's no insurance money! Who would insure *him*?" Sophia gave a scoffing chuckle and jerked her head, indicating Tuggy. "But the idea of those millions kept you around, didn't it? Love. You loved the money, not me. I certainly don't love you, and I'm not going anywhere with you!" She snarled at him, then looked at me. "Or anyone else in this town."

"So, it was all a lie. Us. Fake?" The Chief's face and voice were flat, but I sensed a seething anger simmering underneath.

"You know what they say, friends close, enemies closer," Sophia jeered, shrugging. "You were the perfect stooge. Proud. Gullible. Trusting. I knew you couldn't resist 'saving' me."

"I believed you," the Chief continued, staring at his former lover. "Believed *in* you. Enough to …There's someone else, isn't there? Who?"

Sophia stared back with a contemptuous grin. "I'm not telling you anything. You'll have to deal with this yourself."

"I'm not going down for this alone," the Chief growled. The supportive lover defending Sophia at any cost was gone. Betrayal had turned faith into rage.

They focused on each other, exchanging escalating accusations. Time to go. I took two steps back to the Wheel, stepped up on the platform, and leaned my head next to Tuggy's.

"Ready?" I whispered, bending to remove the long axe. The trapped dollar bill, still miraculously in one piece, flitted to the floor. I unhooked Tuggy's hands from the back and grabbed my phone, which had been sitting on the short wall behind the Wheel. I tapped stop.

Tuggy slid off the Wheel. One hand rubbing his bald head.

I put my phone in my back pocket and glanced at the sad-looking toupee still stuck to the Wheel under the short axe.

"Don't look. Let's go," I murmured, pushing him toward the back exit.

The former lovers were still fully engaged. I looked around once before turning the corner to see the Chief finally pull his gun from the holster. As we hurried out the exit, a loud thunk and an agonizing male groan broke the shouting, as if someone had just buried a hatchet deep into flesh and bone. Two shots quickly followed, then a single female scream as the door closed. Time for 911.

* * *

"Did you have to call me so many names?" Tuggy whined as we slowly walked around to the front. "And that long axe was so close to, you know, the stuff."

"Stop complaining. I had to make it look real, didn't I? And it worked. You needed to see and hear it for yourself. Sorry about the toupee, though," I said, glancing over. "You actually look better without it."

"You think so?" Tuggy asked, both hands now rubbing his bald pate. "I didn't know about the Chief and Sophie. Were there others?"

"Oh, yes," I said, turning to him and smiling.

"Wait, you? But you're a, a…girl. I didn't think she…"

"She used whoever she needed in whatever way necessary. I was just another pawn in her game. I went along because it was also necessary for *my* game. I'm just glad you stayed quiet up there."

"It was hard. I didn't want to believe it. I thought she loved me."

"She loved your lifestyle, not you. You didn't drink any of the beer she gave you, right?"

He shook his head. "Just pretended. She called and met me here tonight like you said she would. How did you know?"

"Because it was my idea."

"She gave me the beer, and we talked a bit until she got a text. She cursed and tore her purse apart, then left, saying she'd forgotten something and would be right back. Told me to finish my beer."

I nodded. "Yeah, that text was from me. I had to get her out of here. See, Sophia was supposed to spike your beer with one of your medications to make it look like you'd washed down your pills with alcohol. Not a smart thing to do, but people do it every day, so it's believable. The spiked beer would make you very nauseous at first. She'd then help you to the bathroom, and when you bent to get sick in the toilet, she'd hold your head under the water until you drowned. By then, you'd be too weak and drowsy to resist. Boom. Accidental drowning."

"I was supposed to die in a toilet?" Tuggy grimaced.

"Yep. She loved that idea, but not the accidental death. She wanted the Chief framed for your murder. I played along by suggesting she steal his badge and that trademark pocket-knife of his. She could leave them under the toilet as if he dropped them while drowning you. Stupid plot, but she went for it. She took both from him one night and gave them to me for safekeeping. I was supposed to put them in her purse this morning, but I messaged her that I'd forgotten them at the beach house where we used to meet. She'd have to go back. I told her to wait ten minutes, then call the Chief about the change in plans. He could drag your unconscious body to the bathroom, put your head in the toilet, and leave. She could drown you when she got back if you were still alive. She liked that idea even better as it implicated the Chief. I had twenty minutes to get you on the Wheel before the Chief arrived and an hour until Sophia got back. Tricky timing."

Tuggy sighed. "It was Sophia's idea about investing in the new businesses. I didn't really get it, but she had a friend at the bank who said it would save us from bankruptcy. I just had to sign everything because the firm was in my name. I thought it was a good thing."

"Her bank friend was in on it, too, of course. They tried to make it look like you were the criminal, not them."

"Sophia was taking the COA money, too?"

"Yes, again with her bank friend. Tuggy, the smartest thing you did was listen to me. It was the best way to get the evidence we needed. But laudanum? How'd you come up with that?"

"I thought that's what you guys said," he shrugged. "Do you really have an accountant friend?"

I nodded. "With her testimony as well as this," I paused, holding up my phone. "We've got them."

"You recorded it all?"

"Up until I untied you," I said.

"Will it work? Will they believe I didn't know?" Tuggy asked.

"I think so. Just tell the truth. Don't downplay your part. You may get some jail time for being so, uh, unreasonably ignorant, but if you help uncover the embezzlement and investment fraud, it shouldn't be much."

"Then back to golfing and my old life?" he asked, hopefully.

We were now in front of the building, and I looked inside the darkened windows. Two sets of legs were barely visible in the shadows, but it didn't appear either was moving. The wooden handle of the long axe protruded into the light.

"Yes, Tuggy, back to golfing and the country club, but we're going to have a talk about your gambling. Now, you ready?" I asked, hearing the sirens getting closer.

He nodded, a wistful smile on his face. I'd bet anything he was already on a putting green somewhere, this business forgotten.

I considered the whole operation. It started when my college bestie contacted me. Her daughter's family was in danger of losing everything in the Ponzi scheme. As the girl's godmother and namesake, I couldn't let that happen. I decided the best way to beat the con-artists was to play along. Go undercover as I had so many times on the job. I borrowed from my 401k, opened the business with Tuggy's firm, and became a victim, preparing for a long bout of mental cat and mouse.

When I realized that Sophia was the brains, not Tuggy, the next step was to become her confidant. I discreetly warned her, as one female to another, to be careful. I suspected Tuggy was into something criminal, which might ruin her life. Sophia immediately recognized the value of having a former police detective as an ally. She claimed Tuggy threatened her to play along with the fraud "or else" at the same time, the Chief blackmailed her into an affair. She didn't know where to turn, blah, blah, blah. I clucked sympathetically, agreeing us girls needed to stick together blah, blah, blah. We devised a plan to get rid of them both. Then I devised the plan within the plan without Sophia. It was a bit dicey, and Sophia couldn't be completely trusted to keep her end, but I figured her ego wouldn't let her quit. If the plan worked, she and the Chief would determine their own fates, not me. And they *had* determined their own fates, I decided, thinking of the two pairs of legs I saw through the window.

Love can be the most dangerous game of all.

I smiled to myself. The business insurance policy I'd taken out on *Axed & Bowed,* covering intentional malfeasance, had been a very expensive, but necessary, precaution. After all, I was going into business with probable criminals. After paying back my 401k, whatever proceeds were left, I'd share with my goddaughter and the other defrauded business owners. Maybe they could redeem their dreams. Maybe I could start redeeming my own, too. Tackle that other unfinished business.

I looked up at the Axed & Bowed sign, which now reflected red strobe-lights as the police and ambulance pulled up. This game was over. The stars were rightfully aligned once again. I felt a sense of peace I hadn't in a long time. Not bad for a hack job.

Story Inspiration:

Being a mystery/crime writer, I tend to view anywhere as a possible murder scene. It's a curse. For example, when others see a peaceful mountain lake popular for its serenity, I imagine a body suddenly floating to the top. In this case, I was at an ax-throwing gallery watching participants eagerly whisk hatchets at various targets for scores. Perfectly harmless. But in my mind, a body was tied to one of those targets. As I wondered who I'd like to put there, "The Hack Job" was born.

WORST DAY EVER

Rebecca Lugones

Rebecca Lugones is the editor of the Rap Sheet newsletter for the Florida Chapter of Mystery Writers of America. She grew up in Miami, a place brimming with stories waiting to be told. This story marks her debut as a published author.

Yerin read the email aloud. "I have your husband. If you want him back alive, you must play a game. You have until seven p.m. tonight to respond. Tell no one. Do not contact the police."

This must be one of Jay's games.

She enjoyed them but never let him know. This game, though, was not fun or funny.

What if it's not a joke? What if it's true?

The email came in after one o'clock, when Jay usually left for lunch. She called his cell. It went to voicemail. After three more attempts, Yerin left a message.

"Jay, I received an email that you've been kidnapped." Yerin controlled her voice. "If it's a prank, it's not funny. Call me back."

Next, she called Pak CyberSecurity Company, Jay's family business. The time on her MacBook Pro read a quarter to two.

The office administrator, Marley, answered the phone. "Pak CyberSecurity. How may I help you?"

"It's Yerin."

"Hey, Yerin, how's the new book coming along?"

"It's coming." Yerin wrote a cozy mystery series featuring Auntie Sun-Young, a Korean American everyone thinks is crazy but is actually clever. Marley was Yerin's cheerleader. "Is Jay around? I couldn't reach him by phone."

"I'll walk down to his office."

Yerin rested her forehead on the kitchen counter. *Why didn't I think of that? I'm not thinking logically.*

"No one's seen him since lunch. He's probably running errands or meeting a client and forgot to put it on his calendar. Do you want to leave a message?"

Tell no one. The phrase ran through her mind.

"Please ask him to call me."

Yerin called Jay's two best buds, Lucas and Perry, and neither knew where Jay was. They'd be in big trouble if they were playing a prank.

Could this be the scam where a fake kidnapper claimed they had your loved one, demanded money, but your loved one was alive and well and not kidnapped at all? She didn't think so because she had spoken to everyone close to Jay, and no one knew where he was. She rubbed the back of her neck.

Yerin searched online for kidnapping scams. Most kidnappers requested ransom money. This person asked her to play a game. This must be a prank.

"I can play your game," she said aloud. "I'm not waiting till seven p.m. to respond."

Straightening her back, she clicked reply on the kidnapper's email and wrote,

Will play your game if every hour I get proof of life first.

She hit send. The pacing began.

* * *

Half an hour later, Yerin received an email. She clicked on its attachment.

A video appeared. Jay sat stonelike on a wooden bench with his hands behind his back. His shirt looked wrinkled, and his hair, which he combed fastidiously in the mornings, stood up like alfalfa sprouts.

Her chest tightened. This didn't look like a prank.

"Yerin, this is not a prank. Pay close attention. I'm okay. I love you." The video stopped.

A text popped up on her iPhone.

This is my game, not yours. You will receive proof of life every morning.

Every morning? How long was this game going to take? Maybe I should call the police.

Another email appeared from the kidnapper.

You have three chances to save your husband's life. Task #1: Guess the correct four colors from these six: Yellow, Blue, Red, Black, White, Green...in the correct order. You have one attempt per task and sixteen hours from the time of this email to solve it. Check your texts for the first clue on where to perform this task.

And remember, DO NOT involve the police!

She checked the time on her watch. *Three o'clock.* She had until seven a.m. tomorrow to complete the task.

Yerin's phone pinged.

Clue: Store

Good Luck, Yerin. Or should I say, good luck to Jay.

The kidnapper added a large laughing emoji at the end.

Store? What does this even mean? She pushed the laptop away from her.

Yerin rested her forehead on the palms of her hands, and her straight, shoulder-length hair encircled her hands like a black curtain.

"AHHHH!"

Okay, she told herself, *you must keep it together for Jay's sake.*

She opened a lined notebook and turned it horizontally. With a pencil, she wrote the word STORE in capital letters and circled it. Next, she drew a line up from the circle and wrote Macy's.

Throwing her head back, she said, "Ugh!" How was she supposed to know which store? It could be a drug store, a hardware store, a computer store. The list was endless.

What did Jay say? Pay close attention. Yerin slid the laptop toward her and reopened the video, watching it several times, first focusing on how Jay said his words. He sounded shaken. The room they kept him in was odd, but she couldn't explain why.

Even if she figured out which store, how could she guess the right colors in the right order?

This is a nightmare.

Yerin yearned for her mom's kimchi-jjigae. Her Korean comfort food.

The time on the microwave was five o'clock. Fourteen hours to go, and yet she felt like she had only fifteen minutes left. Grabbing the notebook, she continued to draw lines from the circle to write different types of stores. She closed her eyes.

* * *

Yerin woke with a start. She rubbed her eyes, disoriented. "Oh, my God! What time is it?" Her watch read midnight. *Seven hours to go.* She couldn't believe she fell asleep.

She looked at the page with the word STORE circled and the lines radiating from it. There weren't any stores open overnight. The word STORE had other meanings. According to the dictionary, it also meant to keep or accumulate something.

Storage places! No. Those places are closed, too. Where else can I store something? A locker! Lockers at the gym, but most don't open until five.

She double-checked the hours of the gyms nearby online. None were open twenty-four hours.

Post office box. Or Amazon lockers. She checked the USPS lobby hours. *Closed.* Both places near her with Amazon lockers were also closed.

There are lockers at the train station, and that's open twenty-four hours.

It was a start, and if the train station was the wrong place, she still had time to get to a gym. *But which one?*

Yerin splashed water on her face to wake up. After putting her hair in a ponytail, she grabbed her purse and a Taser. The train station was not a safe place at this hour.

* * *

Homeless people lie on blankets near each other along one exterior side of the train station with carts or bags full of their life belongings.

Yerin stepped onto the black mat to enter the train station. A man approached her with his hand out. She unintentionally wrinkled her nose at him.

"You smell nice too, lady!" he called out behind her.

Courtesy was not uppermost in her mind.

A few people sat or stood in the lobby. Yerin searched for signs directing her to the lockers. When she found the lockers, she sighed at the sight of so many of them. Many of the lockers had little orange keys with numbered key chains.

These must be the available ones.

Yerin opened the first locker that had a key. *Empty.* She opened one after another until she reached the last one. Having discovered nothing inside, she slumped onto the floor next to the metal doors. Tears rolled down her cheeks.

Was she in the wrong place? Had the kidnapper meant a local rather than a national station? Had she mistaken the meaning of the clue?

Wiping her eyes, she looked at the floor in despair. Black tape running along the base of the banks of lockers caught her eye. Yerin, normally dirt-phobic, crawled, following the tape. Several banks over, she found an arrow pointing up to a column of lockers. These didn't have keys hanging from them.

Was she wrong again? Was the tape only meaningful to the maintenance personnel?

She used her finger to grasp the bottom locker door. No luck.

"GRRR!"

To her left, several banks down, a gray-haired man glanced at her. Her growl must have been louder than she thought.

From her purse, she removed her ring of keys.

Choosing the thinnest key, she slid it back and forth into the bottom of the locker until she had purchase, and inched the door open. With her other hand, she pulled on the side of the door and exposed the locker's contents.

Six small, colorful rubber boats attached to key chains lay on the bottom of the locker. The boats were the same colors that were in the email from the kidnappers: yellow, blue, red, black, white, and green. On the right wall hung four adhesive hooks.

Yerin scanned the locker area. The grey-haired man had left.

Leaning her head against the locker door, she found a small green dot on the hook furthest away from her and a red dot on the one closest to her.

Are the green and red dots a clue? She stared at the boats and sighed. "Choose four colors," the kidnapper wrote. *Here goes.* On the hook with the green dot, she hung the green boat. Her next two choices, white then black, were random. Under the red dot, she hung the red boat. With her phone, she took a picture of her color choices.

"This better work," she mumbled. Worried the boats might fall, she cautiously closed the locker door. Though not religious for years, she made the sign of the cross and walked back to her car.

* * *

Yerin received a text message as soon as she parked in her garage.

2 correct colors, wrong spots.

Shit! Was it the green and the red? No point driving back to the train station. The kidnapper gave her only one chance. How did they know she had returned home?

She stepped out of her garage onto the driveway. In the September weather, the humidity enveloped her.

No suspicious cars or people. Was it a coincidence?

A sense deep within her bones told her no. Thinking of bones, she dragged the weight of her weary body inside and plopped on the sofa.

Phone in hand, she lay and viewed the time. *Two am. Five more hours.*

Little colored boats ran through her mind.

* * *

At four a.m., Yerin awoke. Had she been dreaming about Jay being kidnapped? She checked her email and messages. They proved she hadn't. Despite not feeling hungry, she made a peanut butter and jelly sandwich and ginseng tea for an energy boost.

To distract herself until seven a.m., when the second message would come, she opened her laptop to work on the next book in the Auntie Sun-Young series. Her mind wandered to the kidnapping.

What would Auntie Sun-Young do?

* * *

At seven on the dot, Yerin received an email.

Task #2: You have 12 hours to complete.

Clue: POOL TIME!

Until seven pm. Less time. Jiggling her leg, Yerin waited for the kidnapper's proof of life video. Why would anyone want to kidnap a person and then play a game for their life? Was Jay involved in a criminal act?

Another email appeared. Her neck muscles tightened as she clicked on the video attachment. Jay sat on the same bench and in the same room, looking older than his thirty-one years.

"Hi, Sweetie, wanted to advise you not to use a private eye. I know you can do this. I love you and miss you. Can't wait to see you."

The video stopped. It pained her to see her kind, upbeat husband in that horrible situation.

Jay advised her not to use a private eye. *Was it a clue? What did Pool Time mean?*

One interpretation besides a swimming pool came to mind. Pooling your money. But it required others to contribute to a fund or a kitty. Kitty? Did it mean playing poker at a casino?

She was reading too much into it. Most people thought of a swimming pool. Would she have to arrange little rubber boats by color in a pool? They did not own a pool. What were the ones nearby? Not the ones in a country club because they didn't have a membership. Online, she searched for municipal pools and gyms with pools. Three were close to home. All were open.

Grabbing her purse, Yerin drove to her gym. At the gym, she scanned her membership tag and walked toward the pool. She searched the pool and its area from top to bottom. Nothing.

The other nearby gyms had no pools. Disappointed, she drove to the first municipal pool on her list. Nothing. The same with the other two pools. Was her first guess correct? The casino was further away than the train station.

What am I missing? A few minutes later, she slapped her hand on the steering wheel. *What an idiot! A pool table.* Sleep deprivation impaired her ability to think.

It was too early to go to the pool halls. The ones near her opened at noon.

At home, she rewatched Jay's first video. There was no natural lighting. It could have been day or night. The wooden bench he sat on reminded her of the kind you might find in a diner or breakfast place. Could he be at a diner? Not unless the kidnapper owned the restaurant, and it was after hours. No. The place looks smaller. The floor isn't visible. No other person's shadow. Turning up the volume, she detected an undefinable soft sound.

Something bugged her about this video. Giving up on it, she opened the one from this morning. Again, the phrase not to hire a private investigator struck her as weird. Rewatching the second video, she spotted Jay blinking a lot. To confirm, she opened the first video. Jay was not blinking in that one. *Of course, private eye!* It was a code.

He had been a Boy Scout and learned how to use Morse code. Jay and his brothers had been caught cheating in games using Morse code. Secretly, she had learned Morse to beat them at their own game.

Yerin dragged the slider on the video slowly and observed his eye movements.

The message read, 11122012.

What did these numbers mean? It's too long to be an address. Yerin entered the numbers on Google. A mishmash of results popped up. Answers to crossword puzzles, rug sales, a politician resigned, but nothing meant anything to her.

Was it a date? After a few tries, she came up with 11-12-2012. *What happened on that date?* She scrolled through Jay's social media for the date. One entry popped up.

Worst day ever!

Many friends inquired what had happened. Jay never responded.

At eleven forty-five, Yerin took a shower to wake up. At twelve, she parked in front of Shooters, the first pool hall on her list, and entered.

Inside, she combed through the hall, including the bathrooms, for signs to let her know she was in the right place. Nothing.

* * *

On her way to Cappy's, the next pool hall, she worried the kidnapper had left no clues this time.

Yerin entered the pool hall. Cappy's had a nautical theme with a helm hanging on the wall. A few people ate at the bar. One patron resembled the grey-haired man near the lockers at the train station, but she wasn't sure.

Her heart leaped. Maybe this was the right place. Again, she searched walls and baseboards. Then she spotted the black tape with an arrow on the backside of one of the pool tables. Six solid-colored balls were strewn across the play field—the same six colors—, and a cue stick rested across the rails. She chalked the cue. Could the green and red balls be the right colors she chose at the train station in the wrong place? Two more colors? She studied the table. Yerin bent over, cue in hand, and tapped the black ball into a pocket.

* * *

Like the day before, Yerin received a text message from the kidnapper when she pulled into her garage.

Two correct colors. Only one in the correct spot.

Great! I still don't know which colors. How did the kidnapper know when she arrived at her house again? Outside the garage, she surveyed the neighborhood. Nobody was lurking.

A thought popped into her head. After shutting the garage door, she lay on the floor and slid under her car. In movies, characters put trackers underneath cars. Using her phone flashlight, she found a small box about an inch thick in the wheel well of the front passenger side. She reached out to touch it and quickly withdrew her hand.

Was it easy to remove? Would the kidnapper be alerted if she removed it? Sliding out from under the car, she Googled, **tracker alert if removed**. One article stated that the person tracking her would receive an alert if removed.

Disregard.

Inside the house, she grabbed an energy drink from the fridge and sat in front of her Mac. A good place to start was the Miami Herald. In the search bar, Yerin entered the date and Jay's name. A brief piece from November 12, 2012, appeared with Jay's name.

Cyclist Killed in Collision on Main Hwy

Coconut Grove, FL—Madeleine Swenson, 50, was fatally struck by a vehicle early Monday morning while cycling on Main Hwy. The incident occurred as she crossed the street with her husband, Donald Swenson, riding behind her.

"Maddie looked both ways before crossing. It was all clear. She crossed. When I was about to follow her, a black Toyota Prius hit her," Mr. Swenson recounted.

The driver, identified as 18-year-old Jay Pak, was arrested at the scene and is cooperating with police. Swenson was pronounced dead at the scene. Authorities are continuing their investigation.

Yerin covered her mouth with a hand. Why didn't Jay ever mention this? Poor Mr. Swenson. Yerin thought about how much Jay's death would devastate her.

Donald Swenson must be the kidnapper.

Yerin had many more questions.

Closing her eyes, she imagined what Swenson's house looked like. Was Jay locked in a room? Basements were uncommon in Miami.

Donald Swenson must be about sixty-three. The Swensons were cycling in Coconut Grove. *Let's see if I find any Swenson's around there.* Yerin's search yielded no property results and no social media for Donald Swenson.

Her phone dinged.

Check your email.

Yerin's stomach dropped. *Is Jay okay?* Hands shaking, she opened the email.

Task #3: The rules have changed. You are to shoot…

Shoot? He wants me to shoot someone? Hell no! The room spun. Yerin sat on the sofa and put her head between her knees, breathing in and out slowly.

Get up! Finish reading the email. It may not be what you think.

Feeling better, she lifted herself off the sofa and walked back to her laptop in the kitchen. Fingers trembling, she scrolled to read the rest of the message.

…Hannah Burdock, the county prosecutor. She's attending a luncheon at the Women's Club of Coconut Grove at noon tomorrow. You have until 2:30 pm to perform this task.

I don't need to remind you what's at stake.

Attached is a current photo of Ms. Burdock.

Yerin opened the attachment. The photo was grainy, as if taken off a television. She looked familiar. Hannah Burdock had carrot-colored hair, easy to spot.

How was she going to avoid killing Burdock and save her husband? This was her last chance.

"Shit! Shit!" she said, pacing.

"Ding!" Another video from Swenson.

In the video, Jay's smile did not reach his eyes. "Tell Rivers we won't be able to drive to the real south like we planned. Love you." He was blinking again, but the video cut off after the first few blinks.

Who was Rivers, and how could she find him? How could he help Jay?

In her notebook, she wrote the information she'd gathered from the three videos. She circled the name Rivers several times.

Rewatching the first video, she raised the volume. *A lapping sound.* That's what had been bothering her before. The closed curtains behind Jay swayed. A vision of the little boats in the locker popped into her head. *He's on a boat. The name of the pool hall was Cappy's. Captain, shortened.* If Jay was on a boat, why did it seem like Donald Swenson was leaving her clues to his location? Was this a game within a game?

In the third video, the boat rocked more. *So where is this boat?* She repeated Jay's words from his last video. "Tell Rivers we won't be able to drive to the real south like we planned."

Real south, she understood, because even though Miami was geographically in the south, it was a city, demographically and culturally, not at all like a Southern state.

If he's on a boat, where is he?

She Googled marinas in the area. *Bingo!* She found an address on South River Drive. The Morse code Jay messaged her was a number two. Marina Miami River's address began with the number two. For Jay's sake, she had to be right. As a precaution, she jotted the names and addresses of two other marinas.

She went over several scenarios in her head in which she shot Hannah Burdock. In each one, she either got arrested or, worse, killed. If she died, Jay would be killed. Anyway, the thought of killing anyone churned her stomach. Yerin wouldn't be able to live with herself. How could she get around this dilemma?

Shoot. He said shoot Burdock, not kill her. She'd enter the luncheon, shoot a photo of Burdock, go to the bathroom, and change into more practical clothes. She hoped Swenson would accept her interpretation of the word.

How can I get to the marina? Swenson is tracking my car. Perhaps not Jay's.

Her thoughts were everywhere as she paced. *Is Jay's phone in his car?*

On her iPhone, she went to the Find My app. Scrolling a list of their devices, she found Jay's phone icon and clicked. The app revealed his phone was at his work address.

* * *

Yerin grabbed the spare fob for Jay's car, then drove to the Publix Supermarket nearest to Jay's office building. In the bathroom, she changed her top and put on a cap and sunglasses. Swenson was tracking her car, but was he following her too? Leaving Publix, she walked the two blocks to Jay's office. She didn't have keys to his office, and her only hope was to find his phone in his car.

Yerin's heart dropped when she saw that Jay's car was not in his parking spot, and no other cars were on that floor. She ventured to the next floor and almost shouted when she saw Jay's Audi convertible in the far corner. The car yelped when she punched the button on the spare car fob. *Alleluia!* On the central console, she found Jay's phone. It showed numerous texts and calls.

She hoofed it back to Publix and changed her clothes, then she randomly threw groceries into a cart, so it looked like she had food shopped.

* * *

In the late morning, Yarin drove to the CVS Pharmacy near Jay's work and walked to his car. She moved Jay's car and parked near the Women's Club where Hannah Burdock would be speaking. After, she took an Uber back to the CVS.

Inside the restroom, she changed into a flowing, knee-length dress and paired it with low-heeled sandals. She placed her spare clothes, her wallet, her phone, and Jay's phone in her purse.

At twelve on the dot, she parked her car and entered the club with the camera strap on one shoulder and her purse on the other. A woman eyed her suspiciously inside the dining room. Yerin lifted the camera, and the woman smiled and nodded. As she was searching for the nearest restroom, Marley, Jay's assistant, called.

"Hey, Yerin. Jay hasn't come in. Is he okay?"

"Oh-um, no. He ate something he shouldn't have," Yerin whispered.

"Poor thing. Okay. I'll let his brothers know. How are you?"

"Fine. We'll talk later; I'm at a luncheon."

Down a corridor, she found the bathroom where she could change after she shot the picture she needed.

Back in the lunch area, women were trickling in and excitedly talking to each other. No sign of Hannah Murdoch. It was almost twelve-thirty. She barely had two hours to drive to the marina and save Jay.

At twelve-thirty, Hannah Murdoch arrived. Several women surrounded her. Yerin approached and aimed her camera. A few women posed with the prosecutor. Yerin took the photo. She turned to leave.

"Wait!"

Yerin froze. Did they uncover she was a fake? Were they going to call the police? She turned slowly toward the voice.

"Could you please take a picture of the two of us?" A short blonde woman said.

Yerin smiled. "Sure," she said and took the photo.

"Me too, please," another woman said.

After taking several photos and promising to send the women copies of their pictures, Yerin changed her clothes in the bathroom. She was finally in Jay's car and on the way to the marina.

* * *

At the marina, she had less than an hour to find Swenson's boat and save Jay. Putting on an airhead act, Yerin learned where the boat was docked from the office attendant at the marina.

The old boat swayed in the water. *Uh-oh, I forgot to take a Dramamine.* Quietly, she boarded the boat. With any luck, she'd rescue Jay and be out of there before she got seasick.

Poking her head in the opening, she found Jay lying down on the same sofa from the videos with his legs and feet bound.

"Jay," she said softly as she entered the cabin.

He sat up, open-mouthed.

"What are you doing here? He could be back at any moment."

"Shhh," Yerin said as she sawed at the rope at his hands with a utility knife she brought.

"At last, you found me," said a man's deep voice behind her.

Goose bumps formed on her arms. Yerin turned her head to look at the man pointing a gun at her in the doorway. He was the same grey-haired man she saw at the train station and the pool hall.

"Step away from Jay."

She dropped the knife in Jay's palm and backed away. Donald Swenson yanked Yerin's arm, wrapped his arm around her neck, and pressed the gun to her head.

"I played your game," Yerin said.

"Oh, Yerin, I was toying with you like a cat with their prey. The color games gave you clues on how to find Jay. I was never going to kill him. I'm going to kill you."

Jay's eyes widened in surprise. "That's not what you said!"

"Then why didn't you kidnap me?" Yerin asked.

"What's the fun in that? This way, I can make you both suffer. Besides, it was easier to kidnap Jay. His routine was more predictable. You hardly come out of your house."

"You're angry at me," Jay yelled. "She had nothing to do with this."

"On the contrary. A wife for a wife. When you killed my wife…."

"I didn't kill her. She was dead when she struck her head on the ground. The Medical Examiner said it in court.

"No!" Swenson shouted.

Yerin's shoulders drew up to her ears. The rocking of the boat was making her feel sick.

"Now you'll feel the pain of losing the one person you love most in the world, Jay."

"Let her go," Jay yelled.

"Not until she's dead."

"Let her go, or you'll regret it."

Swenson laughed. "I won't regret…"

Yerin couldn't hold it in. Her mouth opened involuntarily, and a stream of slime and chunks landed on the crook of Swenson's arm around her neck.

He jumped back, shaking his arm in disgust. Jay untied the rope around his ankles. Yerin turned and kicked Swenson in his crotch. He doubled over in pain.

"Police! Hands up!

Yerin and Jay did what they were told.

Swenson raised one arm and said, "Officers, these young people tried to assault me."

"He's lying!" she and Jay said in unison.

* * *

The police arrested Donald Swenson after Yerin showed them the texts and emails from him. A boat captain had contacted the police when he spotted Jay's face peeking through the boat's curtains. He knew Swenson, and he thought it was suspicious that Jay never left the cabin.

At home, even after they showered, Yerin still felt queasy. She drank ginger tea. Yerin and Jay cuddled together on the sofa.

"We were lucky the captain grew suspicious," Jay said, and he kissed the top of her head.

"I had it under control," Yerin smiled cockily. "As horrible as this ordeal was, I plan to use it for my Auntie Sun-Young series."

"Auntie saves the kidnapped victim," Jay said.

"I think I'll let the husband get killed the next time."

"What?"

Jay faked a hurt look, and Yerin laughed.

Story Inspiration:

One of my favorite games as a kid was Mastermind. I loved the challenging use of logic to decipher your opponent's secret code. It provided a perfect structure for this story.

ENDGAME

BV Lawson

BV Lawson's stories have won the Dillydoun Fiction Prize, Short Mystery Fiction Society Derringer Award, Noir Nation Golden Fedora, and Gemini Magazine Awards, and she was a finalist for the Pulpfictional Flash Contest, Hammond Review International Prize, and Tucson Festival of Books Literary Competitions. BV's Scott Drayco novels have also been a featured Library Journal pick and finalists for Shamus, Silver Falchion, Daphne, and Foreword Book Reviews Awards.

The taxi dropped Drayco off on a side street and peeled away as if the driver was eager to scram. Even in the twilight, it was easy to see why. This place was creepy…evil. Tall weeds poked through zigzagging cracks in the broken concrete parking lot, and gang graffiti covered rotting boards over the windows. The grime-coated skeleton of a building looming in front of him was all that remained of the Rancho Lugar Feliz asylum.

Drayco paused for a moment, patting the Glock in the shoulder holster under his coat. Was he making the right call to follow through with this unusual meeting? The client said he needed to be discreet and would make it worth Drayco's time, something verified when a nice deposit was wired into Drayco's account. Plus, there was something weirdly compelling in the man's voice over the phone.

In Drayco's odd synesthesia world, where voices had colors, shapes, and textures, he thought he recalled hearing something similar to—but not exactly like—that voice, with its ochre, sand-covered bubble wrap. It had been driving him nuts trying to recall where and when he'd heard it before, even losing sleep when it invaded his dreams, triggering something deeply disturbing, something primal. But just what it was stayed tantalizingly out of reach. So, he decided to go ahead with the meeting. Maybe he'd at least be able to get a good night's sleep again. And maybe he'd find the answer as to why, deep down, he knew he had no choice.

After slipping through gaping holes in the fence, Drayco spied an opening into the building and picked his way through the maze of narrow hallways and ghostly bedrooms. He had to dodge oil-slicked puddles, terrier-sized rats, and piles of trash from recent squatters. A fire gutted portions of the facility years ago, but the charred smell lingered and almost made him sneeze. Maybe it was fitting that this place, which once housed much human misery, was now suffering its own architectural purgatory.

It was hard not to feel the spirits of those once hidden away within these walls—the homeless, the disabled, the mentally ill. Drayco recalled reading about a group of Marines who once found a box of mummified legs in a freezer here during a training exercise. Perhaps it wasn't the most brilliant idea to meet his mysterious client in such a deserted, lonely setting. But that was the deal.

In the deepest bowels of the building, where only faint slivers of residual sunlight shone through cracked windows high up near the ceiling, he observed a white-haired man, alone—waiting. Drayco scanned the area for anyone else, but the place looked unoccupied except for the two of them.

As he drew nearer, the other man said, "Scott Drayco?"

"Yes, but I doubt your real name is Mr. Smith."

"Jacob Aconi. Perhaps you've heard of me."

Drayco swallowed hard. "You're The Hangman." He'd seen that name many times while still at the Bureau, along with morbid jokes tied to the iconic stick-figure guessing game. The man was a masterful architect of crime, but Drayco's colleagues never had enough evidence for a conviction. That's where Drayco had heard Aconi's voice before, from archived surveillance tapes, although the timbre of the man's voice was now older, thinner, and raspy. Then again, Aconi had been a smoker, hadn't he?

Aconi bowed stiffly. "I'm flattered you recognized me. But fear not. I didn't lure you to this lovely little slice of California's dilapidated history to kill you. Although I do believe a vagrant was murdered in this very place just last year."

"Then why am I here?"

"I need you as a witness." Aconi handed over a manila envelope. "And I want you to deliver that."

The address was in Maryland, the name unfamiliar. "Look, Aconi, if this is a game—"

"Ah, but it's the endgame. Checkmate."

Drayco studied the elderly man, gauging his state of mind. Dementia? He seemed *compos mentis* at first glance. "What's in the envelope?"

"A will, deeds, bank accounts. For my grandson." Aconi pulled something else out of his pocket. Drayco tensed for a moment, his hand instinctively moving toward the shoulder holster, which seemed to amuse Aconi. The older man said, "And then, there's this."

Drayco eyed the little box in the man's hand. "What is it?"

Aconi flipped the box open to reveal a clear, shimmering blue diamond, which sparkled with unusual luster even in the dim light. "Fourteen carats. Such intense color, don't you think? With an impressive, almost perfect clarity. You may not believe it, but it was obtained legally. I want you to give this to my grandson, too."

Aconi waved his free hand around at the crumbling shell of the asylum. "That's why I picked this place. A diamond in the rough. I thought the choice rather merry," and he chuckled.

"I'm not sure I see the humor in any of this."

"Oh, I think you will, in good time."

Would he? It was hard to imagine anything merry about the man standing in front of Drayco, or, for that matter, the building itself. Water dripping from holes in the ceiling thrummed the rusting furnace nearby, creating a kind of muffled heartbeat. The rust contributed a blood-red pigment to the puddle beneath, looking like the remnants of a fresh murder scene. Whatever Aconi had meant by "endgame," this seemed like the perfect setting.

Aconi added, "I used to have a little sideline in the crystal manufacturing business in El Monte. Did you know copper wheels are used in that process? To create what is called intaglio, meaning 'reverse.' The deeper the engraving, the more prominent the object will appear."

Drayco struggled to follow Aconi's reasoning. "Sometimes you have to throw things in reverse to see what lies ahead, you mean?"

Aconi nodded. "You see? Great minds think alike."

"What isn't crystal clear is why you need me for any of this."

"In my line of work, there are few people I can trust. I've heard about you, too. Crime consultant to the cops. Former FBI. In fact, we even crossed paths once, although you never knew it. You're a regular Boy Scout."

"But surely an attorney—"

"My most recent attorney lasted ten years. Then he hired a rather inept assassin to kill me. Needless to say, he's not my attorney, or anyone else's attorney, anymore." Aconi handed over the little box.

Drayco wished he'd rigged a hidden microphone if this was confessional time. Could have helped solve a lot of cold cases. But the man said to come alone and no tech. "Why not give your grandson the envelope and diamond yourself?"

"His mother, my daughter, wisely took him far away. She knew my poison would spill onto him." Aconi laughed bitterly. "Poison. It started when my Romani grandparents died in Auschwitz. My own mother escaped the Nazis, emigrated to La La Land, and married into The Family. Ironic."

Aconi stared at the shadows on the floor cast by the dim light from broken windows, and he visibly shivered. "There are ghosts all around. Here, everywhere. Can't you feel them?"

Drayco suddenly had second thoughts about Aconi's mental state. "You said something about me being a witness. More like a delivery boy, isn't it?"

Aconi smiled, exposing his yellow teeth. "You ever get tired of fighting the universe, Mr. Drayco? Tired of seeing the stars speed away from you, always out of reach?"

"But if you get too close to the sun, you'll still get burned, is that it?"

"I do believe you understand. Then, you've had great losses in your own life, have you not?"

Drayco wasn't surprised Aconi had dug into his own past. But it made him a little angry. There was no reason to drag his own personal traumas into this sordid game. "As you said, ghosts."

"You probably think we're opposites. Yet, we aren't all that different, you and I."

"I don't recall the last time I ordered a hit, or dealt in human trafficking."

Aconi chuckled. "Not that, my boy. We both make our living from crime. But that's what we do. Not what we are. We're explorers. Roving the cosmos, burning fast and bright."

Mobster Existentialism, that was a new one. Drayco stared at Aconi, wondering where this "game" was going. But if there was any chance of bringing closure to some of Aconi's victims, it was worth the risk. "We're human comets with free will? Order is what we make of it?"

"You see? You truly do understand. Even if you don't want to admit it."

Drayco looked around the space, seeing only a few spiders and more of the *beady-eyed*, yellow-toothed rats. "What am I supposed to witness? I have no way of documenting it." He really should have followed his instincts and used a hidden mic.

Aconi unbuttoned his jacket. Strapped to his body was a bomb with enough explosives to take out half the building. Despite Drayco's years of training, a cold sweat broke out on the back of his neck as his pulse rate took a galactic leap. Every instinct screamed at him to run, but this was Aconi's game, and Drayco had to follow the rules, such as they were, if he hoped to survive this.

Time to initiate Crazy Man Negotiations 101. "Does this new little game also have something to do with your grandson?"

"It has to do with everything. Those ghosts—they haunt me, tell me my time is up. That my exploring days are over."

Drayco mentally threw the FBI playbook out the window and improvised. "You want me to tell your grandson he's safe from you. So he won't be haunted by those ghosts of yours?"

Aconi beamed. "I knew you'd understand." He pressed a button on a control device palmed in his hand, and a light flashed bright red on the bomb vest. "And now, you have three minutes to get safely outside."

Drayco clutched the envelope and box and sprinted toward the exit. How to escape via the labyrinth of hallways? He looked for the door he'd left cracked open. Left, straight ahead, right, right, left. How much time had passed? One minute? Two?

Then, he saw it. With one final push of adrenaline, he scrambled through the door and kept on running. He barely made it to safety in a drainage ditch at the edge of the empty parking lot, ducking down and plugging his ears with his fingers, when the heat from the blast wave rolled over him, singeing the hairs on his knuckles.

Once the wave passed, he hauled himself to a sitting position to see the full extent of Aconi's handiwork. Flames rapidly engulfed what was left of the building. There was no earthly way the man had survived that blazing crater.

Drayco checked on the manila envelope and its contents. Undamaged, just a little dirty. The small box was also intact. Would Aconi's grandson want these offerings from beyond the grave? Right now, Drayco didn't really care.

Many scientists said time is an illusion, didn't they? Maybe Aconi's ghosts, the asylum's ghosts—and Drayco's—weren't so far in the past, and "The Hangman" knew that all along. The cold sweat returned, and Drayco rubbed it away as he watched the flames and smoke billowing upward in the winds, upward toward the heavens and beyond.

Story Inspiration:
The protagonist in many of my novels and stories, Scott Drayco, was a classical

pianist forced to switch careers after a violent attack led to a law enforcement career instead. His unusual background and his genetic condition of synesthesia—where he "sees" sounds as colors, shapes, and colors—gives him a unique perspective on the world.

I'm always looking for ways to drop him into unusual scenarios where that unique perspective becomes as much a part of the storyline as the plot. In the case of "Endgame," I wondered what would happen if a notorious, and surprisingly philosophical, mobster took a liking to Drayco, enough to entrust him with one final life-or-death stratagem: a game to reclaim one's soul, albeit via violent means.

DEATH STREAMED LIVE

Stephen M. Pierce

Stephen M. Pierce is a technical writer living in Asheville, NC, whose work has appeared or is forthcoming in Ellery Queen's Mystery Magazine, Bone Parade, *and* Cowboy Jamboree. *His short stories and book reviews can be found at stephenmpierce.wordpress.com.*

Inspector Angel Angelov hadn't played a video game since they came in blocky cabinets, the graphics relying more on imagination than detail, so she felt out of place walking into NCX. The local e-sports tournament and convention had bought the entire Raleigh Convention Center. Not even the law enforcement convention she'd attended last year needed that much space.

The convention had been more welcoming than she expected. As she walked through the building with her lieutenant, weaving between costumed figures, she was stopped constantly for compliments, high fives, and even a request for a picture.

"I didn't know you were popular in this scene," her lieutenant Hector Montaña said with a smile.

"I'm not," Angel shrugged. "I think my son's been to a few small tournaments, but I'm not sure why he'd show people my picture."

They followed A-frame signs to reach the center of the convention, called

The Battlefield, and Angel tried to ignore the greetings that felt increasingly like catcalls. The moment they flashed their badges and entered the double doors, they were hit by a raucous cheer.

The Battlefield was filled with guests, nearly stacked on top of each other. Two uniformed teams sat face to face onstage, separated by a wall of computers. They were shooting each other on a massive screen above. Angel couldn't make sense of the flashy attacks, but she'd been to football games with a less rowdy crowd.

They continued around the audience, pushing past guests lining the perimeter, when the cheers turned into a standing ovation.

A voice boomed through the crowd, "What a stunning comeback! Shiisaa single-handedly takes the win, moving Team Chronologic onto the semifinal round."

The losing team pushed their chairs back and threw their headphones onto the table, but the crowd watched the winners. "Shiisaa" jumped from his chair, raising both hands as the applause washed over him. The rest of his team, all dressed in grey and blue jumpsuits, stood behind him.

Angel and Hector waited by the foot of the stage until they were done. When the audience began to filter out and the players returned to their computers, Angel walked onto the stage. She approached the team's leader, reaching into her pocket.

"Tyler Hirata—"

Tyler raised his eyebrows and let out a low whistle. He stood up, running a hand through his bleached hair.

"You don't gotta be so formal. Everyone here calls me Shiisaa," he said. "So, you want an autograph? I love your costume."

Angel raised an eyebrow. "Costume…?"

"Yeah. You mean you're not dressed up?" Tyler tilted his head. "You look just like Valerie, my main. I was just playing as her."

Tyler turned his monitor, showing a character select menu. A blonde woman holding a massive gun stood on-screen, wearing a police uniform that prioritized sex appeal over realism. Aside from that, she was Angel's spitting image.

Angel understood now why she'd gotten so much attention and why the look in Tyler's eyes disturbed her—he was already lost in his fantasies.

She grimaced and pulled out her badge. "Tyler, we'd like to ask you about your ex-girlfriend Mary Bellerose."

The excitement on Tyler's face drained. He lowered his head and looked at Angel as if about to record an apology video.

"This is about what happened yesterday, right?" Tyler asked. "I honestly didn't even know she was here—"

Hector stepped beside his partner, looking at his notepad. "In a stream three months ago, you said that if you ever saw Mary again, you'd 'beat some sense into her.' You were banned from your streaming site and are still appealing, I believe."

"Look, I won't deny I've said stupid things," Tyler said. "I can get really heated when I'm gaming."

"It seemed an interesting coincidence," Angel said. "I'm sure you know Mary fell from the hotel room where she was staying, but only after the killer slammed a fire extinguisher into her head."

Tyler clenched his fists. His pleading frown turned into a grimace.

"Mary has spoken about your abuse numerous times," Hector continued. "She says you were physical with her, and even after your breakup, you encouraged your followers to 'brigade' her streams and even 'swatted' her apartment."

Angel didn't entirely understand what Hector was saying, but it seemed like Tyler did.

"Were you upset that she was more successful than you? Did you want to prove you were better, once and for all?" Hector asked. "Where were you at the time of her murder?"

"You're putting lots of words in my mouth, but fine. When did Mary take her dive?"

That made Angel's skin crawl, but she only gritted her teeth.

"7:30 p.m."

Tyler turned to the rest of his team, who were busily packing away their equipment.

"Boys, do you think I could have killed Mary at 7:30?"

"Definitely not." One of them stood. "We can all vouch for him."

The other team members nodded in agreement.

"Is that a Valerie cosplayer?" A guy in the back mumbled.

"What's going on here?"

A blonde man in slacks and an ironed T-shirt—the e-sports equivalent of a tuxedo—approached. He provided commentary for the match.

"Reilly, these officers think I killed Mary Bellerose."

"That's impossible. I'm a witness." Reilly said. "In fact, I bet we've got more witnesses right here."

He raised the microphone in his hand and turned to the entrance.

"Excuse me, before you all go—I'd like you to raise your hand if you know what Shiisaa was doing at 7:30 p.m. yesterday."

The guests who'd yet to leave mumbled among themselves, but before long, uncertain hands rose. Roughly half the crowd was vouching for Angel's prime suspect.

"That's ridiculous," she said. "They can't all have been in the room with him."

"They weren't, but they watched him live," Reilly continued. "Yesterday, Shiisaa livestreamed solo practice matches from his hotel room. The stream ran from seven to nine, and his facecam was on the entire time. I was watching, and he never left."

"If that's not good enough for you," Tyler stepped forward, getting as close as he could without committing a felony. "Ask any one of the thousands of people who watched that stream. Mary and I may have had a strained relationship, but I didn't kill her."

"You could have broadcasted a video you recorded earlier."

"Sounds to me like you haven't watched it," Tyler smiled. "If you did, you'd know exactly when that stream was filmed. Until then, could you stay out of my way? We've still got training in progress."

Angel didn't have enough information to respond, so she walked off the stage as Tyler laughed behind her.

* * *

Angel and Hector were back in the hotel room where Mary had fallen from the window. It was only a short walk from the convention. Everything had been left as they'd found it—the overturned furniture, the bloodstained fire extinguisher, and the open window. Hector sat at the kitchen counter with his laptop plugged in, watching a recording of Tyler's livestream.

Tyler was playing the same game Angel had seen on the large screen—apparently a "first-person shooter" game called Resolute—and he was using the Valerie character. Tyler was visible on a screen in the top-right corner, a black controller barely visible in his hands.

"I thought this was a computer game?" Angel asked. "Aren't those played with a mouse?"

"You can get controllers that pair with your computer," Hector said. "Some people like that better."

"Have you figured out why Tyler couldn't have broadcasted a video he already recorded?" Angel asked.

"I did. Turns out around eight, he prank-calls a local pizza joint asking for a 'boneless pizza.' That was one of his classic jokes, apparently." Hector shrugged and shook his head. "We confirmed with the restaurant. Tyler played the phone call on speaker, so there's no chance he faked it."

"Sounds desperate to foolproof his alibi."

"Which means if he really did this, there's a hole somewhere."

They skipped ahead to the exact time of Mary's fatal fall. Angel hoped the murder would turn out to happen between matches, when it would be easier for Tyler to act unnoticed, but it happened right in the middle of a tense round. Tyler leaned close to the screen, completely focused as he fought off four enemy players—pulling off similar techniques to the match today.

"I don't care how good this guy is," Hector said. "No one could play that well while pushing a woman through a window."

Angel approached the window. Beige curtains hung on either side, with rope tiebacks that could be looped around hooks jutting from the wall beside them. A long AC unit was mounted below the sill. The window itself was a sash type. There was enough room to push someone out, but it would be difficult. They'd have to fall out horizontally. Either way, Angel expected these windows would get grates attached within the month.

"I saw something like this in a TV show," Angel said. "The killer needed an alibi, so they started a video call with a background photo of a room in their home when they were right next to the crime scene. These hotel rooms already look the same, so it wouldn't be hard to do."

"That doesn't work here," Hector scratched his head. "It's not a matter of how close Tyler was to Mary. He was supposedly streaming from his own room a few floors down. That's well within walking distance, but the problem is she was killed in the middle of the stream. Even if he was right here, he couldn't push her out."

"And you've checked what network he used with the Internet Service Provider?" Angel said. "That should tell us where he was."

"He was using the hotel's high-speed connection. It could have been any room in the hotel, including the lobby."

"Then the fall's the crux of it," Angel glanced at the window. "Tyler could have beaten Mary right before starting the stream. We know those wounds were pre-mortem, but we can't date them more precisely than that. But we've got loads of witnesses for the fall, and Tyler was under constant surveillance at that time."

"Besides, hotel security busted down this room's door thirty minutes later," Hector said. "If Tyler was still streaming here, someone would have seen him."

Angel looked out the window to the street below. Locals milled about, fixing the extravagantly dressed tourists with frightened glances. The bar-lined sidewalks would be full of witnesses throughout the evening. Tyler likely counted on that.

"There's a chance she could have been thrown from a different room above or below," Angel said. "I doubt anyone on the street could tell the difference, and it would be easy enough to move the murder weapon. Tyler would need access to one of those rooms and a way to get Mary inside."

"That doesn't explain the livestream," Hector sighed and shut the laptop.

"Maybe we should look at other suspects. This could be the work of some deranged fan."

"I'll get the team to look at the lobby's security footage. Maybe we'll identify another suspect," Angel said. "But I find it hard to believe Tyler is innocent. The killer took a big risk throwing Mary from that window. There were more discrete ways to murder her. All they did was make the time of death blatantly obvious."

"Which means our killer had an alibi prepared..." Hector mumbled.

Angel took another circuit through the room. It had a single bed next to the window with freshly tucked, untouched sheets. Mary's phone was still plugged in on the bedside table. She looked at the file Hector brought, and a professional photo of Mary.

She had curly hair dyed red and sharp eyebrows. She was young enough to be Angel's daughter, and that made her heart ache. A week ago, Angel wouldn't have considered Mary's career legitimate. She'd gone through years of training to be a police officer, while Mary played video games. Despite that, they had both forced their way into male-dominated professions, putting themselves at risk. The young woman deserved respect.

"Why was Mary here?" Angel asked. "She must have known Tyler would be at the convention."

"She was accepting an award," Hector said. "From what I understand, Mary had to reinvent herself after Tyler's abuse. The harassment from her followers got so bad she closed her channel. She switched her accounts and became a vtuber."

"What the hell is a vtuber?"

Hector stared at Angel like she was a toddler who'd asked him to explain string theory. "It's basically like—you change your voice and replace yourself with an animated persona before streaming. Usually, an anime girl's...Do you even know what anime is, Inspector?"

"I'll ask my son later."

"Sure," Hector sighed. "The point is, it enabled Mary to keep streaming without anyone, even Tyler, knowing who she was. She could also appear at the convention anonymously, but someone knew."

"Makes sense. This murder was planned, but I don't think anyone came to NCX with intent to kill. That fire extinguisher came from the hall outside, so the killer didn't bring the weapon with them." Angel frowned, glancing at the screen. "But with this vtuber thing, could someone create a fake Tyler?"

"I don't think any rig is that advanced, and someone would still have to be behind the screen imitating Tyler's voice. It might work for a minute, but not for two hours."

Angel moved to the closet, finding a few dresses hung next to a flashy costume. An ironing board rested on the wall beside an open safe. She recalled the safe had been locked when the police arrived. When hotel security staff opened it using a special key, they found Mary's car keys and a tablet.

"Don't you think it's a bit strange this safe was shut?" Angel asked.

"Why do you say that?"

"Typically, you lock up your safe before you leave for the day, right?" Angel asked. "But Mary must have come back to this room before she was killed, and she never opened it again."

"Maybe she didn't need that tablet? Or she came here with someone?"

"Well, she certainly wouldn't let in Tyler or one of his fans…"

Angel stood and closed the closet door.

"I think if I talk to the hotel staff again, I can answer at least one of our questions. After that, I'm going home."

"Already?" Hector asked. "It's only noon."

Angel said, "I need to watch that livestream myself."

* * *

Angel leaned on her fist, her other arm weakly clutching a coffee mug. Tyler Hirata kept talking and talking, saying the most inane nonsense, yet his viewers ate it up.

She didn't understand why people spent hours watching these streams, but she guessed most people left them on while doing something else instead of watching every second like she was.

She'd asked the staff to investigate the guests staying above and below Mary's hotel room and discovered that Reilly, the caster, had specifically requested the room above. That convinced Angel he was involved, but he had an alibi too—he was watching Tyler's stream in the convention center with the rest of Team Chronologic. His role was more subtle, so she still had to break down the stream.

Angel heard the apartment door open. She waved as her teenage son walked in. He locked the door and stopped in his tracks.

"Why the hell are you watching a Shiisaa stream?"

"Ivan, language!"

"Sorry, I'm just surprised. Didn't know you liked that kinda stuff."

"I don't." Angel's chair creaked as she turned around. "You know this guy?"

"Yeah, he's awful. My friends were saying he killed Mary Bellerose yesterday, but I thought they were joking."

"He was our first suspect, but..." Angel turned back to the stream.

Ivan's lanky body crossed the floor as delicately as a cat. He leaned over the dining table and scratched his scraggly chin.

"It's awful," he said. "I watched Mary's streams sometimes. She brought real joy to each game. You could tell beneath all the drama and the deals, she loved her hobby...And I wasn't one of those fans who just thought she was hot. I mean, I didn't think she was unattractive, but_"

Angel laughed. "You can stop there."

Ivan cleared his throat, then squinted at the video, "This was recorded yesterday, at the time of the murder?"

"Yeah."

"But that doesn't make sense," he said. "Look."

He pointed at the screen. It looked like Tyler, still playing as Valerie, somehow caused his gun to glow bright blue and rain explosions on the enemy team. Several players simply evaporated, while the survivors limped away, flashing red.

"See how that guy's flashing? That means he has the 'bleeding' status," Ivan said. "But two days ago, the devs released an update that nerfed Valerie's special so it doesn't cause bleeding anymore."

"Can you run that by me in English?"

Ivan rolled his eyes. "The point is, if Shiisaa really streamed this yesterday, that player wouldn't be flashing like that. This footage had to be from before the game was changed two days ago. The update wasn't advertised much, so maybe he missed it."

"But we know it was filmed yesterday. He made a phone call—"

"Maybe that was faked? I mean, streaming is basically improv."

Angel knew that was impossible because the phone had been on speaker, but Ivan's words still set her brain running. Her lips curled as she glanced at the screen, then she shot up and kissed Ivan on the forehead.

"Ugh, Mom—"

She looked in his eyes. "I think you just blew this wide open for me."

Angel grabbed her keys and swung her jacket over her shoulders. She still had time to get to the convention. As she reached for the doorknob, Ivan shouted after her.

"Does that mean I can drop out to train for my professional gaming career?"

"After everything I've seen today?" Angel shook her head. "Don't push your luck."

* * *

The Battlefield was packed. Angel and Hector had to fight their way through the crowd to see the stage. A cheer rose as Team Chronologic walked to their computers, their opponents doing the same. Tyler Hirata grabbed his controller and sat down, not waiting for an introduction.

Reilly was about to declare the match underway when he stopped. Angel stepped onto the stage and flashed her badge as she nudged him away from the microphone.

"Sorry, everyone. This match is cancelled," Angel said. "Team Chronologic has forfeited. Their opponents will move on to the finals."

"Hey, you can't do that," Tyler said.

The other team bumped fists, but the crowd mumbled, staring transfixed at the blank screen.

"Do you think I'm joking? Go home!"

The crowd broke into a chorus of shouts and boos. Angel realized she might not have handled this well, but she'd wanted to make her suspects' lives as difficult as possible. Tyler's team stood, angry looks on every face. They swarmed the investigators.

"What gives?" Tyler shouted.

"I wanted to save you the trouble," Angel said, "It'd be a shame if you had to cancel the final round because one of your star players was arrested."

"We already discussed this," Tyler beat a fist on his chest. "I've got an alibi."

"This is harassment." Reilly stepped forward. "We know the exact time Mary was killed and what Tyler was doing then. You've got no proof he was involved."

Hector stepped in front of the caster and held out a hand. "You'd best be mindful of what you say. We know everything."

Reilly's face paled. Tyler glanced between, tightly folding his hands. Angel paced across the stage, glancing at the sea of empty chairs.

"The first part was simple," Angel said. "You had to get yourself in the same room as Mary. Your teammate, Reilly, must have helped you. He heard that Mary was here to receive an award. Maybe you offered to give it to her privately, for the sake of her anonymity. Your real goal was getting her to your hotel room, where Tyler was waiting—the room directly above her own."

"Why would I do that?" Reilly said.

"Because Tyler needed to stream from the same room Mary fell from, but he couldn't be at the crime scene when the police arrived. You had to make us think Mary was pushed from her own room, instead of yours. That was easy after one of you came in, messed up the place, and moved the murder weapon inside."

"Too bad you couldn't get into her safe and move her tablet into the room," Hector said. "The fact it was closed suggested Mary had just left, which doesn't make sense if she'd let her killer in. The best you could do was leave all the stuff in her pockets out in the open."

"Okay, fine. Whatever." Tyler waved his hands. "I know where this is going. You think I set up my camera in front of a bare hotel wall, so no one knew where I was streaming from. That doesn't change the fact she was pushed out the window while I was on-camera."

"And don't even suggest I did it for him," Reilly said. "I was with the rest of Tyler's team."

Angel leaned toward Tyler with her hands on her hips.

"You made one huge mistake," she said. "You didn't realize Resolute was updated the day before your stream. We can tell because of the, uhhhh—"

"Valerie's nerfed special," Hector said.

"Yeah, that," Angel said. "But that's still a contradiction. We know you streamed that day because of the phone call."

"But there's an explanation," Hector said. "It's easy to think of a livestream as one video, but it typically has two separate components."

Angel raised a finger. "First, there's the gameplay footage."

She raised another one. "Then, there's the face cam."

Tyler's team started to understand. They backed away from their leader.

"You were never actually playing Resolute during that stream," Angel said. "You recorded the gameplay footage before the tournament, then you played it on your screen like you were watching a movie. From there, it was all improv."

"You turned on your face cam and talked and reacted like you were still playing. You kept your controller off-screen but raised it occasionally, making us think you were using it. You'd given yourself downtime to call the pizza place. You'd been doing this so long, no one noticed the difference."

"I never left my seat," Tyler said.

"No, but if you weren't playing, that left your hands free," Angel said. "When Mary fell, you leaned over. Everyone thought you were focused on the game, but you weren't."

She nodded at Hector, who showed them a photo on his phone of a mechanism they'd created at the crime scene in front of that fatal window. They'd laid one of the tieback cords across the two hooks, so it stretched across the gap, and placed the ironing board in front, one end on the bed and the other on the AC unit, forming a slope straight out the window like a slide.

"Everything you needed was already in the hotel room," Angel said. "You placed the rope over the hooks and fixed it at both ends, so it would hold her weight when you put her on the ironing board. You probably tied several curtain ropes together until it stretched to where you were streaming, then tied that end around the leg of your chair. All you had to do was lean over and untie the rope. It would go slack, and Mary would slide out the window. A murder committed on film, with no one the wiser."

"You can't prove any of this," Tyler shouted.

"We'll see," Angel said. "You can find an excuse for your DNA being in Reilly's room or even in Mary's. But if we find Mary's DNA in Reilly's room, we can charge him as an accessory. How loyal will he be when life in prison is on the line?"

"It was all his idea," Reilly shouted.

Tyler started to run but was soon surrounded by his teammates. Tyler strained against the grip of Team Chronologic, who held him back from Reilly, who trembled at the edge of the stage. More officers climbed up behind Tyler and put him in cuffs, while Hector read him his rights.

The streamer's breathing slowed as he stared at Angel, eyes burning with fury. He looked like he was imagining all the ways he wanted to hurt her. She wondered if Mary had felt the same way when he looked at her.

"You're real clever, pinning this on me," he said. "But I'll fight. Every time I lost my platform, I eventually won it back. You're just another opponent, and I make a living on grinding them beneath my heel."

"You know, Tyler," Angel squinted. "You remind me a bit of my son."

"What's that supposed to mean?"

"I'm guessing you both started out as kids who loved to play video games," Angel mumbled. "But thankfully, he loves people more than games and can accept love. I hope someday you can do the same."

Tyler frowned and bowed his head. Angel watched him walk out the door, his shoulder starting to slump like a child sent to their room after throwing a tantrum. Some kids would never grow up. But Angel thought of Mary and couldn't feel a shred of pity.

"Hey, have you ever played Resolute?"

Angel turned. The other professional gamers had gathered behind her in a semicircle, smiling awkwardly.

"No. Board games are complicated enough."

"Would you like to try?" one of them asked. "The other team would probably agree to re-do this round, and it would be awesome to have a Valerie cosplayer fronting our team!"

She narrowed her eyes. "You're kidding. I don't exactly have a high opinion of this team."

"I know it looks bad, but trust me, none of us liked Shiisaa either. He helped us win, so we went along with his bad behavior. Not the murder part, of course. We never thought he'd go that far…"

The team hung their heads. Angel felt bad for them. They reminded her of Ivan as well, but the portrait wasn't quite as bleak. She supposed there would always be people like Tyler, but for the rest of his team, for Mary, and for Ivan, these games were not about power and conquest. They were about joy, love, and connection.

"I'm not a gamer." Angel massaged a knot in her forehead. "But maybe I'll try it, just this once."

Story Inspiration:

I've played video games my whole life and served as president of my university's game club for a year, so I enjoy seeing mysteries that capitalize on tensions in the competitive esports scene and tricks you can pull with related technology. You don't see these stories often (the only examples I can think of are from Japan), so I wanted to contribute one of my own. I initially came up with this story concept for use in a novel, but when I saw the anthology call, I realized it would work equally well for a short story—and that would give me the opportunity to get the idea on paper sooner.

KILLER INSTINCT

Maya Corrigan

Maya (Mary Ann) Corrigan writes the Five-Ingredient Mysteries featuring a café manager and her energetic grandfather solving murders on Maryland's Eastern Shore. In Book 9 of the series, A Parfait Crime, a killer commits perfect crimes by methods unique in mystery fiction. Maya's stories have appeared in the Chesapeake Crimes anthologies.

I remember the day my tennis coach, Rita, spoke the words that would change the rest of my life—killer instinct. She'd entered my life in 1934, when I was a young teen playing my heart out at the new public tennis courts in Brooklyn. After watching me trounce a boy twice my size, she introduced herself to me. I had no idea then that Rita Richter had played in the U.S. National Championships and was a respected tennis coach.

She quizzed me about my parents, my school, and my ambitions, and then invited herself to my family's tiny apartment. Rita explained who she was to my parents and offered me a job helping her with the clinics she ran for rich kids on Long Island. In exchange, she would give me lessons and a place to stay. My parents were leery, convinced they'd end up owing her money.

"I make enough money giving lessons to people who have no talent," Rita told them. "I've never worked with anyone with the makings of a champion like your daughter. If Elizabeth is willing to put in the time and hard work, so am I."

I spent every summer with her. During the school year, when she taught at a tennis club in upper Manhattan, she found a way to get me on those courts. She touted my skills to the members, turning me into a sought-after doubles partner.

With her coaching, I made it to the finals in a city-wide tournament for high school students. In the third set, with a win just a few strokes away, my opponent tripped and limped off the court. She took a medical timeout, had her ankle taped, and came back. I could have finished her off quickly by forcing her to run from side to side. But I admired her courage for playing through her pain and went easy on her. She won.

After the match, Rita gripped my upper arms as if to shake me. "You need a killer instinct to win. Go after your opponent's weakness. She's your enemy. Your only options are destroy or be destroyed."

From then on, I treated the player on the other side of the net as my worst enemy. With the arsenal of shots Rita had taught me and the killer instinct she'd instilled, I soon earned spots in major tournaments. In 1939, when I played in the French Championships, I met Stefan, the son of a Swiss banker. Handsome and witty, he showed me around Paris. Until then, I'd never realized how much fun I was missing by dedicating my whole life to tennis.

Though he went back to Switzerland, we kept in touch as I trained for Wimbledon. He watched me play in the quarter finals there. After I lost, I consoled myself with Stefan, my first lover. He invited me to his family's chateau after the tournament. He would introduce me to his parents—his mother, who came from an old Swiss family, and his father, who was German, but not a Nazi sympathizer, Stefan assured me.

When I told Rita why I wanted to stay longer in Europe, her blue eyes hardened like ice. "You can't be a champion with a man on your mind. He's a playboy. You've known him for a month. I've invested years in your training. Don't you owe me something?"

She gave me an ultimatum—I had to decide between her and Stefan.

I chose her and tennis. Though surprised at my decision, Stefan suggested we keep in touch. We exchanged addresses and phone numbers.

A week before the U.S. National Championships in September 1939, Germany invaded Poland. That tournament went on as scheduled, and I almost won in the quarter finals. The other major tournaments were canceled until the war ended. Roland Garros Stadium in Paris became an internment camp. A bomb hit center court at Wimbledon.

I felt as if a bomb hit me when Rita resigned as my coach to join the war effort. Her job was so secret that she couldn't discuss it. I assumed she'd be doing intelligence work. She had recommended me as her replacement at the clubs in the city and on Long Island, where she'd been the tennis pro.

I preferred to follow in her footsteps and enlist for military service. When I visited my parents to tell them my plans, I saw how weak and sick my father looked. They hadn't told me about his cancer, fearing that my concern for him would destroy my concentration on tennis.

I had no time for tennis anymore. I moved back to the apartment where I'd grown up to help them. The only bright spot that winter was the Christmas card I received from Stefan. He cursed the war and hoped it would end soon so we could get together.

My father died in the spring, and my mother was too despondent to be left alone. I needed to support us both. With only one marketable skill, I followed up on the leads Rita had left me and taught at the clubs where she'd given tennis lessons.

In 1945, soon after the war ended in Europe, my mother joined an order of nuns, not a surprise to me. She'd always been religious and intended to be a nun before she met my father. As I was clearing out her things from the apartment, Rita knocked on the door. I was overjoyed to see her. We hugged and sat down for coffee at the kitchen table. She asked about my family and offered her sympathies.

Then she put down her cup. "Do you ever hear from Stefan Raimund?"

"The man you forbade me to see." I couldn't keep the bitterness from my voice. "We exchange Christmas cards."

"He succeeded his father as head of a Swiss private bank, where high-ranking Nazis stashed their loot. Now they're fleeing to avoid prosecution for war crimes. They need funds to get away. They may try to resurrect the

Reich in Argentina. We want to make sure that doesn't happen."

I wondered why she was telling me this. "Stefan wouldn't help the Nazis."

"We suspect he's been keeping their loot and the record of their transactions in a vault at his home, instead of the bank. His household staff has been with the family for years. He couldn't count on his bank employees for the same loyalty." She leaned across the table. "I'll cut to the chase. Are you willing to go to his chateau if he asks? You might be able to get information about the Nazi stash and possibly photograph the records. We'll train you."

My jaw dropped. "You want me to spy on him? To gain his trust and betray him?"

"We've just defeated the Nazis on one continent, but if they have the money to move their operations to a different place, we'll have to do it again."

"What makes you think Stefan would want anything to do with me?"

"Why wouldn't he? He's unmarried, still a playboy. Write to him. Tell him you'll be in Switzerland to run tennis clinics. We'll arrange those and hope he invites you to his home again."

I needed to understand more about the scheme. "Why do you need photos of his bank's records?"

Rita hesitated. "The ledger will have a description of each item deposited and the name of the Nazi thief who stashed it there. You're the only one who can get that information. Someday, it might help the victims of Nazi plunder get their property back. It's risky, but you've never shied away from risks."

I agreed to the plan. Rita had given me a purpose, something I could do to help Hitler's victims. I wrote to Stefan about my impending trip to Switzerland. He replied that he'd enjoy seeing me and showing me his family estate.

My training took place in an empty warehouse in Queens. I learned quickly to pick a lock, but safecracking was a skill I never fully mastered. I did better in self-defense training. Years of tennis had developed my strength and coordination. My killer instinct came into play when I defended myself against my instructor. He told me to go easy on him. I also had lessons in photographing documents with a special camera. Finally, I memorized the floor plan of Stefan's chateau. An arrow pointed to the probable location of the vault adjacent to the wine cellar. I had everything I needed for my mission, except armor against falling once more for Stefan.

I met with Rita again before I left for Europe. She gave me the name and phone number of my Swiss contact, who lived above his watch shop in Zurich. I was to call him when I completed my task and turn over the camera and film. He'd get me out of the country as fast as possible.

Rita arranged for me to take an airplane from New York to England, and from there to Switzerland. My first time flying, and I was thrilled. When we traveled to the European tournaments before the war, we crossed the Atlantic by ship. The only cabin Rita could afford for us had been tiny and windowless. With her claustrophobia, she'd spent as little time as possible in the room, even sleeping outdoors on a deck chair despite the cold and wind.

Her plan for my time in Switzerland went off like clockwork. Stefan came to the courts where I was holding a clinic. We had dinner that night. The next day, I moved from my hotel to his chateau. His cream-colored stone home at the top of a hill was a monument to order and symmetry. Six windows flanked either side of a columned portico. The windows above aligned with those on the ground floor. From my bedroom, adjacent to Stefan's, I had a view of craggy mountains.

An impeccable staff ministered to my every need. They showed no surprise at my presence, suggesting he often had lady friends staying there. Only one person made me uneasy—the housekeeper, Frau Vollmer. Hate burned in her eyes when she looked at me. Stefan explained the reason for her hostility. She was mourning her daughter, killed in Germany by an American bomb.

As a prominent Swiss citizen, Stefan escorted me to parties and embassy receptions. No shortage of fine food and wine in Switzerland, and no shortage of Germans enjoying them. Stefan claimed to despise the Nazis. He boasted about how much he charged them to safeguard what they'd stolen.

"Most of them didn't survive the war," he said, "but the bank's fees will continue to accrue until they exceed the value of the items deposited. At that point, those items revert to the bank."

By which he meant himself. As the head of a family-owned business, he could do what he wanted with the unclaimed deposits. "Will you try to find the people the Nazis stole from?"

He shrugged. "An impossible task. If they come to the bank with proof of ownership, I'll return their possessions."

In the unlikely event they had that proof, they wouldn't know where their property was stored unless I succeeded in my mission. Any misgivings I'd had about sneaking into Stefan's vault disappeared. My stay at the chateau tarnished my glowing image of him. I'd expected a playboy, but not a money-grubber.

When a Geneva banker and his wife visited the chateau to attend an embassy party with Stefan, I begged off, saying I didn't feel well. Embassies in the Swiss capital of Bern were an hour away, and their parties seldom ended before midnight. I would have enough time to get into the vault, assuming Stefan's servants retired to their quarters by ten as usual.

I reviewed the chateau's floor plan in my head. At ten thirty, I put on a jacket with pockets stuffed with the tools I'd need to breach the vault. I opened the heavy door beneath the chateau's back staircase with a trembling hand. I expected it to creak like doors in scary movies, but it swung open soundlessly in this well-oiled household. I closed it behind me. By the feeble light of a small flashlight, I went down the uneven stone steps to the wine cellar.

I shone my light down the narrow aisles between fully stocked wine racks. At the end of one row, a rough wood door was recessed into the stone wall. As I crept closer to it, I trained the beam of my flashlight around the doorway, saw the wire that would trip the alarm, and followed it to its source. I pocketed the flashlight and put on a headband with a small light built in, leaving my hands free to work on the wires. After defusing the alarm, I removed the lock picks from my jacket, probed the lock, and selected the snake pick. It would open the lock quickly, leaving no evidence.

The door swung open to a small, empty room. I was dumbfounded. Were the intelligence services mistaken about where Stefan was storing Nazi plunder? Shining my flashlight around the room, I saw a large metal door with a combination lock. I'd never managed to crack a safe quickly in training, but one thing worked in my favor here in the cellar's tomblike silence: I should be able to hear the clicks in the lock.

I fought cramps for the next half hour. Cramps in my hand, stiff with cold and fear, and cramps in my legs from bending to keep my ear against the lock. Finally, the tumblers clicked. The vault door cracked open. Success. I glanced at my watch. Just past eleven. Still time to do what I had to do and get out before Stefan came back from the party. I went into the vault.

In the dim light coming from the anteroom, I could see parcels propped along the right wall. The flat rectangles wrapped in heavy paper had to be paintings. Stacked along the opposite wall were gold bars imprinted with swastikas. On the back wall were floor-to-ceiling shelves holding metal boxes, probably containing currency or jewelry. But where were the records of the deposits?

I looked behind me and spotted a leather-bound book on the shelf just inside the metal door. I took it into the anteroom, flipped the switch for the overhead light, and opened the book. The bank ledger! Names, dates, lists of valuables, all carefully written in black ink.

I fished the camera from my pocket, set the ledger on the floor below the ceiling light, and knelt, positioning myself so I didn't cast a shadow on the pages. I bent down to peer through the lens, making sure the page was in focus, and clicked the shutter. I turned the page, focused, and clicked again, over and over. With only a few pages left, I crouched to turn the next page and froze as a shadow moved over the book.

"So, Fräulein, you are not the nice, sweet American girl you pretend to be. You are stealing from Herr Raimund." Stefan's grim old housekeeper stared down at me with narrowed eyes.

My throat constricted. I couldn't say a word, but I managed to stand up. She pointed to my camera. "Ach, no! Not stealing, spying! In Switzerland, spies go to prison for a long time. There are no tennis courts in Swiss prisons." Her eyes sparkled with excitement. A nasty little smile appeared when she squinted at the page I had just photographed. "So, the Americans want to know the private business of the Swiss banks. But Germans don't want them to know about this, do they? There are worse things than Swiss prisons, Fräulein. If I tell the Nazis hiding in Switzerland what you're doing, they'll kill you, but first they'll torture you."

I suspected she was lying about the Nazis, but I didn't know for sure. A Swiss prison was frightening enough.

With a smug, gleeful look, Frau Vollmer reached for the camera. "So, Fräulein, you give me this camera now. We go upstairs and wait for Herr Raimund."

This vindictive little woman was my enemy. I couldn't let her win. I heard my trainer's voice as if he were in the room with us. "I can show you how to kill someone without leaving a mark on them."

My killer instinct took over. A single hard blow to her chest dropped Frau Vollmer to the floor. I bent down to check on her. No pulse, no heartbeat, no breath. I didn't feel triumphant. If I got away with this, I'd live the rest of my life with the killer inside me.

My whole body shook so much, I could barely hold the camera. But I forced myself to take shots of the last pages in the ledger. Then I closed it, put it back where I'd found it, and locked the vault. I dragged Frau Vollmer's body from the anteroom to a spot between the wine racks, hoping she might not be noticed for a while. Finally, I shut the door to the anteroom and reattached the alarm wires.

Back in my bedroom, I planned my escape. Stefan had lent me a car for my stay so I could get around while he worked at the bank. If I left immediately, his chauffeur-driven limousine might be coming up the narrow road to the chateau while I was going down. How could I explain driving away in the middle of the night? Better to wait until morning and hope that Frau Vollmer's body wouldn't be discovered until later.

After lying awake all night, I was up before anyone else in the household. I slipped a note under Stefan's door, saying I was going to Zurich to pick up my mail at the American Express office. As I came down the stairs, the servants were already searching for the missing housekeeper. One of them translated their conversation for me. Frau Vollmer sometimes raided the wine cellar at night, and she might have fallen down the stairs. I made a quick exit.

I called my Swiss contact from a public phone, met him before his shop opened, and gave him the camera as Rita had instructed. Luckily, there was a plane out of Switzerland that day. He got me on it.

I drove to the airport and parked the car there. Then I phoned the chateau and left a message with the butler. I told him where Stefan's car was parked and explained that my mother had been in an accident and needed me home immediately. I didn't relax until the plane soared over the Alps. Mission accomplished.

The day after I arrived back in New York, Rita debriefed me. Our meeting was all business. She took notes as I answered her questions. Where were the doors to and within the cellar located? How had I broken into the anteroom and the vault? She asked me for the combination of the lock on the vault and a description of what I'd seen. Then she questioned me about Stefan's routine and his household staff, how many lived at the chateau, and where they slept. I asked why she needed those details. She replied that her job was to gather as much intelligence as possible about anyone who dealt with the Nazis.

The OSS would be impressed by my skills and courage, she said. They might call me to set up an interview for future work. That sounded more rewarding than spending the rest of my life conducting tennis drills. I didn't tell Rita how the killer instinct she'd encouraged had come in handy. It was my secret. Taking a life would weigh on my conscience alone.

A letter from Stefan arrived a week later. He hoped my mother was recovering quickly and mentioned that his housekeeper had died of a heart attack. What a relief. No one would arrest me for murder. Stefan wished me well but didn't invite me back to the chateau. A fling was all he ever wanted.

After not hearing from Rita for a month, I dialed the last number I had for her, but her phone had been disconnected. The OSS never contacted me. It was dissolved after the war, and many of its responsibilities were assumed by the new CIA. With plenty of veterans returning from the war, the agency would hire them in preference to a woman.

* * *

Five years after the war ended, I was back in Paris at Roland Garros stadium, where Stefan had first watched me on the courts and turned his charms on me. This time, I wasn't playing but accompanying a young woman I'd been coaching to her first major tournament. She was to me what I'd been to Rita, an athletically gifted teenager who could become a champion. But I never echoed the words Rita had used in her pep talks—enemy, destroy, kill.

After dropping off my would-be champion at the hotel, I returned to scope out the competitors she'd face in upcoming matches. I'd just gone into the stadium when a man called my name. I turned and saw Stefan approaching with a beautiful pregnant woman on his arm. He introduced me to his wife, Mireille, who hailed from Geneva and spoke English with a French accent.

When the introductions were over, he said, "After you left Switzerland, I decided to do what you suggested—try to locate the owners of the stolen loot the Germans had left in my bank. But the matter was taken out of my hands. Expert burglars emptied my vault. Somehow, they knew how to break into it."

Was that my doing? I hoped my surprise at Stefan's news made my blush less apparent. "When did that happen?"

"Not long after you left, while I was spending a week in Geneva. I should have hired guards." He looked disgusted with himself.

As his wife assured him that he wasn't to blame for a burglary, I tried to make sense of it. Rita had told me the OSS wanted photos of the bank records, but she'd picked my brain on how I'd broken into the vault. Could the OSS have stolen back what the Nazis had plundered? No, a government entity wouldn't commit a crime in a neutral country, breaking the sacred laws of banking privacy. I studied Stefan's still handsome face. Maybe he'd engineered the burglary to deprive surviving Nazis of their ill-gotten gains…and fill his own coffers.

After we talked about the upcoming matches, Stefan said, "I'm glad we had a chance to meet again, Elizabeth. When I spoke with Rita this morning, she didn't mention you were here with her."

"I'm not with her. I'm here as a tennis coach. I haven't heard from Rita in years." As a has-been on the tennis circuit, I was no longer of interest to her. "Where did you see her?"

"In the stadium." Stefan described where Rita had been sitting. "She goes to all the majors. She was at Wimbledon last year with the same group of Germans. She and her friends came all the way from Argentina."

I tried to hide my shock. Rita had told me the Nazis would escape to Argentina, a safe haven with a fascist regime. I hadn't realized she'd be among them. The pedestal I'd put her on collapsed.

I wished Stefan and his wife great joy with their child and hurried away, my stomach churning. My visit to his chateau hadn't been an OSS mission, but a hoax. She and her Nazi friends didn't care about the photos I'd taken. They wanted to know how to break into the vault. The Nazi sympathizer had risked my life for her cause…and turned me into a killer. I couldn't forgive her.

I headed toward the stadium section where Stefan had seen her and spotted her mass of blond hair easily. Her friends were loud enough for me to tell they were speaking German. When she left them, I trailed her to the ladies' room entrance. I paused outside the room as two women came out. I looked around to make sure no one was heading for the restroom and then opened the door. When I saw her at the sink, her back to me, my adrenaline surged as it did whenever I faced the enemy.

I reined in my aggression. I'd killed once while doing Rita's bidding and felt guilty ever since. Instead of confronting her, I would set the wheels in motion for her comeuppance.

"Rita! I didn't expect you to be at the tournament." I pasted a smile on my face.

She turned. "Elizabeth. How wonderful to see you. Are you enjoying the matches so far?"

I nodded. "I'd love to catch up with what you've been doing, but I don't have any free time this week. I'm here with the rising champion I'm coaching. How about getting together in New York? You'll be at the U.S. Nationals, won't you?"

She took a moment to answer. "I've been thinking about going there. My parents still live in New York. It's been years since I saw them. I need to give them access to one of my accounts in case their money runs out."

She probably planned to take the money from those accounts back to Argentina. I took a notepad from my purse, jotted down my address and phone number, and handed the note to Rita. "Send me a letter if you decide to come, and tell me when you're arriving. Then I can set aside a time for us to get together."

"I'd like that."

She hurried out of the room, apparently anxious to return to her German friends.

Getting her back in the United States, where she could be arrested for treason, was step one in my plan. The CIA wouldn't bother with her if she'd never had a job in the U.S. intelligence services. But if she'd worked in the OSS, she must have been a double agent and betrayed her country. No intelligence service could ignore that.

Step two of my plan involved an old friend from Brooklyn. I'd run into Joe while visiting my aunt a few months ago in Washington. The skinny, nerdy beanpole I remembered from grammar school had turned into an attractive man. We talked for hours over drinks, but Joe clammed up when I asked about his work.

My aunt laughed when I told her about his silence on that subject. "Most men in Washington talk endlessly about their boring government jobs. The ones who say nothing about their job are in the CIA."

As soon as I returned from France, I called Joe. He agreed to meet me for lunch in Georgetown later in the week.

I hadn't mentioned Rita the last time Joe and I got together, but this time I told him everything about my Swiss adventure except for the part about

Frau Vollmer in the cellar.

After listening intently, Joe asked me for Rita's full name. I did more than that. I gave him a photo of her and me. I noticed his eyes widen slightly when he looked at it. He asked to keep the photo.

Two months later, I received a letter from Rita telling me which day she would fly into New York. I passed on the information to Joe.

For two days following her scheduled arrival, I combed the local papers until I found what I was looking for. A brief paragraph in the *Long Island Star-Journal* reported that a woman who had arrived on a flight from Buenos Aires had been taken into custody when she went through passport control at Idlewild airport.

I smiled. Living in a prison cell would be agony for the claustrophobic Rita. Her pep-talk advice echoed in my mind: *Go after your opponent's weakness.* With the killer instinct she instilled in me, I found a way to destroy her.

Story Inspiration:

"Killer Instinct" was inspired by an incident in Courting Danger, *the autobiography of 1930s tennis star Alice Marble. Her adventure tale of spying in wartime Switzerland has a Hollywood ending, a dramatic chase scene with bullets flying. "Killer Instinct" focuses on character rather than action. The story explores the relationship between a young tennis player and her coach, who plays a dangerous game.*

KARMA CAN BE BOTH

Bruce Kubec

Bruce Kubec was raised in Pittsburgh, PA, but writes full-time from New Smyrna Beach, FL. His writing accomplishments include five award-winning novels and more than a dozen short stories in FWA collections, The Farmers' Almanac, *and several other publications. During non-writing time, he enjoys time at the beach, fishing, and attempting to play golf.*

For the past two years, seven of us met religiously on Friday at noon to play poker. We wanted it to be a friendly game, so we set a limit of $200 as the maximum anyone could lose. Sure, we'd bitch and moan if we lost our stake, but we always showed up ready to play the following week.

That worked well until last Friday.

The game started as usual. A few minutes before 12:00, everyone took their seat at the poker table. Being Vietnam-era Marines, we were punctual SOBs.

Each man arranged his multi-colored chips in their own fashion: Frankie always started with his chips looking like an extended middle finger. The rest of us arranged ours by denomination. Precisely at noon, Jack Spade, who didn't play and wasn't an ex-Marine, dealt the first hand.

The afternoon progressed differently than any other. By 16:50, Alan and

Bill were the only two still playing. In our two years, I don't think it ever came down to only two players at the end. But last Friday, it did.

Alan had $1,195 in chips. Only $205 sat in front of Bill.

I never thought of Alan as one of the better players. Bill, yes, but not Alan. We used to tease Alan that he brought a $200 donation to the table. He'd respond with an F-U, or kiss my grits, but he laughed every time. Each of us could afford to lose $200, and our lifestyle wouldn't change.

Last Friday, Lady Luck sat on Alan's shoulder. He won hand after hand. I wondered if all the alcohol he drank had something to do with it. Normally, he had two, max three cocktails. But, that afternoon, he announced he was getting an early start on celebrating his fortieth anniversary and downed his drinks like they were water. Maybe it allowed him to relax and not overthink things.

Jack, in addition to dealing, functioned as the timekeeper. He made sure we didn't start a hand after 17:00. Most of us needed to be home by 17:30 to have dinner with our wives, or girlfriends.

We are what today's youngsters would call 'Old School'. We're all in our seventies, have wrinkled skin, walk slowly, and wear baggy pants. Being Vietnam vets is what initially brought us together, but our love of poker kept us coming back week after week.

Last Friday, before I knew it, Jack announced, "It's 16:59. Last hand. Agreed?" The rest of us were there, but our consent wasn't necessary, courtesy of Alan. I turned from the golf game on TV and saw Alan and Jack nod.

I looked forward to the game ending. Most of the afternoon, Alan trash-talked more than I had ever heard him do before. When he'd win a hand, he'd make comments like, "I schooled you on that one," or "My parakeet can play poker better than you, and he's a bird brain." He'd then let out a loud "Oorah!!!" I could tell the other guys were pretty much fed up with it, too.

Now, to the final hand.

After Jack dealt the cards, Alan didn't even look at his hand. He donned a shit-eating grin and said, "I don't even need to look at my cards. I know I'm going to spank your ass."

Frankie suggested Alan tone it down a little, but his grin never changed. He used both hands to push all of his chips into the center of the table and announced, "All in."

Bill's head snapped up. "What? You're all in?"

When the five of us heard Alan declare, 'All in,' we turned our attention from the golf tournament on TV back to the poker table. We wanted to see what would happen. Could Alan, the poor poker player, really beat Bill, the much better player? Could the skinny kid really beat up the playground bully?

Jack, the dealer, stated, "Yes, he declared 'All in.'"

The eucalyptus aroma that normally tinged the air was replaced with the combined musk of eight nervous men. The tension in the room thickened, like in the ninth inning, with the bases loaded, two outs and the home team down a run.

Bill nervously bit his lower lip, checked his cards, tapped them on the table's felt, and eyed the dealer's discard pile. I expected him to fold and go home a $5 winner.

And then, Alan flapped his arms and made a clucking sound. You know, like a chicken makes.

Several of us murmured and looked at one another.

"Come on, Alan, that's not needed," Donny said, throwing his hands in the air.

Bill tensed, looked Alan square in the eye, and tossed all of his chips to the center of the table. Hitting the felt, they sounded like fingernails clicking together. "I call."

If Bill lost, Alan would have wiped out everyone. In two years of faithfully playing every Friday, no one had ever walked away with all $1,400. Could Alan accomplish what no one else had done?

I wasn't in the hand, but my heartbeat raced. I saw Charlie wipe his hands on his shorts and leave damp marks.

I think all of us were secretly rooting for Bill. Personally, I was fed up with Alan's attitude and smart remarks. I was willing to chalk it up to the booze talking, but the clucking sound crossed the line.

After Jack dealt the last of the cards, Alan and Bill simultaneously turned their cards face-up.

Bill had three Kings.

Alan had four Aces.

Alan threw his hands in the air like a boxer after knocking out his opponent. "I did it." He looked at Bill and pointed an index finger. "I kicked your ass." He then turned to each of us and repeated in turn, "And your ass, and your ass, and your ass." He ended by doing some sort of ridiculous dance while still in his chair.

Bill's face flushed, and his hands became white-knuckled fists. With a steely glare, he said something along the lines of, "No way you can be that lucky."

Alan pulled all the chips in front of him while saying, "Mine, all mine. Come to me, my pretties." I don't think that was the exact line from *The Wizard of Oz*, but he sounded like the wicked witch. The only thing missing was the cackle.

Bill sat ramrod stiff, eyes as wide as I've ever seen, and his mouth hung open. "My God. How could you beat everyone?" His voice started to quiver and got louder. "Something's not right. No one has ever done that before. No one can be that good." He pushed away from the table and shook his head.

Bill had been sick over the past several years and lost a great deal of strength and weight. Agent Orange did a number on guys like him who were close to the Ho Chi Minh Trail. He had become pretty much skin and bone. I doubt he could carry a 24-pack of beer into the house by himself. His personality changed, too. He'd always been even-tempered, but since the treatments and all, he became agitated easily. We all figured the pain he dealt with was what made the change.

Alan smiled from ear to ear and accepted obligatory congratulations from everyone except Bill.

Bill's disbelief morphed into anger, and he pointed a finger at Alan. "I don't know how or when, but I'm going to get even."

"Okay." Alan smiled, shrugged, and continued stacking his chips.

Bill started to pace, mumbling to himself.

Good thing the two of them were on opposite sides of the table. Bill jabbed his finger in Alan's direction with every word. "I'll get even. I'll get my money back."

Alan maintained his grin. "What are you going to do? Buy a *Poker for Dummies* book?" and then he let out a loud guffaw.

Alan's comment embarrassed all of us. We were supposed to have fun and act like a brotherhood of Marines. Alan's behavior certainly didn't adhere to our code of conduct.

In addition, he made a big show of taking his chips to Henry, the bartender, and collecting the $1,400. Once he had the bills, Alan fanned out the money and giddily told the half-dozen guys at the bar that he had beaten all of us, cleaned our clocks, took us to school, and taught us who was the boss.

I got tired of hearing it and left.

* * *

Saturday morning, Alan's wife, Susan, called. She sounded hysterical. I couldn't understand her. Isaac, her son-in-law, took the phone. "Mr. Tortarelli—

"What a minute, you can call me Torts or Sarge, but drop the Mr. Okay?" My birth certificate stated Franco Aloysious Tortarelli, but the men I served with called me Sarge because of my E6 rank of Staff Sergeant. Friends and neighbors called me Torts.

"Yes, sir, Torts. What Mom's trying to say is that my father-in-law was found dead in his car at the golf course parking lot last night. They think he was strangled."

A bajillion questions ran through my mind. Who would kill Alan? Why would someone kill him? How could it happen in the golf course parking lot? They have cameras, don't they? And the list went on. The more I thought about it, the more my stomach clenched, and my acid indigestion flared.

Isaac brought me out of my stupor, "When he hadn't come home by 6:00

156

last night, Mom called the club looking for him. One of the pro shop folks found him in his car under low-hanging trees in the far corner of the parking lot. When the EMTs got there, they said there wasn't anything they could do; he was dead."

"Your father-in-law always parked there. He said he didn't have to use the AC on the way home if he parked in the shade."

Isaac said, "That sounds like him. He thinks not using the AC saves a few pennies. The police found his empty wallet on the floor, so they think it was a robbery."

"They must have been after the $1,400 he won at poker. He wiped all of us out and made a big deal of it to everyone. Someone at the course must have followed him to his car."

"We didn't know he had won a lot of money. We knew he played poker with you and a couple of other vets. Your address is the only one Mom had in her phone, so we gave it to Detective Sturgill. I believe he's on his way to talk to you."

"No problem. I'll do whatever I can to help find whoever killed Alan. I can't believe he's dead. He was on top of the world yesterday."

Before Isaac and I finished talking, the doorbell rang.

When I opened the door, hot, humid Central Florida summer air rushed in like I had opened a steam room door. Detective Sturgill, from the Jessop police department, stood there. I could tell right away that he was a smoker. The two things I remember most were the badge that hung from a lanyard and the fact that he wore a holstered firearm on his right hip. After my time in Nam and seeing what guns did to human bodies, I swore I'd never own a gun nor allow one in my house. I swallowed hard, realizing I would have to allow a gun in my house for the first time since my discharge.

Fortunately, the detective stepped into the foyer but declined to take a seat in the living room. He didn't waste time and immediately asked what I did after the poker game. I explained that I had gone straight home. Cynthia, my wife, vouched that I had arrived home in time for dinner at 17:30.

He started to ask another question, but I interrupted. "Isaac said Alan's empty wallet was found on the car floor. When he left the poker game, he had at least $1,400. He won the pot."

The detective blinked a couple of times and made a note in his little pad. "That puts a puzzle piece in place. Did you notice anything, or anyone, out of place when you left the clubhouse or while you walked through the parking lot? It doesn't matter how insignificant you think it is."

I rubbed my jaw. "I didn't pay any attention. I was kinda pissed at Alan's behavior and made a beeline for my car. Alan always parked in the far corner, but I park as close as I can."

His eyebrows rose. "What do you mean you were pissed at Alan?"

I hesitated, then told him, "I wasn't pissed at Alan, just the way he acted."

The detective wanted to know specifics, so I shared about how Alan made a big deal of winning. But he rubbed it into Bill especially hard. I didn't want to tell him, but I knew someone would, so I told him Bill had threatened to get even. Feeling bad that I had singled out Bill, I added that anyone from the bar area could have followed Alan to his car. Maybe even someone coming off the golf course.

Detective Sturgill said his associates were speaking with people at the course, and he wanted to focus on our poker group. He tapped his pen on the little tablet a couple of times, then asked, "Do you have the names, addresses, and phone numbers of the other poker players?"

I scrolled through my phone and provided contact information for the other six guys. I saw him put an asterisk next to Bill's info.

When Sturgill left, I texted the guys to inform them about Alan and that a Jessop detective would probably contact them. I asked them to come to my house at 16:00 so we could talk.

When we met, Frankie, who lives two doors from Bill, said he saw the cops load Bill into the back of a police car and drive him away. "I doubt he'll get here. But his hands weren't cuffed, so I hope that's a good sign."

Donny, the retired lawyer, said, "That tells me they're taking him in for questioning but not arresting him, at least not yet. They can hold him in custody for as much as seventy-two hours before they decide to release him or arrest him."

The five of us sat around the living room and shared our conversations with Detective Sturgill. We pretty much told Sturgill the same thing: Bill was pissed at Alan…had threatened to get even…we couldn't believe Bill would hurt someone…we'd let the detective know if we could think of anything else.

My wife, Cynthia, God bless her, served refreshments and let us talk until we mentioned Jack the dealer. She asked, "Who's Jack and why isn't he here?"

"Jack is our dealer. I met him at the bar one day. He told me he dealt poker at the card club up in Jessop and was off on Tuesday and Friday. He offered to deal for us for $20 a player. Said it would help us, and the under-the-table money would help with his debts. I talked to the boys, it sounded good to everyone, so he's been dealing our games for over a year".

I added that Jack Spade wasn't 'one of us,' meaning he wasn't a vet, and I never thought about inviting him. That got me wondering if the police knew about Jack. I asked if anyone had mentioned Jack to Sturgill, and all I got was a couple of shrugs and head shakes.

Cynthia, who is into Tarot cards, raised a hand. "I don't like that name. In the card-reading world, the Jack of Spades can't be trusted. It represents a deceptive individual who may impede your progress or betray you. I always hate seeing that card come up. It normally spells trouble."

Know how something strikes you? Well, Cynthia's words struck me. I had never felt good about Jack. "Things just don't add up. Sturgill said that whoever choked Alan had left a set of bruises, indicating they had strong hands and agile fingers. I'm not sure what that means, but we know Bill doesn't have strong hands. If anything, with what he's gone through the past four or five years, sometimes he has difficulty holding a sandwich or beer bottle, much less strangling someone."

Ernie offered, "Jack brags about being a professional magician and card dealer for over twenty years. Wouldn't that at least give him agile fingers?"

The group agreed.

George spoke next. "You know, I saw Jack's car parked next to Alan's under the trees. I thought that a little odd."

Donny offered, "Shit, you're right. I even mentioned to Jack before we started that I saw his car in the corner with Bill's. He said he wanted the car to be cool when he got in because he tried not to use the AC to save on gas. He needs all the money he can get to take care of his debts. I thought it was a funny way to say it. Debts? Who says that? We all got bills. No one calls them debts."

"You're right. I thought the same thing," Charlie nodded.

Ernie, staring at his hands in his lap, offered, "You know, guys, I never really trusted Jack. About a year ago, Alan and I were playing golf, and Alan, in confidence, told me Jack appreciated our money because it helped pay his gambling losses. I know it's a stretch, but I'm wondering if, with Jack's card experience and ability, he somehow made sure Alan won, if you know what I mean."

George, the smallest of us all, stood. "Gentlemen, I think we need to pay Jack a visit. If he hurt Alan or messed with us yesterday, I think he deserves some old-school punishment." His lips smiled, but his eyes didn't. I thought about him being a tunnel rat in Nam. He had to have a mean streak to survive down there. Going into those tunnels, armed with only a Ka-Bar knife, ten inches of honed steel blade, took some guts.

We agreed to meet at Jack's house in an hour.

I don't know if any of us thought about it; I know I certainly didn't, but we should have called Sturgill right then and told him about what we knew or suspected. In hindsight, I'm sorta glad we didn't.

The others got there before me. When I arrived, I couldn't believe my eyes. Jack had been duct-taped to a chair. With Ka-Bar in hand, George stood next to Jack. On the other side, Fred stood with arms folded across his chest.The scene reminded me of walking in on a couple of guys in Nam 'asking' a squad member if he knew anything about some missing items. I didn't like it in Nam, and I sure as shit didn't like it in Jack's living room.

Jack had tears running down his cheeks. When he saw me, he begged, "Please tell them to let me go. I'm sorry. I didn't mean to do it. I lost my cool."

My chest tightened. "Do what?"

"I need $1,500 to pay my bookie. I was scared. I thought if I made sure

Alan won, he'd give me half of his winnings," Jack shrieked.

I felt like I'd been punched in the stomach. Fred smiled and kept tapping the head of the hammer into the palm of his hand.

Snot seeped from Jack's nose. "Okay, I made sure Alan won yesterday. So what? You guys can all afford to lose a couple hundred. I can't. I thought I could count on him to help me. You know, I scratch his back, he'll scratch mine? When I approached him in the parking lot, told him I made sure he won and asked for half of his winnings, he got all uppity. He said I was full of crap, he won on his own, and he wasn't sharing anything with me. I got mad. One thing led to another. I'm sorry, I didn't mean to kill him. It just happened."

I couldn't believe what he had said. My mind struggled to make sense of it all. It just *happened*? That explained *everything*? It made killing one of our *brotherhood* okay? I had trouble controlling my temper. My heart felt like it was going to beat right out of my chest. I wanted to scream.

Our poker nights were supposed to be games, just for fun. But one of our brethren had been murdered. On top of that, another one of us, an innocent man, sat in jail. His family had to be in shock. Now, a third man had been duct-taped to a chair.

Jack blubbered, "I'm sorry, I didn't mean to do it. I just lost my cool."

The SOB really pissed me off when he said, "You guys better cut me loose and leave. My bookie's collector will be here any minute. Old guys like you don't want to mess with him. You better cut me loose."

I leaned over so that our noses were about a foot apart. "Where's the money?" I asked through clenched teeth.

Jack stiffened and looked at an envelope on the kitchen table. "But, I need it to pay the collector. I'm already past due. He'll hurt me again if I don't pay. Please. I need it."

I checked the envelope's contents: $1,500. "You're not paying him with our money, er, Alan's money." I took $1,400 from the envelope and stuffed it in my pocket. Somehow, I would make sure Alan's widow got it.

Jack needed to be punished. We couldn't do it. But I knew who could and would.

I stood as Marine, tall as I could, squared my shoulders, and said, "Leave him for the collector. Let's go."

George's eyes bulged. He bared his teeth like a mad dog. "But Sarge, he needs to pay. An eye for an eye." He held the Ka-Bar to Jack's throat.

Jack whimpered. "Please, no. I'm sorry. I didn't mean to do it."

I folded my arms across my chest. "We're not in Nam anymore. Vigilante justice doesn't work in the States. Time to bug out."

Frankie stepped forward. "Sarge, you know juries don't believe in the code, like us. Like Ernie said, 'an eye for an eye.'"

I shook my head. "I agree, an eye for an eye. But we're not going to risk going to prison for the few years we have left on earth. He says his bookie's collector is on the way. Let him deal with it. When there's no payment, he'll do things the courts can't."

Jack screamed threats and curses until Frankie covered his mouth with duct tape.

"After the collector visits, I'll call Sturgill and tell him about Jack," I said. The boys grumbled as they filed out. Making sure I brought up the rear, I turned at the door and said, "You'll rot in hell," then walked out.

That was the last time I saw Jack.

A couple of hours after I got home, I called Sturgill and left a message mentioning Jack as our dealer, and gave him Jack's address.

My stomach tightened Sunday afternoon when I saw Detective Sturgill's name on my cell phone. As it turned out, he called to thank me for telling him about Jack Spade. When he heard my message, he did a background check. Jack had been busted twice for extortion of senior citizens, and since all of us, including Alan and Bill, were in our seventies, it raised red flags. Then, while driving to Jack's house, he saw an enforcer for Jimmy Wang driving in the opposite direction down Jack's street.

I asked who Jimmy Wang was. Sturgill said he was into things like bookmaking, fencing stolen goods, hard-money lending, owning a couple of topless bars, and stuff like that.

Well, to make a long story short, Sturgill said he found Jack duct taped to a chair, a bullet hole in his forehead. He put two and two together and figured Jack couldn't pay Jimmy, so Jimmy decided to clear Jack's debt the hard way.

I acted surprised, to the best of my limited acting ability.

The detective said they matched skin cells under Alan's fingernails to Jack and released Bill from custody. He considered the case closed and then asked if there was anything else I wanted to tell him.

I said the only thing that came to mind. "Sometimes karma is a beautiful thing, sometimes it's a bitch. But on rare occasions, I guess it's both."

Story Inspiration:

Ever since I can remember, I've believed: Once a Marine, always a Marine. There's a bond, a brotherhood, amongst those who served in the Corps. Particularly those who saw combat, like the Viet Nam veterans. Even though they may not have served next to one another in Southeast Asia, they're Marines. They're bothers. Like family, they look out for one another. They protect one another. In combat, that's all they had, each other.

The Marine Corps teaches self-reliance. They also instill an attitude of not waiting for someone else to do it—Get your ass in gear and get the damn job done.

I wrote this story to honor Marine vets, particularly the Viet Nam era bunch. I also wanted to show that the lessons learned while in the Corps, carried into their private lives. Even after discharge, when a brother Marine is attacked, they all feel attacked. They form up to find the a-hole who did the wrong and deal with them accordingly. But it's not always about brute force; Marines are a canny bunch. If anyone reading this story doesn't learn anything else, they should learn—Don't ever, EVER, cross a Marine. Otherwise, you could be facing the few, the proud, the Marines. Oorah!

A CROOKED ROOK

JD Allen

JD Allen writes the Shamus Award-nominated Sin City investigation series. She's been president of the FL chapter of MWA, an NC chapter president of Sisters in Crime, and the Chair of the Bouchercon National Board. JD earned a degree in forensic anthropology and a creative writing minor from OSU.

"What a mess," Joan said as she twisted her wrist to ease the pain there. She stood in the opening of the sliding glass door of her Key Colony Beach home, looking in. The quiet little bungalow in the Middle Keys was nothing like her Miami Beach penthouse. Not even ocean-facing but perched on a lovely canal, it offered her anonymous solace from the family business.

Looking away from the deck with its small boat dock, she surveyed the condition of her whimsical beach décor with its sunset pinks, soothing blues, and a splash of palm tree green. A drastic and much-needed contrast to the modern metal themes of her penthouse. A piece of the couch stuffing caught by a breeze tried tumbling toward the open sliding glass. She grabbed it and tossed it near one of the two side chairs, also torn to shreds. The buffet cabinet in the dining area was wrenched from the wall and busted into several pieces. Every mirror and slab of granite was fractured from the force of the sledgehammer currently lying on the master bedroom floor.

"Not how I wanted to spend my downtime," she said. The very young Key Colony Beach police officer that her alarm had inconveniently summoned cleared his throat.

"The CSI tech will be here in a few minutes, Ma'am. She'll check for prints, but I suspect this is vandalism."

Joan could only come up with a short list of suspects. She was shocked that any of them had the brains to find this place or the balls to attack her in the little hideaway. An invasion and personal attack on this intimate level was a declaration. A statement.

"Probably some kids staying at one of the other places along the canal." He appeared offended on her behalf. "I'd like to say we'll find them, but they're most likely already back on the mainland." He checked his notes. "I didn't see any security cameras?"

"Correct." This was her hideout, her sanctuary, carefully hidden from her other assets and business dealings. Only a few in her inner circle knew about it. She'd worried that flying to the Keys, however rare, would possibly draw attention to the hideaway. Driving from Daytona was better. It gave her windshield time—uninterrupted thinking, reviewing business opportunities and those who proposed them, and, of course, her guilty pleasure of blaring the current pop sensations that would be seen as juvenile to the family.

The ancient security system was previously installed, so she'd made it a habit to set it just to scare meddling kids.

"Never thought I'd need cameras."

"Most Airbnbs don't have them. Privacy issues, right?" Without looking up from his writing, he said, "I'm afraid this will be a crime scene for at least a few hours because of the blood."

She would not return anyway. Beyond the extensive damage, her hideaway had been violated.

"Blood?" She hadn't thought the encounter with the intruder had left blood, but her hand was throbbing and cut. She thought she'd kept it out of his view. She looked at it as if she must have missed it. She let her expression ask the question.

"In the master bath. There's blood on the counter. Presumably, one of the vandals got cut when he broke the mirror. DNA doesn't often help with this kind of crime, but we'll collect it."

"Of course." The vandals. *Or I may have gotten overly excited at the end of the struggle with the dead man currently under my dock and cut myself.* "I think I got a nick when I was walking through. It was shocking, you know. Seeing all the damage."

"Don't worry about that right now. From the looks of it, you should make other arrangements for the rest of your stay. I can assist if you need."

He looked a little moonfaced at her. She ignored it. "I can manage. Thank you." As if on cue, her phone vibrated in her good hand. "Excuse me."

Her assistant. She'd texted him the basics. The officer stepped away, and she went to the deck and closed the glass doors behind her. She swiped to answer. "Kenneth."

"Joan. Can you talk?"

"I'm out of earshot of the puppy of an officer in charge here." She leaned over the edge once more to make sure nothing seemed amiss under there.

"Are you sure you're all right? Should I fly down?"

"Other than furious at the invasion of my space." She glanced back inside the glass doors. "I'm fine." The detective was milling about but paying her no mind. "However, I need a cleaning crew. Now. The canal has a good bit of unwanted algae up under the dock just off the back deck. Make it fast. They need to come in from the bay and not be seen from the houses. I'll drop you a pin."

"Oh." He hesitated. She could sense his surprise. She had not told him in her text that an altercation had occurred. "Yes, ma'am."

She scrolled to the correct maps app and dropped the pin for him. "What did you find for me?" Her assistant was fabulous at keeping her together, but there were things she didn't share with him. The family drama. Her brother's propensity to use violence to solve problems. Even those that were better served with diplomacy or intimidation.

Kenneth didn't need to know the depth of their family tension. The real-life chess game she and Derrick had spent their lifetimes playing. To the victor goes the spoils. All the legal and not-so-illegal enterprises. It was always clear the final game would be for the family business. "Have you heard anything? Anyone bragging?"

"It's quiet out there. No one's talking about it. My gut says something…" He didn't finish his thought.

"The only thing left untouched was the right side of the master bed. His stupid little chess piece was on the pillow."

"The Knight?" Kenneth didn't wait for her confirmation. "I don't know what to say. That's a bit of a shock, is it not?"

"It was for a moment." Mostly because her brother made this move. Finding Derrick's blatant message was as hurtful as it was shocking. The siblings had been at odds for the last two years, since Papa died. The old bastard enjoyed his children's power struggle and perpetuated it after his death by leaving conflicting instructions on how the business would be run in the future.

"What's the plan, ma'am?"

She'd won the mantle in a violent coup from within the organization, taking most of the legitimate ventures and leaving him with the grittier end of the portfolio. "I'll enjoy my time in the Keys for a few days and then head home. Where are my reservations?"

"Take some time to consider your next move. Very nice. After I got your text, I did some looking and found you a nice suite at the Isabella Beach Resort on the third floor. It's beachfront, of course. Pictures online look to be your style. It's a destination wedding kind of place, just before that long bridge."

She didn't bother to correct the New Yorker's misnaming of the Seven Mile Bridge, but Google Maps may not have labeled it for him. Right now, she wanted a shower and a drink. "Have them send some wine to the room."

"I did. Veuve Clicquot"

"Perfect. Let me know if you hear anything."

She stepped back into the mess and found the officer in her bedroom. She swallowed down a ball of fury. Losing her cool would do her no good. Her quaint little hideaway was soiled. She'd initiate the repairs, then put it on the market. It was a seller's market. At least she'd make some money for her trouble.

"I'm all set." Her suitcase was on its side by the bed. "I can take this, correct?"

He pulled it upright for her. "Of course. You found a place, then?"

"I did."

He waited for her to reveal that information.

Instead, she concentrated on removing one of the door keys from a Corvette-shaped key ring. "Call me if you need any more information," she read his name badge for the first time, "Officer Dalen."

She turned and left before he could ask her anything else.

* * *

The suite was marvelous. Crisp whites with navy details, a huge fresh floral arrangement. It had a spacious balcony overlooking the Atlantic. Below her were palm trees swaying on ocean breezes. The champagne was fabulous. This was just what she needed. It was a shame she'd only be here for the night.

Joan unbuttoned her black blouse in front of the mirror in the bathroom. Her left shoulder showed the signs of a nasty bruise. She touched it just to feel the pain. To let it sink in. She'd need the anger for what needed to get done. Luckily, the man hadn't hit her face, or she'd have never been able to speak to the officer. The altercation had been a short one. Her attacker, though probably hired for his shooting skills, was dumbfounded when she kicked the firearm out of his hand. As usual, a man underestimated her and paid the price.

"Never take the time to speak to your target." She said to her reflection. What had the man said to her? "Your days as head of the family are done? What an idiot."

The assassin shouldn't have bothered to deliver Derrick's arrogant message or the chess piece. If he'd managed to kill her, leaving the chess piece as evidence was amateur. Derrick knew better. However, he had made more than one poor move lately. He wore his desire to control the entire family business like a Jehovah's Witness's suit. Ill-fitting and unimpressive. His child-like temper tantrums had worsened as well. She'd beat him every time they played chess as kids. It drove him mad. And now she was able to beat him easily. He thought her power moves made him look weak to their rivals and the employees. She never understood why he chose the Knight as a mascot and business logo when he desperately wanted to be King.

A hot shower and clean clothes went a long way to ease the pain in her shoulder and her mind. She refilled her glass and carried the bottle onto the balcony. The cushion on the white rattan loveseat was thick enough to sink into. The view offered a dramatic natural course of sea oats for buffering the coastline from storms, and then a narrow beach. The vegetation in this property section meant no beach frolickers to ruin her view. The dedicated beach area was close enough to her building to make out children's laughter but far enough away not to ruin the experience. Well done, Kenneth.

Her thoughts turned to the problem at hand. The situation was a foregone conclusion, maybe even Papa's strategy, that this modern-day Game of Thrones would eventually lead from the chessboard to real life. The knight on her pillow, as a message, was poor planning on Derrick's part. If the hitman had done his job, why was the knight on the pillow? Who was that message for? Her loyal employees may never have gotten that kind of detail unless Derrick had asked the gunman for photographic proof of death that included the chess piece.

The whole thing made him even less suited to lead Papa's enterprises. Proof of death is also proof of a crime.

The manchild couldn't control his rage. Never had, but she'd thought he was at least competent.

* * *

Driving at 5 am, the trip to Miami was fast. Traffic on the Overseas Highway wasn't jammed with the typical parade of vacationers getting in and out of the Keys. She appreciated the windshield time to consider every angle of the assassination attempt.

Right on time, Kenneth stood at the curb outside the busy donut shop just a few miles from Derrick's compound. She parked across the street and waited for her assistant to cross traffic to join her.

He didn't speak much as she drove, but he wasn't prone to droning on. One of the reasons she'd taken him in. She'd found him getting the crap beat out of him by her cousin Art over a card game. That led to Kenneth needing a new position. Joan liked irritating Art any chance she got, so she hired Kenneth the next day.

Derrick had given Joan a fob for his security gate ages ago so she could sit with his big, mean dogs while he was on one of his excursions to St. Martin with the latest cover model conquest. The dogs were long gone, but she still had the fob. Joan hoped it still worked. There were no other cars in the driveway, but something seemed off.

"What are you going to do?" Kenneth whispered.

"Correct the imbalance." She felt him look over at her. "It's necessary, as much as I'd like it to be otherwise."

She saw movement from Kenneth out of the corner of her eye. He seemed calm, considering. She'd give him that. The man wasn't afraid to ride into a fight with her.

The house, like the neighborhood, slept as they rolled up. That perfect time between deep slumber and the first ripples of awakening.

"You have a plan?"

She glanced from the road to her assistant.

"Of course you do."

She did, but things like this required a good bit of flexibility. Both mentally and physically. She'd like to have a good yoga class before such an endeavor. Nothing like a good stretch to calm the nerves and sharpen the senses. This task didn't give that vibe. On the long ride up, she'd left the sound system silent. Lived in her rage. Visualized the outcome.

He looked down at his watch. "Clean up in the Keys complete."

"Perfect timing," she said as they came to a stop. She squeezed the steering wheel. Was she going to do this? The duality of the need to reciprocate with the closeness of the hit had her emotions dancing through her nerves. She let go of the wheel. "The security system might alert him. I don't know his settings. Whatever happens, follow my lead."

He nodded and got out of the car.

The house was quiet as she made her way through the marble entryway. Kenneth moved along just a step or two behind her. It wasn't until she crossed the oversized living room that she heard music from the party room on the far side of the pool area. No other cars were in the driveway, but he was entertaining someone. The sensory rebounding from going in and out of the South Florida heat made her already electric nerves crackle more. When she pulled the door open, she had her gun ready. She stepped into the ultra-cooled room and stood with her back to the nearest wall.

"Well, you're here," Derrick sighed. This was an odd observation to announce. Her brother seemed more relieved than afraid. Kenneth moved closer to her.

A redhead sat next to her brother wearing the tiny dress uniform of a cover model or centerfold—although she wasn't quite the quality of one.

"I'm disappointed, Derrick," Joan said.

He gave a long nod with a frown. "As am I." His left eye had a hint of a busted blood vessel. His flamboyant flamingo Hawaiian shirt twisted just a bit at the bottom. He was barefoot.

"A redhead?" Joan was sure he'd sworn off all redheads in high school when Kimberly Conner broke his heart by cheating with one of the track guys. She'd found it hilarious that he'd carried the grudge against all gingers this long. But now, she was sure.

He gave her an exaggerated frowning nod. They were not alone. Since the only other person to know where her Keys house was located was also in the room, she was relieved. On the trip up, she'd been able to visualize only two plausible scenarios.

The first scenario: her brother tried to get her killed, which was plausible but would bring complications with their business associates and revenue streams. While he wanted the glory of being the head of the family, Derrick lacked the initiative and patience to manage and run it. He knew that deep down.

"How much do you like this particular ginger, brother?"

"Not much at all."

Joan leveled the gun to heart height on the girl's chest. Of course, the girl squealed. Derrick held her tight around the waist so she couldn't move. That would make the others in the room show themselves. Because Joan knew she wasn't alone. As expected, a curly-headed dude in a Deadpool T-shirt popped up from behind the bar with an assault rifle.

Now she knew her targets.

In her left jacket pocket was a small .380 Pony—her backup. In this situation, she was going to have to go two-handed, even if one was aching and swelling. She shoved her hand in the pocket and gripped the gun. Joan shot twice through the pocket fabric without looking at her target.

The man behind the bar took a split second to react to Kenneth getting hit, going down screaming. His shock took the danger out of altering her aim from the ginger girl to Deadpool's forehead, nicely placed on the front of the man's shirt. Two whipping cracks of the gun firing were only interrupted by the screaming ginger.

"So, it was a tricky Rook and not the Knight who tried to take the Queen."

"She was part of it, Joan," Derrick said, pushing the girl away.

Kenneth groaned. Joan glanced down. He reached for her as if she'd do anything but put a bullet in his head.

Ginger flinched.

"How are you related to these two?"

"I'm not. I um. I was just hired to get," she tilted her head to Derrick, "him to bring me home and leave the door unlocked. You know, to distract him from setting any alarms." Tears fell, but she wasn't full-on crying. Trying to hold her shit together. Joan could tell she was considering the best way to get out of this situation alive. "They said…I thought he was getting punked by his buddies. I swear I don't know anything about anything."

"Joan," Derrick said.

"Shut up."

Joan studied the young woman. She considered her a victim and didn't want to shoot her. She watched her as she calmed herself with deep breaths.

"Give me your driver's license."

"What?"

Joan held her hand out, palm up. "Your purse." It was sitting on the bar. She motioned with the gun in her right hand.

The girl rushed. Joan followed and sat at a barstool next to the shaky girl. She dropped her little wallet twice from shaking so hard. She handed the license over. Joan photographed it with her phone. "Erica. This is insurance. I know who you are and where you live."

"Joanie. She's a witness."

She studied the girl for a moment. "You a stripper?"

Erica nodded. "But I'm trying to get a better job." The girl straightened. Her shaking was all but gone. Impressively calm now, given there were two dead men on the floor and Joan still held a gun. "I have an associate's degree. Business." Erica looked at her feet and tried to cover her mostly exposed breasts, suddenly more embarrassed by her situation and not so much worried over the men bleeding out.

"Take a breath." Joan pointed to a bottle of water. Derrick shook his head at his sister and then searched the Deadpool dude's pockets. Finding his phone in the guy's pocket, Derrick paced to the windows that overlooked the pool and made a call Joan assumed was for a cleanup.

Erica sipped the water and sat on a barstool. She appeared totally at ease now that she was pretty sure she wasn't getting shot. "Business degree? That seals it for me. I have a proposal." She motioned over toward Kenneth's body. "It seems I need a new rook." She shrugged. "I mean assistant. It would be best if you had a way out of the dangerous job you're currently in. Care to join our game?"

The redhead looked at Kenneth, considering the game we played here.

"Do I have to kill anyone?"

"You do not."

Story Inspiration:

I started thinking about female mobsters—what happens when a sister, not a son, takes the reins of the family business? How does power shift when a woman steps into a world ruled by men? The tension, the betrayals, the quiet (and not-so-quiet) battles for control. How far would the men in her own family go to stop her rise—and how far would she go to hold onto it?

GAME OF DRONES

Jane Limprecht

Jane Limprecht's short stories have appeared or are forthcoming in four crime fiction anthologies and Kings River Life Magazine. *Learn more at janelimprecht.wordpress.com.*

Forty-five minutes into my treadmill walk, I spotted the drone behind the Fairfax County recreation center. The fitness room's two-story glass wall overlooked a grassy meadow bordered by a strip of trees. Most of the time, the meadow was empty, apart from the occasional cautious deer, excited dog, or small child trailing an uncooperative kite. It was empty now, except for the drone that hung in the air like a giant insect. Who was flying it?

Maintaining my steady three-mile-an-hour pace, I craned my neck to peer around the treadmills to my right. The glass wall curved enough to show where the meadow met the parking lot. Aha, the drone's person— a ponytailed young man who held a controller and wore oversized black goggles. Even from this distance, I recognized him as my son Sean's longtime friend, Aiden. His dark-blue hair helped make the ID.

Aiden grew up in our neighborhood, and he and Sean studied computer science at nearby George Mason University ten years ago. Sean pursued a career in systems development. Aiden created video games. The two stayed friends and met up now and then.

Right now, Sean was downstairs in an aikido class, no doubt volunteering as the uke, the person who gets thrown around. Every Saturday, he picked me up before class to make sure his unathletic mom worked out at least once a week. Today, he'd arrived a few minutes early to fix a glitch in my laptop. My husband, Jack, was fishing at his cousin's lakeside cabin, and my own troubleshooting skills were limited to "unplug it, then plug it back in."

The drone traced a lazy circle around the meadow's perimeter, occasionally zipping low to cross the field. I checked my treadmill dashboard—two laps left. For the next few seconds, I watched the yellow dot march counterclockwise along the electronic track.

When I looked up, the drone was zooming head-high toward Aiden.

The young man's thumbs sped over the controller while his head bobbed from the handset to the fast-approaching drone. When the drone was a few yards away, Aiden leaped aside. The drone passed his head with inches to spare. Aiden pivoted, ripped off the goggles, then dropped to his knees, the controller tumbling to the ground. As quickly as he dropped, he scrambled to his feet and ran into the parking lot, out of my view.

I jumped at a tap on my shoulder.

"Mom, it's me." Sean chuckled. "Class ended early. I'll hit the weight machines until you're done." His smile disappeared. "You okay?"

I grabbed the treadmill handles to steady myself. "Something's happened outside. Your friend Aiden was flying a drone. I think it hit—I'm not sure. A car? A person?" I pushed the red "stop" button, and the treadmill slowed to a halt. "Aiden looked panicky."

"Let's see if he needs help." Sean steadied my arm as I stepped off the treadmill. Gathering my towel and water bottle, I followed him to the parking lot.

We weren't alone.

Half a dozen people clustered near a man who lay beside a blue Hyundai. Bright red blood stained the pavement where two young women in workout gear knelt by him. A lanky fellow with a squash racket under his arm said he'd called 9-1-1.

"What the—" Sean grabbed my arm. "That's Martin. Aiden's boss. Former boss."

"Oh geez, he exercises in the fitness room. Martin helped me figure out a couple of the machines."

"He runs the game development company where Aiden used to work." Sean checked right and left. "There's Aiden, at the edge of the parking lot," he said, motioning for me to follow.

When Aiden saw us, his words rushed out. "I couldn't control it. It flew at me, and I ducked. Then I saw Martin on the ground." Aiden's hands covered his mouth.

"Aiden, it'll be all right," Sean said. "Did you try to help him?"

"Uh-huh," Aiden said, his voice muffled. "I checked his breathing and tried to press on that cut on his face. Those women ran up and said they were, I don't know, nurses or doctors?" He exhaled heavily.

"I watched the drone fly at you, but I didn't see it hit anyone," I said, as I pointed to the wall of windows.

I heard the ambulance siren getting louder as it got closer. When it pulled up, the EMTs took over Martin's medical care from the two women—Army medics, it turned out. A police officer arrived minutes later.

"Were you and Martin meeting up here?" Sean said. "You're still friends, right?"

"Dude, what are you saying?" Aiden said. "That I decked him with a drone on purpose?"

"Of course not. But the police might ask how you know each other, so be prepared."

Sighing, Aiden said, "I suppose you're right. We're still friends. We were meeting up to play the drone-fighting game we developed when I worked for him. Awesome game. Successful, too."

"Did Martin bring a drone?" Sean asked. "There's one in pieces by the car."

"That's the one that hit him," Aiden said. "Martin planned to bring a drone, but I didn't see it." Aiden raised his hands to his head again and gazed across the meadow.

"Aiden, if you and Martin are friends," I said, "why did you leave his company?"

"Money. I liked working for Martin, but I'm getting married next year. I found a job that pays more. With benefits." Aiden shut his eyes. When he opened them, he jerked his thumb toward the police officer standing by the ambulance. "I'd better go talk to her and find out if I can help Martin. I'll catch you later, Sean."

He took a deep breath, blew it out through pursed lips, and trudged away. I asked Sean to take me home.

"I wonder what'll happen next," Sean said as he beeped his car doors open.

"The police will want to know why the drone hit Martin, how Aiden operated it," I said. "I expect they'll examine the drone controller to see if it malfunctioned. It was clearly an accident."

Sean stared ahead.

"Wasn't it?" I slipped into the passenger seat. "An accident?"

"I'm sure it was. On the other hand, Aiden didn't give you the whole story when you asked why he quit. He told me there was bad blood when he left Martin's company." Sean backed out of the parking space, careful to avoid lingering bystanders. "Aiden was ticked off because he didn't get credit for his work on that game. Drone Strike Command. It's a money-maker."

"Do you play it?"

"No, the DSC game requires some pricey custom drone and a special controller. A cross between a racing drone—light for speed—and a freestyle drone—sturdier for stunts. It comes with goggles for a VR experience. Virtual reality."

"Aiden had goggles on. I wondered why."

"VR puts the operator in the cockpit, piloting the drone. Like you're looking ahead, instead of viewing the scene below. There are points for strikes, avoids, whatever. Obviously, you don't want your custom drone smashed up, so the fighting is all virtual."

"With the fun of flying a drone instead of staring at a screen," I said.

"You got it."

I drummed my fingers on the cup holder between us. "Why didn't Aiden get credit for his work?"

"He said another game developer—his name is Zach—took his ideas and presented them as his own. Aiden got into a beef with Zach about it and told Martin why. Martin didn't do anything."

"Didn't Martin believe Aiden?"

"There was some question about what Zach did. Game development is collaborative. People toss ideas back and forth all the time."

"I suppose you can't always tell who contributed what."

"You're right." Sean glanced my way. "At any rate, Aiden found a better job, and that was the end of it. At least that's what he told me."

* * *

"Aiden quit the job after Martin wimped out on him, Trish," Barbara told me on Saturday evening. "Zach cribbed from my son's work, plain and simple."

"That's lousy. Even if game development is collaborative, the boss should give credit where it's due." I sipped iced raspberry tea on Barbara's screened-in back porch.

"There was another issue between Martin and Aiden," Barbara said.

"What do you mean?"

"Martin dated Aiden's fiancée. Before Phoebe and Aiden got together."

I almost spat raspberry tea down my shirt. "Dated her? Isn't Martin older than Phoebe? As in, older older?"

"Not really. Martin's in his mid-forties, Aiden's thirty, but Phoebe's thirty-five. She and Aiden were friends before they started dating. Aiden kind of—stole her away from Martin." Barbara flapped one hand. "Not in any sneaky way. Phoebe realized Martin's married to his company..."

"And Aiden's a genuinely nice young man who's not wedded to his work," I said.

Barbara smiled for the first time since we sat down. "Phil and I are thrilled they're engaged." Her smile faded. "We're not as thrilled Aiden's gotten into this mess. He doesn't need any more history with Martin, if you get my drift."

I wasn't sure what to say, so I sipped my tea in silence.

* * *

With my husband still at the lake and Sean's girlfriend traveling for work, I invited Sean to Sunday breakfast at one of our favorite family hangouts. For at least fifteen years, Sean had ordered spaghetti with meat sauce for every meal he ate at Athens Greek-American, whether breakfast, lunch, or dinner. Sean munched on his side salad while I divided my pecan waffle, setting aside half for the next morning. I inhaled the aroma of toasted pecans mixed with fresh-from-the-griddle waffle.

"Any news regarding Aiden?" I asked as I poured syrup from a tiny white jug.

"I guess the police questioned him about his work on the drone-fighting game," Sean said. "Like, if there's any obvious reason for the drone to spin out of control. Meanwhile, Martin's in the hospital."

"The hospital? I hope he's all right. They usually send you home unless you're at death's door."

"He got a concussion when his head hit the concrete. They're not releasing him right away because he's on blood thinners." Sean blanketed his spaghetti with grated parmesan.

"Did you know Aiden's fiancée used to date Martin?" I said.

"Yeah." Sean gave me a side-eye. "Is it relevant? And how did you know?"

"I visited with Aiden's mom. She mentioned it." I topped off my coffee with more creamer. "I was thinking, what if that made Martin less inclined to investigate Zach's conduct? Barbara said Aiden stole Phoebe away. I could see Martin downplaying Aiden's complaints because he was jealous, or had hurt feelings. Maybe he treated Aiden unfairly without realizing it," I said. "Would Aiden retaliate?"

Sean looked up from his spaghetti, eyebrows raised. "By hitting Martin in the head with a drone?" He shook his head. "No way. He's a big teddy bear. With blue hair. Funny thing, though, Aiden takes a lot of grief from Phoebe's uncle. Victor somebody. He works for an IT contractor called

Quebnor Systems."

"Quebnor. Who came up with that name?"

Sean tried not to laugh with his mouth full. "It's a subsidiary of this big government contractor. Aiden said they started with Jupiter's moons, but all the pronounceable ones were taken. Same with Saturn and Mars. They gave up and typed random letters to create a name."

"I will never understand the tech contracting industry. But why does anyone care what Phoebe's uncle thinks of Aiden?"

"I don't know if anyone cares. It's just a bummer to have your fiancée's uncle hate you." Sean twirled pasta onto his fork. "Victor's convinced Aiden doesn't take his career seriously."

"The blue hair," I said.

"Or was it green when they met?" Sean tapped his lip and squinted one eye. "The point is, no matter where a game developer works, they're stuck in a dark office crammed with servers and cables. Nobody sees their hair." Sean stabbed the lone cherry tomato in his salad and set the cucumber slice aside. "Anyway, Quebnor offers internships for computer science majors. Routine stuff, to get a toe in the water. Zach interned there."

"Why did Zach end up working for Martin?" I asked. "If Quebnor's part of a much larger company, I would think it offers more job security and better pay."

"Not necessarily. It depends on the contracts they're awarded and the skills they need. Quebnor goes after contracts to develop games for military and law enforcement training. There's even a drone simulator training game designed for law enforcement. With situations they'd encounter when they fly drones. Abandoned warehouses, forests, that sort of thing."

"Would a job with Quebnor require a security clearance? I mean, if we assume Zach wanted to work there."

"Hmm. For entry-level game devs, probably not a full clearance—not top secret or anything. But I expect they'd do some sort of background investigation."

"What if Zach applied for a job at Quebnor but flunked the background check? Some red flag—drug use, let's say. Or maybe I'm way off base and

Zach found his ideal job at Martin's company." I cut off a syrup-soaked square of waffle. "Online games aren't my thing. Scrabble's the one game I really enjoy, and I play it on a flat piece of cardboard with tiny wooden tiles."

"You do the newspaper crossword on your phone," Sean said. "Technically, that's an online game."

"Good point. Just stop me if I ever put on goggles."

* * *

After breakfast, Sean headed back to his apartment, and I drove the short trip to our house. That afternoon, I was walking our Labrador-pit bull mix, Rex, when I noticed Barbara in her driveway. Aiden stood next to her, head down and shoulders slumped.

"Barbara, Aiden, how are you?" I stopped at the end of their drive. Rex took the opportunity to snuffle in the grass. "Did anyone figure out what happened with the drone?"

Aiden exchanged a glance with his mom. "I don't know. The police are asking questions."

"What are they interested in?"

"The drone controller, mostly. I guess they'll examine it for a malfunction. I mean, it must have malfunctioned. The drone stopped responding to my commands."

"This sounds crazy, but could someone have tampered with it?" I tugged on Rex's leash to keep him out of the street. "Was it in your apartment? Your car?"

"That's the thing—I don't own a DSC game. Martin let me borrow the drone and controller in order to play. I picked them up on Friday before his office closed. He said he'd meet me at the rec center with his drone."

"Do the police know you borrowed the equipment?" I turned to Barbara. "If the game was stored at the office, someone may have tinkered with it. Messed up the controls accidentally."

"I don't remember anymore what I told the cops," Aiden said. "I think

I started blabbing about office politics, and Zach, and Phoebe, and who knows what else." Aiden shook his head as he kicked his toe into the dirt. "I should have kept my big mouth shut." He pressed his lips together in a tight line. "Too late for that now, isn't it?"

* * *

"So, Aiden picked up the drone and controller at Martin's office." Sean sat on our front porch step on Monday evening, scratching Rex's ears, while I rocked in the porch swing. He'd stopped by to collect his old camping tent, and I relayed what I'd learned from Aiden and Barbara. "The logical conclusion is that the controller malfunctioned," Sean said. "Except why did it zoom right at Aiden and Martin?"

"I've been wondering…could someone other than Aiden control it?" I said.

"Huh." Sean stopped scratching Rex's ears. "Yeah. If they programmed the drone to accept commands from more than one operator, the second operator could override Aiden's commands. Provided the second operator was within range. Not too far away."

"If there was a second operator, who was it? And what were they doing?"

"Well, if Martin resented Aiden for stealing his girlfriend, theoretically, he could commandeer Aiden's drone, aim it at Aiden, and conk himself in the forehead by accident. But that would be a Three Stooges episode."

"Which this is decidedly not," I said. "What about Zach? Did he want revenge after Aiden accused him of using his work? Although if Zach targeted Aiden, wouldn't he direct the drone to circle back after Aiden jumped out of the way? For another try?"

"You'd think so," Sean said.

I clapped my hands together. "What if Zach targeted both of them? Martin, the intended victim, and Aiden, the intended suspect."

"Whoa, diabolical. Though I don't understand why Zach would target his boss. Martin gave him a pass when he used Aiden's ideas."

"We don't know that. Martin might have confronted Zach after Aiden quit. A little late, but—" I stopped for a moment. "Is there a way to track a second operator?"

Sean tapped a finger against his lips. "Yeah. There is." He patted Rex's head and stood up. "Want to visit the hospital tomorrow? I can meet you there at lunchtime."

* * *

Sean punched the fourth-floor button in the hospital elevator the next day. I straightened the paper flowers in the Star Wars "Death Star" bouquet we'd purchased at the gift shop. The elevator doors opened, and we walked to the intersection of three hallways, where Sean angled left. At the end of the hall, he paused at an open door and rapped gently on the doorjamb.

I trailed behind Sean into a hospital room more spacious than I expected, with a picture window that looked out on the block-long hospital complex. Cushioned on the bed's raised headrest, Martin stared at the TV on the opposite wall. He turned his head slowly when we walked in.

"Sean, my man." Martin attempted a smile, then winced. "Sorry, I'm not at my best."

"How are you doing? We were inside the rec center when you got hurt. Mom saw the drone fly across the field toward Aiden, but you were out of view."

Martin acknowledged the bouquet with a wan smile. "I don't understand this whole thing. The police seem to think the attack was deliberate. They've been asking me about Aiden." In a quieter voice, Martin added, "He apparently told the police about Zach. And Phoebe. And, if I know Aiden, anything else that popped into his mind."

"Trying to help out," Sean said, "and digging himself in a hole along the way."

"You know, at first I didn't believe Zach took credit for Aiden's ideas," Martin said. "After Aiden left, I figured out what happened."

"How did you do it?" I said.

"I went through the code, line by line, and pinpointed where Zach used

Aiden's work." Martin exhaled loudly. "Major mistake, not doing it earlier. I was slammed with new projects, budget worries." He licked his lips. "To be honest, maybe a little jealous of Aiden, willing to let Zach's conduct slide …"

Sean lifted a plastic water pitcher from the wheeled bedside table, filled a paper cup, and handed it to Martin. "I'm positive Aiden didn't direct the drone toward you. And we can prove it—by going through the event log."

Martin grimaced and closed his eyes. "Man, I'm so doped up on painkillers I didn't even think of that." He drained the cup in one gulp, crushed it, and set it on the bedside table. "But I can't do it. The concussion. The docs won't let me read or even use my phone. Believe me, I tried. Got a headache and almost threw up."

"Let me do it." Sean glanced around the room. "Is your laptop here?"

Martin pointed to a cupboard under the TV. "The EMTs brought my backpack with my laptop in it. The drone I brought to the rec center is still in my car trunk, but we don't need it for this." He motioned to the bedside table. "Roll that away, and we can review the log together. Or at least I can pretend to be useful."

After pulling the straight-backed visitor chair close to Martin's bed, Sean powered up the laptop and searched for the DSC file. I cleared a spot for the bouquet and claimed the other visitor chair, a bulky vinyl recliner with a pop-out footrest. I knew how Sean worked—flying fingers, intermittent cursing—so I occupied myself with the tech-related show on Martin's TV. Martin had muted it, which was fine since even the closed captions were gibberish to me.

"There it is," Sean said, his voice urgent. "Where another operator took over Aiden's drone." He pointed at a jumble of characters crowded onto the screen, then held up his hand in a "stop" gesture. "Sorry, Martin, don't try to read it."

Martin frowned, wincing again.

Sean tapped the screen. "There's a sign-on ping from a location approximately two hundred yards away from Aiden." He looked at me. "I can't tell which direction."

"The soccer parking lot?" I said. "There aren't many other parking spots nearby."

"I swear I saw Zach's car there," Martin said under his breath. "It didn't register until now. Sean, you know Zach's—"

"Pride and joy. A 1960 Dodge Dart. Weird brownish-pink color I've never seen on another car."

Martin lay his head back on the pillow. "A lot of things are falling into place. Things I ignored. Or didn't address."

"Such as?" I asked.

"When Zach took the game developer job, I knew he wanted to work for Quebnor. He interned there, but they required a more extensive background investigation for employee hires. The BI could take time, and I figured I'd snap him up while he was available."

"Didn't you do a criminal background check of your own?" I tried not to sound accusatory.

"Sure, I did. Turned up clean. Then, just last week, I learned through the tech grapevine that Zach hadn't been waiting for the results of Quebnor's background investigation. He'd failed it." Martin paused. "He gambles."

I let out a low whistle. "Criminal or not, gambling debts can make you flunk a background check. They pose a risk of theft. Or blackmail."

"E-sports are Zach's game," Martin said. "He bets thousands of dollars. And he loses."

"Do you think he sold Aiden's ideas for cash to cover gambling debts?" Sean asked. "Who would buy some random developer's work on a game?"

"No, I'd guess Zach used Aiden's ideas to get his own work done," I said. "Same as copying someone's homework. But, Martin, could he have also tried to access your company's intellectual property to sell?"

Martin hesitated. "We do have some innovative, and valuable, products under development. Up to this point, we've only created and sold games for entertainment, but we're moving into game design for military and law enforcement training. Zach doesn't have access to that division or its work product." Martin rubbed his hand over his face. "Unless he convinced someone he needed it."

"Who would buy this information?" I asked.

"A company that's developing those kinds of games and doesn't play by the rules," Martin said. "Quebnor, perhaps. They're muscling in on the major competitors for federal contracts."

"What if Zach sold the information to Quebnor or one of its competitors and then realized you were on to him? If he discovered you reviewed the DSC code and found his use of Aiden's work, he'd realize that before long, you'd also learn he accessed other projects without permission." I leaned forward in the recliner. "I've got to ask—why haven't you fired Zach? On top of being a horrible colleague to Aiden, he sounds like a serious security risk for your company."

"Our HR contractor is processing the paperwork even as I'm stuck in this bed."

"I'm no gambler, but I'll bet Zach got wind of that," I said. "So, on his way out the door, he decided to get even with you and Aiden. Attack you, frame Aiden, and, as a bonus, raise concerns about the safety of your drone-fighting game."

Martin gazed out the window and shook his head slowly.

"Did he do this on his own, or was Victor involved?" Sean asked. "Phoebe's uncle, at Quebnor."

"Victor's a hustler," Martin said. "He's willing to undercut and play rough to score contracts, so I can believe he'd buy stolen information and chalk it up to normal business. But I can't believe he'd have me attacked and frame Aiden for it. Blue hair or not."

"We need to take this information to the police. If we're right, Zach assaulted you, set up Aiden, and stole your company's intellectual property to sell to a competitor." I placed a hand on Martin's shoulder. "Are you game?"

* * *

"Here are the matches to light the grill." I handed the box to Sean. "Dad comes home soon, but I'm not sure he's bringing back any fish for a Friday night fish fry."

I pulled a plate of hamburger patties from the fridge, and Sean dumped charcoal into the Weber grill. Homemade potato salad, deviled eggs, watermelon chunks—simple and delicious summer fare. Relaxing into my chair on our back patio, I clicked my phone awake to do the *Post's* daily crossword puzzle. A local news alert caught my eye.

"Zach's been arrested," I said. "He's been charged with attempted second-degree murder, assault and battery…" I skimmed for the crucial details. "Arraignments on Monday."

Sean reached over my shoulder to poke at my phone screen. "Check the end here. Quebnor sacked Victor 'for his role in the purchase of stolen intellectual property.'" Sean pumped a fist. "Good old Uncle Victor."

"He'll have bigger problems than Aiden's hair. You had a huge hand in this. Martin wasn't in any shape to scrutinize the event log." I finished reading the article and clicked into the crossword puzzle. "Want to help me with the crossword?"

"Even if I did, you know I inherited Dad's spelling gene."

"Ah, yes. I can't play Scrabble with either of you." I typed in answers to a few crossword clues, then raised a finger. "Here's one I guarantee you'll know."

"What is it?"

"Five letters. Second letter, 'r.' Clue, 'male bee.'"

Sean cocked his head for a second before he chuckled. "Nice one, Mom. To tell the truth, I never want to hear that word again."

Story Inspiration:

The idea for a drone-fighting game came from a university event where entrepreneurs displayed tech products they developed. I chatted with two enthusiastic young men who had designed a drone simulator training module for law enforcement. They handed me a controller, showed me which button was which, and let me zoom above a deserted industrial park.

Our friendly chat noodled around in my head until this story idea popped up.

My grown children volunteered as "technical advisers" as I invented the game. Now we all want to play it in real life.

ZEBRA FINCH

donalee Moulton

donalee Moulton's first mystery short story, "Swan Song," was one of 21 selected for publication in Cold Canadian Crime *and was shortlisted for a 2023 Award of Excellence. Other short stories have since been published in numerous anthologies and magazines. Her short story "Troubled Water" was shortlisted for a 2024 Derringer Award and a 2024 Award of Excellence from the Crime Writers of Canada. donalee's new book* Bind *came out in 2025.*

My left breast is vibrating. I reach into my pocket for my phone. Then I check to see who's calling. It could be my parents ringing to let me know I'm wasting my life in Nova Scotia as a private investigator. However, it's neither Evelyn nor Charles Montgomery. It's someone called Darnell Sparkes. As I'm about to hang up, I realize I know Darnell. I just have other names for him. Some of them are even nice.

"Great to hear from you."

I can hear Darnell snort down the full length of the fiber optic cable that connects us. "You'll eat those words. I have a job for you."

"I assume it pays."

"I'm a Crown prosecutor. Of course it pays."

The job is straightforward surveillance. The guy under my soon-to-be watchful eye is Jake Hawkins. He has been a bad boy. According to Darnell (and Darnell says he is rarely wrong), Hawkins is part of an armed robbery crew that has cleaned out at least five box trucks in the last seven months. The most recent haul was worth $1.2 million.

Darnell has enough evidence to arrest Hawkins. He's looking for leverage. Hawkins may be good at his own personal criminal enterprise, but he is no mastermind. Darnell wants to flip him. He wants me to find something that will make flipping more appealing than ratting on someone connected to organized crime. What it all boils down to: I will sit in my car, eat potato chips, and collect $125 an hour. I may even get to add a bird to my newly started life list. Easy peasy.

I should know better.

* * *

Jake Hawkins does not lead a wild and crazy life. He's been to the grocery store, walked around the block with an obviously pregnant woman, and now, as I can see through his front window, he's watching Argentina take on Colombia in the Copa América soccer final. I'm playing solitaire on my phone and hoping Hawkins will go upstairs to bed very soon. Then I'll head home, and someone else will take over.

Mr. Laidback does not go to bed. Ten minutes after Argentina hefted a twenty-pound trophy for all the world to see, Hawkins grabs a jacket and walks out the front door. I'm right behind him. We don't go far.

In only five minutes, Hawkins is pulling into a back parking lot behind a strip mall. He gets out of his car and heads to a delivery door. On the other side is a man whose left arm is the size of a fully grown oak tree. I decide to stay in the car. That's prudent. It's also realistic. First, I'm not getting past Groot. Second, I know what's on the other side of that door. When I was a cop with the Halifax Police Department, we routinely raided this poker game. Obviously, that was effective policing.

I'm on my eleventh game of solitaire and wondering if Hawkins is having better luck with his cards. That question is answered in less than three minutes by a swarm of people rushing out the poker room door and heading for cars scattered across the back lot. Hawkins is not among them.

I'm out of my car and booting it toward the entrance. Groot is nowhere to be seen. I go where angels fear to tread. About thirty feet down the hall is the main poker room. It's a mess. Cards, chips, cigars everywhere. Smoke clings to everything.

A plump, dark-haired woman is standing stock still behind the bar, an empty tray in her right hand. She's looking a little green around the gills. Groot and another man are bending over Hawkins. The man I was supposed to be watching is face down on a felt poker table. He's not moving.

The other man with Groot reaches for Hawkins. "Better not do that," I advise. Both men look up, surprised to see me. Maybe surprised I have the temerity (or stupidity) to contradict them. The same look of shock is on the waitress's face.

"I've already called the cops." Well, sorta. I called Darnell.

The Halifax PD is statistically on time. It takes four minutes for the first cruiser to arrive. In that time, I've assessed what I can of the room without touching or moving anything. The only noteworthy item: the three of diamonds within inches of Hawkins's left hand. Maybe it really is the unluckiest card in the deck.

By the time the third black-and-white is in the parking lot, Darnell is beside me. He's dressed in a suit, hair combed, and smelling like something by Giorgio Armani.

I indicate the attire, the put-together package. "Really?"

Darnell opens his arms to take in the illegal poker game, the dead body. "Really?" Touché.

As I finish giving Darnell a rundown on Hawkins—deadly dull until now, now simply dead—the forensic identification team arrives. "You should wear N95 masks," I say to no one in particular and everyone at once. It's as if I've tossed an unpinned grenade into the room. "I think he was poisoned. Likely fentanyl."

There is a flurry of nitrile gloves and snapping of masks. I can feel the look from Darnell. "You left that out of your report."

"I was getting there."

The Crown prosecutor turns to the three people in the room who are not here on official business. A uniform has corralled them into a corner. "Is there any place we can talk privately? We'll need to take your statements."

As if on cue, detectives Mike Donovan and Darius Brooks arrive with notebooks and coffee. We've worked together before. In fact, Mike used to be my partner. Their arrival signals the end of my evening. I'm heading for the door when Darnell stops me. "You're still on the clock."

Three hours later, I tumble into bed.

* * *

I don't know if it's Darnell or the HPD, but 8 a.m. is the preferred time for meetings. It is not my preferred time. Yet here I am with the boys sipping coffee and eating my fourth Timbit, perhaps the world's best donut hole.

"Recap," says Darnell. He nods toward Sully, or more properly, James Sullivan, the chief of Ds.

Mike takes us through what we've learned. Lana Beaumont: 37, waitress, single, regular at the games, served everyone drinks, did not pour drinks. That would be Tommy Callahan, 58, manager of the game, four arrests, no convictions, ties to organized crime. That leaves thirty-four-year-old Groot, whose real name is Manny Rodriguez but goes by Tiny. No arrests. Apparently, like Beaumont, just the hired help.

All three were interviewed separately, but the story is the same. Hawkins was in high spirits. He arrived with an announcement—"I got married!"—and cigars for everyone in the room. When congratulations were out of the way, he settled in to play Texas hold 'em. He won a few games; he lost a few. Anywhere from five to ten minutes after his second rum and Coke, Hawkins is clammy, pale, and having trouble breathing. Then he's not breathing at all. Once the newlywed collapses, the room clears.

"Where are we with locating the others in the game?" Sully asks.

It's Darius who answers. "If they drove to the game, we have their license plate number."

The chief of Ds raises an eyebrow. It's impressive. Darnell grins and nods his head in my direction. "Em was doing surveillance. She got the plates. Uniforms are taking initial statements. Anyone of interest will be brought in."

"And in the meantime?"

"There's the new wife," I say. "She couldn't have killed Hawkins herself, but she may know who wanted to. She may have wanted to."

"We can do a sweep of the house at the same time," says Darius. "If she gives us permission."

I have my fifth Timbit in hand, sour cream glazed, and am heading for the door. "Where are you going?" Darnell wants to know.

"To bed, perchance to sleep," I reply with a wave.

The Crown prosecutor waves me back. "You have a distressed woman to interview."

* * *

Monica Hawkins is short, dark, and very pregnant. Her eyes are red, her face splotchy. She has clearly been crying. This has its pros and cons. When we're upset, we're more likely to share information we might otherwise keep to ourselves. We also anger more easily.

I'm in luck. Very pregnant Monica welcomes me into the living room and offers me a cup of tea. Not my favorite beverage, but opportunity is knocking, and I answer "Yes, please." Over two hot mugs of King Cole—Hawkins's favorite, I'm told—Monica asks for an update. "Do you know who killed Jake?"

She's disappointed but not surprised by my negative response. "We're hoping you might be able to help."

"I've been going over everything I know about Jake, but I don't know anyone who would want to kill him."

"Don't think about 'who,'" I say. "Think about 'why.'"

Monica sighs. I don't know if this request is burdensome or if she's tired. Either way, I push. "Workmates, for instance. Any beefs?"

The look I get from Monica makes it obvious she sees through this ruse.

"Was Jake an angel? No. Did he always walk the straight and legal? No. But his 'workmates' liked him. They drank beer together. They had family barbecues together. They did not poison one another."

"And still, someone poisoned Jake."

One step too far. Monica breaks into tears. I scramble to take the hot mug of tea from her and find tissues. I finally settle for toilet paper. When the tears stop, Monica does not apologize for her outburst, nor should she. But a calm has descended.

She gets up and goes into the kitchen. She returns with a piece of paper she obviously had ready and waiting. "Here's a list of all the guys I know Jake works with, or hangs with."

It's not a long list. As if reading my mind, Monica says. "It's who I know. Jake kept the circle small. He didn't want me to know details about his work."

Smart Jake. "Thanks," I say, tucking the paper in my jeans pocket. "What about the people at the poker game?"

"I didn't even know about the poker game."

"Why do you think that is?"

The King Cole is halfway to Monica's lips. She puts the mug down. There is a decisiveness to the movement. She's going to talk or ask me to leave. Before she has a chance to speak, I dive in. "Monica, you can protect Jake's privacy, or you can help us catch his killer. You can't do both. The choice is yours."

Monica chooses option number two.

* * *

Shift has technically ended, but the boys are back at my place, a tradition that started when a former client of mine was murdered. It's a tradition I don't enjoy.

Over fish and chips from John's Lunch and Tall Ship beer, we lay out what we know. By the time my dining room table is littered with Post-it notes, we've determined we have a lot of information and know very little.

Eighteen people were in the room when Hawkins was murdered, and they fell into three groups: players, railbirds, staff.

The latter were interviewed at the scene and again at Halifax PD. There's nothing to indicate they were involved, nothing concrete to eliminate them from the suspect pool.

We have eliminated suspects from the player pool. Five people were at another table, not close to Hawkins, and they separately confirmed no one left the table. The four other players with Hawkins also didn't leave the table, but only two were close enough to drop something in his drink.

We've also got five railbirds, hangers-on who like to watch the game. Four of these are girlfriends, three of whom were within arm's reach of their men at the second table. Only one was at Hawkins' table, and she has a yellow Post-it note in her honor on my dining room table. The remaining railbird, Logan Hunter, is a runner. His job is to get anyone at the game anything they want from the outside world: cigarettes, food, weed. He's not staff; whoever gets Logan to run pays him (and tips him) for his services.

The chief of Ds is looking at the jumble of colored Post-it notes. We're all watching with interest. James Sullivan often sees what mere mortals miss. Not this time. Sully shakes his head as if to clear away the fog. "So do we have a winner?"

We do not. We have opportunity for several of the people in the room, but no motive. "Monica was helpful here."

"She didn't identify anyone as a possibility," Mike points out.

"No, but she opened the door to motive." Seems Hawkins has lately wanted out of the armed robbery world, looking for something safer now that he had a kid on the way. He was no longer playing to an inside straight.

Hawkins's newfound risk aversion also included drinking and carousing less. He recently gave up hard liquor, Monica said, and hard women.

"Do you think he was lying to her?" Darnell asks.

"I don't know, but I know she thought he was all in when he said he was going straighter and narrower."

"So," Sully says, "we're looking for someone who worked with Hawkins or slept with him."

We stare at the Post-it notes and spend the next two hours narrowing down the list of would-be killers. When we're done, we have three solid suspects.

* * *

Logan Hunter is a bundle of nervous energy. It emanates from his tapping toes, his drumming fingers, and his bouncing body. It's not unusual, of course, to be nervous when you've been brought into a police station for questioning. The questioning is done under the guise of helping Halifax PD, but although he's only twenty-two years old, Logan is no fool. He's been humming around the edges most of his life. He's a pleaser. It's how he survives. Question is, how far would he go to please someone?

We're all agreed, if Logan had anything to do with Hawkins's death, it's because he was paid, he was asked as a favor, or a favor was called in.

Mike and Darius are conducting the interview. I'm in the observation room. Mike is leaning back in a metal chair in the corner. It's an intimidation technique. Darius is kitty-corner to Logan, all smiles. "Thanks for coming in."

Logan doesn't know what to do with this, so he does nothing. Smart.

The silence doesn't faze Darius. "Did you know Jake Hawkins?"

Logan doesn't know what to do with this either. "No. Yes. I mean, I didn't know him, but I knew him."

It takes another twenty minutes to determine that Logan had run the odd errand for Hawkins when he was playing cards, but other than that had no association with him, did not know what he did for a living, specifically, or whom he did it for. I don't think he's bluffing.

Darius switches gears. "What exactly is it you do?"

The confusion on Logan's face is evident. Or maybe it's fear. "I don't know what you mean."

"How do you make money, pay your bills?"

"Oh." Logan relaxes. "I'm a runner."

Mike tips his chair forward. "You run drugs?"

Logan is beside himself. "No. No. No. I run errands. Players need stuff. I get them stuff."

"What kind of stuff?" Darius wants to know.

"Ordinary stuff. Smokes. Booze. Food."

"What if somebody wanted you to drop a pill in someone's drink?" This is Mike.

Logan is horrified at the thought, or at the thought the police know this. "No one wants me to drop a pill in someone's drink." It takes a second. "Oh god. Is that how Hawkins died?"

Neither detective answers. As expected, Logan rushes in to fill the empty space. "Players and railbirds don't want stuff like that. At least not from me. They want stuff they think is lucky or stuff to make them more comfortable. And it can be really specific shit."

Mike and Darius remain silent, eyes locked on Logan. "Man, it's stuff like twelve-year-old Macallan or New York-style thin-crust pizza from Freeman's or nicotine patches and gum. Specific shit. One time, I had to pick up a burner phone so some guy could call his side piece. I had to hold the phone all night waiting for her to call back."

Logan is done. You can see him physically deflating. The three of us feel the same. We fold.

* * *

Tommy Callahan is up next. He arrives on time. With his lawyer. This will be a quick conversation.

Darius and Mike switch positions, although we all know Callahan will not be intimidated. He's already been given a pass on the illegal gaming. Mike asks a few perfunctory questions and, after his lawyer gives the okay, we get a few perfunctory answers.

"Jake played poker occasionally. He didn't win much. He didn't lose much. Not a shark, not a fish."

"As far as I know, everyone either liked Jake or didn't give a damn about him."

"I have no idea who'd want to kill Jake. I know who didn't. Me."

It's time to call it. The detectives are getting nowhere, which we all knew once

the lawyer was in play. Callahan starts to stand. He's not trying to hide the grin on his face.

I lean into the mic. "Ask him about Mo Blake." Blake is our third suspect. The railbird who hovered around Hawkins's table for most of the night, according to everyone we interviewed.

Callahan's response is interesting. "Why do you want to know about Mo?"

Now it's our turn to grin. Mike shrugs. "Humor me."

"Shit. You think Mo killed Hawkins. Not a chance."

"Why not?" Darius asks from his corner of the cramped room.

"I don't even think they knew one another."

"She's an attractive woman," Mike says. "Maybe they knew each other really well. If you know what I mean."

Callahan folds over the table. He's holding his sides, he's laughing so hard. "Oh, please let me be there when you tell that to her wife."

And with that, we're out of suspects.

* * *

Over Costco pizza and Diet Pepsi, we go back to the drawing board. There are fewer Post-it notes and no inspiration in sight. So, we do what cops always do—and investigators hired by chief prosecutors apparently—we start over.

I'm assigned Lana Beaumont. The men in the room, which is everyone else in the room, think women have some magical connection, and as soon as the waitress sees me, she will open up. Like a warm embrace. Let them cling to the myth. I'm getting paid my full daily rate.

Beaumont lives in a small house in North End Dartmouth. She has sweet iced tea and four kinds of cookies waiting on the patio table. It's like two friends wiling away a pleasant afternoon. Maybe the boys are on to something.

When I think she's not paying close attention to me, I pay close attention to Lana Beaumont. I originally thought of her as plump; now I see she's more round all over. Her cheeks are full, her legs shapely, her breasts large. Her pants seem tight, and there is a gap in her shirt where a button strains. The curves are obvious.

"Are you having any luck?" Beaumont asks, bringing me back to reality. I don't answer, just shrug slightly. "Of course," she says, "you can't tell me."

"To be honest," I say, leaning in, "There isn't much to tell. We thought Logan was involved."

"Not a chance," says Beaumont. "He doesn't have the balls. Not to mention he doesn't have a reason."

"We have come to that conclusion. We've also taken Mo Blake off our list."

Beaumont sets her iced tea down. She's laughing so hard the tea is starting to spill. "Oh, you guys are really reaching. I'll admit Jake liked to flirt, but he had sense enough to leave Mo alone."

"That's why I'm here. You were there night in and night out. Someone wanted Hawkins dead. Who?"

For a second, I'm not sure Beaumont heard me. Then I realize she's considering the question. "I've been asked this before. And I've been thinking about Jake's death. None of the other players or railbirds knew Jake well enough to want him dead."

"What about staff?"

"Callahan doesn't want trouble at his game. Tiny is a pushover."

"Let's look at this from another angle. Who could lay their hands on fentanyl?"

Beaumont doesn't hesitate this time. "Everyone."

* * *

We're back at my place. Darius has picked up corned beef and cabbage from Jim's Restaurant, and we're drinking Keith's ale. We're rehashing our notes, tossing theories into the air, absurd and otherwise. We're getting nowhere. Perhaps we're too comfortable.

"Let's call it," Sully finally says. "Maybe some rest will do us good."

It does. At least it does one of us good.

* * *

I text Darius at six the next morning. He gets back to me seconds later. By 8 a.m., HPD's appointed hour, we're back in the conference room. Darius has brought doughnuts and coffee from Tim Hortons. I'm the last to arrive (thought I saw a hermit thrush). Everyone is waiting for me to explain why I called this meeting.

I don't waste any time. "I know who did this."

Mike snorts. "Did you have a visit from the ghost of Jake Hawkins last night? Or maybe a vision?"

I ignore the detective. So does everyone else. Darnell looks at me closely. "Are you sure?"

"I'm sure. I'm not sure I have any evidence. I'm also not sure we'll need any."

"Okay," says Sully. "Let's unwrap those loaded sentences."

"Before we do that, do something for me. Describe Lana Beaumont."

The men in the room don't hesitate. "Sexy." "Attractive." "Hot."

"Got it. You think she's good-looking."

"Very," says Darius. I shoot him a look.

"Describe her physically for me."

Here's what I get: tall, shapely, brown hair, green eyes, not muscular.

"What do you mean by not muscular?"

"Well," says Darnell, "she is a little plump."

"More round than plump," says Mike.

I sigh. "You have all given this woman a lot of thought. Think harder."

It's Sully who comes first to where I have landed. "She's pregnant."

"Shit." This is from Darius. And Mike. And Darnell.

"We'll need more than being a tad plump to make an arrest," says Darnell.

"I can't confirm she's pregnant, but I stopped by Logan's on the way here. Guess who has quit smoking and wanted the nicotine patches and gum?

Guess who was nauseous from cigars the night Hawkins died? Guess who served me four different kinds of cookies yesterday with sweet, iced tea?"

"Oh yeah, she's pregnant," says Sully. "I remember this phase."

"Did your wife kill anyone?" Darnell asks.

"We have a place to start, but we'll need more," says Mike. He's right.

"Beaumont said something interesting when we were talking. I asked about staff who might want Hawkins dead. She said, 'Callahan doesn't want trouble at his game. Tiny is a pushover.' She never mentioned herself."

"Still not enough for an arrest," says Darnell.

"No, but it may be an indication she is itchy to talk." This is Mike. I am reminded again that he is a good cop.

"Bring her in," says Sully.

"She'll know something is up," Darius cautions.

"Find a way to get to her," Sully shoots back.

I cough quietly. "I know a way."

* * *

Lana Beaumont is enjoying herself. She knows exactly what is going on and exactly why she has been called to police headquarters to "answer a few more questions." She also knows we have squat.

I have the corner spot in the interrogation room. Darius is shuffling through a list of questions we've already asked and taking notes carefully as if he has never heard these answers before. Beaumont is playing at being helpful, but her patience is starting to wear. I think she wants to talk, but she has enough smarts to keep her mouth shut.

It's my turn to toss a comment into the mix. "We need to understand Hawkins a little better. Your insight will be helpful."

Beaumont nods. I pull my chair to the table alongside Darius. "Have you ever heard of a zebra finch?" I ask. Beaumont is confused. So is Darius.

"I recently became a birder. Well, really, I've just started my life list. But I've read that the zebra finch is the most promiscuous bird. We understand Hawkins was a zebra finch."

Beaumont stiffens. This may be because she sees where I'm headed. She dismisses my question. "I didn't know him well enough to know."

"But you've seen him dangle women. You've seen him with railbirds. You know he's a flirt. More than a flirt."

"They're all flirts," says Beaumont. "They think women can't wait to take a tumble with them."

"Is there anyone Hawkins liked to tumble with?" I ask. "We hear he's not great when it comes to being faithful. Likes to deal from the bottom of the deck."

Beaumont is still now. It's not fear I'm sensing, but anger. Darius holds up a finger, and the conversation halts. He whispers something in my ear, as planned. "Sorry. Darius is right. He's just pointed out that Hawkins's cheating days are done. He's committed himself fully to his wife. According to her, he said she was the only woman in the world that mattered, that had ever mattered."

I'm thinking Beaumont wants to come across the table at us, at the very least, rant and rage. She doesn't move. On cue, Mike opens the door and ushers in a very pregnant Monica Hawkins. He looks up in mock surprise. "So sorry. I didn't realize this room was taken."

We're not sure if Beaumont has ever seen Hawkins's wife or if she knows about the pregnancy.

Darius waves away the faux mix-up. "No problem."

I turn to Beaumont as if we have accidentally run into each other. "I'm not sure if you've ever met. Lana, this is Monica Hawkins?"

Beaumont has a tell. The look on her face is priceless. She may have known who Monica is; it's clear she has never seen this woman—or her belly—before.

Darius stands up. "Mrs. Hawkins, please let me say how sorry we all are about your husband. Everyone we've spoken with has told us how much he loved you and how thrilled he was about the baby."

Every muscle in Beaumont's body is tense. "That's funny. I never heard him mention her."

"That's not surprising," says Darius. "All the witnesses said how protective he was of Monica. How he wanted to guard her from the sordid side of his life."

It may have been the word "sordid" that clinched things. Beaumont is on her feet. She's yelling with such volume and such speed there is spittle on her face. "He didn't love her. He loved me. He wanted a baby with me. And he got his wish." With this last pronouncement, Beaumont turns triumphantly to Monica.

We've prepared Monica for this. It wasn't easy for her to hear, nor was it a total surprise. Monica meets Beaumont's angry eyes with a steady gaze. When she speaks, it is with dignity. "Funny, he never mentioned you. He said he'd had a fling or two, but they meant nothing."

"I was the reason he got up in the morning," Beaumont screams. It's clear no one in the room believes her. I doubt she even believes herself.

"And yet," Monica says, "he woke up every morning next to me."

"Not anymore," Beaumont hisses.

"He dumped you like a sack of potatoes," Monica says. "He had to pick a woman to cherish. He picked me. He had to pick a kid to love. He picked our kid."

"And look where that got him. Holding a dead man's hand. The one I dealt."

It's Mike who steps in front of Monica before Beaumont can reach her. Darius and I pin Beaumont down. We've got cuffs on her within seconds.

"Lawyer!" she screams.

But it's too late. She's shown her hand.

Story Inspiration

I wrote my first short story, "Swan Song," two years ago in response to a call for submissions from the Crime Writers of Canada. The theme of their fortieth-anniversary anthology was "cold," in the broadest sense of that word. I discovered writing to a theme was fun and productive. It helped me to focus, and at the same time, it opened up a new way of thinking about a crime and the characters who inhabit that world.

E.M. (Em) Montgomery is my first private eye, and "Zebra Finch" is the second story she appears in. The poker setting, of course, was inspired by the theme of this anthology: dangerous games. I toyed with the idea of pickleball or lacrosse, but I know nothing about these sports. Poker, I know.

In the first Em Montgomery story, "Indigo Bunting," she has to solve the murder of an avid bird watcher and becomes interested in the activity. The bird theme has played out—and entitled—all six of the stories to date. I hope you enjoy reading "Zebra Finch" as much as I enjoyed writing it for you.

THE CHESS CONNECTION

Kirlagh James

Kirlagh James, a Maryland native, is a professional proposal writer living and working in Northern Virginia. She incorporates her lifelong affinity for mystery fiction into her debut story, "The Chess Connection."

I rang the bell. Steve didn't answer. I twisted the knob and let myself in as usual, "Steve, I'm here."

He didn't respond. Thinking he might be on the third floor, I took the stairs up to the main living space of his split-level house. The open floor plan provided an unobstructed view of the whole floor straight through the window to the clearing and the woods behind the house. I loved it.

It took me a few seconds to process what I saw in the middle of the floor. Steve was lying unconscious next to the glass coffee table. I started to panic and got lightheaded.

Willing my legs to move, I went to him and checked his pulse. He was cold and stiff. Two years of Criminology and Criminal Justice classes and watching crime dramas did not prepare me to see an actual dead body, especially not Steve's.

After taking a moment to calm down, I called 911.

The operator told me to wait outside for the police to arrive. I didn't want to leave him alone. As I turned to go, I noticed the door to the display case was open. The one where he kept his collection of chess sets. The top shelf had the green and white onyx set he picked up in Afghanistan. The middle shelf housed the jade set from Japan. The third shelf was empty. Where was the Makruk set from Thailand?

I glanced around the living room for the set and any other missing items. The everyday acrylic chess set sat on the gaming table near the window. Steve's phone was on the table next to the couch. He still wore his Rolex and gold chain. Everything but the Makruk set seemed to be here. I went outside as instructed and waited for the police.

Sitting on the hood of my car, I looked down the tree-lined street. Single-family homes sat neatly spaced on both sides of the road. The old, mid-modern neighborhood looked different from the cookie-cutter ones sprouting all over the D.C. metro area.

Steve used to say, "I feel like I set the flux capacitor to 1970 when I drive down this road. I expect Marsha Brady to walk down the sidewalk any minute."

I gave him the blue light stare.

That's when he said, "You need a proper education."

And we spent the day watching Back to the Future and episodes of The Brady Bunch. The memory made me feel like crying, but I couldn't get the tears out.

* * *

The first officer arrived at the house, and I introduced myself. I told him about Steve, and he told me to wait outside until the supervising officer came. He secured the scene.

Another officer arrived a few minutes later, followed by the Medical Examiner. Then a hawkish-looking man in his fifties parked his dark grey Charger across the street and watched.

The second officer began to ask me questions. "What's your name?"

"Katie MacLeod."

"Do you live here?"

"Technically, yes. I use this address for school tuition, but I live at my sorority house most of the year and spend the summers in Connecticut with my parents. This is my uncle's house."

"What happened?"

I repeated what I told the first officer, then said, "I think this might be a burglary too, but I'm not sure. His Makruk set is missing."

"What's a Makruk set?"

"Makruk is Thai chess. It's similar to chess, but some of the piece movements and starting positions are different. His is a wooden replica of a traditional set. The king, queen, bishop, and rook look like round balls with spires on top. The knights look like horses, and the pawns look a bit like marshmallows."

He gave me the stare I gave Steve about the flux capacitor. I did a quick search on my phone and showed him a picture. "It looks like this, only the red pieces are stained black in Steve's set."

"Was it expensive?"

"Not compared to Steve's watch and gold chain. I've seen some sets online for eighty-five dollars up to six hundred."

"Are you sure it's not somewhere in the house? Or maybe he loaned it to someone?"

"I didn't see it, and he wouldn't loan it out. His unit gave it to him when he retired from the military. He took it with him to Thailand last week."

"Thailand?"

"He went to visit some friends and play in a Makruk tournament. His last duty station was the US Embassy in Thailand. He served as the Detachment Commander for the Marine Security Guards there. Retired at the end of last year. He called this his gap year. He wanted to take time to figure out what he wanted to be when he grew up."

* * *

Soon, the street was filled with marked and unmarked Crown Vic police cars, the mobile forensic lab, and neighbors. I stood amongst the onlookers while the police processed the house and canvased the neighborhood. Steve told me the world could be a very hard place to live in. I had to be able to handle anything that came my way. I guess this is what he meant.

The lead detective, Detective Adams, approached us. He was in his mid-thirties and reminded me of a younger version of Steve.

I repeated my story to him, and I got the stare again. I pulled out my phone and showed him a picture. He took down my information and continued his investigation.

The crowd began to thin. Eventually, the man from the Charger joined me on the sidewalk. He was dressed similarly to Detective Adams. He showed me his badge and introduced himself, "I'm Agent Russo, Naval Criminal Investigation Service. Do you live here?"

"Yes, but I am at the sorority house during the school year. My uncle and I have a few seshes every month, eating our way through the day. Sometimes we play chess, but we usually watch sports. Our matches don't usually last long. He slays…slayed at chess."

"I knew Steve."

"Agent Russo, do you think it's strange that his Makruk set is missing, but he is still wearing his Rolex and gold chain?"

"Makruk set?"

"Yeah. It's a type of chess set."

"I know."

"I think you and I are the only two people out here that do."

He nodded. "Not a surprise. Can you point out which one is the lead detective? I need to have a word."

* * *

The Medical Examiner's team removed Steve's body, and the forensics team finished processing the house. Detective Adams said, "The ME is going to perform an autopsy to confirm the cause of death. Looks like natural causes, but he needs to confirm."

I gave him the side eye. "Natural causes? Like a heart attack?"

"Something like that."

"Hard to believe. He's so young. Never had a heart problem."

The detective pulled a notebook and a pen out of his pocket and wrote in it. I couldn't see what he was writing, "There was no forced entry."

"Well, what's the deal with the Makruk set?"

"We're looking into it."

"You don't believe it was stolen, do you? You talked to Agent Russo, right?"

"Yes."

"Yes, you don't believe it was stolen, or yes, you spoke to Agent Russo?"

"I spoke to Russo. We're looking into it."

"Now what?"

"I'll let you know if there are any developments." He handed me his card.

* * *

I needed answers. Time to talk to Ms. Shirley. Lucky for me, we were in tight after chatting away at the St. Patrick's Day party a few weeks ago. Steve used to call her the eyes and ears of the neighborhood.

She lived in a corner house, four doors down from Steve. I found her weeding in the front yard.

"Ms. Shirley!"

"Katie, Katie, I am so sorry about Steve." She gave me a big bear hug, and I started to cry. "He was a good neighbor. He helped me weed and mulch my garden a few weekends ago. I can't believe it!" She pulled out of the hug. "So many strange things happening around our neighborhood. Did the police tell you I saw a dark sedan parked in front of my house about one this morning? I have a lot of trouble sleeping these days."

"A dark sedan?"

"It was kind of sporty. I'm not good with makes and models, but I've never seen it in the neighborhood. It was gone when I got up for the day, about dawn."

"Did you see the driver?"

"No. It was dark, and I couldn't see if anyone was inside."

"Did any of the other neighbors see or hear anything?

"I don't think they did. People seem to be more interested in asking questions not sharing. Couldn't hurt to ask around."

"Thanks. I will"

And I did. I talked to both of Steve's next-door neighbors and the family who lived across the street. Total dead end. It was a hot night, and everyone had their windows closed with the A/C running.

Between the stress of the day and my self-defense class the night before, every muscle in my body was sore, and I just wanted sleep. It was time for me to head back to College Park.

I realized I hadn't set Steve's burglar alarm. I walked back to Steve's house, activated the alarm, and left.

* * *

I woke to chimes ringing at full volume. It was three-thirty in the morning. The security company was calling. I answered. Steve had listed me as the backup when he'd gone to Thailand, and I guess he never changed it back when he returned.

The operator said Steve's house alarm was triggered. They called the police, and I called Detective Adams. He told me he would meet me at the house.

I arrived a few minutes before four-thirty am. Four Crown Vics, with their lights strobing in the darkness, blocked most of the road. Three neighbors stood on the street talking to police, and neighbors within eye shot of the house peered through their windows. Detective Adams examined a ground-level window.

Climbing up the embankment, he said, "Someone tried to get inside through that window using a glass cutter. They didn't make it in. The alarm must have stopped them."

"The Makruk set thief is still looking for something. Do you know what it is?"

"Ms. MacLeod, this is an active investigation."

"Call me Katie. I might be able to help if you tell me what's going on."

"Someone wants something, and they think it's in the house."

I saw Ms. Shirley waving at me from the crowd. She hurried over. "That dark sedan was back again. This time, someone jumped into it and drove off. I didn't get a good look at the person or the plates. It could have been a man."

"What time was this?" Detective Adams asked.

"Close to three-thirty."

"That's when the alarm company called me," I said.

"I'm going to finish interviewing the neighbors," Detective Adams said. "I'll arrange for a patrol car to pass down this street periodically."

"Can you text me when I can go into the house?"

I hung out with the neighbors until the hardware store opened. I needed to find something to cover the window. Then I went to my favorite local diner to drown myself in French fries and coffee.

* * *

I was on my third cup and playing online chess when I spotted Agent Russo standing in the doorway of the diner. He was looking for someone, and I figured it was me, so I flagged him over.

"Agent Russo, are you stalking me?" I said, grinning.

"What? No. Detective Adams said I might find you here."

"Just kidding," I said. I didn't remember telling the detective where I was going.

"He called me about the break-in. I think it's time I fill you in."

"Finally, some answers."

"NCIS is looking into a gem smuggling operation being run through US Embassies, using the Marine Security Guards. We don't know who all the players are. Three months before Steve made his permanent change of station back to the States, the former Detachment Commander recruited him into the operation."

My whole body felt like it was contorting. "Steve, a smuggler? Be serious!

He would never do that."

"I'm afraid he did."

"Is that why someone took the Makruk set?"

"Each piece contained a ruby from the Mogôk mine in Myanmar. Thirty-two rubies, each a carat to a carat and a half."

"That's a ton of guap."

"Guap?"

"Money."

"Yes, Millions in this case."

"How did he pass along the gems? That was over six months ago, and he still has…had the set."

"The pieces unscrewed. The smugglers used a bolt adhesive to secure them, so someone in customs couldn't take them apart with their bare hands. He needed pliers to twist them open.

"His contact left a burner phone in his mailbox and sent him text messages about where and when to drop them."

"A dead drop?"

"In a local park about a half mile from one of the entrances."

"So, his trip to Thailand was another ruby run?"

"He brought the Makruk set with him and swapped it out for an identical set filled with rubies."

"The scheme with the dead drop worked. Why did his contact change their operation and go to Steve's house?"

"Good question. Maybe Steve didn't show."

"The Medical Examiner thinks his death was due to natural causes. Did he die before he could make the drop?"

"Possibly."

"Thank you for telling me about Steve."

"Be careful." Agent Russo handed me his card. "Call me if you find anything."

Now I had two reasons to get back to the house. Fix the window AND find the rubies.

Detective Adams texted; *Forensics is finished.*

I sent him a thumbs-up. Then I texted, *Agent Russo found me at the diner. Told me about the rubies.*

I unloaded the plywood and nails from my car and brought them down to Steve's office. The burglar probably tried to get in through this room out of convenience. It was at ground level and obscured by the embankment. I needed a hammer to board up this broken window.

Entering the laundry room, I was stunned by Steve's organizational skills. Everything from his tools to the laundry detergent was neatly shelved. I found a hammer right away.

My phone gave two short vibrations. Detective Adams texted, *What diner? What rubies?*

I replied, "*The one you told him I was at. He told me about the smuggling ring.*"

After I finished nailing the board over the window, I looked around the room. I knew I should leave, but I might never get this chance again. "Okay, Steve, where would you stash a bunch of rubies? You have a place for everything."

The police didn't find them yesterday. A secret compartment? Close but out of the way. Your bedroom?

I went to the third floor. The sixty-year-old stairs squeaked with every step. In the silent house, it sounded like something out of a horror movie.

When I got to his bedroom door, I felt like I was intruding. I walked across the room, creaking all the way. I never realized how squeaky these old floors were.

I opened the closet, pushed the clothes aside, and scanned the walls, hoping to find something they missed yesterday. No anomalies in the walls. No attic access door.

My phone vibrated twice, announcing another text.

I got down on the floor. Two boards didn't follow the same alternating pattern as the rest. They were evenly aligned, and they made an eight-inch by four-inch rectangle. My heart fluttered. I went to the nightstand, looking for something to lift the boards with, when I saw the last text from Detective Adams. "*I don't know what you are talking about.*"

Starting to think that Detective Adams was crazy, I remembered what I said to Agent Russo at the diner. Was he stalking me? Why?

I tried calling Detective Adams, but the phone went to voicemail.

I continued searching for something to help me lift the boards. I remembered Steve had a knife in his nightstand for protection. Once I got the board up, I could see a jewelry pouch and a cell phone. I got butterflies in my stomach. My hands were sweating when I picked up the pouch. I peeked inside. Shiny red rubies.

I wasn't sure what to do next. I'd never seen a mini hoard of rubies before, and it was more than a bit tempting to dump them out and play with them. I know Agent Russo wanted me to call if I found anything, but I thought twice about it and texted Detective Adams instead, *"I found the rubies and a phone."*

Two more vibrations emanated from my phone. Detective Adams replied, *"Where are you?"*

I texted, *"Steve's house."*

He replied, *"On my way. Be there in ten."*

I sent a thumbs-up emoji.

The tension of the last twenty-eight hours was taking its toll. I lay on the bed and stared at Steve's clothes hanging in the closet. My excitement from finding the rubies quickly turned to grief. It was horrible, knowing I would never see him again. I couldn't hold back the tears. They welled up in my eyes and trickled down my nose onto the pillow. I was a soggy mess.

* * *

Floorboards squeaked, breaking the quiet. My heart rate quickened. I sat still and strained to hear. A few more squeaks. It sounded like footsteps.

My heart started racing faster. Did I forget to lock the door?

It couldn't be Detective Adams. Too soon.

I got off the bed slowly and walked to the bedroom door. A floorboard let out a groan halfway there.

No. No. No.

I stopped and listened. Did they hear me?

I couldn't hear any movement now. I shut the door and made my way to the closet, trying to avoid the betraying board. I was almost there when another board gave me away.

Again, I stopped and listened. I heard footsteps. They seemed closer. I closed the door as quietly as I could. I turned the phone to silent mode and texted Detective Adams again. *Someone's in the house.*

I called 911.

The footsteps were slow but continued to get closer. They must have known someone was here. They had to have come in the front door.

My phone flickered. Detective Adams replied. *Five minutes out. Call 911. Done.* I replied.

I heard the stairs creak one after another until the footsteps stopped on the landing. I heard a familiar voice call out, "Katie, it's Agent Russo."

I almost called out when a text flashed across my phone, and then my stomach turned. *Agent Russo isn't who he says he is.*

It was quiet for a moment, then the squeaky board in the middle of Steve's room cried out. My adrenaline pumped through me like a rocket, and my heart was pounding in my ears. I realized I'd left the knife on the other side of the room.

An instinctive fearlessness within me roared to life, melting away the panic that was trying to take hold. I remembered something from my self-defense class. The doorknob turned. I screamed as loud as I could, grabbed the knob, and threw all my weight against the door, taking Agent Russo off guard. Planting my left foot on the ground, I swung my right foot up into his crotch and punched him square in the nose as he was doubling over. I grabbed the first cable I saw, the phone charger, and tied his hands behind his back. Then, for good measure, I used the electrical cord from the alarm clock to tie his feet together.

I hurried down the stairs and out the front door. I shut the door behind me and ran out into the street. An unmarked Crown Vic was coming down the road.

The cavalry.

Detective Adams got out of the car. "You all right?"

Nodding, I pointed behind me. "Agent Russo. Master bedroom."
Police cars flooded the street for the third time in two days.

* * *

Fifteen minutes later, Detective Adams joined me on the curb. "He's in custody. You did a number on him. The alarm clock tied around his feet was a nice touch."

"Who is he?"

Just as Detective Adams was about to answer, a woman in her late twenties dressed like him approached. "I'm Agent Russo, NCIS."

"You can't be," I said.

"It's true."

"I knew something was wrong when you texted me from the diner. I didn't know you were there," Detective Adams said. "I started making phone calls."

"Then who is in the house pretending to be you?" I said, pointing to the woman.

"I'm not sure," she said. "The smugglers have been one step ahead of us since the investigation started."

"Was Uncle Steve really a smuggler? The other Agent Russo told me he was carrying rubies out of Thailand."

"I can't give you the details. Just know that if Steve hadn't tipped us off, we wouldn't have known about the operation. He was one of the good guys."

Detective Adams extended his hand and helped me up off the curb. "Katie, you held your own in a very dangerous situation today. I'm impressed."

"Your uncle would have been proud," Agent Russo said.

"Detective Adams, shall we find out who's been impersonating me?" As I watched, the detective and Agent Russo walk back to the house, a new level of confidence settled inside me. I knew I could handle anything.

Story Inspiration
  I found inspiration for this story in many places, from my personal life to

crime dramas. In fact, I had so many ideas the story had two prior plots, but these stories didn't gel. I took a step back and settled on the title, "The Chess Connection." And like the movie The French Connection, *I decided the story should be about smuggling. What could get smuggled using chess? Gems! Rubies are my birthstone.*

Research into ruby mining and smuggling led me to Thailand, and I changed chess to Makruk. I needed a way to get the rubies back to the US, and I found it in my experience working with Marines and writing proposals for guard services at US government facilities worldwide. The mid-modern neighborhood where I live brought the setting to life. And Katie, my protagonist, is how I remember all of my confident, passionate, and caring sorority sisters. FYI, I bought my first chess set while writing this story.

THE QUIZMASTER'S LAST ROUND

Kerry Hammond

Kerry Hammond's stories have appeared in Malice Domestic: Mystery Most Geographical, Malice Domestic: Mystery Most Diabolical, *and* Mystery Most International. *Her story, "Strangers at a Table," appeared in the* Best Mystery Stories of the Year *anthology, edited by Amor Towles. Her story, "Sins of the Father," received an Agatha award nomination.*

"A murder, it's a murder of crows," whispered Drew as he tapped his finger on the table.

"Are you sure?" said Tara. "That doesn't sound right."

"Drew is in charge of collective nouns, so we need to trust him," said Katie. They had all agreed that Katie would be the quiz team captain, so when she spoke, it shut down any arguments. Drew smirked. Tara narrowed her eyes and glared at him. Jack just shook his head and smiled.

"Okay, players, pens down." Quizmaster Kirk scanned the room to make sure all pens were indeed down. He was a stickler for the rules and would disqualify a team one second over the allowed time. It sometimes seemed like he went looking for someone to break the rules so he could bring down the hammer.

When time was called, Katie made sure to mic drop her pen in the middle of the table, and all members of The Fearless Four leaned back in their chairs with their hands up. The semifinals were not the time to get disqualified. Not when they were one of only four teams still competing.

"Okay, team, we got this," said Katie. She wasn't just the team captain, she was also the mother figure in the group, the one who smoothed things over and gave much-needed encouragement.

It was hard to believe that the team had been playing for almost a year. Last February, Katie lost her grandmother, a woman who had been more of a mother to her than her actual mother. She took the loss hard, and Drew, Tara, and Jack had tried to distract her. They weren't just her co-workers. They were her adopted family. The group called themselves The Fearless Four and got together after work at least once a week for happy hour or dinner.

Katie found that going out to dinner or drinks with her friends didn't help. It was too easy for her to think about her grandmother and let her mind wander when they were just hanging out and chatting. She needed more to occupy her mind.

One night, while walking home from dinner, she saw a sign for a Thursday night quiz at a bar in her neighborhood. She went inside and registered. Team name: The Fearless Four. She knew she could convince the others to join her. She had only expected it to be a one-night thing.

"Want a drink, Tara? We've got about twenty minutes before Kirk calls the results," said Drew as he pushed back his chair and stood. He was over six feet tall and lifted weights at the office gym every day at lunchtime. He got lots of looks from women, and Katie could tell that he liked it.

"I'll come with you. I need to stretch my legs," said Tara. She and Drew were like siblings, bickering one minute and laughing at an inside joke the next. Tara often gave her opinion on the women Drew dated, and he always took her advice; they were extremely close, but platonically so.

Tara and Drew had agreed to quiz night right away. They were extremely competitive at work, often up for the same sales goal awards at the advertising agency where they worked. Giving them another chance to compete was a no-brainer. Katie noticed that the quiz nights had drawn them even closer. She wondered if sparks would ever fly.

"Those two really make me laugh," said Jack. He pushed his empty glass forward and leaned on the table. Katie nodded and smiled, watching as the two in question walked to the bar.

"I know, me too," said Katie. "I knew they'd love quiz night, but have you noticed them arguing less? You never know, maybe something else will come of it." She gave Jack a wink.

"Matchmaking, are you? I don't know, I can't see them in a relationship. I think they work as good friends, but maybe not as a couple." Jack looked down at his lap, suddenly shy.

Jack could be intense and had been a slightly harder sell for quiz night. He could be self-conscious, too, and in the strangest of circumstances. He and Katie worked as support staff for the agency. Neither wanted the stress of meeting sales goals or trying to sign new clients. They preferred to work on the accounts that Tara and Drew landed. Jack had his go-with-the-flow moments, so even though he was hesitant, Katie didn't have to push too hard to get Jack to agree. It helped that they had been dating at the time.

They had hooked up at the office holiday party and dated for about three months. Katie would have broken it off sooner, but it's taboo to break up with someone too close to Valentine's Day, so she had waited until the end of March. Jack was a nice guy. He just wasn't for her. Katie liked men with strong personalities, and Jack just wasn't that guy. His self-conscious, always doubting himself thing really got to her.

They had stayed friends after the breakup, and things were only awkward for a few weeks.

Jack started dating a girl from accounting a few months later, and by that time, Katie was secretly dating Kirk. She refused to call him Quizmaster Kirk, and it rankled him.

There were sparks between Katie and Kirk when they started chatting that first quiz night, even though they were both dating other people. Neither acted on it immediately. They didn't go on their first date until Katie had broken up with Jack and Kirk had ended his relationship. Katie was the jealous type, so she never asked any questions about Jack's former girlfriend. When it came up, they both called her 'the ex.' Luckily, that was a rare occurrence. The one thing that eased her mind a bit, and made her laugh, was finding out that 'the ex' had gotten a tattoo of a heart with Kirk's initials inside. Who does that? Even Kirk thought that was a bit over the top.

They kept their relationship a secret because they didn't want anyone to think that Kirk played favorites with Katie's quiz team. She hadn't even told the rest of The Fearless Four yet, but she wondered if any of them suspected. Sometimes it was hard to act normal around Kirk, to keep her flirting in check. She also had to turn down invites to after-work get-togethers when she and Kirk had a date.

She really dreaded Jack finding out about Kirk, even though they didn't get together until she and Jack had split. One of Jack's ex-girlfriends had cheated on him, and he took it hard. Infidelity, even the possibility of it, would not go over well. It was one of the only things that cracked his calm demeanor. She also valued Jack as a friend. She didn't want to lose that friendship.

Katie stood up to stretch. It was amazing how tight your muscles got during each round. "I'm going to get a drink too, ready for another one?" she said. She knew that Jack limited himself to one alcoholic drink during the quiz, then celebrated with another when Kirk was computing the final round's scores.

"Yeah, I'll have a drink. It's my turn to buy, though. I'll meet you up there. Need to hit the restroom."

Katie walked up to the bar. "Hey Katie," said Melissa. "Same again?" Melissa was their favorite bartender, and she worked every quiz night. She could mix a mean martini and never poured a beer with too much head.

"Yes, please," said Katie, putting her empty martini glass on the bar. She scanned the room, sizing up her competition. Tonight's game would eliminate two of the four teams. Next week would be the finals, and one team would be crowned the quiz night winners and receive the $1,000 cash prize.

"What do you think about our chances?" Jack returned and sidled up to the bar next to Katie, slipping both hands into his pockets.

"I think we have a good chance," said Katie. "I could see the hesitation on the Quizinators' faces when Kirk asked that question about southern hemisphere constellations."

Melissa set a vodka martini with a twist in front of Katie, which was her usual. "Here you go, hon. What'll you have, Jack?"

"I'll take a pint of the IPA and pour one for Kirk, too, please." Jack always bought Kirk a beer after the final round as a thank you. Kirk didn't drink during the game but loved a beer when he announced the results. Jack always left it on the table across from Kirk, so it was there when he was done scoring and didn't interrupt his concentration. Melissa put two pints down on the bar, and Jack tapped his card to pay. He grabbed one of the pints of beer and walked across the room to deliver it, his one hand back in his pocket.

He returned a moment later to grab his beer. "Kirk says about five more minutes. I think it's a close call; he looks stressed." They both made their way back to the table in time to hear Tara and Drew arguing about whether Turkey was in Europe or Asia.

Katie, the geography expert in the group, ended the fight. "It's both Europe *and* Asia. You're both right, so stop." Each member of the team oversaw a handful of quiz topics and were meant to study up on those topics prior to each game. They had tweaked the categories a few times but had settled on a good mix. Katie was geography, poisons, 1980s TV, world wars, and celebrity couples. Jack was sports, world festivals, classical music, United States history, and literature. Tara and Drew filled in the rest. With a team of only four people, you had to be diversified.

Kirk prided himself on asking things that weren't the norm. He liked to be the Quizmaster that stood out from the crowd. It worked too. He was booked nearly five out of seven nights each week, in different bars across town. Sometimes that only left one or two nights for Katie, but she didn't mind; she didn't like clingy relationships.

"It's time for the final results." Kirk was back on the microphone, and a hush fell over the room. "As you know, only two teams will go on to the finals next week. The other two teams will be eliminated from the competition." Kirk loved announcing the winners. He loved the suspense of it all, the fact that every eye in the bar was on him. He could be such a ham.

"The first team going on to the final round is." He took a swig of his beer, counted to five in his head, then continued. "Trivial Terminators." A cheer went up from the Terminators' table, and the four guys on that team exchanged high fives and chest bumps.

"Only one spot left," said Drew. "I swear, I've never been more nervous in my life."

"Stop being so dramatic," said Tara. We're going to get it, we're just as good as the Terminators."

"And now, the final spot in next week's quiz championship." This time Kirk counted to ten and took a gulp of his beer. He swallowed and set his drink down on the bar. "The final spot goes to The Fearless Four."

Tara and Drew jumped up and did a hip bump and happy dance. You would have thought that one of them had scored a touchdown. Katie let out a whoop, and Jack gave her a bear hug. "Another round of drinks for The Fearless Four—on me!" he yelled.

The Fearless Four spent the next week studying their individual categories. Katie turned down all social engagements and spent each evening with flashcards of questions from trivia games and questionnaires she found online. She and Jack exchanged sets of questions and talked on the phone every night for an hour, asking question after question until a timer went off.

"Do you think Kirk will ask any questions about obscure wars?" asked Jack. "I know you mostly concentrate on World Wars I and II."

"I don't know, he hasn't in the past, but that doesn't mean he won't now."

"Oh, okay. I just thought, you know, that you might, well, know." He broke off, and the silence hung between them for a few seconds. "Never mind, I'm sure we'll be good."

Tara and Drew were so hyper-focused that they stopped arguing at work. Like Katie and Jack, they traded flashcards and randomly, throughout the day, they would pass each other's desk and throw out a question. It was good to see the team working together.

Kirk and Katie decided not to get together or talk prior to the finals. She was busy studying, and he didn't want to give anything away. Katie hadn't studied that hard since she was a college student, but it felt good when she was able to memorize obscure facts about unrelated subjects.

When finals night rolled around, The Fearless Four felt ready. The bar created a custom cocktail for the night: the Quiztini. It was slightly sweet, had a golden hue, and was full of alcohol. Each of the gang decided to get one to calm their nerves. They really wanted to win.

Kirk started with his usual opening remarks and explanation of the rules. Quiz Night was a weekly occurrence, but there were always those who just wandered in for a drink and were therefore unfamiliar with what was happening. Many people came in each week to watch the quiz, but not participate.

When the questions kicked in, The Fearless Four were on fire. Kirk calculated the scores after each of the rounds. At the end of the second round, they were two points ahead of The Terminators. They took a fifteen-minute break, and Drew went up to get another drink. He was having trouble sitting still.

"Two more rounds to go," said Jack. "We got this."

"I sure hope so," said Tara. "At this point, it's not even about the money; I just want to beat The Terminators. They're so smug."

"Didn't you date that Terminator with the blond hair last year?" Katie asked, looking over at the team's table.

"We went out twice," Tara replied. "I don't think that counts as dating. He was just as smug then as he is now, and I want to beat him." She crossed her arms over her chest and gave the other team a sideways glance.

Kirk started the next round with a geography question. "What is the capital of Panama?"

"Panama City," said Katie. Drew wrote it down and gave Katie a tight nod to show he knew she'd have the answer.

The questions flew by, and the team was hyper-focused. By the time they finished round four, there was only one answer they weren't sure was right. When Kirk called time, Drew tossed the pen on the table, and they all leaned back, hands up. It was a relief that the questions were finished, and Katie let out a breath she didn't know she was holding.

They all pushed back their chairs at the same time and headed for the bar. They wanted to grab drinks before the other team, so they could avoid small talk.

Melissa anticipated their orders. Katie's martini was on the counter, and she was pouring two IPAs for Jack. He took one hand out of his pocket, grabbed one of the beers, and headed over to Kirk. When he returned for his glass, only Drew was left standing at the bar, waiting for his Quiztini.

"Like our odds?" said Drew, looking like he needed reassurance.

"I do, man, I really do." Jack knew that telling Drew that he was worried wouldn't help, so he kept it to himself.

When they returned to the table, Katie and Tara were sipping their drinks in silence. To break the ice, Jack asked Tara about her latest boyfriend. He knew she'd met someone on a dating app last month and was miraculously still seeing him. She went through men like Kleenex.

"So, his name is Brett and he's actually kind of nice." She continued to regale her friends with stories about the five dates they'd been on, how considerate Brett was, and what beautiful babies they would have. Everyone relaxed and got lost in her story, forgetting about the quiz for a few minutes.

"Okay, quizzers," said Kirk, walking back to the edge of the bar with his beer. He raised his glass in the air toward Jack as a thank you and took a large swallow. "I'm a bit parched after that exciting game. I know you're all waiting for the scores." Kirk's voice cracked, and he cleared his throat. He took another sip of his beer. "As I was saying–" He coughed again, this time setting the beer down on the bar and putting his hand to his throat.

Kirk dropped his clipboard and fell to the floor in a heap. Everyone in the bar was speechless, and it was a few seconds before Jack yelled, "Someone call an ambulance." The rest was a blur, people moving and shouting. There was a ringing in Katie's ears that didn't subside until Kirk's body had been removed, and she sat across the table from Detective Stone in a booth to the left of the bar's entrance.

"I know it's been a long night, Katie, but I do need to ask you a few questions," said the detective.

"It all happened so fast, I just don't know," said Katie, a tear rolling down her cheek.

"Is it true that you and the deceased were dating?"

Katie looked up sharply. "How did you know?"

"Let's stick with my questions for now," said the detective kindly. "It's true then?"

When Katie nodded, she continued. "How long had the relationship been going on?"

Katie told the detective about meeting Kirk at the first quiz night and how she'd been in a relationship with Jack but that a few weeks later, she and Kirk got together—when they were both single. The detective wrote furiously in a small brown notebook she held in her hand. Katie found herself slowing her speech to give the detective time to write everything down.

"You were in a relationship with Jack when you met Kirk. That must have been awkward when you started dating Kirk and Jack was on your quiz team."

"Not really, Jack didn't know I was dating Kirk. Besides, he's dating someone at work now," said Katie. She didn't want the detective to think she was a horrible person.

"All of your friends knew you were dating Kirk," said the detective. "I've taken all their statements, and they're all worried about you because they know you've suffered a loss." She tipped her head to the side and focused on Katie. "So I'll ask again, was it awkward?"

"No, it wasn't. I swear. I'm totally surprised they knew. If it had been awkward, I would have suspected that Jack knew." The last part sounded more like a question than a statement. She remembered his comment when they were studying, when he wondered if she had knowledge of what Kirk would ask. She also remembered that his mood changed slightly when Kirk's name was mentioned at the office. She'd known him long enough to notice the change but hadn't been able to connect it to Kirk until now.

"Okay, let's switch gears, shall we?" The detective had a way of being firm, but gentle at the same time.

"I understand that Jack always bought Kirk a drink after round four. Did he do that tonight?"

Katie hesitated before answering. She knew that the detective must already have her answer, so there was no use lying. "Yes, he bought him a beer."

"And he always delivered the beer to Kirk at his table, while he was scoring the game. While he was concentrating on the scorecards," she added. Again, this was a statement, so Katie just nodded.

"Katie, I'm going to be straight with you." Detective Stone put her notebook down and pulled her chair closer to the table. The squeak of the chair legs against the floor made Katie wince. "We know for a fact that Kirk was killed with a fast-acting poison. We think that poison was administered in his glass of beer. Do you know anything about that?"

Katie's eyes were as wide as beer coasters. "No, I don't know anything about that. And I'm sure Jack doesn't either, just ask him."

"Oh, we did, we asked him. He claims to know nothing about it. But you see, Katie, Jack was in the perfect position to add something to the drink when he walked it over to Kirk, out of sight of everyone else. Kirk would have been busy scoring the game and wouldn't have noticed. The beer was an IPA, I believe." The detective checked her notes as if she just wanted to make sure she'd gotten it right. "IPAs are on the bitter side, which would be a great way to mask a poison. Once we get the tests back, we'll know what type of poison was used, and we can trace how Jack got ahold of it."

"You can't be serious," Katie pleaded. "Jack wouldn't poison Kirk. As she spoke, she saw two uniformed police officers enter the bar, one male and one female. The male officer pulled a set of handcuffs off his belt and approached the table where Tara, Drew, and Jack sat. He spoke to Jack, and Jack stood up and put his hands in front of him.

"No," said Katie. "You can't arrest him." She stood up, and so did the detective.

"Thanks for your cooperation, Katie. That's all the questions I have for you at the moment."

Detective Stone joined the police officer who had handcuffed Jack, spoke a few words, then led Jack out of the bar. The uniformed officer stayed behind, starting a hushed conversation with his female partner.

Katie went over to the table where Drew and Tara were sitting. "This is bull," Tara said. "Jack didn't kill anyone."

"I know," said Drew. "There's just no way. They've got it all wrong. Don't they?"

"What do you mean, don't they?" Tara looked accusingly at Drew as she picked up her water glass and took a tentative sip. "You don't think Jack poisoned Kirk, you can't."

"Well, I mean, he didn't like Katie dating Kirk. It's always the quiet ones." He looked sheepishly at Katie.

"I can't believe you all knew that Kirk and I were dating. Why didn't you say?"

"It was clear you didn't want us to know," said Tara. "So we pretended we didn't. We figured you would tell us when you were ready. Jack wasn't happy about it, we could tell, but he'd never do anything about it." She put her hand on Katie's shoulder and gave it a squeeze. "It'll be okay, Katie, we're here for you." She put the water glass to her lips, changed her mind, and set it down with a shake of her head. "Do you know why we can't leave yet?" she asked, changing the subject.

"The detective said they want to do some sort of swab for poisonous residue, but their technician is at another crime scene, so we have to wait," said Drew. "Katie, you are our poison expert, can't you figure something out?"

"I know about poisons, but I've never seen anyone poisoned. Besides, I wasn't close enough to Kirk to see anything. Was there foam around his mouth? Was there a smell of bitter almonds? I just don't know. It could be anything. Heck, it could have been olives."

"Olives?" said Drew and Tara in unison.

"Yeah, he was deathly allergic to olives. That's why he only drank beer at the bar, and why I always got my martini with a twist instead of dirty. The bars where he runs quiz night have to agree to not have olives or olive juice on site. He's that good at his job. Quiz nights drive a lot of business."

Before Katie could say more, there was a commotion behind the bar, and everything happened at once. The male police officer who had put handcuffs on Jack stepped onto a barstool and used the leverage to catapult himself over the bar. The policewoman who was with him yelled "catch" and threw a set of handcuffs through the air that he caught with his left hand; his right hand was on Melissa's wrist.

Melissa had a jar of olives in her one hand and was attempting to put it into the purse she held in the other. Before she could complete the task, the cuffs were on her, and the policeman had used a bar towel to take the jar away from her.

Katie's hands were over her mouth as if to stifle a scream, and Drew had moved closer to Tara, putting a protective arm around her. Tara had leaned into Drew, holding onto his shirt front.

"You're coming with us, miss," said the policeman to Melissa, who scowled at the three remaining members of The Fearless Four.

Before the policeman could steer Melissa from behind the bar, they heard a voice and turned to see Detective Stone walking into the bar alongside Jack, whose hands were no longer in cuffs. They were smiling, and Detective Stone was patting him on the shoulder. "Thanks for your help, Jack. We really appreciate it."

The three stunned friends looked at each other and then at Jack. "What's going on, man?" asked Drew. "Are you not under arrest anymore?"

"I never was," said Jack with another grin. "When Detective Stone first interviewed me, she asked for my help. She needed me to play along when she pretended to arrest me. See, she suspected Melissa from the beginning. The medical examiner saw that Kirk wore a wrist band with his allergy on it, and Detective Stone saw a jar of olives behind the bar. The detective is a regular here and has seen that note on the menu that says they don't carry olives.

Jack gave a smile at his friends' rapt attention and continued. "She figured that Melissa was the only one who had access to the jar and was the one who brought it in, but that wasn't enough. Unless Melissa tried to cover it up or take the jar with her, they had no evidence. She figured that if she pretended to arrest me, Melissa might try something. And it worked." He beamed at them, as if the whole plan had been his idea from the start.

"I'll take it from here, nice work both of you," said Detective Stone to the two uniformed officers as she grabbed Melissa's arm to lead her out of the bar.

When Detective Stone and Melissa passed the group of friends, Katie looked down at Melissa's hands, cuffed in front of her. That's when she saw it. On the inside of Melissa's arm, just below her watch band, there was a small pink heart.

Tattooed inside that heart, in a small black font, were Kirk's initials.

Story Inspiration:

I watch a lot of British TV and have seen entire shows dedicated to a group of people who either meet or bond at their local pub on quiz night. I thought I would take this one step further and wondered what would happen if murder were to ensue at such a quiz competition.

LUCKY NIGHT

Robert Lopresti

Robert Lopresti is a retired librarian who lives in the Pacific Northwest. His 120-plus stories have won the Derringer and Black Orchid Novella Awards. He recently edited Crimes Against Nature: New Stories of Environmental Villainy.

I yawned as I stumbled into my hotel suite and hung up my overcoat. I was trying to choose between Scotch and coffee: would I go to bed at five A.M. or try to get through the day without sleep? Neither choice was very appetizing. All-night poker games can really throw off your body clock, especially games as wild as—

"Good morning, Mr. Patterson."

I had turned the corner into the living room, and there he was, a stranger, sitting comfortably on the couch. He wore a nice gray suit that clashed with the bright red ski mask that covered his face. Also, in one gloved hand, he held a big steel gun.

"Who the hell are you?" I asked.

"Sit down, please. I'm here to congratulate the big winner."

He knew about the poker game. I sat down. "Oh. You're here to rob me."

He chuckled, very pleased with himself. "Well, it's not fair for a visitor to take so much money out of town, is it? I'm trying to help the local economy."

So was I. This was my hometown, after all. I had gone to school here and worked for a manufacturer of precision tools for ten years until I finally realized that they were never going to catch up to the modern world.

So, I had moved over two states and started my own company. The company had blossomed, and now I was back home to open a branch office.

I needed someone to run it for me, someone who knew both the area and the business. My two top candidates for the job still worked at the old firm.

Larry had been my best friend there. A great guy, everybody's pal. Too bad he thought budgets were for wimps.

Sam, on the other hand, was a financial genius. With the personality of a dentist drill.

It was a classic business-school question: Do you hire an outside man or an inside man? A people person to bring in customers, or a numbers guy to make every penny count?

The best solution is to hire both, but I couldn't afford that, so I had been in town for three days, struggling to make the toughest decision since I opened my business.

When Sam invited both Larry and me to his weekly poker game, I jumped at the chance, hoping that I'd learn something that would help me make up my mind. And I'd learned, all right.

Larry was as much fun at the poker table as everywhere else, telling jokes, keeping it light. But he was a hunch player, which meant a loser. Late in the game, he bet most of his remaining chips on three queens and lost to my straight, "Ladies, you let me down," he told the cards, and strolled out of Sam's house, still smiling.

Sam, on the other hand, wouldn't have played a hunch if it bit him on his double chin. He knew the odds by heart and with a single glance at the showing cards, he could tell you each player's odds of winning the hand.

But he never looked from the cards to the players. In years of sitting at a poker table with these guys, he didn't know as much as I learned in a couple of hours: that Mike grinned when he was bluffing, or that Carlos strangled his beer bottle when he thought he had a sure thing. So, over the course of the evening, Sam lost, too, and got sore about it.

* * *

I thought about all that as I sat in the hotel suite with the chuckling stranger in a ski mask. Mostly, I thought about the fact that Larry and Sam, my two candidates for district manager, were the only ones who knew I was staying at this hotel.

"Who sent you?" I asked.

Ski Mask shook his head. "If I told you I'd have to kill you, and that's not the plan. Otherwise, I wouldn't be wearing this mask. I'm just going to take your money and run."

"It's a big hotel," I said. "If I call the cops after you leave—"

"You won't." It wasn't easy to look smug in a ski mask, but he managed it.

"An up-and-coming businessman isn't going to admit to illegal gambling. Or to getting ripped off."

He was right, of course.

"Enough chat. Hand over the money, Mr. Patterson."

I sighed. "You're going to be disappointed." I reached a hand into my pocket. Ski Mask raised his gun quickly.

"Just my wallet," I said, and drew it out slowly. I threw it across to the couch where he sat.

He fumbled it open with a gloved hand. Suddenly, his gun hand was shaking. "Thirty bucks? Where's the rest?"

"That's what I'm trying to tell you." I shook my head sadly. "It already went back into the local economy. We had a last round of jackpots, and I lost every hand. When I got a full house, it turned out the dealer—"

"Shut up!" He threw the wallet on the floor as he stood up. "I don't believe you!"

"Then where's the money?" I raised my arms. "Do you think I left it in my rental car? Here." I threw him my car keys.

Ski Mask let them fall to the floor. He was so mad, I thought he would shoot me. "Don't tell anyone about this."

"Not much point," I muttered. He marched past me, and the door slammed behind him.

I went over to the mini-bar and poured a drink. Definitely a time for Scotch.

With the drink safely in hand, I strolled over to the door and bolted it. Then I reached into the open closet and pulled out my overcoat. My winnings were in the pocket, just where I left them.

The fact is, I had done terrific in the last round of jackpots. Sam knew that. He had watched me try to cram the money into my wallet, and when I gave up and stuffed it in my coat, he had said something snide about me getting too rich for my britches. If Sam had sent Ski Mask, he would have certainly told him about the coat.

But Larry had left early. So, it was Larry, my good buddy, who set me up. Too bad for him that his accomplice couldn't read a bluff.

I drank more whiskey. The funny part was that on the drive home from the poker game, I had decided to hire Larry. Not great at math, I figured, but you can trust him. What a mistake <u>that</u> would have been.

Talk about a lucky night.

Story inspiration:

I haven't played poker in nearly forty years. Used to be a favorite activity before I shifted coasts. We mostly played penny ante, which is easy on the wallet but has one great disadvantage: It's easy to call a bluff if the stakes aren't high. Fortunately, most of us were thrifty. Or broke. Or downright cheap.

I was thinking about that one day, and I realized there were other ways to bluff. And to cheat, for that matter. Now my story has made me more money than I ever won playing poker.

SIX QUESTIONS

LaToya Jovena

LaToya Jovena lives in the DC suburbs with her family. Her work has appeared in Ellery Queen's Mystery Magazine, Alfred Hitchcock's Mystery Magazine, *and* Twisted Voices: Stories from Ellery Queen's Mystery Magazine. *When she's not writing, she's taking care of her kids, or scamming.*

People had protested every time a casino opened in the area, but they fought the casino due in court today the hardest, because it had table games.

Their arguments were all the same. The casino would have negative social consequences. People would become addicted to gambling, and crime would follow. So, Lori found it ironic that the casino was the one hurt in this case, the victim of the crime.

It was nine in the morning and already eighty degrees. Menopause would dictate that she wait inside, but Lori wanted a good story and the details necessary to write it.

She heard high heels clicking on the cement before she saw them. Tony was wearing a different suit, but it was still a little too large and a lot too boxy. He looked like he wanted to be a player but fell short. His attorney's suit fit impeccably. Then there was Tony's girlfriend. She was wearing a tight tan high-waisted skirt and a white blouse. On her feet were the signature red soles of some fancy designer. Looking at her shoes made Lori's ankles hurt.

Lori knew everything there was to know about Tony; it was all public record. Tony's attorney wanted to be found. He handed out business cards like orange slices after a kids' soccer game. But Lori knew nothing about the girlfriend, except that while Tony was the criminal, she looked like the player.

The courtroom had never been an interesting place. TV always made it look like some dramatic moment would occur, shocking everyone, but that never happened. Most cases are solved before trial, if the defendant and prosecutor can settle on the terms. Of those that weren't, the prosecution won eighty percent, as they had won this one. Today was sentencing day, sure to be a yawn, but she would get her story.

Both the defense and the prosecution knew the penalty that went with each charge. The judge could choose the minimum, the maximum, or somewhere in the middle. Everyone knew that, too. But there was always shock, awe, and dissatisfaction from someone whenever the sentence was handed down.

Tony was sentenced to eight years. He'd be eligible for parole in two and most likely would get it. Honestly, not a bad deal for stealing nearly a million dollars. Of course, part of his sentence was restitution, but there was no way the casino was getting all the money back.

Tony took the news stoically. His attorney patted him on the back. His girlfriend interlaced her fingers with his. The casino's representatives looked disgusted.

Lori wrote it all down, leaving her opinion out of it, but she had a few. The first was that from what she'd seen, Tony had gotten away with way more than a million. The casino came up with that number because the police found a quarter of a million in cash in Tony's apartment. Cameras had caught Tony pulling the scam four times. But Tony had worked at the casino for six years. It seemed unlikely that he had only started robbing them the last four months of his employment. Most likely, he knew where the cameras were. Lori thought that he only recently got sloppy enough to get caught.

The bailiff approached Tony, while Lori looked for his mother. She had come to court most days but was absent today. She probably didn't want to see them lead her son away in handcuffs.

Tony brought his girlfriend's hand to his lips and kissed it, then one of his hands was pulled behind his back. He let go of her hand like he didn't want to, and the pair stared at each other. Then he was forced away from her and led out the back of the courtroom.

When Tony's girlfriend walked past, Lori expected to see tears. Instead, she saw something else entirely. An expression Lori could only describe as relief. Who was this girl? What was her game?

Lori hustled after her. Her Tevas were nowhere near as glamorous as the girlfriend's fancy red bottom soles, but they were comfortable, and she had gotten them on sale at DSW.

The girlfriend exited the cool courthouse, and Lori followed her into the satanic heat of Maryland in July. The sun was so bright her eyes watered, blurring her vision, but Lori could hear the click clack of the girlfriend's shoes heading to the parking lot.

"Miss," Lori called.

There was no response, which wasn't shocking to Lori. She was used to being ignored, but that wasn't what this girl had done. It was as if she hadn't heard Lori at all. If Lori hadn't known any better, she would have assumed the woman was deaf.

"Excuse me, Miss," Lori called again.

She didn't go faster. She didn't slow down. She just continued her strut.

Lori had enough to submit her story to the Beltway Bulletin. She had watched the whole case from gavel to gavel. She had a few spicy details to keep readers interested. For instance, the casino still didn't know how Tony had done it, but they did know how he had spent the money. The prosecution had bombarded the jury with photos of private flights, diamond-encrusted jewelry, and multiple luxury cars. Readers would also be interested to learn that most of Tony's fancy stuff was seized, and now up for auction to help with his restitution.

Her editor would be pleased, post her story to the blog, and pay her the paltry sum they had agreed upon. And that was okay. Lori didn't do it for the money. She did it because she had always wanted to be a reporter, before life sent her in a different direction. That was why she was chasing this supermodel wannabe through the courthouse parking lot. This woman, whoever she was, was the real story.

Lori watched the girlfriend approach an SUV fitting her aesthetic and climb in. The SUV turned on, pulled out of the parking space, and crept out of the parking lot.

Lori ambled over to her own car, a ten-year-old Nissan, parked in a handicap spot due to her bum hip. The girlfriend had gotten a head start, but traffic was slow, so she hadn't gotten far. She spotted the SUV at a red light. It was a Porsche. The windows were tinted dark. The license plate read Ontario. Lori quickly wrote it down, wondering if it was a rental. She couldn't tell if the girlfriend knew she was being followed until they hit the beltway, once there, she floored it. There was no way Lori's car could've kept up with the superior horsepower, but the construction gods smiled down on her, causing delays due to constant road improvement.

Traffic cleared, and they continued south. When the girlfriend took the exit for the National Harbor, Lori was right behind her and not the least bit surprised when the girlfriend parked and made her way over to Lori's car.

"Why are you following me?" the girlfriend asked, towering over Lori in her stilts.

"I have a few questions for you," Lori responded calmly.

"No comment."

"You don't even know what the questions are."

"I don't have any comment on Tony's case," said the girlfriend. "Whatever it is, you're going to have to ask him. I saw you in court at the sentencing, so I'm sure you know where to find him."

The girlfriend took a step back from Lori's car. She looked like she assumed the conversation was over.

"Why do you have Ontario plates?" asked Lori.

The girlfriend didn't respond, but her mask of coolness had slipped. It was only for a moment, but a good reporter listened to everything an interviewee said, and not just with words. "If you keep following me, I'm going to call the police." The mask was firmly back in place.

"These are public roads, Miss. Anyone with a valid license and registered vehicle can drive on them. The police will tell you the same thing. Why don't we go inside and grab a bite? That way we can talk more comfortably."

"I don't eat McDonald's," she replied, looking over at the golden arches. "How about Fogo De Chão? It's right down the hill. You need to pay for my parking."

Lori did everything she could to keep her own mask in place, but her excitement showed. She could see it in the way the girlfriend looked at her.

* * *

"Parking shouldn't be more than ten dollars," said the girlfriend as they walked from the parking lot. "Do you have cash?"

Lori dug out the emergency twenty-dollar bill she kept in her purse. One never knew when something could happen that would make cashless payment impossible.

"Thank you," said the girlfriend, when Lori handed her the bill. There was no mention of change.

The doors to the restaurant were heavy. The hostess perked up when she saw Tony's girlfriend.

"Hi, Natalie," she said in greeting.

Lori had her second clue, a name. Natalie.

Lori followed Natalie to a table with a spectacular view of the Capital Wheel and the water shimmering in the sunlight beyond it. Natalie made eye contact with the hostess, who nodded.

Lori had just put her bag in one of the seats when Natalie walked away.

She sashayed over to the most extensive salad bar Lori had ever seen. Yes, there were all the leaves and fixings for salads, but there were also potato salads, bean salads, meats, cheeses, and even parfaits. Lori couldn't help but wonder how expensive this restaurant was and how she was going to pay for it. There was no way the blog would expense it.

Natalie seemed determined to make sure every color of the rainbow was on her plate, then she sashayed back to the table.

Lori loaded her plate and grabbed a parfait in a chilled glass before she was done.

There was a bottle of sparkling water on the table. Natalie's glass was filled to the brim with clear bubbles.

A waiter appeared as Lori sat.

"Would you like something to drink, Miss?"

"Diet Coke, please."

Natalie was cutting everything on her plate into bite-sized pieces. Beets, orange bell pepper, starfruit, broccoli, and even a purple fig all fell to her knife. Only the blackberries held their integrity. Her focus was admirable. Who was this girl, and what was her game?

"Thank you for meeting with me," said Lori, before taking a bite of the best potato salad she'd ever had.

"Thank you for the meal, I guess," Natalie replied, just as a huge skewer of meat appeared next to her.

Pieces of meat were sliced onto a fresh plate while Lori looked on in awe. There was more than just the salad bar. There was also meat brought directly to the table. And Lori would be footing the bill for all of it.

"Lamb, miss?" asked the waiter.

"Sure."

As soon as the waiter, who Natalie explained was called a 'gaucho,' walked away, a real waiter appeared with a small dish of what looked like bright green Jell-O.

"If you want anything other than lamb, you should let them know," said Natalie. "It's all I ever eat. I don't know if they'll bother to bring anything else."

If Lori wasn't using her mouth to chew, she was certain it would have been hanging open. "Do you come here often?"

"Is that what you want to ask me?" Natalie was cutting her lamb into bite-sized pieces. "Just trying to be personable."

"I only agreed to this meal to get you to stop following me. Once I'm done eating, we're done speaking. If I were you, I would use my time wisely."

"Me paying for the meal should have some bearing," Lori said with a huff.

"Nothing is ever free." Natalie smeared a little of the green stuff on a bite of meat and chewed it.

"Okay, I have a few questions about your connection to the casino case."

Natalie stabbed something on her vegetable plate and popped it into her mouth. She stared at Lori, but she didn't say a word.

"Care to elaborate?" Lori continued.

"You said you have questions. There are only six questions. Who, what, when, where, why, and how."

Lori's face felt hot. Natalie was right. She should have come prepared with a list of questions. Even thinking of what to ask her on the ride there would have been beneficial, but she had been so focused on catching her, she hadn't spared a thought to think about what she would do when she caught her.

"Okay," began Lori. "Who are you? What is your relationship to the defendant?"

"I'm Natalie. Tony is my boyfriend."

Lori had asked, and Natalie had answered, but there was no new information shared. This wasn't going to do. Natalie continued to eat, while Lori continued to think.

If someone had asked Lori who she was, she would have said she was a mother, grandmother, and retiree, who was pursuing her passions now that she had time. Mothers raised children. Retirees had retired. Criminals committed crimes. What a person did defined who they were.

"What do you do?" Lori asked.

"I take care of myself and the people I care about."

"Do you work?"

"Everyone has to earn a living."

"When did you meet Tony?" Lori took a bite of lamb. It was exquisite.

Natalie put down her fork and looked out over the water, squinting back in time. "About a year ago, I guess." She picked up her sparkling water and took a long sip, leaving a pink lip print on the glass.

According to the prosecution, Tony's crimes started four months ago, just eight months after meeting Natalie. That couldn't be a coincidence, but Lori had been there every day of the trial. An accomplice was never mentioned.

"Where did you meet him?"

"I was eating at one of the casino restaurants after getting a massage. He came over to my table."

"How was it dating him?"

"He's a great guy. He took really good care of me. I liked making him happy." Natalie had been chewing bite-sized pieces as she listened to and answered questions.

Lori wondered if that was really all she was going to eat. Would she want dessert? Could Lori afford dessert?

"Why did Tony steal from the casino? Why did you stick beside him? I mean, you must have your pick of suitors." The words fell out of Lori's mouth in a rush. She was running out of time, and she hadn't learned anything.

Natalie picked up her glass of sparkling water and slowly sipped. The wait was excruciating for Lori, but Natalie didn't put her glass back down until it was empty.

"You'd have to ask Tony why he stole from the casino," said Natalie. "I stuck by him because it was the right thing to do."

A waiter appeared behind Natalie. He grabbed her bottle of sparkling water and poured it into her now-empty glass.

"Hi, Steve," said Natalie, looking up at him. "I'm about to head out. Thank you so much for your help today. My friend will be taking care of the bill when she's through." Natalie gestured at Lori before standing to her feet.

The waiter, Steve, smiled and nodded before walking away. Then Natalie was gone too, without so much as a thank you.

At first, Lori was too shocked to speak. Then she was angry, furious even, especially when she saw the bill. She barely tipped and went back for an extra plate of potato salad that she was too stuffed to eat. Finally, she felt guilty both for taking her anger out on the waitstaff and for being a bad tipper, but the feeling didn't make her any richer. She didn't have enough to tip more.

The drive back to her 55-plus apartment community was clogged with traffic heading to the beach, and to make matters worse, she had to pull off the highway twice to find a bathroom. Maybe it was a good thing she had met her husband, gotten pregnant, and dropped out of college. It appears she would have failed at being a journalist if she'd had the opportunity to pursue it. In fact, it seemed like she was failing at all the things she had always wanted to do. All the short stories she had submitted had been rejected. She'd always thought she would have made a good chef, but she struggled in the cooking classes her community offered. She had lagged in swimming and had no rhythm in dancing. Journalism was the last thing on her list, and it seemed like she was about to fail at that as well.

"Hi, Lori," a man called as she made her way to her apartment.

"How you doing, Tom?"

"Just left the greens. Break any big stories? I can't wait to read them."

You and I both, was what Lori thought, but what she said was, "I'll be sure to let you know when I go to press."

Lori let herself into her apartment, kicked off her shoes, and headed straight to the shower. She was drenched in sweat. The air conditioner in her car had been broken for the last two summers, and she didn't have the money to fix it. By the time she was clean and moisturized, she barely had time to boot up her MacBook for her first call.

"Hi, Grandma," screamed her eldest grandson.

"Hi, Buddy," Lori replied. She could see the Willis Tower out the window behind him. "I got a few books from the library. Do you want to pick one to read?"

"I want to read them all."

Eventually, Buddy settled on *Abdul's Story* and *Jose Feeds the World*. Then there was a FaceTime call with her daughter-in-law in Atlanta. Paul Jr. had just learned to roll over and was using his new skill to explore his surroundings. Lori laughed much harder than necessary.

It was said that when you have a daughter, she's yours forever, but when you have a son, he's only yours until he's married. Her sons, both cliches, had moved to the cities where their wives' parents lived, but those wives' birthed sons of their own.

"It comes at you fast," Lori said to her daughter-in-law. "Right now, his surroundings are inside your home. Blink twice, and his surroundings will include the whole world."

She clicked off the call with a sigh. She didn't want to see her grandchildren on FaceTime. She wanted to read to them in person, take them to the playground, and get ice cream. She wanted to help babysit while their parents went on the kinds of dates that keep marriages strong and give children a solid foundation.

Lori had a niggling feeling that the reason she had been failing at all the things she had always wanted to do was because she hadn't really wanted to do them.

She had found success as a mom. She had excelled at organizing playdates and birthday parties. She had gleefully taken her children to every extracurricular activity and summer camp. She had even found ways to trim the family budget, or earn more money, to help pay for vacations.

Lori was a great mom, and under different circumstances, she would be a great grandma. But how did one change their circumstances at sixty years old?

She headed to the kitchen to make her evening cocktail, catching sight of her bag and the notebook inside. Lori may not have had a way to be a more involved grandma, but she did have a way to be a better reporter. She had enough information to get even more. Seeing her name in the byline of some in-depth series wouldn't heal her wounds, but it was better than what she had. Lori started with the Ontario license plate number.

* * *

Even though her sons were grown and gone, Lori hadn't been able to break the habit of waking up early. With no steady job, she usually went to the gym first thing, but not this morning. Today, she battled traffic with everyone commuting to work on Route 50 and I-495. After much delay, she made it to Alexandria.

All the facts about Tony, and his crimes, were public record, including his address. It seemed obvious to her that a girl from Toronto, who had met Tony in a hotel, would be staying at his place.

Tony's girlfriend whipped the door open when Lori knocked, her eyes going wide when she realized it was Lori standing there, and not whoever she was expecting.

"I'm not answering any more questions," she said, once she recovered her composure. "This isn't a public road. If you don't leave, I'm calling the police."

At that moment, a cold drop of water hit the top of Lori's head. The skies had been gray for the entire hour she had spent driving to Tony's place. It looked like it was finally ready to rain.

"No, you won't," said Lori, pushing her way inside the apartment.

It was gray. Gray hardwood. Gray sofa. Gray accent wall.

Lori looked out the window and watched rain fall on the Porsche Macan. She heard the apartment's door close. When she turned towards the sound, she saw two giant boxes near the door.

"Looks like you're moving," said Lori.

"Seriously, lady, what do you want?"

The high heels were gone. She was wearing sneakers, leggings, and a tank top. All of it looked new and expensive.

"I think you want to hear what I have to say, Larenn," said Lori. "I have answers to all six questions."

With a flourish, Lori walked over to the couch and sat down. Larenn, formerly known as Natalie, crossed her arms and leaned against the wall across from Lori.

"Who you are is hard to pin down," began Lori. "But your high school Facebook page calls you Larenn Charles. There are other social media accounts for you, of course. Natalie has a TikTok. Tiffany has an Instagram. And Stephanie is very active on X."

"Twitter," Larenn blurted out. "It's still Twitter."

Lori couldn't help but smile. How funny that a woman who changed her name like other people changed clothes would insist on something being called by its birth name.

"Where are you from?" Lori didn't wait for an answer. "Toronto. You attended one of the best STEM high schools in Canada, but you didn't graduate. You've been all over the U.S. since then. Nevada. Mississippi. Louisiana. New Jersey. Places that all have one thing in common, but I'll come back to that in a minute.

"What do you do?" Lori looked around the apartment. It was spotless, as if Larenn had spent all night making sure there was no trace of her. "What you do is the one question you answered honestly yesterday. You take care of yourself and the people you love. Very good care, it turns out.

"The reason you didn't graduate high school is because you got pregnant. You had to earn money. You had a baby to take care—"

"Don't talk about my son," Larenn snapped. Her eyes were cold.

For a moment, Lori wondered if she was pushing too far, but she hadn't gotten what she wanted yet. She had to follow her game plan.

"Why not?" Lori asked, with faux innocence. "All of Toronto is talking about your son. He may be better at soccer than you ever were with technology. And we both know you were very, very good with technology.

"Because you took what you knew to casino after casino. You seduce a dealer and teach them how to rob the casino blind. Eventually, they get caught, just like poor Tony, and you flee back home to Toronto.

"How you do it is unclear. I mean you're beautiful, finding a dumb guy is the easy part. I just don't understand the tech part. I guess if it was easy to understand everyone would be doing it, and you wouldn't be able to have all this nice stuff." Lori gestured towards the Macan out the window.

Larenn's eyes bored into Lori's skull.

"Why is obvious," continued Lori, undeterred. "All reward, with no risk for you. What I couldn't figure out was the when. That's why I had to rush over here today. I had to know when you were leaving. I know the answer, now."

"I didn't do anything," said Larenn. "If I told you to go rob a bank right now, would you do it? What about if I slept with you first? And if you did it, would I really be the one to blame?"

"You don't have to convince me. You would have to convince the police."

Larenn looked from Lori, to the door, and back again.

Lori hoped she was doing a good job of holding in her smile. "I have two sons of my own. They're grown and gone now. Out there in the world, working their own careers. No more need for their mother."

The look on Larenn's face made Lori worry she was going to vomit.

"My grandkids need me, though," Lori blurted out, not wanting Larenn to dwell on being taken away from her son. "It's just that my grandkids live so far away. Chicago and Atlanta. I just have Social Security and my deceased husband's pension. The blog is more something to do than a way to earn money.

"I do okay, but there's no money for extras, flights, or hotels. I could drive. It's not that far, per se, but my car is so old it would probably break down on the way. And where would that leave me? I don't have any money to replace it, and I live in Annapolis. It's not exactly a hub of mass transit."

Larenn raised her gaze from the floor to Lori's eyes.

Lori looked out the window.

Not a word passed between them.

There was an expensive-looking handbag on the kitchen counter. Lori had recognized the brand, Chanel. Larenn walked over to it, pulled out a stack of money and a key fob. When Larenn got closer, Lori saw the Porsche logo.

"It's all I have. This is for my son's tuition."

The money made Lori salivate, but knowing it was the tuition for Larenn's son pulled at her heart. Could she fault Larenn for doing all she could to give her son the best life possible? But then Lori remembered something, something Larenn herself had taught her.

"Nothing is ever free." Lori took the cash and the keys. "I'll send you my address to transfer the registration. You can keep the handbag. It's not really my style."

Story Inspiration:

"Six Questions" was inspired by four events, in four different jurisdictions. The first was making a new friend at a party in NYC. The second happened outside Washington, DC, when the same friend told me about the Dangerous Games anthology. I was intrigued.

Later, I was at home flipping through streaming services when I stumbled upon Hustlers, Gamblers, and Crooks *on Max. This is where I met Gino Muscara. Gino robbed a now-defunct Atlantic City casino of about $1000 a day. He got off with a $250 fine. I was inspired.*

Finally, my family took a trip to Toronto. We got to stay in a light-filled condo, minutes away from all the tourist attractions. I became inquisitive. What would I be willing to do for my kid to grow up in this condo?

Side note: No casinos were harmed in the creation of "Six Questions."

DEAD HAND, NO JOKERS

Sharyn Kolberg

Sharyn Kolberg is the ghostwriter and author of many bestselling nonfiction books. Moving into fiction, her short stories have appeared in Ellery Queen's Mystery Magazine, Mystery Magazine, Black Cat Weekly, *and others. She has just completed her first mystery novel and is working on her second.*

When I woke up that morning, I never expected that just hours later I would be down on all fours in a stranger's house, staring at a woman who looked like she might be practicing Pilates but who was more likely dead.

I put my ear to the woman's face, listening for the sound of breathing, if only faint, and hoping to feel even the smallest hint of warm air coming out of her slightly open mouth.

I got what I expected. Nothing.

The room started closing in on me, and now I couldn't breathe. It was like I was having a sympathy death. Everything went blank, and I couldn't make sense of anything I was seeing. I pulled myself up, clutching the edge of the dining room table, and then plunked myself down between the arms of the captain's chair, took my cell phone out of my pocket, and dialed 911.

The woman lay on her back, her hands at her sides, her eyes wide open. There wasn't any blood that I could see, no ragged bullet hole in her low-cut butter-yellow cashmere sweater, no telltale knife sticking out of her chest. She did look very surprised, though, as if her last thought had been "If I'd have known I was going to die today, I wouldn't have shown so much cleavage." On the ring finger of her lightly clenched right hand, she wore a tasteful pear-shaped diamond set in platinum that no burglar worth his salt would have left behind. I must have jostled her fingers, because two faded Chinese Mah Jongg tiles fell softly to the wall-to-wall.

They were from a good set, bone and bamboo, not like the plastic tiles from the Mah Jongg set my mother had used when she played with "the girls" every Friday night all those years ago. The girls had played for nickels and dimes; I remember once, my mother had made a celebratory chocolate pudding for dessert in honor of the 85 cents she'd won the night before.

I wondered what the stakes might have been in the game the woman in yellow had been playing. I assumed this was Sheila King, who'd answered an ad I had placed on Facebook Marketplace to sell my late Aunt Rita's old Mah Jongg set. Sheila King had asked me if I'd like to bring my aunt's set over so she could look at it. She gave me the address and told me to be there at 1:00.

I was there five minutes late, set in hand. The door was open when I arrived. Maybe I shouldn't have, but I walked into her house. I called out for Sheila King but got no answer. Aunt Rita's set was heavy, with its full set of tiles and racks in a faux-crocodile box. I put it down next to the dining room table, and that's when I saw the woman lying there.

* * *

I called 911. Did the minutes always go this slowly when you were waiting for emergency assistance? I decided to take mental notes of everything around me so that I could answer any questions the police might have, but I was interrupted by a noise behind me. I jumped out of the chair and saw a young woman standing in the doorway, a blue crop top covering two tiny breasts and exposing a bejeweled belly button, with a tiny skirt covering very little of her tiny body. She said, in a tiny voice difficult to hear, "What did you do to my mother?"

That's when I saw the tiny gun in her hand.

I was twice her size, at least, and could probably have knocked the gun out of her delicate hand with no more effort than it took to brush a crumb off a table. I thought twice about doing that, though, because small as the girl was, a bullet is a bullet.

"I didn't do anything to your mother," I said. "I found her there on the floor. Paramedics are on the way."

She made eye contact for a few seconds, then dropped the gun and ran up the stairs. I took a deep breath, left the weapon where it was, and followed her. It may have been a foolish move, but it wouldn't be the first time curiosity compelled me to ignore my better judgment.

I tiptoed as stealthily as I could to the doorway of an upstairs bedroom, which was now being disrupted by the young woman, who was standing at a dressing table, pulling open drawers, spilling out jewelry, and flinging assorted items of lingerie around the room.

"It's not here, it's not here, it's not here," she mumbled as she lifted the bed skirt and searched under the bed.

"What are you looking for?" I asked. I should have kept quiet, I know, but the poor girl looked so distraught I almost wanted to help her search. She glanced at my reflection in the mirror and spun herself around. "Who the hell are you, anyway?" she asked.

"I'm Cookie. Cookie Sneiderman," I said. I've always felt that Cookie was an inappropriate name for an adult, especially a plus-size woman like me.

I wondered why it took her so long to ask who I was. That would have been my first question. But she seemed much more concerned about whatever it was she couldn't find.

"Your mother answered my ad on Marketplace," I said. "I'm selling my Aunt Rita's Mah Jongg set." As if that was the most important event of the day.

* * *

I didn't know what happened next, except that I found myself lying on the bedroom's lush burgundy carpet, my head throbbing, a balding, brown-eyed giant standing over me with a worried look on his familiar face.

"Cookie? Is that you?"

All I could see was a blurry image of Charlie Brown standing over me. No, wait. It wasn't Charlie Brown. It was police detective Bronwell Mendez. I knew him from high school. Star quarterback on our winning team, and our class valedictorian. During our school years, we had purposely avoided each other. He was known around school as Brownie, and there was an unspoken agreement between us that Brownie and Cookie would never hang out together.

Now here he was, calling my name, and here I was, puddled out on the floor of a stranger's bedroom.

"Cookie," he said again, "are you all right?"

"I think so," I said, slowly sitting up. "I'm just confused. Where is she?"

"She who?"

"The young woman who was here. She had a gun and—"

"A gun?" said Brownie. "Maybe you should start from the beginning, okay?"

"Okay. I walk into this house, practically trip over Sheila King's dead body, let her doll-sized daughter sneak up on me with a gun, watch her ransack this room, then, next thing I know, I wake up and see you standing over me." That seemed pretty succinct to me.

Brownie knelt beside me.

"Who's Sheila King?" he asked.

"Sheila King! Sheila King!" I yelled. "The dead lady in yellow downstairs with the cleavage and the Mah Jongg tiles. I followed her daughter up here and watched her throw things around the room...."

I swung my head around faster than I should have, as throbbing pain thundered through my eyeballs. The last rays of the afternoon light were sparkling through the window. There was nothing on the bed, the chairs, or the carpet. The room was neat, tidy, undisturbed. I was the only thing out of place.

Brownie frowned. "It seems like you had a rough day here, Cookie, but I gotta tell you. There isn't any lady in yellow downstairs, dead or otherwise."

"What do you mean, there's no lady downstairs? I saw what I saw, and I know what I know. Look," I said, "Sheila King called me this morning, gave me this address, and said she wanted to buy my aunt's old Mah Jongg set. She was supposed to make me tea."

I don't know why, but that hit me hard. I had never even met Sheila King, but I was sorry she was gone. I thought about the last hour of her life, an hour she'd spent waiting for me to comb my hair and put on makeup. One minute she was planning to put the kettle on the stove and deciding whether to use the mugs or the fine China, and the next minute she was on the floor, dead in her own dining room. If I hadn't been so concerned about concealing the circles under my eyes, I might have gotten here early, and maybe Sheila King would have met me instead of her maker.

I suddenly realized that Brownie was talking, and I hadn't heard a word.

"…no crime here, as far as I can tell," he was saying, "except maybe trespassing on your part."

"I wasn't trespassing," I said. "Sheila King invited me here."

"Yeah, well, there's only one problem with that," Brownie said. "This isn't Sheila King's house. According to the neighbors, it belongs to Mr. and Mrs. Sidney Cooper, who are on a month-long cruise to Rio De Janeiro. So technically, you're trespassing."

He offered his hand to help me up. "I'm fine," I said, trying to think of how I was going to get him to look the other way while I struggled to stand. I didn't want him to watch my clumsy attempts to rise from the floor.

Brownie sighed, left the room, and waited for me at the top of the stairs. I followed him down to the dining room, which was, just as he had said it would be, bereft of bodies.

"She was right here," I said, pointing to the spot. "Right here on her back with her eyes wide open."

"Well, she's not there now," Brownie said.

"I can see that," I said, annoyed at his gentle tone and condescending attitude. "I'm telling you she was right there. Do people usually call 911 and report dead bodies just for fun?"

"It happens," he said.

This was not going well. I looked under the dining room table, as if the body might have accidentally rolled underneath. It was almost too dark to see anything under there, but I could see what wasn't there. Aunt Rita's set.

"It's not there, it's not there, it's not there," I said, echoing the tiny tater tot in the upstairs bedroom. I turned to ask Brownie if he had a flashlight, but he was off talking to his men in the hallway. They looked at me, nodded, and walked out the door.

I looked under the table again. Nothing—except a small white object that caught my eye. I nudged the object with my foot. It was a Mah Jongg tile, a green dragon beautifully carved on an off-white background. I started to call out to Brownie, to yell, "See, see, this proves it," and then I thought, "Proves what?" All it proved was that some careless Mah Jongg player dropped a tile, and it fell under the table. I slipped the tile into my jacket pocket and straightened up just as Brownie came back into the room. Would he even believe me if I told him about Aunt Rita's missing set? I didn't think so. A missing corpse was bad enough.

"Come on, Cookie," he said. "I'll drive you home. You can come back and get your car tomorrow."

* * *

I took an Uber back the next morning. I was expecting to see yellow police tape and blue and white squad cars around the house, but once again, my expectations were not met. Then I remembered that, according to the police, there had been no crime. What I did see, besides my Honda Civic in the driveway, were several cars parked in front of the house. The old curiosity/good judgment conundrum came into play again—and curiosity won out once more. I walked up to the house and rang the doorbell.

I was greeted by a middle-aged woman wearing a tee-shirt that read "Mah Jongg Is My Therapy." She was dripping with earrings, necklaces, and bracelets made of old Mah Jongg tiles.

"Oh, good," she said. "You must be the new player Sheila King told me about. I'm Caroline Neuberger. And you're…?"

"Cookie. Cookie Sneiderman," I said.

"Come on in and take a seat," said Caroline. "Sheila said you were just a beginner, but we don't care. We love to teach!" She introduced me to the two other women seated at a folding table set up in the living room: Myrna, a stout woman in her forties wearing a too-tight black pullover, and an older player named Annette, whose gray-streaked hair was pulled into a messy bun at the nape of her neck.

"I wonder where Shelia is," said Annette. "It's odd that she invited us to play here and then just didn't show up." They clearly did not know about Sheila's alleged demise and subsequent disappearance, and I wasn't sure I wanted to be the one to tell them. Maybe I could get some info from them first.

"It's a good thing Sheila gave me her extra key," added Myrna. Neither of them seemed overly concerned about Sheila King's absence.

The women did, however, seem anxious to bring me into their fold. It was as if they were a cult, and I was a prospective convert—they seemed determined to make me into a player. The first thing they did was lay all the tiles face down on the table and shuffle them around. I was immediately thrown back to my teenage years. The clacking of the tiles was just as it used to be, even though these tiles, made of plastic with shallowly engraved and painted numbers, pictures, and characters on them, looked very different than the bone and bamboo tiles I saw yesterday.

Caroline brought her Mah Jongg card to the table and sat down. "Let's start," she said. "We can talk while we set up."

I found it all fascinating. To play, you try to match up tiles you've randomly picked to a hand on the Mah Jongg card that's sent out every year by the National Mah Jongg League. These women had obviously been playing together for a while. I don't know how they were able to do it, but even as they played, they carried on a conversation, naming each rejected tile as it was discarded.

"I really can't understand what happened to Sheila. She really liked this house—it's one of the nicest ones, isn't it, Annette? *Two dot*," Myrna said.

"For sure," Annette answered. "*Nine crak.*"

"One of the nicest ones?" I asked, confused, throwing down a five bam.

"Oh, yeah," said Annette, "Didn't you know? Sheila is a realtor for high end houses. She recommends the client travels for a month so she can show the house without them around. In the meantime, she moves in, and we get to play our weekly games in somebody else's mansion. *One crak.*"

I was playing along as best I could, even though I really didn't have any idea what I was doing. I threw down a tile I didn't think I needed, and we continued playing as the ladies started asking me questions about how and when I'd met Sheila King, and did I know why she hadn't shown up today. I told the ladies all about my adventure the previous day.

Myrna looked horrified at my story. "How could you not tell us this as soon as you came in? Didn't you think we'd want to know if our friend is dead?"

"That's just it," I said. "I'm not sure she is. When I came downstairs, she had disappeared."

"Came downstairs? Disappeared?" Myrna asked. "You're not making sense, Cookie. Start from the beginning."

She was sounding annoyingly like Brownie, and, even though I didn't want to go through the whole story again, I thought they deserved to know about their friend. So, I told them everything.

"That's weird," said Annette, "because we never go upstairs in other people's houses. And Sheila doesn't have a daughter."

* * *

"Oh yes she does," said a familiar voice coming from the dining room. Caroline must have left the front door unlocked when she let me in. The young woman must have slipped in while we were busy playing. She was, once again, scantily clad and pointing her small silver gun in my direction.

"Oh, for goodness sake, Gina," said Caroline. "Put that thing away. You're not scaring anyone, you know."

She was scaring me a little. Myrna had turned chalk-white, and Annette looked like she was about to pass out, but Caroline didn't appear to be bothered at all. In fact, her steely-eyed stare was scarier than the little gun. She kept her eyes right on Gina until the girl put the firearm into her purse.

It was deadly quiet in the room until Myrna finally spoke up, her voice reed-thin and shaky. "What's going on, Caroline?"

"Nothing that need concern the two of you," she said to her friends, then turned her eyes toward me. "You, on the other hand, have stuck your nose where it doesn't belong. Did you take something from this house yesterday, Cookie? Something that didn't belong to you?"

I thought about the dragon tile still in my jacket pocket from yesterday. I wasn't sure I should show it to them. On the other hand, I was—once again—curious. Maybe Caroline could tell me if the tile was important.

"I found this," I said, reaching into my jacket pocket to get the dragon tile. "Is this what you need?"

"This looks like it came from Sheila's set," said Annette. "Where did you get it, Cookie?"

"I saw it lying on the floor yesterday when I came to meet Sheila. It's been burning a hole in my pocket since then."

"Well then, I'm sure you'll be glad to give it to me," Caroline said. "I can return it to Sheila at our next game. I bet she's frantically searching for it."

I wouldn't take that bet.

"Oh, that's okay," I said. "I'd rather take care of it myself."

Caroline made a sudden move and grabbed for the tile. I jerked my arm back, and the tile slid through my fingers, landing with a crack onto the slate mantlepiece. The bone and bamboo split apart, and we all watched as powdery white substance spilled onto the hearth.

Caroline was the first to speak. "Gina," she said, "scoop that up and find something to put it in. See if you can get it back into the tile so we can paste it together again." Gina got down on her knees and followed Caroline's instructions. "He's going to kill me if we don't have all of it."

"Yes, he is," said a tall, well-dressed gentleman walking into the living room. He was holding Aunt Rita's Mah Jongg set in one hand and a big black gun in the other. I didn't know which of those surprised me more. Myrna and Annette were shaking in their seats, eyes glued to the man with the gun.

"Hello, Sidney," said Caroline, calmly. "Welcome home."

"I hope you ladies are enjoying the use of my house," he said.

Myrna and Annette now looked embarrassed as well as scared. I had no idea what was going on, but I knew I wanted to get Rita's set out of Sidney Cooper's hand without taking a bullet.

"Um, excuse me, Mr. Cooper," I said, curiosity getting the best of me again, "but I think we all want to know what's happening here, and why you have my aunt's Mah Jongg set."

"I don't," said Annette squeakily, and Myrna shook her head in agreement.

"Sheila wouldn't stick to the plan," said Sidney. "I had her tiles all fixed up, and then she had to get greedy and take three of them for herself. Maybe she thought I wouldn't notice. But I did. And I took care of Sheila. I found two of the tiles, but one was still missing. I sent our daughter to get it back."

"*Our* daughter?" said Cookie.

"Mine and Sheila's," he said, turning to the girl still kneeling on the hearth. "But you couldn't find it, could you, Gina?"

"No, Daddy."

"So, what did you do?"

"I saw the other set after you bopped Cookie on the head, so I took it for you. I thought it was Sheila's and that you might want it."

Caroline had taken Aunt Rita's set from Sidney, placed it on the dining room table, and opened it. Even in their frightened state, Annette and Myrna couldn't help admiring the tiles.

"Look," Murna said, "It's the same vintage as Sheila's old set!"

Caroline spoke up. "I'm guessing Sheila thought she might be able to switch some of Aunt Rita's tiles in place of her own," she said. "She probably thought no one would find out until after the drugs were delivered."

"Thank you both," said Sidney. "Gina, why don't you go outside and wait in the car?"

She hesitated for a few second, which was apparently too long for Sidney.

"Go. Now," he said. She did.

"Okay, ladies," he said, sweeping the gun around the table, "we all need to go for a little ride. Come on, get up."

Sidney grabbed my arm and pulled me close, then pushed me in front of him, pointing his gun at my back, warning Annette and Myrna that if they tried any tricks, I would be the first to pay the consequences. And they would be next.

Annette and Myrna rose slowly to their feet and started walking toward the front door. Caroline followed behind them.

Time slowed down and sped up all at once. My heart raced and slowed, raced and slowed. My legs were full of cement. I thought I heard sirens in the distance. Suddenly, the image of Brownie tackling an opposing quarterback came into my head. I spun around and rammed into Sidney Cooper like this was the final play in the Super Bowl. He landed on his stomach, rasping and grunting. The gun flew out of his hand; I grabbed it and pointed it at Caroline. She stopped in her tracks. Myrna and Annette ran to the curb.

I sat on Sidney.

He was big, but I was heavier.

The more he struggled, the harder I sat.

* * *

While this was going on, Myrna called 911. This time, the police arrived before I could even take a breath. Three cars screeched to a stop. Brownie popped out of the first one, helped me up off Sidney Cooper, and, after speaking to me, Myrna, and Annette, arrested Caroline, Sidney, and Gina.

Brownie walked me back to my car. "I'll have to see you tomorrow to take your official statement," he said, and paused for a moment. "I guess I could come by your house if you don't want to come downtown."

"I guess you could," I said. I could feel my cheeks turning pink. "How did you get here so quickly, anyway?"

"I was already on my way. I went to your house, but you weren't home. I thought you might have come here to get your car. I wanted to let you know we found Sheila King in a nearby pond. She was dead from a drug overdose; somebody—probably Sidney—had moved her there. You were very brave today, Cookie. You flattened Sidney like a pancake, and you probably saved your friends' lives. Good job."

Now I could feel my cheeks turning bright red. Myrna and Annette were waiting for me at the curb. They both started talking at once, fawning over me and asking if I was all right and if I wanted to join them for tea and coffee cake. Coffee cake sounded good to me.

"Just one more question before we go, Cookie," Myrna said. "Wanna play Mah Jongg tomorrow?"

Story Inspiration

As an avid Mah Jongg player, I've been playing for more than twenty years. It's a game, like life, that combines a lot of strategy and more than a bit of luck. You have to learn to play the hand you're dealt—but also to pivot when circumstances allow. Sometimes you win, sometimes you lose.

I've been wanting to write about Mah Jongg for a long time, but never seemed to find the right setting or character. I eventually created the character of Cookie, put her in a novel, and there she sat for several years while I figured out what to do with her.

The inspiration for this story came while watching an old British series about a pregnant PI who encountered many obstacles due to her weight and condition. That led me to the idea of an insecure, overweight character who learns to use her "weaknesses" to her advantage. She may not be the best at choosing a healthy meal, but she is one smart Cookie.

ESCAPE THE MONEY LAUNDERERS

Chris Chan

Chris Chan is an International Goodwill Ambassador for Agatha Christie Ltd. He is the author of the Funderburke and Kaiming series, including Ghosting My Friend *and* She Ruined Our Lives, *published by Level Best Books. He has also written the mystery criticism books:* Murder Most Grotesque *and* Some of My Best Friends Are Murderers.

I may be a teacher, but I'm the first to admit that lots of the best parts of high school take place outside of the classroom. Thankfully, many of my co-workers agree with me, which is why at least once a semester, we arrange for a day off for special excursions that allow our students to have supervised, wholesome fun doing activities that are arguably educational. That's why on a crisp early October afternoon, I was on a bus with a few dozen freshmen, taking them to a newly opened escape room company, Puzzle Paradise, on the west side of Milwaukee.

My boyfriend, Funderburke, and I are big escape room fans. During the past month, we'd played and won all five of their escape rooms on double date nights with my parents. These are not shoddy, uninspired rooms. None of those bare, beige cubes of office space with a modicum of furniture and a bunch of prefabricated puzzles, mostly consisting of various kinds of locks. These are the most immersive escape rooms I've ever visited, with incredible production values. The "Jungle Temple" game does an amazing job of replicating the rainforest. The "Time is Running Out" room has you surrounded by gigantic gears inside a massive clock. The "Labyrinth" room sends you right into the world of Greek myths, and "Mini Golf" has you solving a murder mystery at a kiddie amusement park and playing arcade games for clues. By far, my favorite room is "Aniseed Avenue," a parody of *Sesame Street* that has you exploring a familiar-looking neighborhood and solving puzzles with the help of talkative puppets. There was a sixth room in development, but the theme was a closely guarded secret.

I should point out that all of Puzzle Paradise's escape rooms have a human element. Each room has at least one actor in the room with you at all times, whether that person is out of sight, controlling the puppets, voicing jungle birds, or playing the Minotaur, a night watchman, or an amusement park employee. At pivotal points in the game's narrative, the actor provides clues or background information, and often some laughs, before slipping away and leaving the players to their own devices.

Puzzle Paradise took over an abandoned strip mall, and they must have spent a small fortune refurbishing it and setting up the incredibly realistic rooms. There were only three cars in the substantial lot, which I figured belonged to the employees. The students split up into five teams and started playing. As I knew all the answers to the puzzles, and the students preferred to play without a teacher present, I hung out in the lobby. The other two chaperones were in the restroom with a bit of stomach trouble after some ill-advised fast-food breakfast sandwiches. I'd brought a book, but the main desk clerk caught my attention. She hadn't been there when I'd played the rooms recently. She was a five-foot-one girl in a hoodie made for someone two hundred pounds heavier than her, with sandy hair that had been cut into a ragged fringe by a barber who didn't understand how to use scissors properly. She looked so nervous that I decided that minding my own business was overrated, so I slipped my book back into my purse, smoothed out the bunched-up portions of my royal blue sweater dress, and crossed over to her.

"Hi."

She seemed startled. Tugging at the cuffs of her hoodie, she managed a nervous, "Hey."

"I'm Nerissa Kaiming, a teacher chaperoning this field trip. Nice to meet you."

"Welcome to Puzzle Paradise." Not only did she not make eye contact with me, but her mind seemed like it was in a different time zone.

I pressed for some basic information. "What's your name?"

"Oh! It's Tabitha Achen. My family runs this business."

"Really? That's cool. Why did your family start the business?"

"Well, my Dad's an engineer and my Mom's an artist. After Dad got downsized, they decided to go into business for themselves. My sisters and their boyfriends are all actors, and they take care of the game master work and in-game acting." She managed another indecipherable syllable, silenced herself, and proved unreceptive to my attempts at small talk.

I was just about to give up and go back to my book when I looked out the window and saw a burly man with his hands on a woman's throat. "Call 911! Now! Tell them there's a man attacking a woman outside."

Rushing out into the lot, I screamed, "Let go of her!"

The assailant turned and leered at me. "Get back into the building, babe, and forget you saw anything."

I wasn't about to take orders from him, so I whipped out my personal safety alarm from my key fob and activated it. I pointed the speaker towards his head, hoping the shrieks would rupture his eardrums.

"Turn it off!" he howled, clapping his hands over his ears.

I ran forward, grabbed the woman, who had fallen to her knees, gasping for breath, slipped an arm under her shoulder, hoisted her up, and started pulling her towards the building. After a couple of yards, the attacker lowered his hands and growled at me. Calling me a vulgar name, he reached into the pockets of his cheap jeans and pulled out a switchblade.

I grabbed my purse, reached into the side pocket, pulled out my bright red pepper spray gun, and shot him in the face.

Fortunately, the wind was at my back, so none of the spray blew towards me. While the attacker writhed on the ground and screamed, I dragged the woman into the escape room building, ordered Tabitha to lock the door, and helped the gasping lady into a chair. "Do you need a doctor?" I asked her.

"No," she wheezed. "No doctor."

"Well, the police should be here soon." I turned towards Tabitha, and from her expression, I knew at once she hadn't called. "You didn't phone 911, did you?"

"I can't. You don't understand, we can't get the police involved." Tabitha said.

I didn't understand what was going on, but I didn't like it. After fifteen minutes of trying to get them to fill me in, all I learned was that the injured woman was Tabitha's mother. When I pressed further, the injured woman waved me away, saying, "You don't understand. If we just give them their money, it'll be fine. Now, please, no more questions."

After being rebuffed by the woman I'd just rescued, I looked through the window and saw a mugger was still writhing on the ground. Because these women were reluctant to bring in the authorities, I ducked into the restroom and called the police myself.

When they arrived ten minutes later, the attacker was right where I'd left him. They asked me a few questions, I showed them my permit for the pepper spray gun, and I politely declined one of the officers' invitation to dinner, informing him I had a boyfriend.

The officer's female partner rolled her eyes at him so hard I thought she'd dislocate her optic nerve. After shaking off my rejection, the male policeman asked where I'd gotten my alarm and pepper spray gun. I explained that they were presents from my boyfriend, who believes that gifts should be practical and that the greatest gift of all is the gift of self-defense. I have chosen to view that as romantic.

When I led the pair of them into the building, Tabitha and her mother insisted that everything was fine, and they refused to answer any of the officers' questions. When my efforts to persuade them to change their minds proved fruitless, the officers provided me with their contact information and left.

Before I could speak to the clearly frightened women, my students started filing out of one of the escape rooms. They'd won the "Jungle Temple" with over twelve minutes to spare, and they were followed out by the game master, who also provided the voices of the parrots and the talking stone idol in the temple. I could tell she was related to Tabitha, only she was six inches taller and had a much better hair stylist. I introduced myself, learned that her name was Adalina, and after she took a photo of my triumphant students, I led her off to one side and explained the situation to her.

Adalina was furious. "Why didn't they talk to the police? I've been telling them to ask for help for a month now."

"Have you had a problem with muggers in the parking lot recently?"

"Oh, whoever that guy was, he's not a mugger. He's a hired goon for some low-lifes."

I thought I understood now, "Are they forcing you to pay protection money?"

"No. They're making us launder their money."

Before she could say more, her mother ordered her to reset the room and forbade her to talk to me. Neither Tabitha nor her mother would look at me after that, and the lobby was getting crowded now that another team of students had emerged victorious.

As I plotted my next move, one of my students handed me a slip of paper, telling me that it was from one of the escape room employees. Unfolding it, I read, "CALL ME AT 3:30 THIS AFTERNOON IF YOU CAN—ADALINA." Her phone number was printed underneath.

After we took the students to a Mexican restaurant for lunch, they got to have a little fun at a nearby arcade before going back to school. Once there, I tracked down my boyfriend, Funderburke, who's not only the Student Advocate and a leading member of the school security team, he's also a licensed private investigator. Normally, he uses his skills to perform background checks on potential employees and to help students in difficult situations.

I explained the day's events to him, "I know a little about money laundering. Back during Prohibition, bootleggers bought laundries to cover up their ill-gotten gains, but I don't understand why they needed to own legitimate businesses."

"They must make their illegal profits look like legitimate income." Funderburke leaned back in his chair. "Criminal enterprises are supposed to make money. But unless you want to go all Scrooge McDuck and save your cash and swim in it, you've got a problem. If you spend money you can't account for, the IRS is going to pounce. Of course, these criminals want to buy cars and boats and designer clothes and a whole lot of other luxuries. They made that dirty money to spend it. But if your only official source of income is a minimum-wage job at a fast-food restaurant, it's hard to explain how you can buy a Mercedes and so many diamond rings you can't raise your hands over your head. If the IRS hears about this, they're going to ask questions, and when you can't account for your riches, odds are the government's going to confiscate your nice stuff and throw you in prison."

"So laundering money is all about coming up with an explanation for how you got all that cash?"

"Exactly. If you're cynical, like me, you might think that certain forces in the government don't care if you break the law, if you let Uncle Sam take his cut. If you pay taxes on the proceeds of your ill-gotten gains, you're less likely to be audited. But to appease the taxman, you must have a source of income to explain your newfound wealth. Most of the time, that means buying a business. You mentioned the laundries bought by bootleggers. There was a report a few months back about Milwaukee businesses that are fronts for money laundering. For example, dive bars that never have more than two customers at a time. Criminals bought these businesses or forced the proprietors to do their bidding.

"Anyway, on a normal night, these dive bars sell forty bucks' worth of drinks at a time. But when the money launderers' accountants get involved, suddenly they're selling more than five hundred dollars of cheap beer a night, more on weekends. Of course, they buy the least expensive beer they can find to make it look believable, so that's an added expense, but between claiming markups on their booze and people spending, say, five bucks for a basket of popcorn, and so forth, at this hypothetical bar, money launderers can claim an imaginary five thousand bucks a week, so two hundred sixty thousand a year.

"Of course, this won't hold up to scrutiny if a competent investigator notices the bar only has three customers a night who each ordered one Pabst Blue Ribbon. But if they pay the taxes on that two hundred sixty thousand, often the powers that be turn a blind eye.

"And you can't claim one tiny bar is pulling in a million a year, so you have to run the money through four taverns."

Now I understood. "An escape room company would be a perfect front for money launderers. Their business model requires them to schedule bookings throughout the day, but most of the time, even the most popular escape rooms can only book twenty, thirty percent of the available slots. So, they've got a lot of empty one-hour appointments. Puzzle Paradise is open seven days a week. They've got five rooms. Unless it's a holiday weekend and lots of tourists are visiting, they probably have three hundred slots going unfilled each week, minimum. Eight slots to a room, but you can book a private room for two hundred fifty dollars. That's seventy-five thousand a week…" I took a moment to finish up the math in my head. "Three million, nine hundred thousand a year. Wow. Actually, that's not right. There's usually a thirty-minute gap between bookings so the staff can reset the room. But still, the numbers work as a rough estimate."

"Of course, no auditor is ever going to believe that an escape room operates at maximum capacity every day for a full year," Funderburke said. "Especially if some investigator stakes out the parking lot Monday through Wednesday and only sees nine cars in the lot during business hours. To make it believable, the money launderers could probably run a million dollars annually at the absolute most, and probably a lot less if they wanted to stay under the radar."

I agreed. A glance at my watch told me it was time to call Adalina, and soon we were FaceTiming her. She quickly confirmed our suspicions. Her parents had gone into debt to build the business, and they'd turned to some shady people for a loan to keep afloat until Puzzle Paradise became profitable. Unfortunately, it was taking longer than they'd hoped, and a month ago, the loan sharks had given the family an ultimatum. Launder money for them, or Puzzle Paradise would burn to the ground, and the loan sharks would take the insurance money.

"Do you know the source of the cash being laundered?" Funderburke asked.

"No idea. They didn't say. They just told us that if we did as they said for six months, we'd be even and we'd never hear from them again. They'd dissolve the partnership."

This confused me. "Partnership? What partnership?"

"Oh, I didn't mention. They made my parents sign a contract for some sort of short-term partnership."

"To give their supposed profits a veneer of legitimacy," Funderburke said.

Little tears started forming in Adalina's eyes, "They told us that we couldn't go to the police, otherwise the authorities would seize and shut down the business. But they can't do that, can they?"

"Unfortunately, they can," Funderburke replied. "There are a lot of cases where innocent people have lost everything due to inadvertent connections to criminals. There was this one case where a motel owner allowed the police to use his business to set up a sting. After the authorities got what they wanted, the motel was seized under asset forfeiture laws based on some technicality."

"So, we can't go to the police, because the loan sharks strong-armed themselves into a partnership? We have to launder their money and hope we don't get caught?"

Funderburke ran his hands through his hair. "How much money have they made you launder so far?"

"About fifty thousand dollars."

"If they want you to launder for five more months, at that rate, that means they have about three hundred thousand dollars to launder," I calculated.

"But that much money in such a short time?" Funderburke shook his head. "A halfway competent forensic accountant would catch that in ten seconds. By tax time, the criminals would have split with their laundered cash, and the next time Puzzle Paradise gets audited, they'll be caught trying to explain an influx of three hundred thousand dollars that shouldn't be there."

"So, we're stuck," Adalina's face sagged. "If we don't knuckle under, the business gets flambéed. If we do as we're told, the tax assessors will chew us up and spit us out. Either way, Puzzle Paradise is doomed. And we're almost ready to open our sixth room."

"What's the theme?" It wasn't the most relevant question, but it slipped out before I could think about it.

Adalina told me, and a germ of an idea popped into my mind. I started brainstorming aloud, Funderburke joined in, and soon, we had a plan.

The miscreants habitually paid Puzzle Paradise a visit after close of business every Friday to ensure the laundering was running smoothly and leaving more money to be laundered the following week. Apparently, they wanted the business to create the impression that most players walked in without a reservation and paid cash, and presumably bought merchandise like snacks and T-shirts.

Normally, I would have advised going to the authorities. But seeing as how the criminals had already latched onto the business, I agreed with Funderburke that the possibility of some sticky-fingered bureaucrat deciding to seize the business was above zero, and with high odds of an auditor catching the laundering later when the criminals were gone, the Achens would be left holding the bag. So, we had to find a way to get the Achen family out of trouble. After some brainstorming with Funderburke and Adalina, we developed my idea into something vaguely resembling a feasible plan. The more I thought about it, the more preposterous it sounded. By the time I realized the potential holes in the plan, it was already Friday night, and Funderburke and I were holed up in the control room of Puzzle Paradise with Adalina. It was too late to change course.

The entire building was wired with closed-circuit television, a necessary step for viewing the escape rooms, but Puzzle Paradise also kept an eye on the lobby and parking lot. Mr. and Mrs. Achen were at home after Adalina had convinced them to take the night off and let her handle the weekly meeting. The unwanted guests usually stopped by around ten-thirty, but when the clock hit a quarter to eleven and there was still no sign of them, I started to worry that they would be no-shows. I was about to suggest calling it off when two men walked through the unlocked front door and pushed their way inside the building.

"Showtime," I murmured to myself, adjusting the collar of my black leather jacket.

Both men were a shade under six feet tall. One had a shaved head that didn't suit him– judging from the stubble on his scalp, he still had about sixty percent coverage, and he should have kept what he had on the top of his head and lost the ill-advised goatee. The other guy seemed to think that wearing dark glasses in the middle of the night made him look tough and intimidating. He was wrong.

"Hey! Anybody there?" Sunglasses-at-Night guy bellowed. Adalina tapped a button on the control panel, and ominous music started playing down the corridor.

"Hello?" The two men strode down the hall towards the music. They soon found their way to the door of the yet-to-be-opened room and followed the music inside. They soon saw two piles of cash sitting on wooden chairs, illuminated by spotlights from the ceiling.

Shaved Head & Bad Goatee headed for the left pile of cash, and Sunglasses-at-Night approached the one on the right. "Hey, this is—" Before Sunglasses-at-Night could announce that it was just play money, two iron-barred doors slammed behind them. The two men whirled around and discovered that they were both stuck in individual cells. After shaking the bars unsuccessfully and screaming, the door leading to the corridor thudded shut, and the dim lights rose just enough for them to see the details of the room.

I haven't mentioned it yet, but the theme of the yet-to-be-opened room was "Murder Basement." One of the most popular themes of escape rooms is the den of a serial killer. Picture the goriest, grisliest, most stomach-churning horror movie you've ever seen. This "Murder Basement "room was twice as terrifying. Not only was the room filled with fake blood and the remains of previous captives, but Adalina opened the vents and released a disturbing odor of decay and rusted iron. I knew what was happening, and I was ten yards away in a different room, but the scene on the screen still freaked me out.

We let the men shake the bars of their cells for a few minutes before the secret door slid open in the far corner of the room, and the character known as "The West Side Flayer" entered. Adalina's boyfriend, Jaime, was a lot better-looking without the mask that was made from fake internal organs. His coveralls looked like they were drenched in gore. Until that night, I was not aware that there was such a thing as rubber chainsaws that could whir and screech without possessing the ability to cut anything tougher than butter.

"YOU WILL PAY FOR YOUR CRIMES!" The West Side Flayer shouted in a voice that sounded like a talking garbage disposal.

Both of the imprisoned men looked like they were in need of clean undergarments. Shaved Head & Bad Goatee sank to his knees and begged for mercy.

"CONFESS YOUR CRIMES AND I MIGHT SPARE YOU," the Flayer hissed.

So Shaved Head & Bad Goatee spilled his guts. He confessed to sending hired goons to beat people who couldn't pay their debts, he admitted to making out with his brother's girlfriend (From the response on Sunglasses-at-Night's face, I realized the two of them were siblings. Once Sunglasses-at-Night took off his shades, I saw the resemblance.), and in addition to other sordid acts I needn't mention here, he also confessed to stealing more than three hundred thousand dollars from a drug dealer and forcing the owners of Puzzle Paradise into money laundering. The brothers seemed to be new at loan sharking, as the Achens had been among their first customers. They'd scraped together enough of a stake to start lending, but most of their customers had skipped town without paying, and when a shady acquaintance of theirs left his car unlocked, they'd seized the opportunity, but realized they'd need to launder it to pay off their own debts. So, they'd forced the Achens to sign a contract making them limited partners, and the money laundering process began. When Mr. Achen threatened to go to the police, they sent that hired goon after Mrs. Achen.

By the time Shaved Head & Bad Goatee cleansed his soul, Sunglasses-at-Night had scraped together enough brain cells to realize that this wasn't actually a real serial killer and told his brother to shut his mouth. That's when Adalina used the intercom and told her boyfriend to take off his mask, and she joined him in the room.

"Your entire confession has been taped through the closed-circuit television," Adalina informed the brothers. "However, if you two turn over all of the documents giving you a stake in the business, plus all of the remaining money, and never speak the Achen family's name again, then the recording won't be turned over to the police."

When they balked, she reminded them, "If I publicize the recording online, the drug dealer, who no doubt has access to hired goons of his own, will find out and start looking for his money."

After whining and negotiating, Sunglasses-at-Night was released while Shaved Head & Bad Goatee stayed in the cell, and he returned an hour later with all the copies of the documents granting him and his brother a limited partnership in Puzzle Paradise, plus a briefcase with the remaining money. After they released Shaved Head & Bad Goatee, his brother tried to grab the money back, but a little whirring from the convincing, but useless rubber chainsaw convinced them to abandon the cash. The brothers signed a note declaring that the Achens owed them nothing and rushed out into the night, after Adalina and her boyfriend promised not to give the tape to the police.

But Funderburke and I didn't make that promise.

After a slightly edited audio version of the confession was slipped to a friend of ours on the force, the brothers were arrested. The police didn't play the recording, but they created the impression that someone had seen them take the money from the drug dealer's car. After Shaved Head & Bad Goatee started begging for mercy, they cut a deal to testify against their drug dealer acquaintance. Of course, they hadn't turned over all the money, so the hundred thousand they'd kept, including the money already laundered, was confiscated as evidence. The names of the Achens and Puzzle Paradise were never mentioned. Adalina was reluctant to part with the cash we'd extracted, but I convinced her that no good could come of keeping drug money, and the Saint Mark Ji Tianxiang Center for the Treatment of Addiction received an anonymous donation of more than two hundred thousand dollars.

A few weeks later, my parents, Funderburke, and I played "Murder Basement," compliments of the Achens. I don't care for grisly, horror-themed rooms. But we won with two and a half minutes to spare.

Story Inspiration:

About a decade ago, one of my best friends, who I've known since the second grade, introduced me and another one of our friends from high school to escape rooms. Over the years, other friends from school have joined us as we've played nearly every escape room in the greater Milwaukee area. During the pandemic lockdown, we played lots of online escape games together, and for some time, I've been toying with the idea of writing an escape room-set mystery.

A recent scandal about local bars being used as money laundering fronts got me thinking: what other businesses might be covers for nefarious deeds? After a bit of thinking, I realized that escape rooms were an ideal business for criminals to exploit. I drew further inspiration from a real-life case (not in Milwaukee) where a hapless burglar broke into an escape room company, not knowing what was inside, and wound up getting stuck in a cell in a "serial killer's murder basement" room. Unable to escape, he freaked out and was forced to call 911 for help.

It should be obvious how these real-life inspirations fueled my story.

THE QUEEN OF PICKLEBALL

Daphne Silver

Daphne Silver is the Agatha Award-winning author of the Rare Books Cozy Mystery Series. Her latest book is The Tell-Tale Homicide *from Level Best Books. Learn more and join her newsletter at www.daphnesilver.com.*

I had just collected our bags from the Forester when my wife Judy raced towards me, yelling, "Hal, call the police!"

I dropped the bags to dig my phone out. Pickleball paddles, balls, and whatever else Judy had crammed in spilled across the parking lot.

"What's going on?" I asked.

Judy hunched over, breathing heavily, and staring down at her ridiculous red sequined sneakers. She had convinced me to buy them, saying they reminded her of the ruby red slippers her namesake Judy Garland wore.

She pointed towards the court. I held my hand up to block the morning sun, but I couldn't see anything unusual. "What am I telling the police?"

"Mattie…"

"Mattie Crenshaw?"

She nodded, steadying herself on her knees. Strange since she was such a powerhouse on the court. Sure, it was another doozy of a Florida morning, but she must have run hard. I found her water bottle in the mess and tossed it to her. The bottle fell to her feet.

"Is Mattie okay?" I asked.

She shook her head. I left the Pickleball equipment lying by the Forester, pocketed the unused phone, and headed over to explore. I would call as soon as I knew more of what to tell them, and it was apparent Judy couldn't help.

There, lying across the court's kitchen, was the body of Mattie Crenshaw.

It was probably rude, but my first thought was how this would impact our chances of winning this year's Pickleball tournament. I'm also sure it wasn't polite that I snapped a few photos of the scene with my phone, but I didn't touch anything. Besides, rushing now wouldn't help Mattie. The pool of blood and glassy open eyes were enough to confirm her deceased state.

I called 911. I made a few additional calls, including to league president, Bob Furino, the gym's front desk, and a few players. Better to be on top of the details, I told myself. I didn't know if Mattie had any family in the area.

Then, I headed back to Judy to make sure she was okay. My wife leaned against the Forester, gulping the water. I turned on the car and suggested she sit in the air conditioning.

"How are you so calm, Hal?"

I shrugged. "We're all simply doing the best we can."

"Is she really…"

"Appears so."

"Who would do such a thing?"

I didn't respond, but several names came to mind. No one liked Mattie. She was a nuisance at best. We all put up with her for a single reason: she won.

The police arrived, but not before several other players did. Having recovered, Judy took over the duties of informing those whom I hadn't called yet. I noticed some serious crocodile tears flowing.

I spent the next few hours talking with the police. Then I regurgitated my description to the county detective. Wishing to be helpful, I suggested the cleaning company one of our players ran, since the court was such an unusual surface. Besides, Lynn Albee was one of my accounting clients, so I knew she could use the work.

* * *

Each morning afterwards for the next week, Judy played Nancy Drew, announcing a different suspect at breakfast. This morning, she decided Mattie had been killed by her old partner, Althea Turin.

"Remember when Mattie dropped Althea for Jenny? I don't think she ever got over that." We sat in the kitchen. I sipped my coffee and made small noncommittal noises of understanding.

Yesterday, she thought it was the Yoders, Mattie's neighbors. I made the mistake of asking why, and Judy blabbered on about property line disputes. When I pushed back that it was hard to imagine property line disputes with townhouses—especially those with fences already in place, Judy pivoted and argued about construction permits.

After that, I stopped asking.

"We should move, Hal," Judy said while cleaning up. "Go to a different development. Get a bigger place. Not this tiny, cramped townhouse with people attached on both sides."

"That seems overkill. How do we know the murderer lives around here? I don't see how spending a fortune on a larger place is going to make things better."

I snapped open the *Orlando Sentinel* and buried my face in it. Judy muttered to herself, but I wasn't going to indulge such fantasies when they involved emptying our bank account. Being semi-retired meant keeping to a budget, but Judy didn't see it that way. She pictured a Hollywood retirement, as if we had gone down a yellow brick road.

"You're shortchanging our present for an overly optimistic future," she said.

"I'm doing what?"

"You heard me. You think we're going to reach the age of 115 or something. Well, I don't even want to reach 115. How about this? You relent a bit on the budget, and I'll promise to kill myself on my ninetieth birthday."

"That's ghastly."

I grew tired of her little dramas. When we were young, I had found her imagination attractive, compared to my logical approach. She had pushed me to be spontaneous and less cautious. I'd never even been outside the country until she convinced me to join her on a whirlwind trip to Mexico. We honeymooned there a year later. These days, though, her antics were less fun and more frustrating.

It didn't help that the court remained closed, and we struggled to find somewhere else to play, especially being so close to the start of the tournament.

I'd started playing Pickleball because Judy won lessons during a silent auction at a local museum. I wasn't pleased with how much she'd spent, but since the deed was done, it'd be worse to let the lessons go to waste. It surprised me to discover how much I enjoyed the game. The gym and league fees were more than I wanted to spend, but it was a small luxury that we could afford on our budget.

My cell phone ringing pulled me back to reality.

"I just wanted to say thank you, Hal," Lynn Albee said. "I heard you were the reason we got the contract to clean up the court. Thank you for thinking of us, even with such, well, chaos happening. You always keep such a cool, level head."

"My pleasure," I replied. We chatted a bit longer, and Lynn confirmed that the court would reopen soon.

Once I hung up, Judy jumped in again. "It was *her*, wasn't it?"

"Her who? Lynn? That was Lynn Albee." I got up to refill my coffee cup. It was a surprisingly decent coffee that came from a new client. A rich flavor with notes of caramel and chocolate. Maybe I'd order some bags for holiday gifts.

"Yeah, Lynn. It was her. I bet she killed Mattie." My amateur detective poured herself a second glass of orange juice. She stood at the kitchen counter and looked out the window, towards Mattie's now vacant house. She wore those silly red sequined sneakers. What a relief the courts would reopen, so she could wear them there instead of at home.

This imaginative speculation had gone far enough. "Lynn didn't kill Mattie any more than Althea or the Yoders. Why would you think that?"

Judy *tsked* me. I really didn't care for that clicking sound. So patronizing. "For the money."

"What money?"

"To clean the court. You mentioned that Lynn's company… What's it called? Carnation Cleaners? Anyway, you mentioned she needed new business." Judy placed her hands on her hips. I sat down at the kitchen table and debated ignoring her entirely. She'd just keep talking anyway. She was nothing if not persistent.

"You think Lynn is going around killing people with the hope that she'll get the clean-up contract? That isn't a great business model."

Judy sighed. Although she conceded, she wasn't going to be happy with me today. I didn't look forward to navigating the thin line between her defensive heart and overly imaginative mind. So, I threw her a bone. "But I get your point that money could have been the motive. How about this? I handled Mattie's accounts and those of several other players. It wouldn't hurt for me to review them."

Judy came over and threw her arms around my neck. She kissed the top of my forehead. I must have made the right offering this time. Besides, the more I thought about it, the more I wondered if there were any clues in their accounts. Someone had killed Mattie. Money can be a powerful motive.

"I'll head there later this morning." I maintained a small office just outside our neighborhood. A little far for a walk, but an easy bike or car ride. Several of the players used my accounting services.

"Today? Thank you. That'd be great." She kissed my head again. I couldn't help but smile. As much as Judy could be wearing, I still sought her approval.

* * *

I didn't get to the office until much later. We both had errands to run, and it was my turn to handle grocery shopping. At the Publix supermarket, I ran into league president Bob Turino in the produce section. He sported a tropical-patterned shirt and flip-flops. Typical Floridian uniform, yet they still struck me as strange choices compared to his full white beard.

He kept picking up an orange, turning it over, and putting it back. I've never been a fan of fruit touching. I've always gone with a visual examination to reduce the spread of germs.

Besides, this was Florida. Didn't he have a few orange trees growing in his backyard? Even with our tiny plot, we still managed to have two healthy trees. Their fruit was always better than the variety here, even the so-called organic ones.

"Well, I'll be. Hal Johnson. Good to see you." Bob thrust his hand out. The same germy hand that had touched half the fruit in the store. However, I knew that social pleasantries required me to shake it, so I did, all the while mentally adding sanitizer to my shopping list.

"How you doing, Bob?"

"Honestly? I've been better. Losing Mattie is going to be a real blow to our chances this year. You know…" Bob leaned in close enough that I could feel his breath on my ear. Pleasantries or not, I leaned away. One of the other things I enjoyed about Pickleball was that it was not a hand-to-hand sport. Everyone kept to their zone and stayed within the game's parameters. It would have been lovely if the world worked in the same way.

Undeterred, Bob spoke in sotto voce. "We've got a little pot going if you want in."

"A pot? On what? Who's going to win the tourney?"

Whenever Bob laughed, he reminded me of a retired Santa Claus. He had a deep laugh that required both of his hands to hold his significant belly. Given his weight, it was amazing how adept and agile he could be on the court. He was one of the best. Not as good as Mattie Crenshaw, unfortunately, but none of us were.

"No, no," he said. "Okay, so maybe a bit macabre, but we've got a little bet on who killed Mattie and why."

Well, that was surprising. And intriguing. "How many people are in?"

"Half a dozen so far. There's a few—maybe more—coming in. You only need a grand to enter, so it's a nice return. If we're all wrong, then the money will go towards a charity we choose. So, either way…" He held his hands out like a scale, trying to balance.

"That's a lot of money."

"I thought so too, but my wife said the reward was too promising."

Bob was right. It was a macabre project, but if enough people entered, the payout would be decent. Was it decent enough to risk putting in something?

"How do I enter?"

Bob's smile turned wolfish. "Glad to hear you're in, Hal. That'll convince a few others to join. Hoping we get it up to twenty grand if we can."

"Who's we?"

"We've got a secret website going. A place where you can post your theory and make an entry. My granddaughter set it up for us. She promises me that it's super private and can't be traced."

He told me the address but said I couldn't write it down. "Just memorize it. She says to use an incognito browser to enter."

While I thought it was all bizarre, my curiosity got the better of me, and I knew I'd check it out sooner than later.

In the parking lot, I ran into Mike and Olivia Yoder heading into the shop. They followed me as I took my bags to the Forester.

"Bad news about Mattie, isn't it?" Mike said.

"We've been struggling to think who'd do that to her?" Olivia added.

"Wasn't she doing work at her place?" I asked, thinking about Judy's theories.

"I think she had a few projects planned, but I don't know if she'd started any." Olivia shrugged. Mike nodded. I wondered if they were being completely truthful, but I'm no human lie detector.

Mike said, "Hal, have you seen…the, uhm…"

"The website?" Olivia added.

"This one is…special," said Mike.

"Like *one thousand dollars entrance fee* special?" I asked. Mike visibly relaxed. "I just spoke to Bob about it inside. But I haven't seen it yet."

"Oh, okay. But you're going to do it, right?"

"Not sure yet."

"Neither are we," Olivia said with a too-wide smile. Even I could tell she wasn't being truthful this time. They must have already ponied up.

* * *

As soon as I got into my car, I logged onto the URL from my phone. The page was simple. A blank field with the instructions to type in my initial idea about who killed Mattie and why. I had to pay before you saw anyone else's first guesses.

My curiosity clawed at me, and even with the painful cost, I paid. Once inside, I saw we were already up to thirteen people. Everyone used fake names to hide their identities. The theories were all over the place. A few echoed things that Judy had suggested. The craziest one was that I had been sleeping with Mattie and killed her to end things. That took me aback. I had originally thought I'd share the page with Judy, but after seeing such nonsense, I knew I'd have to keep this to myself.

* * *

When I got to my office, I found it a complete mess. Boxes were turned over, and my computer monitor was broken. Looked like a brick had gone through it. The CPU tower was missing as well. I had password-protected everything and backed it all up, but maybe that got destroyed, too.

Notably, I was missing my paper files on Mattie Crenshaw, Lynn Albee, Bob Furino, and several other Pickleball players. Meanwhile, my files on unrelated businesses seemed completely untouched.

I sat in my chair and called Judy using the desk phone. I reached her on the second ring and explained the situation. As always, her big heart and even bigger imagination flowed through the receiver.

"Oh, Hal. I'm so sorry! Someone must have figured out that you'd have records. You're right. This is about money. Do you think Mattie owed money to someone? Or that someone owed it to her?"

"I don't know, but it doesn't mean that isn't the case," I replied. A thought tickled at the back of my brain. I put the phone on speaker and got up. I ran through the remaining files to see if there was a particular one left. I was surprised to find it there, apparently unnoticed by the perpetrator.

"What'd the police say?" she asked.

I didn't respond because I became engrossed in studying the file. At first glance, one might think everything was fine financially. But there was a somewhat unusual expense line that ticked up month over month, starting about three months ago. I should have noticed it long before today. It's my fault I missed it.

"Hal?"

I continued to ignore her as I turned to the income lines. If I had paid more attention, I might have noticed the sizable amount of money flowing in as well. Nothing obvious in one payment or another, but numerous trickles hidden across several lines that added up to an unexpectedly high number. While I was annoyed at missing these details, I also felt a strange amount of respect for the person hiding everything in plain sight.

"Hal!"

Finally, I put the papers down and focused on Judy.

"I called you first. I'm going to call them next," I said. That wasn't entirely true. I had determined there would be one additional call I'd make ahead of the police. "I'll call you back later, okay?"

"Of course. I'll be waiting."

I next called my lawyer, Jock Lymon. I explained the situation, wanting to make sure I wouldn't be in trouble. He wasn't sure.

"C'mon, Hal," Jock said. "I don't know if a jury of your peers are going to accept that as an oversight. You're normally so meticulous. They'll think either you were in on Mattie's death or that you're incompetent at your job. Neither's great, although at least incompetency would keep you out of jail."

"Thanks. I'll think about it."

After our chat, I sat back and considered my options. I debated calling Judy back, but I decided to wait and discuss what I had uncovered with her later in person.

Instead, I scanned through the secret website forum. It looked like most people thought the killer was probably one or both of the Yoders. I saw the references to property lines and permits that Judy had mentioned. And apparently, someone theorized that Mattie was sleeping with Mike, too.

After seeing my name pop up in such a way, I didn't know how much credit I gave to that idea, but it didn't mean it was untrue. Of course, the Yoders' files were missing from my office as well.

A few new threads popped up. One continued to push the Yoder theory, but now it contained new, private financial information.

"The Yoders' house is seriously underwater," wrote someone going by the name RUBYRED. "They bought before the rest of us, way back at the height of the market, and are struggling with equity issues. A real house of cards. Mattie knew, and she was trying to get them to sell their place. They didn't want to do it, but she knew all about their finances. She wanted them gone and the house to be hers." The author listed a few more financial details that likely came from my stolen records.

I studied RUBYRED's profile. The same author had recently crafted several additional threads, using more information that had been included in my accounting files. It appeared Mattie had been blackmailing more than a few people in our league.

"Well, I'll be," I said to no one.

* * *

I stopped on the way home to pick up a bottle of Judy's favorite red wine and a bouquet of roses. I debated getting some good chocolate as well, but I wasn't sure if she'd be happy about them or upset that I was "destroying her figure." Her moods could be uncertain. I had assumed that they would improve when we retired, but unfortunately, it seemed like her emotions became even more untethered.

She was in the kitchen again, reading the newspaper. "Look at this write-up, Hal! I think the police are probably going to arrest Mike soon. It makes sense. Scorned lover, money troubles… everything!"

I came over and kissed her cheek. I presented her with the wine and flowers.

"What's all this? Are we celebrating?"

"Sure, we can call it celebrating. I'm celebrating you."

"Aren't you sweet? Thank you!" She got up and found two glasses and the wine opener. "By the way, what did the police say about the break-in?"

I hesitated for a moment but told her. "I never called them."

She stopped and turned. "You never called them? Why didn't you call them? I bet it was Mike Yoder who did it. I bet they found his fingerprints everywhere."

"You're probably right. Not sure how you arranged that, but I have full faith that you could do it." I came over and took the glasses and opener out of her hands. She watched me with big doe eyes, but didn't stop me. I opened the bottle and poured two glasses. I went heavy on the pour. She took the glass from me but didn't drink it. I held mine up to her in a mock salute.

"How…how'd you figure it out?" Her confused expression turned to fear, mixed with a touch of anger. I needed to tread carefully.

"Oh, I don't know everything. I don't know when you got to the gym that day or even how you did it. But Mattie must have been blackmailing us. Well, you. Although I'm not sure why you didn't tell me."

I paused, realizing my error. Judy interjected something, but I interrupted her. "No, no, of course. It's because you were using my files. *You* were blackmailing several of our friends. And Mattie found out."

Judy sipped at her wine and laughed. "She was extorting *me*. She said she'd reveal what I was up to if I didn't pay her." Her voice sounded odd. Instead of the peppy wife I'd known for over forty years, her tone was flat, if not dour. "And her price was going up. Way up. I hadn't done that to anyone. Just a little side income, that's all. An understanding between friends. But Mattie's requirements meant I was going to need to hustle more out of the rest of the gang."

"But why? We didn't need it."

"No, *you* didn't think we needed it. You are comfortable with us living in this cramped cottage of a townhouse, always cooking at home, and taking one tiny vacation to see our kids once a year. Every time I've suggested we do something more, you've always pushed back, saying it's not being…what's the word you'd use…*pragmatic*." She sighed and gulped at her wine. Then she asked again, "But how did you figure out it was me?"

"Out of all the files you took from the office. You didn't take ours. I found the expense line you had disguised as a 'Vacation Fund.' It increased rather drastically in the past few months."

"I didn't think it was necessary to take *our* file. It's your office." She grabbed the bottle of wine and poured a generous refill.

"And you were named after Judy Garland, Miss *RUBYRED*. I know that the *Wizard of Oz* is your favorite movie." I didn't mention her stupid sneakers.

I watched her as she downed the glass and refilled it a third time. Mine remained on the table.

"Ah, you found the forum. I didn't think you'd spend that much money," she said.

"We splurge on occasion. For the right reason."

She looked at me carefully. "We don't have to tell anyone."

"And let you implicate Mike Yoder?"

"Or one of the others." She waved her wine glass around casually, almost as if she was asking me to choose whose life to destroy.

"No, I don't think that's a good idea. But I also don't want to see you go to jail either." It was a conundrum. In one day, I had discovered that my wife of more than forty years had murdered a person and blackmailed who knew how many others. All so that we could live her version of a better life. It was a lot to process.

"So, what are you going to do?" she asked.

I sat back in the seat and tented my fingers. The damage was done. Did I think she would do it again? Probably not, although I couldn't be certain. I had underestimated her. I needed to treat her differently. This time, I needed to be the spontaneous one.

Eventually, I replied, "Nothing. Absolutely nothing."

"I'm sorry?"

"But only if you stop going after people using my files—or any other gossip or intel or anything else. And no more pushing that it was the Yoders. If you can do that, then I'm going to help you cover things up. Starting with an extended vacation to Cancun until things quiet down around here. Well, unless you prefer Cabo," I said.

Judy gasped and knocked over her glass of wine. She darted over to me and embraced me as if we were twenty-somethings on our first date again. After a few deep kisses, I gently pushed her away and said, "And we aren't implicating anyone else either."

She pouted. "Fine. But I want to win that prize money. It'll help with the costs."

I laughed and agreed. We pulled out our phones and peeked at where things stood. Not including the both of us, there were over twenty-five other people who had already entered. It seemed word was spreading quickly. How high would the pot go?

"Actually," I said, "I have a suggestion." I remembered what Bob had said would happen to the money if no one's theory proved correct. I figured that the people entering the betting pool already knew they were risking their money. If it disappeared, then that was on them for gambling.

"Oh?" Judy had wandered over to grab the paper towels and came back to clean up the spilled wine. I got out the bottle of spray cleanser.

"I think it's time to start a charity," I said. "Something in Mattie's memory. We can set it up from any resort with a solid internet connection."

I figured it wouldn't be hard to convince the others to let me handle the details, since so many of them already trusted me with their money. No one knew about the so-called break-in. As I thought through the logistics, Judy finished cleaning up and placed the flowers in a vase.

* * *

It didn't take all that long to get the first steps organized. As I suspected, the others were more than happy to let me manage things. While I worked on my computer at the kitchen table, Judy packed. Or tried to pack. She struggled to limit herself to a single carry-on, even though I warned her numerous times to keep things as light as possible.

"But what about everything else?" She waved her hands around the house. We had gone through a similar tête-à-tête when we downsized to this place.

"That's not the same as reducing yourself to one microscopic bag," she'd argued.

"We'll take care of the rest later," I replied.

She tsked. "But when? How?"

"Right now, I need to focus on getting this money squared away. Then we need to leave for the airport by…" I checked my watch. "By 1 p.m. sharp."

Judy rolled her eyes. "The point of all this was to have a more relaxed life. Now you're telling me I can't keep any of my things and that I'm on a strict schedule? Not to mention how I'm not allowed to talk to any of my friends. You won't even let me call our kids to alert them." She pouted.

"It's not safe," I replied.

"When will it be safe?"

I sighed, but closed my laptop and stood up. No reason to irritate my little murderess further. I put my arms around her and felt her fall heavy onto them.

The doorbell chirped. I dropped my arms, nearly jolting Judy to the floor. Had I become a smidge nervous? I shook my head. This wasn't like me.

Judy picked herself up and headed to the door. I put my hand out, touching her arm. She looked at me, confused, but I shook my head and put a finger to my lips.

"Why?" she mouthed.

"Safety," I whispered.

"What?"

"Safety," I repeated, slightly louder.

She scowled at me.

The doorbell chirped once more. Her gaze ping ponged between the door and me. Crossing her arms, she fell into her seat at the table.

The doorbell didn't chirp again.

* * *

We made the flight. Barely, but we got on. Judy alternated between freezing me out and peppering me with inane questions about logistics. On the taxi ride to the resort, she ignored the beautiful scenery and kept her arms crossed firmly, sulking the entire time.

Our hotel room was gorgeous with a stunning view of the crystal blue ocean. We had a private patio, occupied by a sun-gazing iguana. I dropped our bags on the fluffy, soft bed and explored the place. There was a generous bathroom with one of those rain showers I'd always wanted to try. The television on the wall was larger than ours. Not too shabby.

"You know, Hal," Judy said, "this room is much smaller than our townhouse. I had wanted to go bigger, not tinier."

"It's bigger than a prison cell."

She hmmphed, obviously unimpressed with my joke.

"We don't look out over the ocean back home," I argued.

She shrugged. "The beach is a golf cart drive away."

"And this place is all-inclusive. So all the food you could ever want."

She didn't respond.

"Besides, you wanted to travel more," I replied.

She sat on the edge of the bed, putting an arm on a suitcase. She was quiet for a long time, but it felt different from the plane ride over. Finally, she spoke, "But this is it."

"What do you mean?" I asked.

"There is no more travel."

"I don't understand."

"We can never leave here, can we, Hal?"

"What?"

"You said this was bigger than a prison cell."

"I was joking, Judy."

"But you're right. It's the nicest prison cell in the entire world. But that's still what it is."

"What on earth are you talking about?"

She studied the polished tile floor. Then she laughed. "Jail is all-inclusive too, you know."

"I suppose that's technically correct," I said slowly. "But I doubt the food compares. And they certainly won't have any wine."

Her head fell to the right side. "That's true. But we're still stuck here."

"We're not stuck. You're being dramatic," I said, regretting the phrase as soon as I said it. She popped up off the bed. Although not as tall as me, she managed to glare right into my eyes.

"We are stuck. In a tiny room. Unable to contact anyone else. Just each other. For eternity."

"You'd prefer the alternative?" I asked.

Her mouth gaped.

"No," she said finally. "But I would like you to recognize what this is. We've traded one prison cell for another."

I shook my head. "An all-inclusive luxury resort on a beautiful beach is not a prison cell."

Judy rolled her eyes.

The room phone rang. Again, my body jolted as if lightning tore through it. We both stared at the phone. Should we answer it? Or should we let it ring?

"It's like the doorbell all over again," Judy said softly.

"We'll let it go to voicemail," I replied.

She shrugged and wandered over to the patio. The iguana ran off.

The phone rang a few more times before finally silencing. Yet I knew it would ring again. Someone would come to the door. Someone else would check on us.

"Huh," Judy said. "We're right next to the pickleball court. Wish I had brought my sneakers."

I joined her on the patio, watching two couples sparring off. My stomach sank. One couple looked nearly identical to the Yoders. The other reminded me of Bob Furino and his wife. We had gone so far, and yet, it felt like we were still in Florida.

Maybe Judy was right.

This was the nicest prison cell in the world.

Story Inspiration:

My dad's passion for the game inspired "The Queen of Pickleball." He plays almost daily, teaches in his community, and has become a true pickleball advocate. It's inspiring—but I couldn't help wondering what would happen if a friendly match turned deadly. A real dill-emma!

Acknowledgments

Big books take big crowds to put together, and this one is no exception.A big thank you to Heather Graham. She not only provided the opportunity for my first published story many years ago, but she also wrote a great story for this anthology. Thank you to Shawn Reilly Simmons and her major domo, Deb Well, at Level Best Books. You guys are amazing.

A big shout-out and thank you to our head judge and project manager, Pat Hernas, whose skills as a former librarian proved to be invaluable. She also drove the development of the story selection rubric. Without her help, this anthology wouldn't have been possible.

To our esteemed judges—Sharon Long, Janet Kuchler, and Kim Hammond. It's not easy combing through story piles to discover diamonds. A big thanks for your hard work and discernment. Janet is owed an additional thank you, and some wine, for helping me through multiple re-reads. Thank you to Linda Farrell, Donna Andrews, and Barb Goffman for being there when I needed help.

And thank you to Jeffrey Deaver for telling me the secrets to writing short stories one afternoon at Bouchercon. This was a game-changer. And here's a shout-out to Mystery Writers of America, Sisters in Crime, and the Short Mystery Fiction Society for great support. Great organizations every mystery writer should join.

And thank you to my family: Pat Lacy, Bev Lacy, Todd Dorman, and Shawn Jennelle. Love you guys.

About the Editor

Deborah Lacy learned to strategize eight moves ahead by playing chess in a cutthroat league during childhood. She now applies those skills to life and writing. Her short stories have appeared lots of places, including *Alfred Hitchcock's Mystery Magazine, Blood on the Bayou,* and *Mystery Most International.* She's served on the local organizing committees for Left Coast Crime, and the world's largest mystery convention, Bouchercon. In her spare time, she invents dice games and throws a mean fondue party.

AUTHOR WEBSITE: deborahlacy.com

SOCIAL MEDIA HANDLES:
  Instagram: @deborahlacy
  Threads: deborahlacy
  BlueSky: @deborahlacy.bsky.social
  Facebook: deborahlacy